AGAINST THE TIDE IMPERIAL

JAMES YOUNG

This book is a work of fiction. The names, characters, places, and incidents are products of the writer's imagination or have been used fictitiously and are not to be construed as real. Any resemblance to persons, living or dead, actual events, locale or organizations is entirely coincidental.

AGAINST THE TIDE IMPERIAL
TEXT COPYRIGHT © 2020 JAMES L. YOUNG JR.
IMAGES COPYRIGHT HELD BY AUTHOR AS OF 2020

ISBN: 9798571927994

All Rights Are Reserved. No part of this book may be used or reproduced in any manner whatsoever without written permission, except in the case of brief quotations embodied in critical articles and reviews.

PICTURES

Standard Ship Diagrams

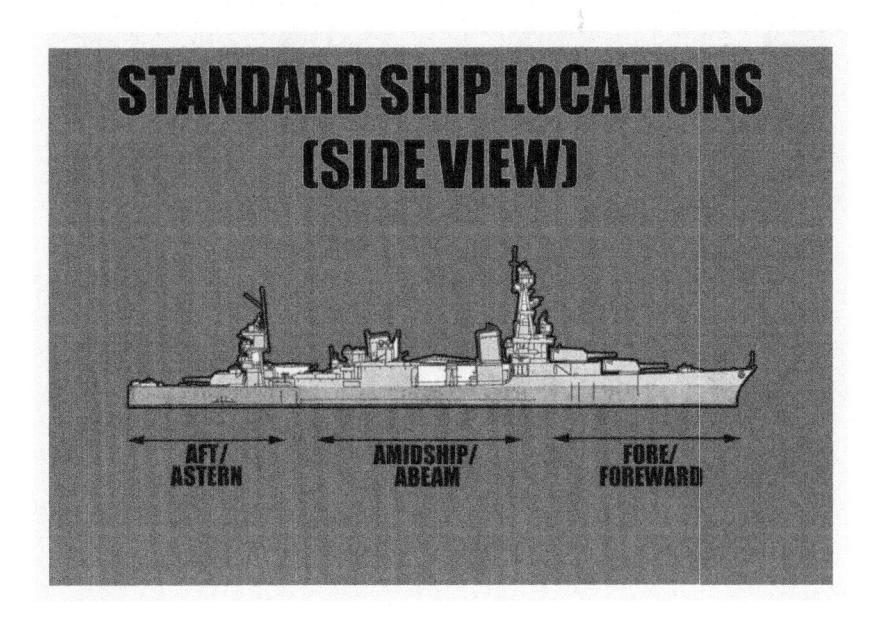

STANDARD SHIP LOCATIONS (SIDE VIEW)

AFT/ ASTERN — AMIDSHIP/ ABEAM — FORE/ FOREWARD

STANDARD SHIP DEFINITIONS

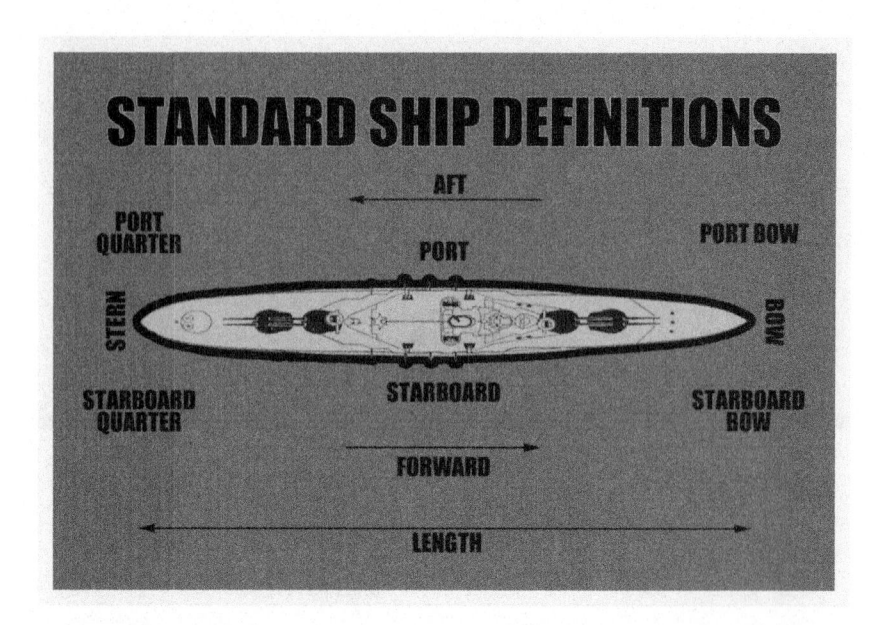

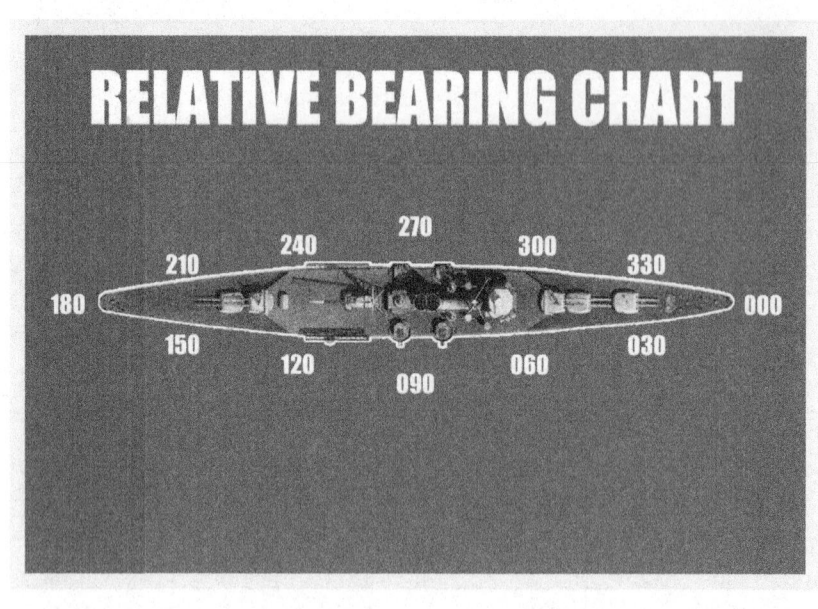

AFT

PORT QUARTER

PORT

PORT BOW

STERN

BOW

STARBOARD QUARTER

STARBOARD

STARBOARD BOW

FORWARD

LENGTH

RELATIVE BEARING CHART

270
240   300
210   330
180   000
150   060   030
120   090

INDIAN OCEAN THEATER OF OPERATIONS

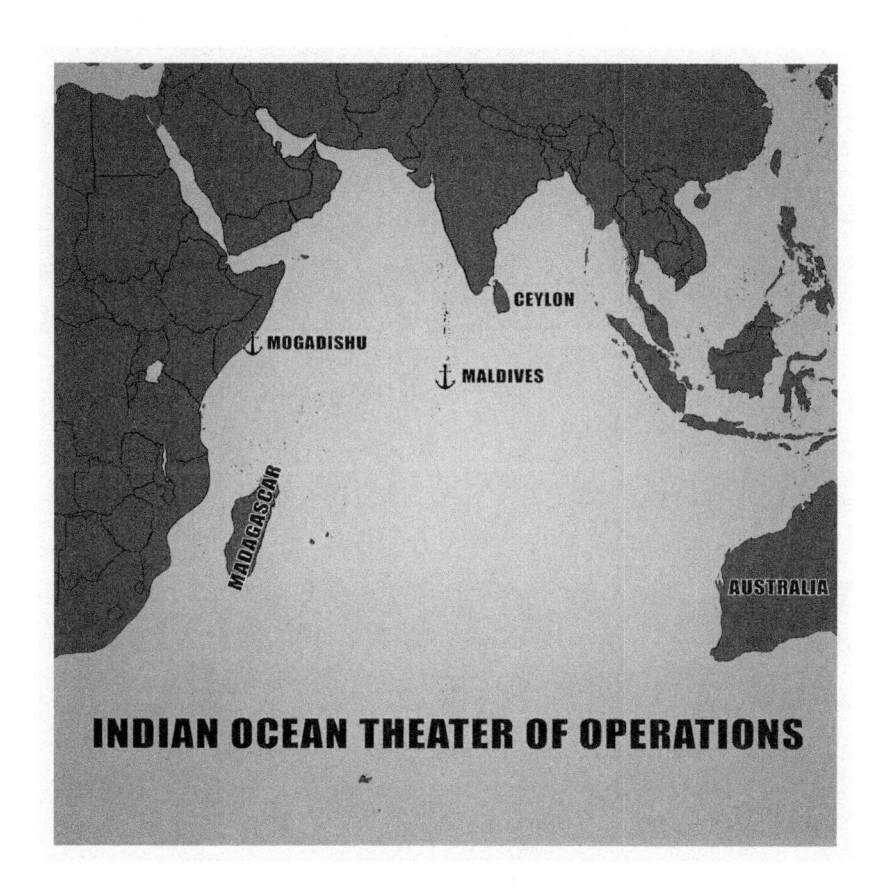

1
TO THE SHORES OF MADAGASCAR

Who will remember, passing through this Gate,
The unheroic Dead who fed the guns?
Who shall absolve the foulness of their fate—
Those doomed, conscripted, unvictorious ones

— **SIEGFRIED**

U.S.S. HOUSTON
0345 LOCAL (2045 EASTERN)
MOZAMBIQUE CHANNEL
23 JULY (22 JULY) 1943

MURDER WAS NEVER *one of my strong suits*, Captain Jacob T. Morton, skipper of the heavy cruiser U.S.S. *Houston*, thought. *But damn if I'm starting to get the hang of it.*

"Contact One continuing on course oh four zero true," the talker said, his voice seemingly loud in the gloom of the *Houston*'s bridge. "She continues to be followed by Contacts Two through Twelve, range holding steady at twelve thousand yards."

"Contact One" was the first of two large blips on the U.S.S.

Houston's radar. Jacob did not completely understand the new fangled rotating antenna mounted on the heavy cruiser's superstructure. What he did understand was that it allowed Lieutenant Commander Willoughby, his gunnery officer, to lay the heavy cruiser's guns on the correct bearing and greatly assisted in guessing a hostile vessel's speed. With visibility just below eight yards, the *Houston* would have to wait to fire once positive identification was made.

Totally oblivious, and clearly used to the Indian Ocean being their bailiwick since the war resumed. Well, we're about to change that. The Italians had inherited several of Great Britain's colonies in the aftermath of the Treaty of Kent. While some considered that document to have ended what had been deemed the Second World War, Jacob had problems with that terminology.

The fact that the Brits lost the Second Battle of Britain and some asshole seized his niece's throne doesn't mean it's not the same conflict. I'm sure as hell not fighting to put some teenager back in Buckingham Palace.

"Destroyers should be going in anytime now, Captain Morton," Commander Osborne Farmer, Royal Navy, stated. The officer was staring intently at the stopwatch in his hand. "I have faith you're about to be made a prophet."

I don't know if he's being facetious or is actually hopeful I'm right, Jacob thought, nodding at the Commonwealth officer's comment. A tall, gaunt man with a scarred face thanks to a German shell, Commander Farmer was a liaison officer from Her Majesty's Commonwealth Ship (H.M.C.S.) *Repulse*. The older battlecruiser, flagship of Task Force (TF) 24.2, was eight hundred yards behind *Houston* in the pre-dawn haze. Following the *Repulse* at similar intervals was the H.M.C.S. *Exeter*, and then the U.S.S. *Nashville*. Six destroyers, the Commonwealth *Garland*, *Griffin*, and *Hasty*, along with the American *Porter*, *Phelps*, and *Winslow*, had surged forward into the mist to launch torpedoes. Four more DDs, the U.S.S. *Farragut*, *Dewey*, *Monaghan*, and *Preston*, continued to maintain an anti-submarine screen around their larger charges.

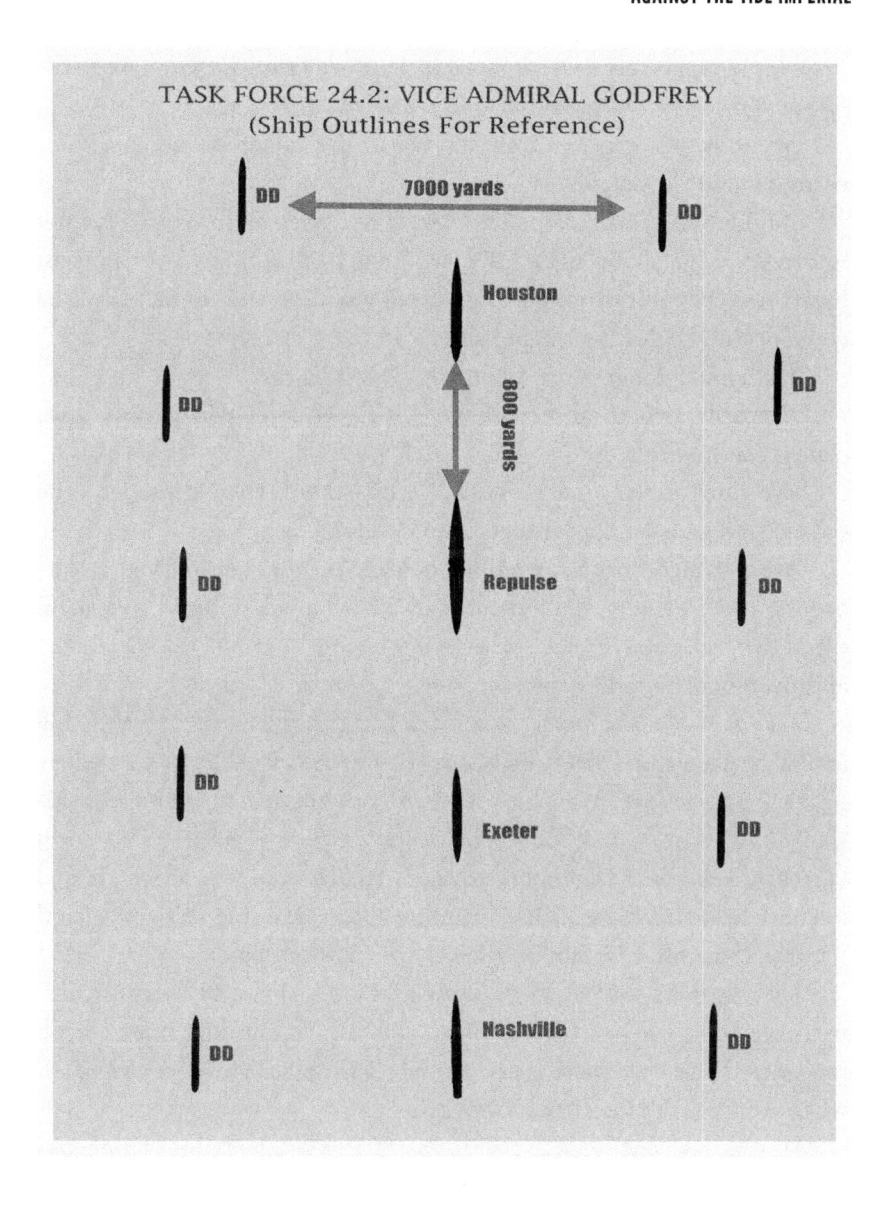

TASK FORCE 24.2: VICE ADMIRAL GODFREY
(Ship Outlines For Reference)

DD ←—— 7000 yards ——→ DD

Houston

DD ↕ 800 yards DD

Repulse

DD   Exeter   DD

DD   Nashville   DD

I didn't expect anyone to actually read that tactics proposal for our next combat operation. Nevermind attempt to carry out.

"Sir, lookouts can see Contact One," the talker stated, his voice rising a couple of octaves.

"Bloody hell, those torpedoes would not have arrived yet," Farmer muttered as Jacob brought his own binoculars up. The ever present haze prevented him from getting a good visual on the contacts, but he could just make out two shapes similar in size to the *Houston*.

"How much longer?" he asked.

"Probably two to three minutes," Farmer replied anxiously after glancing at his watch.

"We don't have time to wait," Jacob stated, then turned to the talker. "Tell guns he may engage Contact One."

"Aye aye, sir," the talker replied quickly. As the man relayed Jacob's orders, the *Houston*'s captain brought his binoculars back up just in time to see one of the darkened shapes starting to signal the approaching American cruiser.

Well, we're about to answer that signal in a way you're not expecting. Tall and wiry, Jacob had been nicknamed "The Stork" due to his gangly physical appearance. As many a boxing opponent had found out, his frame's awkwardness belied a relentlessly aggressive nature. The vessel currently sending a lazy query towards the *Houston* was about to find out just how much Jacob had ingrained "hit hard, hit fast, hit often" into the crew since he had become the vessel's captain.

The *Houston*'s searchlights illuminated a vessel roughly her own size with all four turrets trained fore and aft. From her lines, Jacob recognized she was Italian, not British, and felt slightly less guilty at what was about to be a brutal shock.

My God, they don't even have their turrets manned. His observation was immediately followed by the brilliant flash of *Houston*'s No. 1 and No. 2 turrets unleashing six 8-inch shells.

The unwitting target of the *Houston*'s ire was the Italian heavy cruiser R.M.S. *Trento*. A contemporary of the *Houston*, the vessel was similarly armed with four pairs of 8-inch guns, faster, and roughly two thousand tons greater displacement. Unfortunately for her crew, her designers had never foreseen a situation where the vessel would be caught flat-footed, at night, and with the crew not even at battlestations. Even worse, in order to gain her impressive speed, those same designers had skimped on her armor protection.

For all these reasons, Lieutenant Commander Willoughby's opening salvo was particularly devastating despite hitting with only two shells. The first punched into the *Trento*'s superstructure and exploded in the captain's day cabin, killing him and several other other personnel manning her anti-aircraft batteries. The second hit stabbed into the cruiser's forward boiler room, causing a great gout of steam that broiled the space's engineers as the ocean poured in.

"STARBOARD THIRTY DEGREES," JACOB BARKED. "SIGNAL THE *Repulse* and let Vice Admiral Godfrey know that we are engaging Contact One."

As the talker acknowledged his orders, Jacob quickly stepped into the compartment aft of *Houston*'s bridge. Previously part of the captain's day cabin, the yard workers in Sydney had converted the compartment to house the new radar equipment. Jacob had ordered the *Houston*'s operations department to also install a temporary plot that he could quickly reference in the midst of battle without departing too far from the bridge.

Jacob quickly took in the developing situation while the *Houston* jumped again from another full broadside. If the group followed his proposed action orders, *Repulse* would likely take Contact Two under fire, leaving *Nashville* to engage destroyers or other escorts.

"Make sure guns knows where our destroyers are," Jacob said, then ducked back onto the bridge as the main battery thundered again. This was followed by the secondaries firing starshells and the *Houston*'s searchlights winking out. The reason for the latter decision became readily apparent as four shells landed roughly five hundred yards short of the heavy cruiser.

"Helm, zig zag, standard pattern," Jacob ordered, bringing up the binoculars again. The roar of the *Repulse*'s 15-inch broadside was audible aboard the *Houston*, and he watched the large shells head downrange towards their target. To his dismay, he saw the that *Repulse* was also engaging the *Trento*.

Goddammit, he thought, even as two of the battlecruiser's hits wrecked the Italian cruiser's forward turrets in a massive fireball. *So much for distribution of fire.*

THE *TRENTO*'S CREW WOULD HAVE HAD MUCH MORE UNFAVORABLE things to say about the Allied' vessel's gang tackle. Lt. Cdr. Willoughby, having found the range with half of his second broadside, had put another five 8-inch shells into the cruiser's hull. The onslaught had killed many of the crew as they were stumbling out of their berths and trying to respond to the general quarters alarm, smashed the rudder machinery, and set the cruiser's aviation fuel storage afire. With the *Repulse*'s assault setting her forward armament ablaze, the *Trento* was rapidly becoming an inferno from stem to stern.

The focus on the Italian vessel had saved her companion, however. The H.M.S. *Arethusa* had joined the convoy after carrying a new ambassador from King Edward's London to Pretoria. Appalled at the escort commander's lackadaisical attitude, the *Arethusa*'s captain had maintained much better readiness than the *Trento* or the the five Italian destroyers accompanying her.

Recognizing the massive waterspouts indicated the presence of at least one capital ship, the *Arethusa*'s officer of the deck immediately put his helm hard about and began making smoke. By the time her captain made it to the bridge, the light cruiser's crew was mostly to battle stations, her 6-inch turrets had swung out, and the vessel's torpedo tubes were at the ready. Passing down the far side of the three merchantmen and tanker that made up the Italian convoy, the light cruiser waited for clear targets. As the U.S.S. *Nashville* opened fire with her fifteen 6-inch guns, the American cruiser's lack of flashless powder outlined the vessel's form.

. . .

"Nashville is engaging Contact Seven, possible destroyer," the talker shouted over the din of *Houston*'s main and secondary armament. Before Jacob could respond, the destroyers' initial torpedoes finally began to strike after their long runs. Before his eyes, two Italian destroyers erupted, their acceleration and turn towards the Allied force having carried them into torpedoes intended for the convoy. Jacob, looking at the clock, was briefly shaken to realize it had been barely ten minutes since radar had first detected the convoy.

"*Repulse* is ordering a forty-five degree turn to starboard to allow the destroyers to close," the talker relayed. "Formation will turn when we do."

"Acknowledge," Jacob said. "Helm, starboard forty-five."

"Training pays off, sir," Commander Farmer stated, his voice conveying the same awe that Jacob was feeling.

Jacob nodded his assent. Admiral Hart, Commander-in-Chief of the Southwest Pacific Area, had initiated a vigorous training regimen in the aftermath of his vessels' performance during the Dutch East Indies Campaign. His immediate subordinate, Admiral Victor Crutchley, Royal Australian Navy, had ruthlessly enforced the standards Hart had set forth. Vice Admiral Godfrey, Her Majesty's Commonwealth Navy, in turn made Crutchley seem like a kind, benevolent soul.

Three relieved captains and people realized the man was serious, Jacob recalled. *Getting most of one's navy destroyed will do that for–*

"Sir, the *Nashville* is taking fire!"

Jacob rushed out to the starboard bridge wing, looking down the *Houston*'s length to where the *Nashville* continued to lash out at a flaming vessel on the horizon. Starshells were drifting down around the light cruiser as a group of splashes was just subsiding. Another salvo arrived around the *Nashville*'s stern, and Jacob watched as the vessel's turrets stopped firing. After a moment, they began to orient towards very faint, distant flashes on the far side of the Italian convoy. As two shells hit forward along her hull in a flurry of sparks, the *Nashville*'s own stern turrets belched a bright retort towards her assailant.

What in the hell is out there? Jacob was still considering that question when, with a bright fireball, one of the convoy's vessels exploded in flames.

"*Repulse* is ordering all large vessels to retire to the northeast," the talker stated.

"Acknowledge," Jacob repeated, then gave the necessary orders to the helmsman. As the *Houston*'s bow came around, Jacob was treated to a better view of the *Repulse* as the battlecruiser turned to follow the American heavy cruiser.

Whatever fired at **Nashville** *clearly thought better of that plan.*

THE *ARETHUSA*'S CAPTAIN, AFTER BRIEFLY ENGAGING THE *Nashville*, had indeed determined that discretion was the better part of valor. Setting a course due south, the light cruiser quickly accelerated to her top speed. Remaining unsighted by the southernmost division of advancing Allied destroyers, the vessel vanished into the gloom.

The other escort vessels were not so lucky. The *Euor* and *Pegaso*, after blundering into the salvo meant for the convoy, to torpedo impacts with heavy loss of life. Their compatriots aboard the R.M.S. *Carlo Mirabello* and *Augustus Riboty*, initially saved by virtue of being on the far side of the convoy, had been illuminated by the *Nashville* attack on a hapless collier and the burning *Trento*. That had been enough for the *Garland*, *Griffin*, and *Hasty* to engage. The subsequent arrival of the *Porter*, *Phelps*, and *Winslow* had sealed the two destroyers' fate, the Italian crews barely getting off a handful of salvoes before both vessels' guns were silenced. As they were pounded into helpless wreckage, first the *Mirabello*, then the *Riboty* burst into flames.

With the escort dispatched, the destruction of the remaining merchant vessels was simply a matter of firing a shot across their bow. After pointed discussion with signal lamp, each merchantmen's crews took to their boats as prize crews boarded each vessel from the Allied destroyers. Moving quickly and surely, these men lay scuttling charges on each Italian vessel, then returned to their destroyers. Ten minutes later, over 50,000-tons of shipping was headed for the bottom of the Mozambique Channel.

The destroyer crews were returning to their parent vessels when the *Trento*'s fires reached the heavy cruiser's forward magazines. The brief inferno that followed the fireball was swiftly quenched as the heavy cruiser plunged bow-first into the depths. As her flaming stern slipped beneath the waves in the rolling cacophony of shattering bulkheads, sizzling decks, and escaping steam, the crews of the *Porter* and *Phelps* could hear survivors crying out in the darkness. Hurried consultation with the bridge and *Repulse* led to the two destroyers cutting free rafts and floatation nets for their Italian counterparts, but the pair of destroyers soon joined the rest of the Task Group in heading northeast.

"Sir, the *Repulse* is signaling for all vessels to set course for point Wideawake," the talker said, his words slurring slightly with fatigue as the adrenaline began wearing off.

That was intense and violent. I hope the flyboys do as much damage to the French when the sun comes up in a couple hours.

"Officer of the Deck, I'm going to look at the plot," Jacob said. "You have the con."

"Aye aye, sir," Lieutenant Mitchell, the current OOD, replied.

"We didn't quite manage to follow your plan, Captain Morton," Commander Farmer observed as he entered the darkened compartment a few moments later. "Still, I'd say that your theory about letting the destroyers attack first would probably have worked if the rest of the task force had been slightly further away."

"Well, to be fair, we weren't facing an enemy with radar," Jacob replied. "But yes, if I was writing the suggestion again, I'd recommend 10,000 yards' range along the line of advance, 15,000 yards lateral separation might work better."

Farmer pursed his lips.

"The risk of getting confused as to who is who increases a great deal at that range," the RN officer pointed out. "Doesn't do much good to get torpedoes off if that's immediately followed by one's own heavies blasting you to smithereens."

Jacob nodded at the man's words.

"Well that's always the risk, isn't it?" he observed grimly. "I do wish we'd had time to engage whomever fired upon the *Nashville*."

"I am reasonably certain we do not want to be in this channel come daylight," Farmer said. "Those two squadrons of bombers in Mozambique could make us rather uncomfortable with the carriers busy striking Madagascar."

BLUE ONE
VB-11
40 MILES NORTH OF DIEGO SUAREZ
0710 LOCAL (0010 EASTERN)

DAMMIT, FINALLY, LIEUTENANT ERIC COBB THOUGHT, CHAOS swirling around him. *After the Germans nearly kill me, the English make me sit through a surface battle, and the Japanese nearly paralyze me, here I am getting to dive bomb some assholes at last.*

"Thach you son-of-a-bitch, get these fighters off us!" Lieutenant Commander Eric Hitchcock, the squadron commander, shouted over the radio. Eric didn't hear the response from Commander Jimmy Thach, Fighting Five's commander, but he could see why Hitchcock was incensed as yet another French fighter slashed through Bomber Squadron Eleven's (VB-11's) formation. The Frenchman's slipstream buffeted Eric's bomber, the wind chill in his face through the *Dauntless*'s cockpit.

It's cold as hell out here. He grunted in amusement at the relatively inane observation in the middle of a battle. Yes, being in a different hemisphere took some getting used to, but he was going to be plenty warm if someone set his *Dauntless* on fire.

"Red, Blue flights, we have the heavy cruiser!" Lieutenant Commander Hitchcock, barked, tagging the squadron's first six bombers to go after the French vessel below. "Green, Yellow, get those damn destroyers."

VB-11 planes had lifted off the U.S.S. *Yorktown*'s deck barely an hour before. As the reserve squadron for Task Force 24, VB-11 had been armed with armor-piercing 1,000-lb. bombs and ordered to stand by for launch orders. According to Commander Montgo *Yorktown*'s CAG, they were either to be committed against installations that survived the onslaught from the U.S.S H.M.C.S. *Victorious*, and H.M.C.S. *Ark Royal*'s initial attack against the French naval base at Diego Suarez, or attack units attempting to flee. When reconnaissance aircraft had sighted a heavy cruiser and two destroyers just outside the harbor's mouth, the latter had clearly been decided.

"Red One, bogey at your five o'clock!" someone warned.

"Goddamit Green Four, get the hell back into formation!"

"Yellow Two is hit!"

The insanity of VB-11's squadron net was a distant distraction as Eric looked down at the French heavy cruiser turning wildly beneath them. He dimly heard his tail gunner, Radioman First Class Willie Brown, shout a warning about two of the French fighters coming in from seven o'clock high, but did not break from his preparations. As Brown cursed and opened fire with his twin .30-caliber guns, Eric watched Red flight pitch over into its initial dive.

Red One was hit, he thought, seeing smoke streaming back from the squadron commander's aircraft. Lieutenant Commander Hitchcock was a first grade asshole, but Eric had watched enough men die already in this war.

"*Sir, break right!*" Brown screamed. Eric reacted instinctively, skidding the laden SBD to starboard. It was not a moment too soon, the roar of an aircraft engine suddenly loud as radial-engined French fighter plunged past their port wing tip. Eric had a brief flash of a spiderwebbed canopy and a red smear on the glass.

Holy shit, Brown! Bringing his eyes back forward, Eric realized they had overshot his intended push over point.

Goddammit! Moving quickly, Eric extended the *Dauntless's* dive brakes. The metal structures extended from the wings, immediately slowing the SBD just before Eric pushed the nose down. Looking through the windshield, he saw with great relief that the French cruiser had reversed course to throw off Red flight's dive. Black puffs of smoke burst around the lead three dive bombers, tracers arcing up towards Lieutenant Commander Hitchcock's smoking aircraft.

Pull out you idiot!

As if the man was hearing Eric's mental plea, the trapeze cradle underneath Hitchcock's aircraft extended to swing the 1,000-lb. bomb clear of the SBD's propeller arc. Before the device could finish, a French heavy shell burst just underneath the SBD's starboard wing. As if smacked by an angry toddler striking his toy, the wing flipped upwards then snapped off, fluttering back in the wind. With the sudden loss of lift on that side, Hitchcock's *Dauntless* snap rolled, its bomb arcing off crazily under the forces.

Dammit! Nausea rising up, Eric ignored the rest of the outcome as he bent to his own bombsight. Manipulating his own bomber's stick and rudder, he aligned the crosshairs on the French cruiser just as Red Three's bomb hit its bridge. Debris and what he could only assume were some members of the French cruiser's crew spewed out of the brown-black fireball. Focusing on the ship, Eric gently manipulated the *Dauntless*'s rudder to keep the now circling ship within the aim point.

"Four thousand..." Brown began counting down, looking at the altimeter mounted in his position. "Three thousand."

Thank God you're alive. Eric saw the flashes of the French vessel's automatic weapons winking up at him. With a sharp *crack!*, one of the vessel's 90mm anti-aircraft shells exploded off their port wing. Eric felt and heard fragments pepper the airframe, but did not take his eye off the sight. With minor adjustments to his stick, he kept the aim forward of the now-burning bridge.

"Twenty-five hundred..." Brown said, his tone clearly indicating it was time to release the bomb. With his aimpoint just behind the French tri-color painted atop the second turret, Eric toggled the bomb release. The *Dauntless* buffeted slightly as the 1,000-lb. bomb swung out into the slipstream, then lifted as the half-ton weapon was released. Eric immediately hauled back on the stick, vision darkening as the blood rushed from his head.

THE VESSEL WAS THE FRENCH CRUISER *SUFFREN*. WITH HER CAPTAIN dead on her bridge, command of the vessel had fallen to her executive officer. Unfortunately, the French officer was not made

AGAINST THE TIDE IMPERIAL

aware of his new promotion in a timely manner. It was only as the cruiser was taking no evasive action and there was no communication with the bridge that the commander realized the damage that had been wrought forward. By that time, Eric's bomb was completing its descending arc that terminated between the *Suffren*'s two stacks.

The 1,000-lb. bomb had been intended to penetrate a capital ship's decks. As such, it pierced the *Suffren*'s decks all the way to the forward fire room before detonating on that space's deck. Unlike the unfortunate *Trento* a few hours before, the *Suffren*'s boilers burst, the vented force adding to that of the American high explosive to burst internal bulkheads and the vessel's sides. With the cruiser moving at twenty-five knots, the sea's force flooded the space so quickly that those in the midst of being scalded to death were mercifully drowned by the chilling waters.

Blue Two's bomb, released high and early, exploded off the *Suffren*'s starboard bow. Close enough to shake the cruiser and pierce her hull in the bow, the sum effect was to detract even further from the vessel's buoyancy via the insidious gradual flooding forward. Blue Three's weapon had the opposite problem, being released so low its fuse barely had time to arm before hitting the extreme end of *Suffren*'s stern. Passing through the structure, the weapon detonated between the rudder and middle prop, rendering both useless. Shuddering, the heavy cruiser remained locked in a starboard turn.

THE BLUE GRAY OCEAN SEEMED TO BE RUSHING UP TOWARDS HIM until it was lost below the *Dauntless*'s rising nose. Eric could feel the aircraft still sinking as his sight dimmed, the g-forces of his pull out shoving the blood from his head.

Oh fuck. Simultaneously with a massive blast that shook the SBD, the dive bomber leveled off a scant twenty feet above the water. Eric quickly closed his dive brakes and shoved his throttle forward as tracers arced above his canopy.

"Ow! Goddamit!" Brown shouted from behind him.

"You okay, Brown?"

"Got some metal landing in the cockpit, sir!" Brown replied. "You hit that bitch right amidships!"

Eric ignored the urge to turn and look back at the cruiser. Instead, having gained some airspeed, he brought the *Dauntless* around to the designated heading for rendezvous and checked for his wingmen. Ensign Stanley Van Horn, Blue Two, slid into position on his starboard side, but Blue Three was ominously absent.

"Blue Three, Blue Three, Blue One," Eric said, keying his microphone.

"This is Blue Three!" came the confused voice of Ensign Robert Strange, *Yorktown*'s newest dive bomber pilot. "I'm north of the target, Blue One, where are you?"

Eric started to make and angry comment then stopped himself.

You were once a scared nugget too.

"Head to the rendezvous point, Blue Three," he said sharply.

Only after he'd confirmed the survival of his men did Eric glance over his shoulder back towards the French cruiser. The vessel was slowing to a stop, her stern ablaze and a long slick of oil trailing behind her. One of the large *Fantasque*-class destroyers accompanying her was in even worse shape, its forward third a mass of flames. Its sister ship was circling at a distance, Green flight having apparently failed to damage it.

If that captain hasn't flooded his—

The violent explosion was a demonstration of what happened when an out-of-control blaze converted a magazine's potential energy to a thermodynamic process. The destroyer's bow, mostly separated by the blast, was severed by the press of onrushing water as the *Fantasque*-class continued to steam forward. With her bow gone, the vessel quickly began to flood, and Eric watched as it began to settle into the Indian Ocean.

"All Pegasus units, check in with status," Lieutenant Commander Scott Brigante called over the radio in his thick New York accent.

I don't know why we couldn't just use Haymakers on the radio, Eric thought. *That was another one of Hitchcock's dumb ideas.*

"Red Two, one down."

"Blue Flight, all accounted for," Eric checked in.

"Green Flight, one down," Lieutenant Drake Ramage, Green One, followed.

"Form up on me," Brigante said. "Calling *Yorktown*."

Blue Three slid into his position at that moment. Eric winced as he looked the *Dauntless* over, seeing several holes in the fuselage and wings. Despite its current resemblance to a colander, the SBD was only streaming a slight bit of smoke.

Unless he's really unlucky, doesn't look like anything is going to become a more serious problem. Still, better check.

"Blue Three, you look like the moths have been at you over the winter," he called. "What's your status?"

"The engine's lost a couple of cylinders and McCannis caught some shrapnel," Strange reported. "But I can get her back."

Not like you have much of a choice. Eric looked down at the seas below, then shook his head. *If exposure doesn't get you, the sharks will.* Their Royal Navy counterparts had taken some relish in explaining to the Americans just how shark-infested the waters below were this time of year. While Eric had sensed the Fleet Air Arm officers might have been having a lark, he was in no mood to test the theory.

Those poor French bastards, there's about to be a couple hundred of them going for a swim.

"How many hits did we get on the cruiser?" Brigante asked over the squadron net.

Well shit.

"Blue Two looked like he missed close forward, Blue Three right under the stern," Brown said.

Guess I'll take that as the gospel. Eric passed along the report as VB-11's surviving *Dauntlesses* slowly climbed back to 14,000 feet.

"Wonder if our mail will finally catch up with us?" Brown pondered, scanning the skies behind them. *Yorktown* had left Pearl Harbor in mid-May bound for the South Pacific. Their mail had caught up with them precisely *once* since departing Pearl.

Not the mail folks' fault. I'm kind of amazed her props haven't fallen off as many miles as we've steamed.

"Probably not until we get back to Australia or resupply catches up with us," Eric said, continuing to keep his eyes peeled. "We basically fell off the ends of the Earth as far as Pacific Fleet is concerned."

Brown chuckled bitterly.

"Yeah, well, I'm not sure if you officer types have noticed, but we're kind of in the *wrong ocean*."

"We go where the enemy is," Eric noted, his tone conveying that this wasn't a conversation he was super interested in holding. "The Frogs and Italians were leaning awfully hard on the South Africans, so we want to remind them the Mediterranean is *north* of here."

"Awfully expensive geography lesson today," Brown replied, then added a very delayed, "Sir."

He was good friends with Hitchcock's gunner, Eric reminded himself, taking a deep breath to keep from jumping down his gunner's throat. Movement at their altitude on the northern horizon caused the young officer to grab his stick harder. As the dots closed, he recognized them as an outgoing gaggle of *Wildcats*, *Avengers*, and *Dauntlesses*.

"Looks like the Brits are going to finish that cruiser off," Eric said. He recognized the *Ark Royal*'s squadrons due to the distinctive yellow-chevroned rudders and charcoal gray paint on the fuselage.

I guess the Commonwealth's work on figuring out a color scheme we Americans can recognize at a distance is progressing well, Eric observed. There had been some rather ugly friendly fire incidents in the Atlantic between USN and Royal Navy forces, some of which had contributed to the Allies losing the Battle of Iceland as several papers had dubbed it.

Nothing like 14,000 dead sailors and soldiers to generate some reforms.

"I hope they put that bitch on the bottom," Brown muttered angrily.

"That makes two of us," Eric replied. The ensuing silence told him it was best to let Brown grieve alone

I hope we do get some damn mail. I wonder what in the hell Jo and Patricia are up to.

Dry Dock No. 1
Pearl Harbor

1000 Local (1500 Eastern)
24 July

Patricia Ann Cobb, a.k.a. "Tootsie" or "Toots" to her four brothers, could feel the dockyard workers' eyes on her as she followed Vice Admiral Halsey down Dry Dock No. 1's sides. Taking a breath, she pushed the men's gazes from her mind and listened to what the acting commander-in-chief, Pacific Fleet, was saying.

"Your drawings and plans in the flesh, Ms. Cobb," the older man said, his eyes almost twinkling under his bushy salt-and-pepper eyebrows. With a grand gesture, he pointed to the repaired side of the U.S.S. *Maryland*. The coat of fresh paint applied to the battlewagon's side helped to hide the fact that her repaired section was visibly different in weathering compared to the rest of the plating on the armored belt.

"Thank you, sir," Patricia said, feeling color rise to her cheeks. She'd been hired on as a draftswoman a scant five weeks before. In that time, her previous experience helping a local architect when she was a young teenager had translated well to drawing ship repair plans. That, in turn, had helped the dockyard crews figure out ways to more efficiently repair the *Maryland*'s damage and likely saved several men's jobs.

"I think it was a team effort, Admiral Halsey," her boss, Frances Carter, stated. The short, stocky civilian stood just behind Patricia, his broad bulk straining the coveralls he'd been given. His balding brown hair was plastered with sweat, and his beetle brown eyes were narrowed as he spoke.

I have the urge to shove this man, Patricia thought, controlling her facial expression. Carter had been over her section for less than two weeks, and already Patricia hated the man. Insufferable, chauvinistic, and with a tendency to not watch where his hands were placed, Carter wasted no opportunity in reminding the four women working for him they only had jobs due to the need for the workshop's men elsewhere.

"I didn't say it wasn't," Halsey observed flatly.

Patricia recognized that tone, having heard it in several meetings. It was a noise as distinctive as a safety being taken off a deer rifle.

Gotta be easier and less painful ways to commit suicide, Patricia thought, then started to smile at one of her brother Nick's favorite sayings. The youngest Cobb was…somewhere, she had no idea where. The *Plunger* had left on a war patrol back in May, then not returned to Pearl Harbor.

"Something amusing, Miss Cobb?" Vice Admiral Halsey asked, startling Patricia.

"No sir," she said quickly. "I was just thinking about my brothers."

Halsey's face softened.

"I wish I was out there with them," the man said grimly. "Any of them."

"Thank you, sir," she replied, her draw thick with emotion. "It means a great deal."

I'm glad Nick's fiancée is the Submarine Commander's secretary, Patricia thought as Vice Admiral Halsey gestured for the *Maryland*'s captain to lead them on. *As I'm pretty sure I'd be the first person she'd tell if the **Plunger** was overdue.*

"Watch your step, Miss Cobb," her escort, a young ensign, said as she made her way to the gangplank laid to *Maryland*'s side. Per Halsey's orders, the battleship's crew continued with their feverish repairs, doing their part to make sure the battlewagon was ready to sail as soon as possible. Still, the shrill notes of a bosun's whistle cut through the air as Halsey crossed to the teak deck. Patricia tried to ignore the rather obvious crimson stains near the deck's edge, their faint outlines making their origins readily apparent.

"Welcome aboard, sir," Captain David Bursa, *Maryland*'s current master, stated as he came to attention then saluted. A thin man of average height, Bursa wore the khaki duty uniform of an officer overseeing work rather than the crisp dress whites such a visit would usually entail.

"Thank you, Captain Bursa," Vice Admiral Halsey replied, returning the salute. "Don't let us get in the way of anyone's work."

"Aye aye, sir," Bursa replied with a nod.

The next hour was spent crossing up and down decks as Captain Bursa took the party to the areas where *Maryland* had caught her two torpedoes during the Battle of Hawaii. In both cases, Patricia was amazed at how smoothly the repairs had been added, with the starboard hole being particularly good work.

"She'll be ready when the time comes, sir," Bursa finished, discussing the additional modifications that had been made to *Maryland*'s equipment since she was already in dry dock.

"The time is coming sooner than I'd like," Halsey replied, running a hand through his hair. Bursa nodded in acknowledgment, realizing his superior was not going to say anything else with Patricia and a couple other civilians present.

Of course, he doesn't realize that his sailors aren't quite as circumspect about keeping their mouths shut, she thought. *Jo could probably tell us all the exact date the **Intrepid** is due into port, when the **Maryland** will be floated out of drydock, or that the **King George V** and **Nelson** are expected to arrive from the Panama Canal any day now.*

Whether all that information was accurate was, of course, another matter. That it was even being discussed raised Patricia's hackles.

"Well that's enough of us being in your hair, David," Halsey stated. "I will see you at captain's call tomorrow morning."

"Aye-aye, sir," Captain Bursa replied. "Ensign Devereaux, if you'd be so kind as to take Mr. Carter and Miss Cobb topside?"

Devereaux nodded, came to attention, and saluted. Captain Bursa and Vice Admiral Halsey both returned the gesture.

Probably want to talk about the state of the hull, Patricia mused.

"If you'll follow me," Devereaux said, his tone clearly indicating it was not a request.

The bright Hawaii sunlight actually hurt Patricia's eyes as they returned to the *Maryland*'s deck. Blinking away the brightness, she looked down towards Battleship Row...and saw a strange, broad-beamed vessel steaming slowly down the channel towards Ford Island. Patricia did not need to see the large, white ensign fluttering from the warship's mast to know it was a Commonwealth battleship.

Damn thing looks like an oil tanker, not a battleship. All of its turrets forward like that seems to make no sense. Still, glad to see another battleship.

"Well, looks like the Royal Navy has arrived," Carter said snidely. "How nice of them to…"

"It would probably be best for everyone if you did not finish that thought, mister," the ensign said lowly but firmly. Patricia fought to hide a smirk as she heard Carter take in a deep breath as about to argue, only to find the young officer regarding him with a hard set face.

"One of my brothers got to spend some time aboard their vessels," Patricia observed, studying the new ship intently. "I believe that one's the *Nelson*?"

"Or *Rodney*," the ensign stated. Patricia could see the man was being purposefully obtuse.

At least someone here understands security.

"How did your brother end up on some Limey ship?" Carter asked derisively. "Is he a damn monarchist like our president?"

"Eric got shot down by the Germans," Patricia stated flatly. "When the King got killed."

Carter snorted.

"Seems like we're going through a whole lot of discussion to settle which pair of buttocks get to sit on a throne in London," the man muttered lowly.

Patricia saw her escort's face color.

"Ensign Devereaux, perhaps it's best if we take our leave," Patricia said. To her surprise, Carter ignored her.

"It appears we have a difference in opinion on this war's usefulness, Ensign," Carter continued.

Devereaux smiled.

"I think that my opinion is irrelevant. Congress has declared war in response to unprovoked attacks against us."

"*Unprovoked?*" Carter asked. "We basically gave the English all the weapons they could carry, provided them with the boats to carry it with and, if the papers are to be believed, conspired with Great Britain on how to go about killing Germans, all the while loudly proclaiming our neutrality."

Where in the hell did Captain Bursa and Vice Admiral Halsey go? Patricia thought, glancing around in a near panic.

"That's *quite enough*," Ensign Devereaux barked, causing several nearby sailors to pause in what they were doing to watch. Carter, realizing he had pressed things a bit far, shut his mouth and stared back at the young officer.

Is this how people are seeing the war now? Carter was correct in what the mainland papers were saying. In the aftermath of the USN's twin defeats off Iceland and Hawaii followed by the loss of the Philippines, Guam, and Wake, many were questioning how the United States came into the war. The bombshell that the Roosevelt administration had been apparently conducting secret talks and strategic planning with Her Majesty's government as far back as *1940* had led to an uproar.

Senator Lindbergh is calling for hearings, Patricia thought. The Republicans just might have the votes to force them in **both** houses.

"Let us go, Miss Cobb," Carter said after a long moment. "Would hate to disturb Ensign Devereaux from his delusions."

Patricia moved towards the gangway, the speed of her passage causing her dark chestnut hair to fall out of its bun. Muttering as she walked, she reached up and grabbed her tresses before they attempted to stream like their own pennant behind her. When she crossed onto the edge of the dry dock, she paused to finish fussing with her hair while Carter crossed far more slowly behind her.

"Tell me, Miss Cobb, do you support this war?" Carter asked as they walked towards the waiting automobile.

"I have four brothers and my fiancé fighting in it, Mr. Carter," Patricia said, barely keeping her tone civil. "I don't really have the option of *not* supporting it."

Carter looked at her with a cool air of assessment.

"I was brought out here to Hawaii from a lucrative job in California," Carter said after a moment. "I was next in line to be a foreman at Mare Island when my bosses determined I would be more valuable correcting inefficiencies in the shop out here."

I cannot imagine whatever would make your boss send you all the way out here, Patricia thought wryly.

"I am telling you this so you understand that I mean every word of what I am about to say," Carter continued. "If you ever interrupt a discussion I'm having with someone again, I'll fire you on the spot. No one will question it, no matter how much Vice Admiral Halsey seems to have taken a liking to you. Understand?"

Well fuck you, Mr. Carter. Patricia did her best to keep the anger from her face and tone as she responded.

"Yes."

Carter looked at her with a raised eyebrow. Patricia continued looking at him in her best airhead debutante.

"I'd always heard Southerners were raised with manners," he said finally. "But no matter. I also understand that my predecessor, before he got sent to Australia, had you come in at nine o'clock. Your hours are now six to four, with an hour lunch break. As you know, there's a war on."

IJNS AKAGI
SINGAPORE
1200 LOCAL (0030 EASTERN)
25 JULY

THE POUNDING OF RAIN ON THE CARRIER'S FLIGHT DECK WAS audible as Vice Admiral Tamon Yamaguchi stood on the vessel's bridge. He fought the urge to smile, but his heart filled with joy as he looked at the long, flattopped shape easing its way into the harbor.

Shokaku, it has been so long since we have seen each other. At last the Kido Butai is complete once again. Then, after a moment, that reflection sobered him. *Well, as complete as numbers make us.*

Zuikaku, the *Shokaku*'s sister ship, had been lost at the Battle of Hawaii. Hit first by American submarine torpedoes then finished by a squadron of their *Flying Fortresses*, the carrier had gone to the bottom of the Pacific with many of her aircrews. *Shokaku* had been struck by the same submarine that had holed her sister. Due to being able to maneuver, however, she had managed to evade the B-17s' attentions. Instead, the larger carrier had received multiple bombs from the U.S.S. *Hornet*'s air group shortly before the rest of the *Kido Butai* had put paid to that vessel as well.

Hawaii went almost perfectly for carriers attacking an alerted enemy. **Hornet**, **Lexington**, *and* **Saratoga** *sunk along with several of their battleships.* He gazed out once more towards the open ocean beyond Singapore's breakwater. *So why do I feel like a man about to be overwhelmed by an incoming tide?*

He did not question how their German allies got their information. However, it had been accurate for the most part, so he had no reason to disbelieve that his force had landed a heavy blow upon the Americans. Coupled with the losses that the Imperial Japanese Navy had inflicted during the Dutch East Indies campaign, Vice Admiral Yamaguchi and his peers had run amok for a little over three months.

Perhaps it is the news that an enemy task force is on the loose in the Indian Ocean and I am just now confident that I could deal with it. Intelligence had stated that there were at least two, and possibly as many as four, Allied carriers running amok near Madagascar. Given that Yamaguchi had placed three on the bottom of the Pacific and had to strain to keep air groups for six fully operational, it was astounding how quickly the Allies were recovering combat power.

I cannot sink them quickly enough.

"You seem very reflective, Yamaguchi-san," Admiral Isoroku Yamamoto observed beside him. "I believed you would need to be restrained from running up and down the flight deck in joy now that *Shokaku* and *Taiho* have joined you."

"I am merely doing math, sir," Yamaguchi allowed. "The enemy will probably react strongly to our Ceylon operation."

"I can only hope so," Yamamoto stated. "So far we have split the honors with your counterparts."

I think the first fight off Ceylon was a victory, Yamaguchi silently disagreed with his superior. *I'd have traded **Shoho** for just about any other carrier in this war, and we definitely sank the **Furious**.* Yamaguchi had seen the camera footage of the British carrier rolling over to starboard after taking three torpedo hits in quick succession.

"With the *Yorktown*, *Victorious*, *Enterprise* and *Ark Royal* confirmed to be on other side of the Indian Ocean," Yamamoto said, "I am sorely tempted to send you south to see if you could convince the *Illustrious* to come out and fight."

"I have enough pilots fighting land-based aircraft, sir," Yamaguchi said stiffly. "I don't need to go picking a fight in Australia."

Yamamoto smiled as his subordinate continued.

"We have spent the last three months scraping together air groups, and one carrier would not be quite enough to justify that fight. Ceylon will bring them all out, then we will kill them."

Yamamoto nodded at Yamaguchi's proclamation.

"It is a shame that the refineries in the Dutch East Indies were so damaged," the senior admiral stated. "Otherwise we would not care about Ceylon."

"I was shocked at how much oil the Germans gave us from the Persian Gulf oilfields," Yamaguchi noted. "It would be nice to have access to that oil again."

"Instead we have Ceylon cutting that off like a fish bone in our throat," Yamamoto noted. "No matter. Hopefully this will end things in the Indian Ocean for the British."

It would have been easier if we could have persuaded India not to lease Ceylon, but there's no way we could replace the British grain shipments. How India was going to feed herself after the Japanese seized Ceylon was not Yamaguchi's problem, but he still felt a slight tug at his conscience.

"The Army still has delusions of invading northern Australia," Yamamoto stated, changing the subject.

"I shudder to think of the problems we would have if those idiots were still in charge," Yamaguchi spat. "In some ways, the Soviets did us a favor."

Yamamoto gave his subordinate a sideways glance.

"I think there are several thousand soldiers still missing who would disagree with you," he observed, then held up his hand before Yamaguchi could protest. "This, of course, versus the million or so that would still be stuck in China as snakes trying to swallow an elephant."

Snakes that would be, in turn, consuming far more resources than they produced. At least the Southern Operations will eventually begin to pay for themselves once we get the Americans to accept the new world order.

"Ozawa-san believes that we should split the *Kido Butai*," Yamamoto said, referring to Vice Admiral Jisaburo Ozawa.

"Of course he does," Yamaguchi replied sarcastically, then bowed slightly. "Sorry, sir."

Yamamoto smiled knowingly.

"It is as if I knew another admiral who once complained loudly about a superior's inability to effectively control this very force," he observed drily. "Hopefully Ozawa will never be proven as prescient as that officer was."

Yamaguchi nodded, keeping his mouth shut. Yamamoto, seeing that his point had been gently made, continued.

"Ozawa is concerned what will happen if the Americans counterattack again towards Wake," Yamamoto said. "We cannot trust in our submarines managing to sink a pair of battleships every time."

Dammit Ozawa. Ozawa had a point insomuch that the carriers remaining with part of the battle line had never been intended for a general fleet action. However, Yamaguchi knew there was a significant difference in what he could do with four aircraft carriers versus six, especially with Allied forces in the Indian Ocean.

"Never fear, Yamaguchi-san," Yamamoto said after a few moments. "I reminded him if he had not let *Ark Royal* get away from him off Ceylon the first time, you would not have to worry about numbers so much."

That had to sting a little bit.

"I pointed out that, with *Ryujo* being out of dry dock much earlier than anticipated, he will have plenty of airpower to keep Ceylon suppressed if we follow the plan."

The hard rain continued to rattle against the *Akagi*'s bridge windows, the wind starting to pick up as well. As he watched the tugs take over maneuvering the *Shokaku*, Yamaguchi was glad that he did not have that thankless job.

"Ugaki-san is driving the staff hard to finish the planning for Operation I," Yamamoto said, gesturing towards the battleship *Musashi* roughly a half mile away. "His assumptions include that you will need time to work *Shokaku* back into your force."

"We can work her back into operations on the way to Ceylon," Yamaguchi said. "I know that every day we wait, the Americans grow stronger. I would prefer that we help them see the error of their ways before the giant grows robust enough to simply smother us with his size."

Yamamoto nodded.

"It is sometimes hard explaining to people who have never seen their factories just how much potential the Americans have," Yamamoto stated soberly. "I will tell Ugaki to plan on this force initiating operations in a week rather than three."

Well, here's to hoping that my gamble is correct, Yamaguchi thought. *For if I am wrong, I may truly regret this decision.*

"With six carriers to their five, plus Ozawa-san's flight decks, I like our odds," Yamaguchi said. "Especially if we can capture airfields on Ceylon before they can react."

BREMERTON NAVAL SHIPYARD
WASHINGTON STATE
1100 LOCAL (1400 EASTERN)
26 JULY

"WELL, I SUPPOSE IT BEATS FLYING THEM ABOARD," MAJOR ADAM Haynes, United States Marine Corps, observed drily as a crane lifted the last of his squadron's FM-2 *Wildcats* aboard the escort carrier U.S.S. *Chenango*.

Got birds just in time to put them on a ship and catch a ride to Pearl Harbor. His squadron had been without aircraft for much of the previous three months.

"I think it'd be easier with her than some other vessels," Captain Samuel Cobb, his squadron deputy, replied grimly. Converted from an oiler hull, the *Chenango* was actually a fairly long vessel as escort carriers went. Although not even an untrained eye would mistake her for a fleet carrier, Adam could appreciate that the Navy wasn't sending his squadron to the Pacific in one of the "floating coffins" that he'd watched depart for parts unknown two weeks before.

I think both the Cobb brothers would have mutinied if they had, Adam thought, glancing sideways up at Sam. Which would be a whole lot of man to try and force on a vessel.

Sam and his twin brother, David, had been formerly assigned to VMF-14. Their unit had been almost completely annihilated when a Japanese I-boat torpedoed the U.S.S. *Long Island*. Although both of the large men were putting on a strong front, Adam had the feeling neither was pleased about returning to Hawaii.

Of course, I'm not pleased about having to land on a damned postage stamp in the middle of the ocean. The Navy had initiated a crash course for he and any other Marine who had not qualified on carrier landings during their induction process. As a man who had been in his fair share of combat and then some, landing on a carrier was still the most terrifying thing Adam had done.

"Are you still planning on giving the squadron three day's liberty?" Sam asked. The question startled Adam, as Sam had struck him as someone who did not care much about such things.

"I imagine I will, yes," Adam replied. "You and your brother going somewhere?"

Sam laughed.

"I guess he didn't tell you yet," Sam said. "Sadie has *finally* arrived in Seattle."

Adam face broke into a broad smile.

"About damn time," he stated flatly. "I thought I was going to have to get you brother out of jail if personnel had screwed up his dependent paperwork one more time."

"Can't really blame them given that those idiots in Honolulu screwed up the marriage certificate," Sam allowed. "Not that I'd tell David that to his face."

David and Sadie Cobb had gotten married just before the two brothers were bundled off to the West Coast at Vice Admiral Halsey's explicit direction. Realizing that it had only been dumb happenstance that three of the four Cobb brothers had not been slain in less than thirty days, Halsey had clearly believed sending the twins on a war bonds tour through Washington State was a way to keep them safe. Sam and David had short circuited that plan by accosting Adam in a restaurant

"Wise plan," Adam observed. "I still remember the suicidal moron who was flippant about her not being on the *President Coolidge*."

Sam chuckled, and the sound was surprisingly dark. The *Coolidge* had been carrying the first load of dependents from Hawaii when she pulled into Bremerton. Due to wartime secrecy, Sadie had not been able to inform Sam that she'd been bumped from the vessel due to her paperwork not being in order. The Navy lieutenant in charge of the manifest had basically implied that maybe the newest Mrs. Cobb had gotten cold feet and decided not to join her husband after all.

"Only reason there wasn't a murder was we were raised not to hit a woman," Sam stated. "I still think that nurse had probably never received such a thorough butt-chewing without a single word of profanity."

"I think Vice Admiral Halsey underestimated you yahoos when he sent you here," Adam said. "You probably would have been just fine if you'd stayed in Hawaii."

Sam shrugged.

"He was trying to do us a favor. Plus, I don't think the Navy wanted another publicity black eye after losing those brothers on the *Arizona* and *West Virginia*. Apparently those five brothers on the *Juneau* got split up as well."

"So any idea where your other brothers are?" Adam asked.

"Eric's off somewhere with the *Yorktown*," Sam said. "Last letter we got from him mentioned the Indian Ocean."

Adam gave Sam a cocked eyebrow at that one.

That's a bit of a security breach.

"Not in so many words," Sam hurried to explain, correctly reading his commander's look. "Toots used to love running around in moccasins when we were kids. He mentioned he was off to get her some new shoes out of the ocean."

Adam shook his head.

"As for Nick, who knows?" Sam said. "No one's heard from him since he went aboard *Plunger*. His fiancée was nervous for some reason, and I heard the sub's last executive officer cracked up because her captain was insane."

"Isn't that like saying water's wet?" Adam asked, incredulous.

"I don't follow?"

"You're talking about a group of men who, of their own free will, get into a big metal can and dive hundreds of feet under the ocean," Adam explained. "I know I'm not exactly one to talk about rational choices, but that seems a bit mad to me."

Sam shrugged.

"Nick says it's not all that crazy unless you screw up. He's always been kind of vague about what that means."

"I imagine anything that lets more water into the submarine than the captain intended would be a screw up," Adam replied. "There's a reason I prefer flying to anything to do with water."

Sam looked up at the carrier, then back at Adam.

"So I'm guessing you're about as upset about this as David and I are?"

"Not quite," Adam replied.

A young lieutenant exited the *Chenango*'s gang plank and started looking around. Tall and gangly, the man scanned the dock, his face somewhat concerned. Seeing Adam and Sam, the officer strode over and saluted.

"Major Haynes, I am Lieutenant Palmer, Officer of the Watch," the man said. "Captain Damon sends his compliments, and understands we will not see any of your squadron until Sunday morning."

"That is correct," Adam replied. "By authorization of Rear Admiral Dalton."

"Understood," Lieutenant Palmer replied. "Captain Damon also wanted me to pass along that the carrier will be leaving at 1000 on the dot Monday morning. Please have your men sober, aboard, and prepared for that departure, sir."

Adam smiled at that last bit.

"Tell the good captain we are indeed aware of our duty requirements," he said without rancor. "If anyone fails to make movement, I understand there's a procedure involving the keel for that."

"Aye aye, sir," Palmer replied. He came to the position of attention and snapped off another salute. Adam returned it, then turned to look at Sam.

"You heard the man," Adam said as Palmer walked off. "See you Friday night, go ahead and start your pass."

"I was planning on helping you provide the safety briefing to the squadron," Sam protested.

"I think I can cover 'don't beat your spouse, don't get publicly intoxicated, please don't kick the Army's ass even if they deserve it, and don't make any babies unless you intended to'," Adam observed. "Anything else I don't cover isn't probably going to be important anyway."

Sam shook his head.

"With that, sir, I'll see you on Friday afternoon," Sam said. "I'm going down to Olympia to check on someone."

That certainly sounded somber. Also not my business, as he's grown.

"You can bring that *someone* over to my house Friday afternoon if they can get away," Adam said. "Going to have a picnic, according to Norah."

Sam smiled at the mention of Adam's girlfriend.

"I'll see, sir," Sam said.

SIX HOURS LATER, SAM FOUND HIMSELF WONDERING IF THIS WAS THE best idea he'd ever had as he walked through the early summer evening to a small, nondescript ranch house on Olympia's outskirts. A single beat up Packard was in the drive, and the house's well kept garden was seemingly indicative of a meticulous home owner or owners. A child's bicycle lay carelessly on the walkway, causing Sam to stop and do a double take.

Do I have the right address? Did she mo...

"I'm sorry, sir, let me get that out of your way!" a harried voice said from the next yard over. Sam turned to see a small, diminutive Asian woman come running over from her front porch, quickly wiping her hands on the apron wrapped around her blue dress. "Harry has been told many times not to leave his bicycle in Mrs. Bowden's yard!"

"Oh it's alright," Sam said, holding up his hands. "I don't want a young man to catch a tanning on my behalf."

"No, it most certainly is not," the woman replied. Sam realized she had a hint of an English accent. "I have warned him several times that our neighbor does not need to come stumbling out of her house in the middle of the..."

The front door opening stopped Sam and the woman both in their tracks. Beverly Bowden stood on the front porch in a terry cloth robe, her mouth wide open as she took in Sam standing there in his Marine khakis.

"I know this is a total surprise, but if a woman writes you a couple times a week, the least you can do is make sure she's doing okay," Sam said by way of greeting. Beverly quickly closed her mouth, then turned to her neighbor.

"Myla, please don't hold it against Harry that he left his bicycle there," she said breathlessly. "I distracted him by offering him some cookies, then he tore off after Leto."

Myla looked at Beverly, then Sam, then back at Beverly. The woman's face started to soften in concern.

"Oh no, Mrs. Bowden," Myla said, clasping her hands together. Beverly, initially not following, realized what Myla believed was occurring. The American quickly reached out and grabbed her neighbor's hands.

"No, that's not why he's here," Beverly said, then paused. "I...I've already had that visit."

Myla looked confused, then quickly caught on.

"Oh no...I...I just assumed that when you said your husband was a Marine that he was overseas," Myla said, clearly embarrassed. "I'm so sorry."

"Don't be," Beverly said gently. "I don't...I'm still getting used to it myself, so I don't correct people that I mean he passed. I didn't want to burden you with my troubles given Ian is still out there."

Who is Ian?

"I'm sorry, I'm being rude," Beverly said, as if awakening from a dream. "This is..."

She paused to look at Sam's rank.

"...Captain Samuel Cobb. He was in my husband's squadron."

Myla turned to look at Sam, her smile cautious.

"Greetings Ma'am," Sam said, nodding and bowing slightly.

"As you can hear, Sam is not from around here," Beverly said with a slight smile. "Neither is Myla, as you can also tell. Myla's husband, Ian Ferguson, is a member of Her Majesty's diplomatic corps."

"Pleased to meet you, Samuel," Myla said, extending her hand. Sam took it gently, then was surprised at Myla's firm grip.

"If you give me a moment to get decent, I'll have you inside for some coffee," Beverly said. "I was just getting ready to walk down to the store to grab some fish."

"I can walk with you," Sam said. "I think I know exactly what store you're talking about. I walked by it on the way in."

"You walked?!" Beverly asked, then caught herself with a laugh. "Of course you mean from the train station. Sorry. I just woke up. Be right back."

Sam watched as Beverly disappeared back in her house. Turning to Myla, he smiled sheepishly.

"She wasn't expecting me," Sam said by way of explanation.

Myla chuckled at that.

"Clearly," she replied, giving Sam an inquisitive look. "I did not know that there were Marines in Olympia."

"I'm down from up north," Sam said smoothly. "She told me that she'd arrived in Olympia about a month ago; I figured I'd come pay my respects."

Myla nodded at his vagueness, even as her inquiring look deepened.

"I understand the need for security," she said. "Ian has always been secretive as well. He could be in Tibet, he could be in India."

"India?" Sam asked, surprised. He pondered asking the follow-on question of what Myla was doing in Olympia.

"Her Majesty's government is considering moving to Vancouver," Myla said, apparently reading his expression. "We moved there briefly, then Ian was asked to come down here on a matter he could not tell me about. We'd been here only six months before he was detached to go to India, then the war resumed."

"I'm sorry to hear that you are separated by his duty," Sam said sadly. "That's really unfortunate."

"Well, America is a much better place to spend a war than Usurper Hong Kong," Myla observed.

Sam was saved from responding by the door opening to reveal Beverly in a red gingham dress. She'd brushed out her long brunette locks and applied very subtle make up. In her flats, she barely reached his chest, but exuded a presence that far belied her size.

The head nurse returns. Sam's eyes burned slightly as he remembered

Beverly sneaking Toots, David, Nick, and himself in to see Eric after his younger brother had been injured on *Hornet*.

"I would hope I don't look that horrible, Sam," Beverly said softly. Startled, he looked at her and saw a twinge of sadness in her own brown eyes.

"You don't look horrible at all," Sam said, his face warming as Beverly smiled.

"I better get back inside before my pie burns," Myla said hurriedly, sensing the tenseness. "If you see that son of mine while you're walking, tell him he better get home, no matter what that cursed dog has them up to."

Sam looked at Myla and nodded.

Beverly may have saved him from a talking to about the bike, but he's definitely going to get gnawed on about being late for dinner.

"Will do, Myla," he said. Beverly put on a hat that matched her dress, then took Sam's left arm.

"Shall we, Captain Cobb?" she asked.

"Lead on, Mrs. Bowden," Sam replied, then kicked himself.

A few blocks of companionable silence later, Beverly finally spoke.

"So I was not expecting you to come find me, obviously," she said. "I just wanted to tell David and you thank you for what you did with gathering the belongings."

"It was the least we could do," Sam replied earnestly. "I...we..."

"If you're about to say you're sorry, don't," Beverly said, her tone edgy. She took a deep breath. "And if you're going to feel guilty, that's stupid."

Sam looked over at Beverly, seeing that her eyes were wet.

"Max told me once that anytime you go up in a plane, you're taking your life in your hands," she continued, her voice raw. "I knew what he did for a living, I saw what could happen firsthand after the battle."

The Battle of Hawaii was an eye opener for a lot of us.

"Knowing and having to face it are two different things," Sam stated, his own voice catching as he recalled that horrible morning.

"I can only imagine how horrible you feel," Beverly replied. "I heard the scuttlebutt that you were in the landing pattern when it happened."

"Yes," Sam replied. He shook his head as if a mosquito was buzzing around it, trying to stop his mental replay of the *Long Island*'s demise. Beverly squeezed his arm.

"They told me that Max had just returned to the ready room when the torpedo hit," she said. "He probably never even knew what hit him."

Who the fuck told her all those details? Sam seethed, both angry at the security breach and the morbidity of explaining to a widow just how her husband had died.

"I asked," Beverly said, as if reading his mind. "I begged the chaplain to find out for me, as I had horrible nightmares of Max slowly drowning as the carrier sank."

Sam patted her hand, then returned the salute of a pair of passing Army soldiers.

"We need to talk about happier tidings," Beverly said. "How is David? Did they ever finish moving his wife to the States?"

"Sadie arrived really early this morning," Sam said. "He caught the train down to Seattle to meet her. Haven't heard from him since."

"I can only imagine," Beverly said, giggling. "I hope you won't think less of me if I admit to that being the part I liked the most about Max coming back from a tour."

Sam shrugged.

"You were a happy couple," he said with a smile. "Reminded me of my parents in a lot of ways."

Beverly swatted his arm.

"I'm not that old, thank you very much," she said, aghast

"Well obviously not in *that* way," Sam replied. "Just two people who clearly loved each other a lot."

"His mother always believed he could have married better," Beverly said. "She let me know it, too."

"Well that's just stupid," Sam said. "Maj…Max clearly loved you. I think that's all that was important."

"Loretta wanted grandchildren," Beverly said. "The comment came out in a fight about Max wanting to go to Hawaii for his next duty station and me being fond of the idea."

Gee, what it is it with mothers being mean to their children just because they're going to Hawaii? Toots and Mom are still really stiff about one another, and that's been almost a year.

"Mrs. Bowden sounds like a mean hag," Sam said.

"Well, both of them are," Beverly allowed, then continued before Sam could argue with her. "I did remind the woman that maybe the problem was her, given how her husband ran off and now her son was running away as well."

Sam sucked in a pained breath.

"So, tell me, who won the catfight?" he asked, bemused. "I can only assume you, seeing as how you have both your eyes still."

"I won for two reasons," Beverly said archly. "One, we went to Hawaii. Two, Max spent his mother's Christmas gift money on a nice necklace for me the next day."

"I bet that went over like a lead balloon," Sam observed.

"She never brought up the topic again," Beverly said. "I think that Max had a talking to with her as well."

Their conversation was interrupted by furious barking and laughter coming from below the foot bridge they were standing on. The two of them went to the side and looked over the railing. Below them, they saw two young girls, a half-Asian boy who clearly favored his mother, and a very wet, muddy German Shepherd.

"Oh my word, that boy is going to die when he gets home," Beverly breathed, then said, louder, "Harry, Leto, your mother says for you both to get home *right now*."

Harry looked up in surprise from where he was playing with his two young friends in the mud. Sam was quite certain that the two young girls were sisters, their similar curly hair and freckled faces giving away the relationship more than the matching patterned jumpers.

"Yes, Mrs. Bowden," Harry said. Leto, recognizing Beverly, sprung out of the mud and began scrambling up the bank towards them while barking excitedly.

"Leto!" Harry called after his companion. The German Shepherd stopped in its tracks, tongue lolling as it looked at Beverly, then back at Harry.

"You don't need to get Mrs. Bowden muddy," Harry admonished

the dog. The animal lowered its head in submission, wagging its tail slowly as its master caught up with him.

Well-trained dog. Harry produced a treat from his pocket, then scratched Leto's ears. His two friends giggled and also petted the dog, who licked them both in turn.

You'd never realize there was a war on, Sam mused. Which is the point of fighting those bastards out there.

"You left your bike on my sidewalk again," Beverly called. "You can't keep letting your mom know I'm giving you cookies like that."

"Yes, Mrs. Bowden," Harry said, sheepish. Beverly made a shooing motion, then turned back to Sam.

"Let us not tarry, Sam, it's getting late."

"You know, if you'd like, I can buy you dinner," Sam said. "Probably easier to find a restaurant than to cook at this point."

Beverly gave him a smile.

"Why Samuel Cobb, are you asking this widow on a date?"

Sam scuffed his feet, then stepped back slightly from Beverly.

"I didn't mean to give that..." he began hurriedly.

"Well, and here I'd heard all these tales that you were a ladies man," Beverly said, shaking her head. "I assure you, I will not mistake dinner as anything other than a friendly gesture."

"I just would not want any likely suitors to think it was anything other than a meal with very pleasant company," Sam said.

Beverly looked around.

"Who else are we picking up?" she asked, then outright guffawed at Sam's pained expression.

"I have my shift in a couple of hours," she stated. "Don't stand there wondering what to say for too long. Most places are kinda slow now, and I think you actually want to enjoy your food."

*U.S.S. P*LUNGER
*0400 L*OCAL *(1500 E*ASTERN*)*
*P*HILIPPINE *S*EA
*27 J*ULY *(26 J*ULY*)*

CLICK...BOOM! CLICK...BOOM! CLICK BOOM!

The rumble of depth charges had persisted for over twenty hours. Cruising at 280 feet and rigged for silent running, the U.S.S. *Plunger* was far below the Japanese barrage. As he took a shallow breath, however, Lieutenant Nicholas Cobb could tell that the air quality was starting to reach the dangerous stage.

"You'd think that *maru* was carrying their entire payroll and their ancient ancestors' ashes," Commander Titus Emerson spat. If they were going to be this upset, they really should have guarded her better."

I swear to God, sir, I could punch you. Nick, having been the officer of the deck when the convoy was sighted the day before, had quickly determined the solitary *maru* with three destroyers as her escort probably wasn't worth attacking.

Should have known that Commander Emerson would feel differently. Normally that wouldn't be a huge problem, as any sane man looking through the periscope would have done the same math I did.

"Sir, I think three destroyers guarding her was more than enough," Nick replied lowly. "Most people turn and run at that point."

"Good thing we're not most people, XO," Emerson said happily. "That *maru* sure did put on one hell of a pyrotechnic show when she went up."

Yes, I'm sure we just hit some really important target. Too bad none of us are going to live to talk about it at this rate.

"Sir, they're making another run," the sonar man said resignedly.

"We must be leaking *something*," Chief Petty Officer Luke McClaughlin, Chief of the Boat, snapped. "Otherwise how are those fuckers tracking us?"

Emerson gave Chief McClaughlin a disapproving look at the man's language. Before the commander could say anything, the next batch of depth charges gently shook the boat rather than delivering the sharp jarring of near misses.

"How many charges does that make?" Emerson asked, turning to Ensign Paul Griswold. The boat's most junior officer, Griswold had been put in charge of tracking the explosions.

"That's two hundred charges, sir," Griswold said, licking his lips as he consulted his notes. "The majority of them have not been close."

"Looks like we're all still learning our jobs, even on their side," Emerson remarked. "Continue on this current heading. Eventually someone's going to decide those destroyers have another job."

We can only hope so. Looking around, he noted the condensation within the boat seemed to be increasing. In addition to simply making it hard to breathe, the declining air quality meant it was quite clear the *Plunger* was filled with unwashed, sweating human beings.

I don't even want to know how hot it is in here. Unlike his brothers, Nick was a very thin, wiry man. The *Plunger* was still more than humid and warm enough to make him uncomfortable without extra bulk. Some of the crew's larger members looked perilously close to heat exhaustion, and he'd already informed the submarine's officers to ensure they were forcing hydration.

"Lieutenant Cobb, what do you think that vessel was carrying?" Ensign Griswold asked quietly. Nick had not been aware the young officer had slipped over from his spot near the plotting table.

"Explosion that heavy? I'd guess it was some sort of ammunition. But that's awfully odd for a single ship to have an escort of three tin cans."

Griswold looked thoughtful as he contemplated Nick's comment.

"You think we killed some big wig?"

"One could only hope," Nick replied. "But generally their admirals fly the same as ours do."

"Damn the luck," Griswold replied with a smile. "Had a fantasy it might have been Hirohito himself."

Nick gave the junior officer a look while reminding himself to, as his mother would say, 'be kind to those less intelligent.'

"I'm reasonably certain he'd be on one of those big new battlewagons intelligence keeps going on and on about," Nick replied. "Sure we'd be crazy enough to attack her still, but probably would have taken more than one fish."

"Strange that we only got one hit out of three. I thought for sure we had a good set up."

Well, that's a conversation for another day. Probably not with you, either.

Emerson, having conducted four patrols, was keeping track of how many of their torpedoes seemed to either miss or, worse, just bounce off the target. Nick's predecessor had gone stark raving mad in part because Emerson's attack on a destroyer had seen just such a dud. Rather than diving, Emerson had coolly remained at periscope depth and fired two more torpedoes down the throat. One of those *had* worked, blowing the enemy vessel's bow off.

*Too bad **Plunger** hadn't stuck round to finish her off. Of course, hanging around within aerial distance of Truk was probably ill-advised in any case.*

"Sir, I have two sets of screws moving off," the sound man reported.

"Hmm," Emerson said, then double-checked the plot. "Well, I counted three cans when we opened this dance. Let's increase speed to four knots, starboard sixty degrees."

"Starboard sixty degrees, aye aye," the helmsman answered. The acceleration to four knots was hardly noticeable as Eric shifted over to the other side of the plot.

"Read my mind, XO," Emerson said quietly. Nick looked down at the plot, noting that they were at least thirty miles from land in water that had a reported depth of four hundred feet.

"You're seeing if there's a destroyer that is now sitting silent just waiting for us to surface," Nick said. "By turning from our current path, we're going to figure out two things. One, if we're leaking strong enough for them to see it on the surface, he's not going to stay stationary long. Two, if that last run was cover for him to get into position, taking us to starboard hopefully opens up the range far enough for us to come to periscope depth and take a shot at him."

Emerson's grin broadened.

"We'll make a submarine commander of you yet, Lieutenant Cobb," Emerson said. "Starting today. You have the conn."

Wait, what?! Despite his sudden panic, Nick kept his facial features expressionless.

"Aye aye, sir." Turning to look at the plot one more time, Nick tried to visualize where the enemy destroyer might be.

He wouldn't want to be too close to where he'd think we might come up, Nick mused. *Be too hard to depress the guns to give us a broadside and even destroyers don't accelerate that rapidly from a standing start.*

"Sound, how fast did it sound like those tin cans were moving away?" Nick asked.

"About the same as their runs, sir," the sonar technician replied.

"Tell me when you don't hear their screws anymore," Nick stated, then turned to look at Griswold. "When that happens, Ensign Griswold, you start a stop watch. Tell me when twenty minutes has passed."

"Aye aye, sir," Griswold said.

Nick once more looked at the plot.

Don't want to get too far away if he's where I think he might be. Just close enough for the torps to arm.

"Set torpedo depth for three feet," Nick ordered.

"Three feet, aye aye."

Once more I am glad that Emerson took it upon himself to stop using the magnetic warheads. That decision had raised some eyebrows within the SUBPAC staff, but Rear Admiral Graham had backed it given the reports from the Philippines-based boats and his own submariners experience in the war.

Too bad that asshole down in Brisbane won't let his boats do the same. He pulled his mind back to the present, realizing that the lack of oxygen was starting to make it hard to focus.

"Screws have faded, sir," the sonarman said.

"Thank you," Nick stated, noting the clock. "All stop."

"All stop, aye aye," the helmsman replied.

It was an incredibly long twenty minutes in the silent submarine. Nick spent the time running and rerunning through how he wanted to conduct the attack, if there was indeed one necessary. He resisted the urge to look to Commander Emerson for guidance.

The man wants me to run the attack, I'm going to run it. I just question the logic of having me earn my spurs against a destroyer.

"Time, sir," Griswold said.

"Periscope depth," Nick said.

He barely heard the planesmen's acknowledgment, listening as the submarine's compressors forced air into the water tanks. The *Plunger* lurched slightly as she began to rise, causing Nick to grab the edge of the plot table as he strode over to the periscope.

That would be my luck. Fall and hit my head on the damn edge of the table during my first attack run. Reaching the edge, he knelt down on the deck.

"Up periscope," he ordered, extending his hands to catch the handles as the device rose. Putting his eyes to the scope, he rode it up as it extended to its full height. There was nothing but darkness initially, the *Plunger* still slowly making its way up from the depths. Nick heard the dive crew manipulating their controls, taking particular care not to broach the boat. Gradually, the waters began to lighten, then with a rush the *Plunger's* periscope was through the surface into the dawn...and getting pounded by sheets of rain.

That might explain why they moved off. He quickly rotated the scope, noting that he could not see more than one thousand yards, at best. Spinning once more slowly, he did quick calculations in his head and considered the changed situation.

Weather forecast said there would be a front coming through our area today or tomorrow, Nick thought. *Looks like it arrived early.*

"Standby to surface," Nick said, not taking his eyes off the periscope as he continued to swivel. "Minimal bridge crew, keep the decks awash. Remain rigged for dive."

As the crew acknowledged, Nick felt someone push his binoculars into his side. Keeping his eyes on the scope, he took them, quickly slipped their carrying loops over his head, then resumed scanning. The rain continued to lash at the periscope, making it difficult to discern shapes in the gloom. He was continuing his second sweep when a bright flash nearly blinded him.

"Goddammit," he said, jerking back in shock. Blinking his eyes, he had a moment of horror as he realized the bright light may have been a searchlight scanning the boat. Just as he was about to order the boat back into the depths, two more bright flashes occurred just inside his field of view.

"Lightning," he said aloud. "We just got near missed by freaking lightning."

There was nervous laughter around the control room. Satisfied there was nothing within visual range, Nick brought his head back from the scope.

"Take her up," he said, then turned to Emerson.

"Sir, do you wish to resume control of the boat?" Nick asked. Emerson smiled, and Nick belatedly realized the man was amused at him.

Well, you're the one who usually has me remain on the periscope rather than go topside whenever we do this drill. Emerson seemed to consider his choice for a moment, then broadened his grin.

"I'll take the scope," Emerson said. "You've earned some fresh air."

"Aye aye, sir," Nick said. He climbed up to the conning tower's hatch as Emerson took his place at the scope. The *Plunger*'s CO continued to scan the horizon as the conning tower broke the surface. Nick quickly pushed the hatch open, the rush of air like ambrosia even as he was thoroughly soaked. Pushing out onto *Plunger*'s bridge, he was swiftly joined by the lookouts and Ensign Griswold. After five tense minutes searching the horizon in the pouring rain and listening, Nick was finally confident that the intensifying storm meant all three of their assailants had moved off.

"Rig for surface," Nick said into the *Plunger*'s voice control. "All ahead flank on diesel."

As the *Plunger* finished blowing the last of the water from her ballast tanks, Nick was suddenly barely able to keep himself erect. Gripping the edge of the bridge, he took a couple of shuddering breaths as the strain of the last few hours lifted from him. The sound of the *Plunger*'s air conditioners and diesels starting up was a welcome one, and he took another grateful deep breath of sea air.

"Good job, XO," Emerson said as he came up from below. "We'll get off a report to SUBPAC in an hour or so when we're totally sure we're clear."

"Yes, sir," Nick said, his drawl pronounced.

"You go ahead and hit the rack," Emerson stated. "I'll have someone wake you in six hours, then we can trade places."

"Aye aye, sir," Nick said, then yawned. "Do you still want to take her back south towards Luzon?"

"No," Emerson said. "I think heading the opposite direction of the destroyers might be a smarter plan."

What have you done with my commander?

"The last orders we received before we started our attack were ordering us to head back to Midway immediately," Emerson said lowly. "I was about to acknowledge before we attacked that ship. I'm going to see if there's something else heading down towards the Philippines before I cut the patrol short."

"Aye aye, sir," Nick said with a nod. "No reason to go back with almost half our fish."

"Exactly my line of thinking," Emerson stated, grinning again. "I think this pairing is much better than the last one, Cobb."

I don't know if that's a good thing or bad, Nick thought. *But two patrols in and we haven't managed to get ourselves killed yet.* Counting the vessel that they had just dispatched, *Plunger* had managed to sink three confirmed vessels and damaged another two. Although Nick imagined their German opponents laughing politely behind their hands, that score made *Plunger* the second most successful submarine behind Brisbane-based *Wahoo* at the moment.

Speaking of crazy people, that 'Mush' Morton is a real wild man.

"Thank you, sir," Nick returned. He gave a nod, then left the bridge. As he slid down the ladder to the control room, his mind turned to the "other Mortons," i.e., his sister's roommate, Josephine, and her father, Jacob. The duo were no relation to Mush, but the common last names had linked them in Nick's mind since he'd first heard of the latter.

Small world, this war I wonder if Captain Morton has met Commander Morton in some capacity? News of her father's promotion and the potential upgrade of his Navy Cross to a Medal of Honor had reached Josephine as Nick was headed to Midway aboard *Plunger*. She and Patricia had made it a point to keep writing letters to all of the Cobb brothers and Patricia's fiancée, Ensign Charles Read.

Mail call will be nice. Nick yawned as he began taking off his wet clothes. He dried off as much as could be possible in the still humid submarine, then slipped into his bunk. *I hope those knuckleheads are someplace safe.*

2
GOD (AND LION) SAVE THE QUEEN

Only we die in earnest, that's no jest

— **WALTER RALEIGH**

Baron Flight
0800 Local (2230 Eastern)
Ceylon
28 July (27 July)

THERE ARE *moments in a man's life when it is appropriate to question one's own sanity*, Squadron Leader Russell Wolford thought to himself as the *Mosquito*'s engines roared loudly in his ears. Tooling around with a cyclone in the offing is probably as good as indicator as any that I've lost every last one of my marbles.

Baron Squadron, as his unit of twelve *Mosquitoes* were known, had the unenviable mission of making sure a hostile Japanese force was not hoving over the horizon to catch Ceylon by surprise. To date it had been a fruitless mission, but the intelligence types kept swearing that the Japanese would be showing up any time now.

Unfortunately, they've been saying that since the start of the war, apparently. Which is likely why there's a touch of 'cry wolf' among the units that have been here since our former friends from Nippon got rather violent.

He looked out over the Indian Ocean to the southeast, fighting down a sense of foreboding.

Those of us who have had the misfortune of meeting the 'other Imperials,' on the other hand, are not so sanguine. It had been several months since the Dutch East Indies had fallen. More than enough time for the Japanese to reconstitute their forces and prepare for the next push.

"Baron Leader, Portal Leader," Russell's headset crackled.

"Who in the bloody hell is Portal Leader?" his pilot, Flight Lieutenant Carl Bellingsley, stated angrily, his Welsh accent growing thicker with the tension of keeping the *Mosquito* level in the growing turbulence.

I am certainly crazy for bringing Bellingsley with me when I formed No. 505 Squadron, Russell thought. *He has a terrible temper, never pays attention to my briefings, and complains about everything.*

"The *Sunderland* squadron," Russell said, hoping his exasperation carried in his voice. He looked at the map, then keyed his radio.

"Portal Leader, Baron Leader," he said.

"I have attempted to send traffic to the Press Box twice," came Portal Leader's clipped voice. "Have sighted and attacked one hostile submarine, position follows."

Russell quickly took down the information, noting 4°56' N, 86° 41' E was well outside of any friendly submarine corridors. Looking out at the growing clouds and doing some hasty calculations, he realized that the *Sunderland* was much closer to the approaching typhoon than his own aircraft.

"Roger, Portal Leader," Russell replied. "Will relay. Bloody ballsy chasing a sub in this weather, mate."

"Roger, thank you," Portal leader replied, chuckling. "Pretty sure we missed the bastard thanks to the crosswind."

"Understood, will pass along," Russell stated. He checked the code book, reading over the different columns in the gathering gloom.

"Tough racket flying those *Sunderlands*," Bellingsley stated, his voice full of exertion as the *Mosquito* once more passed through heavy turbulence.

"Especially in this mess," Russell replied.

Then again, he is the best stick in the squadron, if not the Wing. Russell regarded the other three *Mosquitoes* spread out in left echelon at half mile intervals, noting their movements looked much rougher than his own aircraft's. Like fingers of an outspread hand, the *Mosquitoes* were the RAF's swing to make contact with any Axis surface forces.

"Baron Leader, Baron Three. I am low fuel."

Russell sighed. Baron Three was a former *Lancaster* pilot who was still getting used to the *Mosquito*'s quirks. As a result, he consistently managed to run out of fuel roughly forty miles short of their sector's end.

Going to have a word with that lad. At some point things go from being a mistake to a habit.

Once more, Russell gazed out the window, fighting down the sense of being in over his head. He wasn't exactly new to squadron command. It was just that the last time he'd been in charge of one it was because his predecessor had died, they were neck-deep in Japanese, and range had not really been a problem in the Dutch East Indies. Having his own squadron, especially straddling the uneasy division between being at war without actual regular contact, had been hard to adjust to over the last month and half.

"Baron Flight, let's head back to home," Russell said, trying to keep his voice level.

"Wasn't that the third submarine contact the flying boats have had in the last week?" Bellingsley asked out of the blue.

Fine, he's not only a good stick, he sometimes observes things that apparently escape my notice.

"We'll have to check with the intelligence section when we get back," Russell said. "It does seem like there are quite a few submarines around these days."

"Likely wanting to get a lick at any convoys up from Sydney," Bellingsley replied. The *Mosquito* went through a lurching series of ups and downs, and Russell was suddenly glad they were climbing back up to cruising altitude.

"Wouldn't surprise me," Bellingsley grunted. "It's not like our blokes aren't trying to do the same to theirs over in the Indies. Difference is, I doubt the Japanese are going to put up with food riots if a convoy doesn't make it."

Yes, but it seems like we're barely keeping the lid on things on Ceylon. The natives, as they say, are getting restless. Her Majesty's government, in order to still the Usurper's influence, had been shipping massive amounts of grain from North America to Ceylon, then from there to India in order to pay for the lease. Of course, the colonial government had believed it was a great idea to husband the grain in Triconmalee rather than distribute it to the countryside. For safety reasons that *certainly* had nothing to do with attempting to suppress the incipient nationalist rebellion that had grown bolder with India's independence.

Good thing we got two extra divisions of Australian troops with tanks in the convoy that brought us up as reinforcements. Otherwise, I'm not sure this would still be a friendly base.

"So how long until the Japanese show up?" Bellingsley asked after almost a half hour of silence.

"You sure it won't be the Italians?" Russell half-joked.

"You're the brass, you tell me," Bellingsley replied. "I half hope it is the Italians, especially as our side was winning quite handily in the desert until Jerry stepped in."

"I don't think the Italian Fleet would make it all the way out here without getting chewed up by our carriers," Russell replied. "Ol' Mussolini's boys would be smart to continue haunting the Med."

"You know that," Bellingsley stated. "Our fleet knows that. But the question is, do *they* acknowledge that?"

"Well if what happened to the Yanks is any indication, it is generally a bad idea to chase carriers with battleships," Russell said.

"So it will be quite amusing if the Italians come out into the Indian Ocean to challenge?"

Russell pursed his lips.

"I'm not sure if *amusing* is the word I'd use for it," he replied. "Perhaps shocking is a better adjective."

"I don't care what adjective we use, as long as it's the other side doing the dying."

Russell considered admonishing his pilot, then let it go.

Kind of strange how a few months of combat changes a man. Russell recalled Bellingsley being shocked at his hoping the Queen would give the Usurper the traditional traitor's fate upon regaining her throne. Burying many of his friends and standing up a whole new squadron appeared to have profoundly changed his pilot.

*Or maybe it's talking to some of the Australians who **just** managed to get out ahead of the war restarting.* Although 'escaping' might be too strong a word for the individuals' repatriation, the dozen or so Army men he'd met on Ceylon had opened his eyes to others' viewpoint. While the men following the Usurper were certainly misguided, if not foolish, the blokes on the other side were still former comrades-in-arms.

Lots of bitterness in this war. Way too much time spent far away from home for most of us.

I.J.N.S. AKAGI
1200 LOCAL (0030 EASTERN)
SINGAPORE
28 JULY (28 JULY)

THANK THE HEAVENS, IT FEELS GOOD TO BE BACK, LIEUTENANT ISORO Honda thought as he stepped onto the the *Akagi*'s hangar deck. It was brutally hot and humid in the structure, the stiff ocean breeze keeping things just on the positive side of hellish. Slinging his sea bag over his shoulder, Isoro headed towards the *Akagi* fighter squadron's ready room. He was almost to it when he came upon two of the fighter squadron's pilots standing near their *Shiden* fighters. Seeing him, both men came over.

It's almost like they were waiting for me. Honda tried to hide his concern as he studied the two men. To his relief, he saw that one was a warrant officer, the other a petty officer.

"Welcome back aboard, sir," Warrant Officer Taisei Oda said, saluting Honda. Isoro returned the gesture, giving Oda a clearly measuring glance. Nodding once at the man, Isoro then turned to the NCO on Oda's right. Petty Officer Airi Takahashi came to attention and also saluted Isoro.

New wingmen, Isoro thought with slight disdain as he once more returned the gesture. *Breaking in new wingmen is **exactly** what I want to be doing when we go to Ceylon.* His previous wingmen, Warrant Officers Sawato and Watanabe, had been detached from *Akagi* to serve as leavening for the *Taiho*'s new air group.

We are having trouble keeping bodies in airplanes. The current batch of pilots who had come down from Japan aboard *Taiho* consisted of the third wartime class of fighter pilots. While each was highly trained, Isoro could not shake the feeling that another three months of losses like they'd suffered in the Indies would completely disrupt the training pipeline.

We lost the equivalent of four graduating classes in fighter pilots alone. Who knows how many bomber pilots died.

"Where is..." Isoro began to ask, only to be interrupted.

"Honda!" Commander Mitsuo Fuchida, *Akagi*'s commander air group, shouted happily from across the hangar. Isoro came to attention as the man strode over, two of his squadron commanders in tow. Isoro did not recognize either man as he saluted.

So much change.

"Lieutenant Commander Maki, Lieutenant Commander Ogawa, this is Lieutenant Honda," Fuchida said. "Honda was our leading ace during the Dutch East Indies campaign and is rejoining us after some time with the *Raiden* project."

Both men gave Honda a respectful nod.

"Lieutenant Commander Maki will be taking over the *Suisei* squadron, while Lieutenant Commander Ogawa will be leading the new *Tenzan*s."

*So, those **were** the new bombers I saw on the airfield when we landed!*

"How is the new fighter?" Maki asked, referring to Mitsubishi's A7M. "I have heard a great deal about it, but have not actually seen it. When will it be fielded?"

"I do not know, sir," Isoro said. "It is supposed to be replacing the

Zero with the land-based units soon, but there were still problems with the prototype."

Namely the engine had a tendency of deciding to quit working if you put it through too tough of paces, Isoro thought. *But, like the **Shiden**, they'll figure it out.*

"Everything has teething problems," Ogawa said. "The *Tenzans* have had their issues, but those are minor given the improvement over the B5N."

They are far braver men than I. No matter what the improvement, I would not fly straight and level into the teeth of anti-aircraft fire for anyone.

"We will have a chance to test everything soon enough," Fuchida said. "Vice Admiral Yamaguchi has asked permission for us to leave earlier so that he may attempt to find the Allied carriers as they return from Madagascar."

Isoro looked at Commander Fuchida in confusion, causing the latter man to realize that Honda had not been briefed before leaving Japan.

"We are departing for the Indian Ocean," Fuchida said. "Operation C, the seizure of Ceylon, will begin in four days. Submarines have already been dispatched to establish a scouting line."

"Understood, sir," Isoro stated. "However, I do not understand the reference to Madagascar."

"At least four Allied carriers are attacking our Vichy and Italian allies along Africa's east coast," Fuchida stated. "The intention is to raid Ceylon, then go to find them once they respond."

Raiding land bases when they are expecting us is always dangerous. He was certain that their opponents would have reinforced Ceylon with whatever assets they possessed. After his experiences in the Indies, he did not relish dealing with well-prepared defenses. Especially when those defenses were probably manned by enemy who would realize retreat was impossible.

"You look as if you are thinking about something, Lieutenant Honda," Fuchida said, startling Isoro.

"The enemy, sir," Isoro replied. "Do we know what forces are on Ceylon?"

"We are not certain," Fuchida said. "In any case, it will be only a brief attack in passing."

Isoro nodded.

"The Fifth and Sixth Carrier Divisions will be accompanying the transports," Fuchida said. "They will get to deal with anything we leave."

"Hopefully that will not be much," Maki stated. "I would hate to fight four enemy carriers while still having to worry about what is behind us."

I think we can all agree on that. There are limits to how many aircraft we can handle. Once again, his mind turned to the Dutch East Indies. By the end of the campaign, the *Kido Butai*'s squadrons had begun to be ground down despite their victories. Although he expected any carrier battle to be more episodic than drawn out, once more considering attrition gave him pause.

I am not a coward, just cautious.

"The good thing is that there are two British and two Americans," Fuchida observed. "I doubt that they have established procedures between themselves."

Honda wished he could share his CAG's confidence.

Established procedures or not, that is still a great number of aircraft. Although at least the majority of our pilots are experienced, while the Americans will have had to replace their losses from Hawaii.

H.M.C.S. Victorious
1320 Local (0620 Eastern)
Western Indian Oceans
29 July

THE FLIGHT DECK WAS NOTICEABLY WARM BENEATH ERIC'S FEET, THE armored metal absorbing sunlight far quicker than its wooden American counterparts.

"Welcome aboard, *Leftenant* Cobb," Commander Abraham Martin stated, extending his hand. Eric shook it, reminding himself that the Royal Navy had designated their flight decks to all be no salute zones.

The restriction made sense and was something he wished the USN would adopt.

The flight deck should be a place people are less concerned about rendering the proper greetings than making sure no one walks into a propeller.

"Thank you, sir," he replied. "I understand that you have message traffic for Vice Admiral Fletcher?"

"Yes, yes we do," Martin replied. "Vice Admiral Cunningham had some questions regarding tactical procedures during a fleet action."

Find the enemy, bomb the shit out of him. Not that hard.

"This vessel had previously worked those out with Vice Admiral Halsey during our exercises off British Columbia, but it appears that Vice Admiral Fletcher has some differing views on things," Martin continued.

Namely Fletcher seems to believe every fourth day is a tanking day, whereas Cunningham appears to want to get on with jabbing the shit out of his former countrymen at every turn?

"I would say that Vice Admirals Fletcher and Halsey have always been two very different people, sir," Eric allowed. "As soon as you get us refueled, I'll be happy to take the message traffic back to *Yorktown*."

"Of course," Martin replied warmly. "Until then, would you care to join a few of our officers for a drink?"

"Certainly, sir," Eric replied. "Would it be possible to get my gunner one as well?"

"I'm certain a 'medicinal ration' can be obtained for him from the surgeon," Martin replied with a smile. "Follow me, we'll go to eight oh four's wardroom."

Eric could understand both sides. The last thing he wanted to happen was an enemy fleet show up unexpectedly with most of the task force lacking any fuel. However, Fletcher took things to an extreme, rotating either the *Yorktown* or *Enterprise* out on a regular basis. While the tankers were only a couple hundred miles behind the task force, refueling was still a time-consuming process when Vice Admiral Cunningham clearly wanted to surge ahead and strike Mombasa after basically razing Madagascar.

I think the French are going to be loathe to send anything back to that island anytime soon, Eric thought, smirking. Between the surface sweep by the

Repulse and carrier strikes, the fleet had bagged the *Suffren* and *Trento*, hunted down the *Arethusa* just as that vessel was reaching South African territorial waters, then doubled back and sank another Italian convoy.

"I understand it was your squadron that found the *Arethusa*?" Martin asked.

"No sir," Eric said. Martin looked at him with a puzzled expression, so the American explained. "I'm from Bombing, or VB-11. It was Scouting, i.e., VS-11 that found her."

Lieutenant (j.g.) Charles Read, one each, as a matter of fact, Eric thought, feeling a bit of pride at his future brother-in-law. Charles had sent off a textbook sighting report, got it acknowledged, then proceeded to put his 500-lb. bomb right beside the Usurper cruiser.

Too bad I missed the strike thanks to flying antisubmarine patrol. Although I got to make up for it on the convoy.

"Ahhh," Martin said. "Squadron nomenclature is always a funny thing."

"I freely admit I can't keep track of your squadrons, sir," Eric said as they moved down a passageway.

"Eight hundred series are operational carrier squadrons," Martin said. "The Air Ministry reassigned numbers back in June, so now even squadrons are fighters, odd are bombers."

"Ah," Eric said. "In any case, our squadron was the one that attacked the convoy, not the cruiser."

"Ahh," Martin said. "Good work on that, really made a mess of that escort before the torpedo bombers went in."

"That we did," Eric stated. "Although I think those destroyers thought we were friendly before we started diving. Makes it a lot easier to put a bomb on target when someone's not firing at you."

"Indeed," Martin said. "Bad week for Italian destroyers. I don't know how many they started this week with, but they've got seven less thanks to you Yanks and Vice Admiral Godfrey's force."

Eric smiled at the gallows humor as they stepped into No. 804 squadron's wardroom. Unlike the lighter, haze gray of the *Victorious*'s passageways, the 804 wardroom's bulkheads were painted a sky blue, with the squadron's crest on the far wall.

Swift to Kill. Apt motto for a fighter squadron, although I'm not sure about the tiger clutching a sword as the emblem.

"All right you lot, we've got a Yank among us for about a half hour," Martin said. "Some of you may have heard of the famous *Leftenant* Eric Cobb..."

To Eric's surprise, there was a round of cheers, with several of the men standing up to come clap him on the back. He shook hands with several of the officers in a whirlwind of introductions, then had a shot of whiskey shoved in his hand.

I guess people like you when you've allegedly saved part of their fleet from defeat, Eric assumed. *I still say that they would have sighted the Germans before they were able to bag the Royal family, but if it keeps getting me drinks I'm not going to argue.*

"To Her Majesty!" someone shouted. Eric lifted his glass, then tossed it back with his companions.

Now I understand why I got tagged for this.

"Gentlemen, Vice Admiral Cunningham!" someone shouted. The room quickly came to attention as a tall, balding man entered the room. Seeing Eric, he quickly extended his hand.

"*Leftenant* Eric Cobb, it is my pleasure to make your acquaintance," Cunningham said, his accent holding a slight trace of his Scottish origins.

"Thank you, sir," Eric said.

"I am glad that Vice Admiral Fletcher finally sent you over," Cunningham said, gesturing for his aide. The man pulled out an envelope, and Eric was surprised to see that it was affixed with an official wax seal. His astonishment turned to awe as he realized that the seal was not just any one, but the actual royal seal of Her Majesty, Queen Elizabeth. There were a couple of gasps behind him as others made the same recognition.

"Now I can finally tell Admiral Tovey to stop sending me dispatches regarding mail not addressed to me," Vice Admiral Cunningham said with a smile. There was a wave of laughs around the small compartment.

"I am always glad to reduce message traffic," Eric stated with a slight smile. "Although I am not sure what Her Majesty's return address is."

"Well, seems that there's an ill-mannered gentleman occupying her regular residence," Cunningham replied with a wry smile, reaching inside his jacket. "However, I am certain if you send it to our embassy in Washington it will get to her."

"Thank you, sir," Eric replied with a slight neck bow. Cunningham was about to reply when there was the sound of running feet and a male voice asking for individuals to make way. Moments later, a young Royal Navy officer stood in front of the British flag officer.

"Sir, message from Admiral Tovey," the ensign said, face red from running downstairs. Vice Admiral Cunningham took the message flimsy, his expression indicating it had better be an important one. Peering at it, his face paled. The British admiral looked up at the ensign, then down at the flimsy, and read it again.

"Who else has seen the particulars of this message?"

"Only the communications desk, sir," the ensign replied. "And the captain."

"Immediately repeat this message to all Commonwealth vessels, captains' eyes only," Vice Admiral Cunningham said. "Tell them to inform their crews of its contents within the half hour after they have had time to digest it. Do you understand?"

"Yes, sir," the ensign replied, then repeated the particulars of what Vice Admiral Cunningham had ordered. Cunningham waved the officer away, then visibly gathered himself before turning to the assembled group.

What in the hell has happened? Eric wondered, feeling butterflies in his stomach.

"Gentlemen," the admiral began, "I have grave news. An assassination attempt was made on Her Majesty this morning in New York City. Early reports are that the assassins were Americans. They missed her, but that Prime Minister Churchill and Admiral Pound are both at a local hospital in grave condition."

Eric was suddenly breathless, a shock like a block of ice in his stomach. He took a couple steps backwards as there were several murmurs and curses in the wardroom.

Who would try to kill the Queen? Why would they attempt to kill the Queen in New York of all places?

"Lieutenant Cobb, are you all right?" Martin asked, placing his hand on Eric's shoulder.

"I will be," Eric said, his voice cracking. He turned to the wardroom.

"I am so sorry," he said, tears welling in his eyes. "I am so sorry for my countrymen."

Martin put his hand on Eric's shoulder.

"It's all right lad," the man replied, swallowing. "There are more than enough of you out here with us right now."

HAYNES RESIDENCE
1200 LOCAL (1500 EASTERN)
TACOMA, WASHINGTON
29 JULY

"ADAM HAYNES, WILL YOU TURN THAT RADIO OFF AND GRAB ME SOME potato salad, please?" Norah Hedglin asked from the kitchen door. The redhead stood in a blue polkadot dress with her hair up in a bun, dark blue earrings that matched her eyes completing the ensemble.

When a smart, beautiful woman asks you to turn off the radio, she's really saying that it's not doing any good to sit here and grow progressively more angry at something you can't control, Adam thought, turning the appliance off. He reached into the refrigerator and pulled out the large bowl of potato, then grabbed a wooden spoon to serve it with. The sound of the rain lashing against the large bay window that opened to his backyard made him smile ruefully.

So much for one last picnic. Or the rainy season allegedly taking a break in July.

There was a peal of thunder, and the rain intensified.

But at least it's not Florida, or we'd all be sweating to death inside this place. As it was, the mild Northwest summer was even cooler than they'd expected, which made the inside of the house quite pleasant.

Norah walked up behind Adam as he sat the potato salad on the table, wrapping her arms him from behind. She ran her hand down the front of his pants, causing him to jump in shock.

"See, took your mind off things for about a half second," she said, exhaling as she brought her arms back up and hugged him.

"You're a little bit of a minx, you know that?" Adam said, turning around to embrace her.

"Only with you," Norah replied, looking him in the eyes. "You make me feel safe enough to be one."

Adam was about to respond when the doorbell rang.

"That would probably be the Cobbs," he said. "I imagine both of them, if previous experiences hold." Reluctantly, Adam let her go and headed for the door.

"You're always so jealous of them," Norah observed. "They're twins. It's not surprising they often seem to be of like mind and action."

Yeah, that doesn't change the fact it's downright creepy sometimes. But it's a big part of the reason I've let them stay in the same flight rather than make them each take one. One didn't break up a winning team just on a whim.

Opening the door, he was surprised to find only David and a woman he assumed to be Sadie Cobb. As Norah had requested, all of the Marines had come in civilian clothes, with David opting for a dark red button-up shirt that matched his wife's burgundy cocktail dress.

Well, Sam wasn't lying when he always ribbed David about marrying a beautiful woman, Adam observed as introductions were made. He took the covered dish from Sadie's hands as Norah came forward to greet the newlyweds.

"I have heard so much about you," Norah said, taking Sadie's hands. The brown-haired, slender woman looked mildly concerned for a moment, glancing between Norah and her husband.

"All of it good," Adam said, smiling at David's momentary discomfiture.

"Oh thank goodness," Sadie said with a laugh. "I was afraid Sam had been going on and on about how mean I was."

"Having known Sam for only two months, I cannot say that he definitely deserved whatever you did to him," Norah said. "I will say I'm very predisposed to believe Sam deserved it."

"Speaking of Sam, where is he?" David asked, looking around. "He sent a telegram saying he was going to be here by…"

As if summoned, a black taxi drove up to the end of their driveway, a familiar hulking form in the rear passenger side. Hopping out before the vehicle had even stopped moving, Sam Cobb drew the flaps of his raincoat tighter. Reaching inside the garment, Sam produced a long black umbrella, then opened it and walked around to the driver's side rear door.

Okay, who is she? Adam wondered, seeing a tall, Asian woman standing beside Sam. He handed off his umbrella to the woman, then moved around to the passenger's side door. It was opened, and another umbrella passed out to Sam. The large man opened the umbrella as the passenger turned and gave the driver money. It was obvious the taxi driver was pleased, as he nodded vigorously at something the passenger said before waving at Sam.

All right, I should have known Sam would bring two women.

"Holy shit, that's Beverly Bowden," David said. Everyone but Sadie looked at him.

"Who?" Norah asked, then realized there was no time for David to answer. She pushed the screen door open and waved at the approaching trio.

"Come in, come in!" she said, her Missouri twang deepening.

*Why Miss Hedglin, I'd never realize you were in full "Who the fuck are **these** people?"-mode,* Adam marveled, also smiling as Sam held the door open for the two women behind him. The short brunette in the lead was barely through the door before David threw his arms around her, ignoring the rain beaded on her black coat.

"Beverly!"

"Hello David," the woman replied, her voice deep with emotion as she hugged David back. Letting him go, she turned to Sadie. The younger woman threw her arms around the brunette as well, her eyes wet.

"Sadie, you'll soak your dress," Beverly said.

"I don't care," Sadie replied. "It's so good to see you again."

I feel like I'm missing something here, Adam thought.

"Hello, my name is Myla," the Asian woman said, her accent

causing Adam to smile. "Myla Ferguson." She reached inside of her oversized bag and brought out two large bottles of wine.

"Norah Hedglin, and you are certainly welcome here with those!" Norah said with a smile, taking both bottles from her and handing them to Adam. Adam looked down at them and nearly dropped both.

"I see that you are familiar with wine, Mr...?" Myla said with a smile as she shrugged out of her coat to reveal a dark blue, knee-length dress.

"Haynes," Adam said. "Adam Haynes. It may surprise you, but I allegedly own this place."

"Well, at least until he finally bows to the inevitable and asks Norah to marry him," Sam said in the middle of embracing his sister-in-law.

Adam's face warmed as Norah's colored almost to match her hair.

"You know, Sam, you talk a great deal about marriage for someone who has never been close to the altar," David observed.

"Common refrain with fighter pilots," Beverly stated. Adam saw a shadow of pain and sadness cross the woman's face.

Wait a second. Wasn't Bowden their former squadron commander's name?

"Do you have a washroom?" Beverly asked lightly. Norah, having picked up on the same expression reading as Adam had, quickly stepped past him.

"I'll show you," she said, leading Beverly away. There was an awkward silence afterward that was finally broken by Myla.

"Yes, those are Chateau Lafite," she said to Adam. "My husband secured them when we were leaving Hong Kong, and my son has nearly broken them at least a dozen times. From what Sam has said about you the last two days, this seemed like appropriate company to drink it with."

It was Sam's turn to blush as everyone turned to look at him.

"You know, it's nothing I wouldn't say to any of you," he said thickly. "But thanks, Myla."

"You bought my son a slingshot, Sam," Myla replied. "Now my child who you have known for less than forty-eight hours won't stop talking about wanting to be a fighter pilot and has already killed two squirrels. Which is a big deal when you're eight."

Sadie turned and looked at Sam in horror.

"Samuel Michael Cobb!" she exclaimed.

"Look, it's not like they don't kill tree rats in Kansas," Sam said, spreading his hands plaintively.

Sadie glared at her brother-in-law.

"Not for fun, and not at *eight*," she said.

Adam saw David giving his wife a sideways glance, worry a little plain on his face. With the sixth sense most spouses have, Sadie whirled to look at her husband.

"I can *hear* you thinking back there, David," she said, her tone reproachful. "Our son does not get a slingshot before he's ten."

Adam looked sideways at Myla, who was also looking at him. The Englishwoman smiled slightly with a twinkle in her eye.

Okay, so I'm not the only one who heard it, he thought. After a brief moment of consideration, he gave in to his impish side.

"Coca-cola for you, Sadie?" he asked. Sadie turned to look at him, shock on her face.

"How did you kn..." she started, then stopped as she realized what she had just done.

"Major Haynes, I have just met you, but you are a terrible man," Myla said, then turned to Sadie to speak with great conviction. "He did not *know* until just now."

David looked at his wife, then at Adam, then at his wife.

Oh shit, apparently David did not know either, Adam realized, feeling stark raving horror at what was unfolding in front of him. *Sorry about that, lad!*

"Did not know what?" Norah asked, walking into the room. She saw the look of surprise on David's face, Sadie blushing, and Myla glowering at Adam.

"I was going to tell you tonight," Sadie said quietly, starting to smile.

"Your boyfriend, in an act of utter perfidy, has just let a rabbit out of the bag," Myla observed almost simultaneously, her smile pure poison as she looked at Adam. "A dead one, as a matter of fact."

There was a moment of silence as Norah processed what Myla had said and the rest of the group waited for her reaction.

"*Adam! What have you done?*" Norah asked, realization causing her voice to rise.

"I did not..." Adam began.

"Oh you bloody did!" Myla cut him off, laughing. Norah glared at Adam.

To the table, to the table right now, he thought, turning away.

"I'm not sure it's a boy," Sadie said quickly behind him. As he sat the bottles down, Adam saw David break into a stupefied grin. Beverly chose that moment to come back out, her make up redone.

"It sounds like you guys are having a party out here without me," she observed, then saw the matching smiles on David and Sam's face.

"One of them smiling like that is bad enough," Beverly continued. "But both of them? I clearly need to get right with the Lord."

"I'm pregnant," Sadie said haltingly.

Beverly's face lit up.

"Congratulations!" she said, embracing Sadie once again. "I would ask how far along are you, but that's kinda obvious."

Sadie laughed, then rubbed her stomach.

"Yes, crossing on a boat was not fun," she observed.

"I can imagine," Myla said, turning slightly pale herself.

"Well, too bad you're not down in Olympia," Beverly said. "I could fuss over you in the ward."

Norah turned from where she was busying herself in the kitchen.

"You're a nurse?" she asked Beverly.

"Yes, I am," Beverly replied. "You as well?"

"Yes, obstetrics," Norah said. "I also did surgery for a year."

Beverly gave Norah a speculative look.

"I'm older than I look," Norah said with a smile, then gestured over at Adam. "Should have seen his face when I told him my true age."

"We just thought Major Haynes was robbing the cradle when you started going out," Sam said.

"It's not like I'm *that* old," Norah replied archly. "Thank you very much."

"I love you Americans," Myla said, her amusement with the social chaos in front of her.

"As a people, we do try to keep it unpredictable," Adam replied.

Norah still gave him a cross look, and he slightly shrugged his shoulders in return, face pained.

I am in so much trouble, he winced inwardly. *I think if I wasn't about to leave for several months I'd be sleeping alone tonight.*

"I'm going to be an uncle," Sam said, still smiling. Sadie, remembering how the conversation initially began, turned to look at him.

"Yes, and you will *not* give our son a slingshot," she said, then continued seeing Sam grin. "*Or our daughter.*"

THE NEXT THREE HOURS PASSED PLEASANTLY, FILLED WITH WINE AND good food.

I'm glad I asked Beverly to come up here, Sam as he stood in the kitchen making a sandwich to take with him for dinner. The widow Bowden was engaged in an animated conversation with Norah over some peculiar nursing requirement Washington had. David and Adam were locked in an intense game of backgammon, the fifth in a series after they'd each won a pair. Sadie leaned against her husband's shoulder, smiling at some joke David had just made that Sam did not catch.

"It's like the world is totally normal outside," Myla observed from beside him, her voice low. "That there's not a war on, that half the people in this room are about to go off to fight in it, and not all of them will come back."

Sam turned to look at Myla, unconsciously drawing away from her bald truth.

"Sorry, I'm just feeling a bit maudlin," Myla said, then held up her wine glass. "I mean, I'm drinking the wine my husband swore we'd open when he returned."

"I'm sorry," Sam said, feeling the urge to sweep Myla into his arms due to the forlornness in her voice. She held up a hand.

"Save that for the woman you *can* comfort, Sam," she said with a smile. "It is greatly appreciated, but I am afraid if a man touched me right now I'd swoon into his arms. Beverly would be justified in poisoning my entire garden if I did that."

Wow, she's a blunt one, Sam realized, watching as Myla blushed then looked steadfastly at the wine glass in her hand.

"Okay, so I will not be drinking any more wine this afternoon," she said, setting her glass down.

"I'm sure your husband is just having difficulty getting word to you," Sam said earnestly. "Now I wish we hadn't opened that second bottle."

"Ian has been missing for four months in the northwest corner of India," Myla replied flatly. Sam's eyes widened as she continued.

"His aircraft was overtaken by a storm and is likely scattered over the side of a mountain somewhere. I do not have the heart to tell Henry, so I have not told anyone else until just now."

Sam gripped the counter in front of him, feeling the blood run from his expression.

"Wipe that look off your face, you'll make the other curious," Myla whispered in, smiling as if Sam had said something quietly amusing. Sam immediately followed her orders, turning back to his sandwich and forcing a grin of his own

"I was actually about to tell Beverly the day you came down," Myla said. "That was part of my shock in finding out that she is a widow."

Sam finished putting the second slice of bread on top of his sandwich as he listened.

"So, I came along in part because I needed to see if there was a light at the end of the tunnel," Myla continued. "Well, you have both convinced me that one can heal."

"But we're..." Sam said hurriedly.

"Oh no, I'm not saying you guys are a whirlwind of perfumed letters and heated glances that's waiting to happen," Myla said. "But you have been good for her these last couple of days."

"I hope I haven't given her the wrong impression," Sam said quietly. "I don't want to her to think I'm interested in a relationship."

"She's no more ready for a relationship than she is ready to fly to the moon," Myla observed. "Indeed, part of her will probably feel guilty about having fun, but she needs to go on living."

Myla laughed at that last part.

"I know I feel a bit like the kettle talking about the pot here," she said. "But part of me is still holding out hope Ian will walk through that door, pick up his son, and then ask me how the last year has been."

"That could still happen," Sam said hopefully. Myla smiled at him kindly.

"Thank you for saying that," she said. "If it does, I promise to write you a letter saying you were right. But I, for one, have lost almost all of my hope."

"Sam, could you bring out the turntable from the cabinet behind you?" Norah asked. "I think we could all do with some music."

"That sounds like a great idea," Myla said. "Allegedly Sam here is quite the dancer."

"Whoever told you that apparently has iron bars for their feet," Sadie said.

"Thanks Sadie," Sam replied. "I may have imbibed a bit at your wedding before dancing with the bride."

"Which wedding?" David asked, getting a playful slap from his wife.

"Which wedding?" Myla asked.

"Civil and church ceremony," Sam said.

"I found him to be quite the charming dancer," Beverly said, standing up. "If he hurries up with that record player, I might be sober enough to avoid making him catch me."

Sam looked at the four empty bottles of wine sitting on the dining room table.

Sadie didn't have any, I have had maybe a couple of glasses, and David's been being very careful how much he drinks so he can drive home, Sam mused. *No wonder Myla, Major Haynes, and apparently Beverly, are all three sheets to the wind.*

"That's not hurrying," Myla said quietly.

Sam smiled in response, then went to go get the appliance.

I better just shut up and embrace what the universe is throwing at me, I guess.

Honolulu Public Library
1400 Local (1900 Eastern)
Honolulu
29 July

"Well, you look like you're ready to stab a few people in the throat," Josephine "Jo" Morton said as she stood up from the bench in front of the local library. "I sincerely hope it has more to do with the reason you're a couple hours late rather than anything I've done."

Jo almost ducked back behind the bench as Patricia glowered at her.

"I may kill that man," Patricia spat.

"To think a few weeks ago I would have had to ask you which man you meant in particular," Jo replied. "Your fiancée, one of your brothers, *the two sailors who keep looking at your ass like we're not standing in front of a reflective glass.*"

The two men in question jumped at Jo's barked tone, both blushing. Jo continued to glare at the duo, her olive complexion preventing her face from coloring so she could have maximized the angry effect.

Bad enough you guys sat there for the last thirty minutes without even giving the woman in green a second glance. But the minute Miss Alabama here walks up in a yellow number and suddenly you're unable to tear your eyes away? Jo clenched her jaw, nostrils flaring as she continued giving both men an intense glare.

"Sorry," one of them muttered as they both hurried into the library. Jo usually worked at the far smaller Pearl City Public Library, but had agreed to cover a friend's shift due to the little matter of childbirth.

Sue Ellen doesn't need any more on her plate, Jo thought. *Not with her husband, like seemingly everyone else who was at this place a few months ago, somewhere in the Pacific.*

"VICE ADMIRAL FLETCHER'S FLEET ON RAMPAGE!" a newsboy cried, holding up the latest copy of the *Honolulu Star-Bulletin*. "ITALIANS FLEE CARRIERS!"

Or perhaps elsewhere. Her brow furrowed, thoughts turning to where

Italians could be possibly running from Fletcher before Patricia interrupted.

"You know, I'm not going to spend my half day off listening to you poke fun at me," Patricia snapped, then caught herself and drew a deep breath, exhaling slowly. "Okay, I'm sorry, I should not be taking my anger out on you."

"Your new boss is an asshole," Jo replied. "It doesn't help he's got you working insane hours with an odd schedule."

"Well, apparently that stopped today, and I got a half-day off as well," Patricia noted. "I don't know who complained or if it was just a case of someone in payroll noticing the odd times, but he got quite the ass- chewing."

Jo kept a poker face as she looked at her friend.

*It's funny that the daughter of a lawyer who has watched me pull several tricks out of the proverbial hat has no inkling just how her overbearing boss got set up It's almost like I don't know **anyone** in the Navy besides her brothers.*

"Have you heard from Eric?" Patricia asked as they stopped before crossing a street.

"No," Jo said, exasperated. "For Christ's sake, Patricia, you think I wouldn't have mentioned hearing from him? Especially since he's on the same ship as one Ensign Read, the man you've been raging against for not writing?"

Patricia shook her head, laughing.

"You're right, that was idiotic," she said. "I swear, I feel like we're just tossing letters into the void."

"I did hear from Dad though," Jo continued brightly.

"Finally!" Patricia said. The two of them stepped into *The Flying Pineapple*, their planned lunch destination. Both women stopped as they entered the bustling room, shocked at how busy it was. Jo felt several sets of eyes pass over them, but studiously ignored the gazes, stares, and outright leers as she got the waitress' attention.

"Just the two of you?" the woman asked, looking at Jo and Patricia with a familiar smile.

You'd think we ate here quite a bit when Patricia still worked at the library.

"Yes," Jo said, smiling back.

"Miss, you can come sit by us," a British accented voice stated. Jo looked over at the table and saw that there were four "tars" sitting at it, their dark uniforms contrasting with the USN whites and khakis that were all around the bar.

"No thank you, we'll wait," Jo said politely. She was turning back to the waitress when a New Jersey-accented voice piped up.

"What's the matter, you too good to just sit down with some sailors?"

Jo ignored the comment, making sure the waitress had heard them.

"Hey lady, I'm talking to you!" the voice said again, this time touched with a bit of anger.

"And if you speak to her like that again, you'll be seeing the inside of your ship for the remainder of your stay!" a voice cracked across the room. There was dead silence as the captain who had spoken stood up from his table. Jo did not recognize the man, which was a rarity within the Pacific Fleet.

"Actually, sir, I think whomever said that and anyone sitting at his table are done eating lunch *right now*," a second voice cracked, this one belonging to a senior petty officer who was also coming to his feet. There was a parting of the Red Sea moment as everyone near the wisecracking sailor quickly moved away.

Might as well have an arrow over his head, Jo thought.

Patricia giggled beside her, a delicate hand covering her mouth. The sailor, a dark-haired man with acne-ridden facial features and beady dark eyes briefly looked towards her, angry at being laughed at. It was a bad mistake, as the chief strode over to him.

"What ship are you off of?" the chief snapped. The sailor slowly rose to his feet, trying to work his face into impassiveness. After a moment, he realized he should be at a position of parade rest when addressed by an NCO.

"The *San Francisco*," he replied sullenly.

"Oh, the old Frisco Maru," the petty officer said, drawing some hard looks from the men with the mouthy sailor. "Funny, I might know a couple of chiefs on her. *How about you and I take a walk back?*"

The man's tone made it clear he wasn't asking a polite question. Suddenly, the sailors glaring at the man, and the two other petty officers who had joined him from their own lunches, almost tripped over themselves leaving.

"I think you might need some help with having this sailor find his liberty boat," one of the chiefs said. "Right after he apologizes to these two young women."

Oh he's fit to be tied.

"I'm sorry, Miss," the man said, his voice cool.

"Why, he sounds almost completely contrite," one of the other chiefs said. "Why, he's so sorry, I think he wants to buy her lunch."

Oh no, that's a bit excessive. She was about to speak when the young man reached into his pocket and pulled out a bill.

"I think this will cover it," he said, slapping the money down on the table. "Enjoy your meal, ladies."

"Thank you," Jo said, meeting the young man's eyes. She had never seen someone say *fuck you* with their gaze before, but there was clearly a first time for everything.

"Let's go, sailor," the chief said.

"Thank you, chief," the captain said. Jo realized the man had three of his officers with him, all lieutenants and lieutenant commanders. "I'll almost forgive you insulting my future vessel."

The chief, to his credit, didn't even flinch.

"I think it was the sailor's mistreatment of these fine young women talking, sir."

"Certainly," the captain replied. "Mistreatment I'll be happy to deal with it in the morning after taking over from Captain Callaghan. Maybe when I'm consulting with this man's division chief."

"Aye aye, sir," the petty officer replied. He turned back to the now-pale sailor.

"Looks like your timing and ability to place both feet in your mouth are impeccable," the petty officer said. "Start walking."

Jo watched as the two men left. The captain watched them go, then strode over.

"I apologize for that man, Miss..?"

"Morton," Jo said. "Josephine Morton, Captain."

The man did a double take, then laughed.

"Jacob Morton's daughter," he said. "I can see your mother in you now that I hear the name!"

"Thank you," Jo replied, feeling her cheeks warm.

"I'm Captain Fischer," the man continued. "Mel Fischer. Your father was the gunnery officer on the *Augusta* when I was the executive officer."

"Oh!" Jo said, her memory jogged. She noticed Patricia talking to one of the man's accompanying commanders.

"Where is he now?" Fischer asked.

"He's captain of the *Houston*," Jo replied, sort of surprised that Fischer was not aware of what had been going on.

"Captain?!" Fischer said. "Well I'll be dam—"

Jo smiled as the man caught himself.

"He's been very fortunate," she said quietly. "Lucky to be alive, really."

Fischer nodded at her comment.

"I've heard the East Indies was a very difficult time for everyone involved," he said. "*Augusta* was the vessel the *Houston* replaced, so it could have just as easily been us as her if the war had started a couple years earlier."

Maybe if it had started a couple of years earlier my father would have been safely in charge of his own destroyer rather than getting injured on someone else's cruiser, Jo thought. Oh well, worked out for him in the end.

"Sir, we have a four o'clock appointment with Vice Admiral Halsey," one of the other officers, apparently Fischer's XO, said quietly. Fischer looked at his watch then smiled apologetically.

"Until next time, Jo," he said.

"It was great catching up," she replied, then felt kind of silly. She watched as the man and his group of officers walked out of the diner. Whether spurred by her incident or the normal ebb and flow of a work day in Honolulu, *The Flying Pineapple* had mostly emptied out.

I feel sorry those British sailors had to see that, Jo thought, mildly ashamed at her countrymen. The hostess took them to one of the table that had been wiped down, offering them both menus.

"I'll have the ham and bacon sandwich," Patricia said even before she slid into one side of the booth.

"I'll have the BLT," Jo added, the hostess writing both down before she walked off.

"Sailors are getting out of control," Patricia observed angrily. "It's getting so I don't even want to go out anymore."

*To think that this is **with** the whorehouses staying open. I can't imagine what it'd be like if Vice Admiral Halsey and General Short had actually listened to some of those Stateside moralists.*

"Too many sailors, not enough women," Jo replied aloud. "If we were Stateside we wouldn't even be noticed."

Patricia made a haughty sound.

"Fine, *some of us* wouldn't even be noticed," Jo amended with an eye roll. To her credit, Patricia had the decency to look mildly embarrassed at her vanity.

"Still, you're right," Jo said. "The librarians walk everywhere in pairs or more now when they're out. A couple of them even make sure to take taxis rather than just walk a few blocks at night or catch the bus if it's particularly late."

"Too many men doing nothing," Patricia said. "My mother used to always say that a bored man would sooner set a field on fire than do anything useful."

"That's a little extreme," Jo said, then got to thinking. "Although you're right, it's not far off from 'idle hands are the devil's workshop.'"

"There's a reason the boys learned to never say, 'I'm bored' when Mom was in ear shot," Patricia said. "That'd usually lead to *everyone* getting some chore assigned to them."

"I still say your mother should be sainted," Jo said. "I love your brothers, but I can't imagine growing up in a houseful of their younger selves."

"There were advantages," Patricia said. "I miss having someone to walk me back from the Navy Yard or go to the beach with. Not that I've had time to do any swimming lately."

Jo looked around to make sure no one was nearby, then back at Patricia.

"I heard there's a new admiral on his way out here," she said. "New guy, was in the elephant graveyard for the last five years."

"Elephant graveyard?" Patricia asked, mystified.

"Where they send old admirals on the retired list," Jo said. Seeing Patricia still looking confused if not slightly terrified, she continued. "It's not a literal graveyard, if that's what you're asking. It's just a list of admirals that the President can call upon if he needs to replace someone on the active list."

"What difference will bringing in some retiree make?" Patricia asked. "Isn't that an insult to Vice Admiral Halsey?"

Jo shrugged.

"I don't make the rules," she said. Their conversation was interrupted by the waitress coming back out with their order. The brown-haired woman sat it down, along with a bottle of soda apiece, then sat down next to Jo and Patricia on an empty chair.

Rebecca, Jo thought. *Her name is Rebecca.*

"I'll be so glad when this shift is over," Rebecca sighed.

"I imagine you're making some amazing tips, though," Jo observed.

"Here's the kind of tips I've been making: Sailors can pinch your rear end without even moving their arms or their buddies seeing who did it," the woman said grimly. "I think they're lucky my husband is working triple shifts, or he'd probably come to lunch to kill the first man he saw place their hands on me as an example to others."

"They can't keep him repairing ships forever," Jo said.

"You'd think not," Rebecca said, lighting up a cigarette. "But I swear to God half the Navy got beat up by the Japanese back in the spring."

"Odd how quiet it's been since then," Patricia said. She was about to say something else when a man came running into the diner.

"King's dead!" he shouted, twisting his hat in his hands. "Admiral King is dead!"

3

THE NIGHTMARE SLIPS ITS MOORINGS

Whoever commands the sea, commands the trade; whosoever commands the trade of the world commands the riches of the world, and consequently the world itself.

— **WALTER RALEIGH**

HEDGLIN RESIDENCE
0530 LOCAL (0900 EASTERN)
BREMERTON, WASHINGTON
30 JULY

"I THINK I may have had too much to drink last night," Beverly said, her breath rustling the hair on Sam's chest.

Oh shit, Sam thought. *Here comes the regret.* To his shock, Beverly slid up, grabbed his face in both of her small hands, then kissed him. Getting over his initial surprise, he responded in kind, running his hands down her back.

"Because I don't remember a whole lot other than Norah shoving us both in a taxi with a key to this apartment," she said after a moment. "However, you being an impeccable gentleman, I think I literally had to take my dress off for you to get the hint."

"I do not think," Sam said, kissing her on the forehead, "that is called a hint anymore at that point."

"Well, after about the third slow dance with you poking something into my stomach, I figured you were interested," she said. "I'd been interested since the third glass of wine."

"So you're saying it's the fruit of the vine that has led you down this treacherous path to sin?" Sam asked.

"No, I'd say it's my husband getting himself killed, three months of coming home every night alone sobbing myself to sleep, then the meddling of my neighbor," Beverly said, sighing as she nuzzled Sam's neck. "Then, yes, the wine."

There was the sound of a flushing toilet from somewhere upstairs.

This place isn't quite a dive, but it's certainly not a top of the line building. I hope we don't get Norah in trouble.

"Sounds like someone else is up," Beverly said. "By the way, where is Myla?"

"David and Sadie took her home," Sam replied, causing Beverly to shake her head ruefully.

"That poor woman does not need to listen to those two rutting like crazy," Beverly observed guiltily. "I am such a bad friend."

"I think Myla is utterly fine with what you did," Sam said, drawing a poke from Beverly.

"What *I* did?" she asked.

"Fine, what *we* did," Sam replied sheepishly.

"Why Sam Cobb, are you ashamed of me?" Beverly asked. Her tone was joking, but Sam could sense the genuine concern underneath the question.

"I would never be ashamed of you, Beverly," Sam said.

I hope she can tell I mean every word of that.

Beverly searched his face, her eyes narrowing in the pre-dawn gloom.

"I am, however, ashamed of my brother and his inability to realize how far low sounds carry," Sam said. Beverly raised her eyebrows at that, then realized what Sam was alluding to.

"Yeah, there are things I could have gone to my grave without hearing him say when Sadie and he were courting," Sam said. "I can only imagine it's ten times worse now that they're married."

Beverly looked wistful for a moment, then changed her expression.

"What were you thinking?" Sam asked.

"It's not nice to pry into a woman's mind," Beverly replied. "You'd think you'd know that with a sister."

"If you were trying to find a way to kill the mood, that was pretty close to a direct hit."

"Sorry," Beverly said. "I didn't mean to get cross with you."

"No, I was meaning mentioning my sister," Sam quipped, drawing a playful slap from Beverly.

"So, not to truly kill the mood by being practical, but did we use a rubber last night?"

Sam pointed to a small trash can next to the bed.

"Yes. I don't think we need any more little Cobbs running around in nine months."

"The doctors figured it was my fault Max and I didn't have kids," Beverly said quietly. "So you may have wasted that one."

"It was more than one," Sam said sheepishly. "I am really feeling like I took advantage of you last night, or was a very bad performer."

"Men," Beverly said, rolling her eyes. "You assume I have some back catalog that I'm grading you against?"

Sam squeezed her.

"I was not thinking about anyone else but present company," he said.

"I was totally wondering if Clark Gable was as dreamy in a...*ow*!" Beverly started, stopped by Sam pinching her buttocks.

"It's not nice to tease, Beverly," Sam said. "I—"

He was momentarily thrown off his train of thought by a very firm grip and stroke around his manhood.

"I have never teased a man in my life, Sam," she said, grabbing the back of his head with her free left hand. With surprising strength, she pulled him in and brought his mouth to hers while still urging him to hardness. The two of them shared a sense of urgency as she rolled over, hooking her leg behind him and shifting him into alignment.

"I don't..." he started to say, feeling her warmth beckoning him.

"I know, and I don't care. In, now," she breathed, bringing both of her legs around him. In a mutually satisfying movement, Sam followed her instructions.

THE SOUND OF A KEY IN THE LOCK JERKED SAM back to wakefulness. Both he and Beverly started to move, leading to them bumping their heads together.

"Ow," Beverly said, starting to giggle, then breaking into laughter. Sam, after a moment, followed suit.

"Well glad to see you guys are awake," Norah called down the hall. "Sam, your boss says you better ensure that lovely woman you're with gets a new outfit so no one questions her morals at the hotel."

Clearly no finger wagging from that direction, Sam thought, surprised at Norah's cheerful tone.

"Are you two decent?" Norah asked from the direction of the living room..

"Not at all," Beverly called back cautiously, looking around for her clothes.

"Nevermind, question answered," Norah said laughingly. "There is a robe that will probably fit you in the closet, Beverly. Sam, you just might be out of luck."

Beverly got up out of the bed, briefly trying to wrap the sheet around her before simply laughing and standing in front of Sam in all of her nudity. He successfully fought the urge to wolf whistle, instead rolling over to sit on the edge of the bed behind her while Beverly searched for the robe in question. Sam ran a hand down her back, causing Beverly to shiver.

"You stop that right now, Sam," she whispered fiercely, finding the robe. She turned around as she put it on, giving Sam a mock disapproving look as he openly ogled her.

"I'm going to go get our clothes. Then we are going to take Norah out to a nice breakfast."

"That sounds like a good idea," Sam said. "Except I'll buy you both breakfast."

"I hope you don't think it's too forward, but I'm thinking of asking Norah about openings up here at Bremerton hospital," Beverly said. "I'd like to help deliver babies."

"Norah really likes it as a place to work," Sam observed. "So I think you'd enjoy it."

"You don't feel like I'm..." Beverly began.

"You are a grown woman, and I enjoy your company," Sam said, causing Beverly to raise an eyebrow and smirk. "More than that, thank you very much."

"But I'm pretty sure that didn't hurt?" Beverly said, leaning in to kiss him.

He slid his hands inside the robe, only to have them swatted away.

"Breakfast."

"Yes, Ma'am," he replied.

Beverly left the room and went down the hallway. Sam heard a murmured conversation then some laughter.

In some ways I think we should get Major Haynes to come along. Unfortunately, that wouldn't be proper. Lonely is the commander.

"Norah says it's nonsense to go out to a diner, we might as well have breakfast with her," Beverly said.

"I think that sounds like an excellent idea," Sam said, reaching to take the pants from Beverly's hands. She pulled them back, smiling.

"I just wanted to look one more time," she said sadly.

Oh shit, Sam thought, recognizing an imminent crying jag when he saw one. He swiftly wrapped Beverly in his arms as she started to sob, her tears hot against his chest.

"Is everything all...oh, sorry!" Norah said, quickly ducking back out of the room. Beverly started giggling and sobbing at the same time, the juxtaposition triggering a bout of hiccups.

"Sorry, Sam," she said, sniffling. "It's just...I've been walking through a haze for months. And just for a moment, when I was taking a picture of you in my head, I felt such guilt, then such joy, then..."

"Then Norah walked in and saw more of me than she ever wanted to," Sam bemoaned. Beverly looked up at him.

"Well, I hope she enjoyed the view," Beverly said lightly. "I certainly have."

Sam blushed.

I hope she did not. That would be a little bit awkward flying with Major Haynes.

"I don't want to put you on the spot," Beverly said. "But I'd like to stay in touch, wherever you go."

Sam hugged her tighter.

"This wasn't just some random fling," he said. "If it's possible, I'd like to stay in touch as well."

"Well, glad we got that settled," Beverly said teasingly. "Although I think you'd be a hard man if you'd said you didn't want to talk to me."

"I'd be a foolish man," Sam replied. "I try to avoid doing foolish things in life."

"We better get out and eat breakfast before it gets cold," Beverly said.

"Yes," Sam said. "Also, we don't want to go walking around in the same clothes that we came here with too late in the day."

"Good point," Beverly replied, letting him go. The two of them dressed quickly and efficiently, then went out to the kitchen where Norah was just finishing placing some bacon on a plate to the side.

"Myla left a note saying she'd come here with a change of clothes for you, Beverly," Norah said.

"That was nice of her," Beverly replied, her tone surprised.

There was a knock on the door.

"I'll watch the eggs," Beverly said, stepping to the pan. Norah wiped off her hands and went to open the door to the hallway. Standing there in his khakis with a grim look on his face was David. He held a garment box in his hands, and Sam saw a pale, puffy faced Sadie and fear-stricken Myla behind his brother.

I don't even need to know what he's about to say.

"When do we need to be dockside?" he asked.

"Major Haynes said as soon as possible," David replied. "To quote him, 'That includes time for a shower and getting dressed.'"

"Goddammit, he didn't say anything to me," Norah snapped.

"He got the phone call from Bremerton just after you left, apparently," Sam said. "Major Haynes did not sound happy at all."

"It's been a rough couple of days for him," Norah said with a grimace. Sam could see that the woman was attempting to put a strong face forward, but her quivering lower lip told him that she was fighting to hold back tears. Turning to Beverly, he saw that Norah was not the only one nearly overcome with emotion.

I hate seeing a woman cry, Sam thought angrily. He went and tenderly kissed Beverly on the forehead.

"Oh dammit Sam," she sobbed, dropping the spatula on the stove and embracing him. Sam hugged her fiercely back as they stepped out of Norah's way.

"I have to go," he said. "I don't *want* to go."

"I know," Beverly said. "Sooner you go, sooner you can come back from wherever they're sending you."

"Come in out of the hallway, David," Norah said. "There's plenty of eggs for Sadie and you as well."

David followed Norah's direction as Sam let Beverly go. He grabbed his uniform and headed for the washroom. As he hung the garment up and started the shower, he had an epiphany that made him shake his head.

Somewhere, some Japanese pilot is probably getting himself ready to face me as well. Well I hope I get a chance to make your widow cry, you son of a bitch.

I.J.N.S. *AKAGI*
0852 LOCAL (2122 EASTERN)
STRAITS OF MALACCA
2 AUGUST (1 AUGUST)

FIRST IN LINE WERE THE FLEET'S MINESWEEPERS. THE VESSELS HAD already passed down the straits at least a dozen times in the last twenty-four hours, their crews meticulously sweeping the ocean with binoculars. Now the ten vessels steamed in line abreast twenty-five miles ahead of the *Kido Butai* with the simple intent of sacrificing their hulls rather than having a stray mine hit a carrier's.

Behind the minesweepers were a swirling contingent of antisubmarine vessels. Too slow, old, or poorly equipped to maintain station with the fleet, the submarine chasers, auxiliaries and, in one case, a captured Dutch gunboat all churned the waters through which the Imperial Japanese Navy's main body would go. Having already sank one unfortunate Dutch vessel three days before, the force hoped to duplicate its success if any Allied vessels were lurking in wait.

Finally, there were the *Kido Butai*'s own destroyers. Each vessel's commander was well aware that the *Zuikaku*'s loss had begun with an American submarine landing several critical torpedo hits. Although objectively the price of doing business in an enemy's home territory, *subjectively* each destroyer captain involved had felt a great sense of shame and personal responsibility. For this reason, each of the men had whipped their crews into a frenzy of hyper-awareness, with all hands possible on deck searching for a tell-tale torpedo track of possible periscope sighting.

JAMES YOUNG

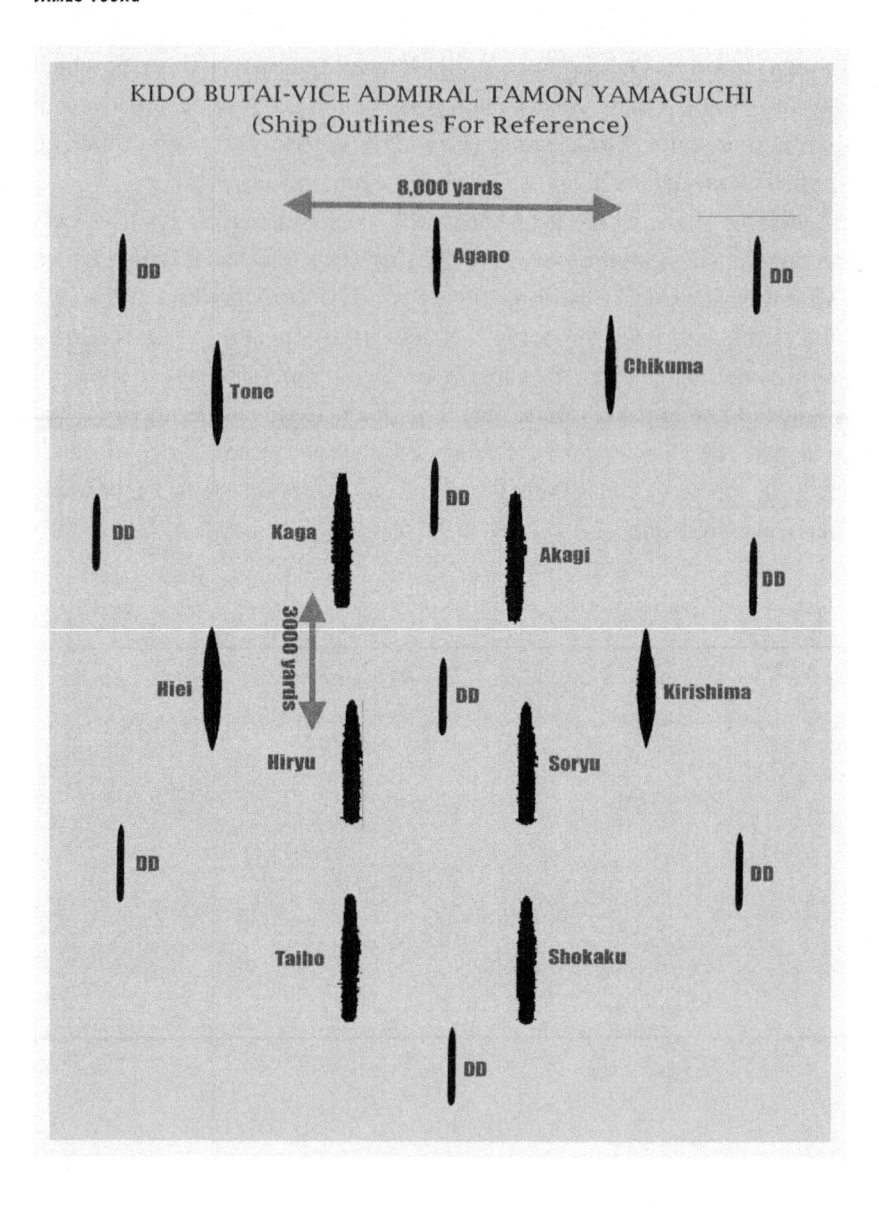

STANDING ON THE *AKAGI*'S FLAG BRIDGE, VICE ADMIRAL Yamaguchi looked on at the frenzied activity with grim satisfaction.

Some fleet commander may be willing to trade a submarine for a carrier, he thought. *But I am not sure that the submarine commander feels the same way.* Attacking the *Kido Butai* in the current circumstances would be almost certain suicide given the likelihood such an action would be responded to immediately with a storm of depth charges.

"Sir, the staff is ready," his aide, Lieutenant Commander Honoka Kuki said from the compartment's rear. Yamaguchi nodded in acknowledgment.

They can wait a few more moments, Yamaguchi determined, feeling the morning sun starting to become warm on his face. *This is a moment I have anticipated for far too long to leave it so quickly.* The strait's narrowness made the *Kido Butai* seem even more powerful, the battleships *Kirishima* and *Hiei* leading both carrier columns. As smoke poured from both battleships' funnels, Yamaguchi reflected on the fact their sister ship *Kongo* lay on the ocean floor a few hundred miles to the southeast, while the *Haruna* was still being repaired in Singapore's drydock.

I hope the Germans are right, and the Americans' Pacific Fleet cannot sortie for another month due to a lack of oilers. Otherwise, Admiral Yamamoto is going to be most upset. Although the *Shinano* had just finished working up and could ostensibly sail forth with the rest of the battleline, the *Kirishima* and *Hiei* represented over twenty percent of the IJN's available battleships.

I told Admiral Yamamoto that I intend to bring the Allied carriers to battle even if I have to chase them across the Indian Ocean to do it, Yamaguchi thought. *If the Americans attempt to retake Wake or, even worse, launch an attack against the Marshalls, we might as well be on the other side of the moon.*

Shaking his head to force those concerns from his mind, Vice Admiral Yamaguchi turned to go back inside the *Akagi*'s island. The newly promoted Rear Admiral Tomeo Kaku, former captain of the *Hiryu*, called the gathered group to attention. Yamaguchi waved them down as he regarded the large map of the Indian Ocean. Wooden pieces represented the *Kido Butai*, the yet to depart transport fleet,

Vice Admiral Ozawa's carrier force and, finally, known Allied and Axis dispositions.

The Italians have surprisingly moved south with three of their battleships and two of the British escort carriers, he noted. *They may serve a useful purpose of exhausting the enemy if well handled.*

"Who is in command of that force?" he asked, pointing at the vessels as he sat down at the head of the map.

Rear Admiral Kaku briefly consulted his notes.

"An Italian admiral named Iachino, sir," Kaku replied.

I do not recognize the name, Yamaguchi thought.

"It would be most helpful if we could coordinate our efforts with him," Yamaguchi stated.

"It is unlikely he will leave the radius of land-based air support," Rear Admiral Kaku observed after once again consulting his notes. "Especially versus a superior enemy force."

"That would be prudent, given what the Germans accomplished against the Americans during their engagement," Rear Admiral Chuichi Hara, commander of the *Kido Butai*'s Fifth Division, stated. A large man, Hara dominated his corner of the map opposite of Yamaguchi with both his physical presence and almost palpable mental resolve.

"Unfortunately, hiding underneath an umbrella of land-based airpower does us no good," Yamaguchi said. "Remove his vessels, please."

Several staff officers complied with Yamaguchi's directive as he and his division commanders continued to regard the Allied force on the mapboard.

"So, what do we expect Fletcher to do next?" he asked the gathered group.

"Sir, intelligence believes that Fletcher should have struck Mombasa by now," Kaku replied. "It has not happened as far as we know."

"Perhaps events in New York have caused a pause in operations?" Hara mused.

"Unlikely," Kaku stated.

"Also unimportant," Yamaguchi stated, waving as if brushing away a fly. "First let us discuss Ceylon."

The staff attendants shifted around the map to be better prepared to move the wooden blocks representing the *Kido Butai*. As they did so, Yamaguchi regarded the ten miniature aircraft blocks present on Ceylon. Carved to represent the types that intelligence believed were present, Yamaguchi noted a pair of four-engined, another duo of twin-engined, a single flying boat, and three single-engined miniatures.

"The enemy has recently reinforced Ceylon with additional aircraft via convoy," Kaku began. "As you can see, there are an expected eight squadrons totaling roughly one hundred aircraft."

The officer moved the three single-engined aircraft to the east of Ceylon.

"Our intelligence indicates these are two squadrons of *Hurricanes*, one of *Spitfires*," Kaku stated. "The *Hurricanes* are recent models, but still inferior to both the *Shiden* and *Zero* fighters. The *Spitfires* may be able to match either."

Several of the gathered aviators stiffened at that, but Kaku ignored them. There were far too many dead pilots and shattered aircraft dotting the Dutch East Indies to merit stroking proud men's egos. The *Spitfire*, as well as the cursed *Whirlwind* and American *Lightning*, had all come as an unpleasant surprise during the last campaign.

"The twin-engined aircraft are the type the British call the *Mosquito*, while the four-engined aircraft are two squadrons of their heavy bombers they call the *Lancaster*."

Kaku paused again as the staff officers moved the *Lancasters* several hundred miles out into the Indian Ocean, then the *Mosquitoes* a lesser distance.

"From captured documents, interrogation, and examination of enemy capabilities, we believe this is how far these aircraft can reach out into the Indian Ocean," Kaku stated. "Thankfully, they cannot operate in daylight against us, and will likely be ineffective at night."

Yamaguchi looked up at that, eyes narrowing.

"Based on what?" he asked sharply, causing Kaku to stare at him, mouth open.

"I do not understand, Vice—"

"The British nearly sank one of Ozawa's vessels and consistently harassed our ships during night operations throughout the Indies," Yamaguchi snapped. "They also managed to hit Ozawa's fleet at night during the Battle of Ceylon. So why do you think they cannot strike us at night?"

The steady thrum of *Akagi*'s turbines was the only sound in the compartment for several long seconds.

Time to make my point clear, Yamaguchi thought, feeling rage welling from within him.

"We will not win this war by ignoring our enemies' capabilities and inconvenient facts," he barked, standing up. "You will prepare another briefing in the next hour which actually reflects what we have learned the last three months. If you are too stupid to do so, I will have you relieved and sent to a post more befitting someone of your lack of imagination. Am I clear?"

Kaku had come to rigid attention. The man's face colored as the *Kido Butai*'s commander finished, his dark eyes focused on the bulkhead in front of him.

"Yes, Vice Admiral!" he responded.

"Rear Admiral Hara, a word please," Yamaguchi said, striding for the exit out of the briefing room and onto the flight deck. There was the scraping of chairs as the staff came to attention while he walked out onto the flagship's teak deck.

Well at least the pilots are getting some rest, Yamaguchi thought. The structure was cleared of aircraft, the prevailing winds blowing at a ninety degree angle to the *Akagi*'s current path of travel. Far above, gaggles of land-based interceptors, both Army and Navy, kept a watchful eye over the departing *Kido Butai*.

"Sir?" Rear Admiral Hara asked from beside him. Vice Admiral Yamaguchi turned to regard the man.

"Walk with me," Yamaguchi stated. He gave both their aides a stern look that clearly indicated the invitation did not extend to them.

"I wager you cautioned against even starting a plan that did not take into account our opponents' use of this new invention 'radar,' didn't you?" Yamaguchi asked once they were halfway to *Akagi*'s bow.

"Hai," Hara replied, clearly uncomfortable.

"Then why did Kaku ignore you?" Yamaguchi pressed.

"He believed, with proper timing, that we could stay outside of the enemy's range, then close to launch a dusk strike on Ceylon," Hara stated.

Yamaguchi turned to him, eyes wide.

"Where did he expect our pilots to land?" Yamaguchi asked, his voice rising. Hara looked at him in some shock.

"Sir, our pilots are qualified to land at night."

While factual, surely I am not the only one who can see the debacle that would become, Yamaguchi thought, clenching his fists.

"Yes, and if I wanted to kill one out of every ten of them, it'd be much more efficient to just go belowdecks with a pistol right now," he spat, then extended his finger. "You and Kaku-san will figure out a plan that has us striking at midday, not dusk. I do not care if we have to nearly empty the destroyers' fuel tanks rushing in at high speed."

Hara gave a short neck bow.

"Also, I will state this now," Vice Admiral Yamaguchi said, suddenly having an epiphany. "If we sight enemy ships while we are attacking Ceylon, we will launch on them *immediately*."

Hara nodded again, his face clearly showing his disapproval.

"Our primary targets are carriers," Yamaguchi explained. "If we only hole their flight decks on the first strike, we can still surely launch another before they repair from that one."

"But sir, what of the battleships reported to be with Fletcher's force?" Hara asked.

"Even with the *Sandaburo* warheads that were sunk en route to Singapore, I am confident we have more than enough weapons to destroy the carriers," Yamaguchi stated. "The battleships are not going to steam over two hundred miles and attack us once we damage their carriers and remove their air cover."

Rear Admiral Hara looked as if he was considering disagreeing with his commander, but reconsidered.

Sandaburo warheads had been manufactured based on a chemical formula shared by the German *Kriegsmarine* with the Imperial Japanese Navy. The Germans, in turn, had obtained it from the British as part of the Treaty of Kent.

"I will inform the staff of your orders, sir," Hara said stiffly, coming to attention and saluting.

Yamaguchi returned the salute, watching as the man moved back to the *Akagi*'s island. He turned back forward to see a pair of minesweepers making a depth charge attack on a suspected contact two miles off of the *Haruna*'s port bow. The *Kido Butai*'s own destroyers were not participating, the vessels' captains adhering to their orders to save ordnance for the battle group's journey into the Indian Ocean.

If only we could put the Sandaburo explosives on our depth charges, Yamaguchi mused. *I am sure the Americans would truly be so grateful that their allies had given us the means to enhance our ordnance then.* Whether something had been lost in the multiple transfers, the Germans had not shared the full formula, or a combination thereof, the Japanese ordnance factories had been unable to manufacture enough of the explosives for torpedoes *and* anti-submarine weapons. The maru which had been blasted into oblivion on the way to Singapore had been carrying almost two months' worth of production.

Stupid American submarines, Yamaguchi seethed. *What kind of idiot attacks a cargo ship escorted by three destroyers?*

Looking out into the Strait of Malacca, the Japanese Vice Admiral took a deep breath and shook his head.

The same kind of idiot who attacks an entire task force by himself, that's who, he thought, recalling how the *Zuikaku* had been lost. *Which is why those minesweepers are probably busy murdering whales and fish.*

TWELVE HOURS AFTER THE *KIDO BUTAI* HAD PASSED THROUGH THE Straits of Malacca, in the evening's darkness, the Strait's waters bubbled and frothed. In the center of the maelstrom of bubbles and expelled water, a dark shape pierced the ocean's surface. In the gloom of the darkened, cloudy sky, the hull of the H.M.C.S. *Torbay* was barely visible despite the glistening water pouring from the hull.

As its hatch clanged open, the *Torbay*'s crew rushed towards their deck gun. With her air so fouled that many of the crew had lost consciousness, the submarine's commander was unable to even countenance attempting to flee underwater. Having waited until long after the screws of the various light craft clearing the strait had passed, the *Torbay* was going to go down fighting on the surface if the need arose. But first, she would transmit the news of the massive, dangerous monster that had passed overhead.

Several long, tense minutes later, her message having been transmitted three times as the submarine made her way southward under diesel power while charging her batteries, the vessel's commander finally breathed a long, shuddering sigh of relief. Regardless of what happened, *Torbay* had achieved her mission. The lack of similar transmissions from her sister ship, H.M.C.S. *Truculent*, led the *Torbay*'s crew to consider their fellow sailors' likely fate.

"Set course for Darwin," *Torbay*'s skipper said. "I don't think Ceylon would be a good place to visit anytime soon for any of Her Majesty's Ships."

U.S.S. Plunger
1000 Local (1600 Eastern)
Midway Island
4 August

"Sir, I'm not saying that I necessarily think what you did was wrong," Chief Petty Officer McClaughlin said as he leaned against the *Plunger*'s bridge railing. "I just think telling Rear Admiral Graham we could head back out without a refit wasn't a good idea."

Nick took a deep breath and watched a gooney bird come in for an awkward landing. The sea fowl made one of the ass over tea kettle touchdowns it was known for, then quickly got back to its feet like nothing had happened.

"Out with it, XO," Commander Emerson said.

"Sir, I'm in agreement with Chief," Nick said simply. He gestured towards the *Plunger*'s stern. "Our hull may not technically be holed back there, but the divers mentioned we've clearly got some buckles and spots where she's going to start leaking soon—"

"That's old age," Emerson snapped.

"Sir, that's getting the shit depth charged out of us at least three times since the war began," Chief replied, his tone rising. "Yes, she's an older boat, but it's hardly like this is a Sugar boat or the damn *Nautilus*."

He looked sheepishly over at Nick.

"Sorry sir," he said.

"No problem, Chief," Nick replied. "The old lady gave us good service."

Commander Emerson fumed while Chief McLaughlin and Nick finished their exchange. More worrisome, the *Plunger*'s commander seemed to be considering his next words carefully. For such an outspoken man, that meant what was coming next was probably going to be a doozy.

"Lieutenant Cobb, has it occurred to you that a long time in the yard may lead to your reassignment to Stateside construction?" Emerson asked.

That wasn't what I expected him to say.

"Given your past achievements, it may even lead to you being assigned to a War Bond tour."

Nick could almost feel Chief McLaughlin's eyes upon him. Both the Chief and Commander Emerson were well aware that Nick had just barely managed to get out of Pearl in front of reassignment orders straight from the Navy Department. Given the Navy's string of losses in both the Atlantic and Pacific, the service's image was taking quite a beating. It was apparent that some individuals wanted a feel good story to sell to the nation. Whereas the *Nautilus*'s former CO, Commander Jason Freeman, had been reassigned as U.S.S. *Herring*'s master and was thus unavailable, there were plenty of lieutenants available for reassignment to *Plunger*.

That confirms part of the reason we rushed out of Pearl last time was to keep me out ahead of the public relations posse. Which is kind of a shitty thing to do to the crew at large, but there it is.

"Sir, while the thought of getting stuck at Mare Island exhorting a bunch of construction workers to do their utmost does strike me as a fate worse than death," Nick said drily, "I'd rather do that than actually kill the crew."

Commander Emerson's face colored.

Might have pressed a little too hard on that one, Nick realized. *But it needed to be said.*

"Sir, if the *Fulton* could fix us, I'd be all for it," Chief McLaughlin said, gesturing to where the submarine tender lay anchored. There were already four submarines tied up alongside the large vessel, with two of the pigboats taking on torpedoes as the *Plunger*'s command team had their huddle.

Emerson's lips pursed until they were almost white, and a vein throbbed in his neck.

To be honest, maybe it's time you took a rest also.

"I will inform Captain Davis that, in the opinion of my XO and Chief of the Boat, the *Plunger* is materially defective," Commander Emerson bit out. "I am sure we will receive subsequent orders to return to Pearl Harbor for repairs."

"Sir, I–" Nick began.

"Both of you are dismissed," Emerson cut him off. "Please allow me time to receive our follow on orders before informing any members of the crew or the wardroom."

Both Nick and Chief McClaughlin came to attention and saluted. Commander Emerson returned the salute crisply, at which point Nick and Chief McLaughlin both made their way down to the *Plunger*'s deck, then off the boat.

It was a tense ten minutes as they walked, Nick returning the salutes of other submarine crewmen and passing Marines. Even though scuttlebutt had it that the Japanese Fleet was away in the Indian Ocean, the reinforced USMC battalion that garrisoned Midway seemed to be in a state of constant preparation and anticipation. The roar of a flight of *Wildcats* passing overhead at medium altitude caused Nick to spare a thought to Sam and David.

Looks like I might be joining those idiots in Seattle soon.

"Sir, permission to speak in confidence," Chief McLaughlin nearly hissed.

"Yes, I think he's dangerously close to a crack up also," Nick said without preamble.

Chief McLaughlin nodded, exhaling heavily in relief.

"Thank you, sir, for backing me up. I understand how much you do not want to be trapped back on the mainland."

"I want to be lying on the bottom of the ocean even less," Nick stated. "Despite the protestations I occasionally may make."

"Do you think that they'll actually send you back now?" Chief McLaughlin asked.

"If Rear Admiral Graham has his way? No. Commanding officers can claim needs of the service to a point, and I think Vice Admiral Halsey will back him up."

Chief McLaughlin nodded at that statement as the men reached the water's edge.

"How soon do you think it will be until Vice Admiral Halsey's replacement arrives?"

"To be frank, Chief, I thought his replacement would already be at Pearl," Nick stated. "Vice Admiral Halsey doesn't strike me as the type of man who needs to be manning a desk. While he's not Commander Emerson aggressive, Vice Admiral Halsey's an attacker."

"Interesting that we haven't been attacking, then," Chief McLaughlin said.

Nick shrugged.

"We started to attack and the Japanese sent the *California* and those two escort carriers to the bottom," Nick observed. "There's also that rumor that something big is about to happen in the Indian Ocean, plus the damn German submarines continue to cause all sorts of problems off the East Coast and near the Canal Zone."

Nick looked out over the Pacific and took a deep breath.

"For all we know, someone *is* attacking," he stated. "Just not us at the moment."

U.S.S. HOUSTON
0545 LOCAL (2245 EASTERN)
100 MILES NORTHEAST OF MOGADISHU
5 AUGUST (4 AUGUST)

I THINK WE'RE ABOUT TO ROUSE SOME FOLKS FROM A MISPLACED SENSE OF security, Jacob thought, gazing astern as the *Houston* made a lazy turn to starboard in the predawn darkness. *Especially if they weren't, for instance, expecting surface ships to come a callin'.*

Task Force 25, as the new surface group was now called, was a much stronger force than the one that had terrorized the Mozambique Channel. In addition to the heavy cruiser's normal companions, the large, hulking shapes of the U.S.S. *Massachusetts* and U.S.S. *Indiana* now loomed astern of the H.M.C.S. *Repulse*. Although both battleships' crews were just slightly less green than a bed of kelp, their eighteen 16-inch guns more than tripled TF 25's available firepower.

Certainly makes a potential encounter with what the Italians allegedly have in Mogadishu a little more even. The two new cruisers that came up with them will also help. The *Baltimore* was a heavy cruiser like *Houston*, while the *Tallahassee* was a "light" cruiser that displaced over 2,000-tons more than Jacob's vessel.

"I must say, sir, Vice Admiral Fletcher has surprised me somewhat with his aggression," Commander Farmer observed.

Jacob detected a slight sense of nervousness in the man's voice, and the British officer busily scanned the skies to the west.

"Well, I don't pretend to be able to read Vice Admiral Fletcher's mind," Jacob observed. "But I do think the possibility of an Italian Fleet gathering behind us finally became something he just couldn't ignore."

Farmer gave a curt nod.

"I must say, however, that Vice Admiral Cunningham would have appreciated knowing of Fletcher's intent to raid Mogadishu before the rest of the fleet departed for the Maldives. Especially with the Japanese sighted entering the Indian Ocean a week ago."

Well, maybe Vice Admiral Cunningham shouldn't have explicitly questioned Vice Admiral Fletcher's courage, Jacob thought. *Especially since it's the damn* **Prince of Wales**' *short legs that have him concerned half the time.* It was not hard to see the differences in British and American design philosophies with regards to their capital vessels and expected range. Having an Empire the sun never set on meant the Prince of Wales' designers had assumed all Royal Navy vessels would be within easy distance of a friendly port. The Indian Ocean's vastness and South Africa's recalcitrance had shown that assumption's inherent errors. The range problem had been further exacerbated by several crew practices with regards to not using certain fuel tanks.

I don't care how worried they are about seawater getting into the boilers, you can't just opt not to use thirty percent of your battleship's fuel.

"I think it's precisely that carrier battle that has Vice Admiral Fletcher deciding it's time to get the Italians out of Mogadishu," Jacob replied. "With *Victorious, Ark Royal,* and *Eagle,* he has three carriers to the four the Japanese are expected to bring, plus the aircraft on Ceylon. I think the odds are much better than even."

Further discussion was cut off by furious signaling from the *Massachusetts.*

"Looks like our friends are on radar," Jacob noted. "Now here's to hoping the Italian or German in question isn't blind."

Farmer looked at the rapidly lightening sky above their head.

"I think it would have to be almost a divine curse, like something out of the Old Testament, to miss a fleet this size," the British officer said grimly.

Very true, with three capital ships in this task force. But had to put something sufficiently large to be able to take care of itself if it came to that out here. Besides, if the enemy's swinging at us, they're going to miss the carriers.

One hundred miles to the northeast, the U.S.S. *Yorktown* and *Enterprise* lurked with their escorts. Unbeknownst to Commander Farmer or any other British officer, the new carriers *Bonhomme Richard* and *Independence* were roughly sixty miles to that group's south and moving at high speed to join up.

Interesting how Second Fleet snuck half their strength all the way down the Atlantic, then around the Cape of Good Hope without anyone noticing, Jacob thought. *Even if Vice Admiral Fletcher's been explicitly ordered not to subject those forces to 'undue risk.'*

"I almost feel sorry for the poor bastards when that spotting report arrives," Jacob observed. "Going to have to make some hard decisions at that point."

The general intent was for the search aircraft's report to flush anything in Mogadishu out into the open water for TF 25 to deal with.

This was preferable to aircraft attempting to put torpedoes into vessels moored in a harbor with torpedo nets up and arrayed.

Assuming we can find the enemy once he puts to sea. That's not always as easy as the flyboys make it sound. Or, for that matter, that what's in the harbor is what the intelligence types think.

"Well, we've got the right commander for the job," Commander Farmer said. "Vice Admiral Godfrey will chase the Italians all the way to Mombasa or Port Said depending on which way they go."

Jacob nodded his agreement even as he tried not to think what had happened to the last Commonwealth admiral that chased an Axis fleet.

Admiral Phillips died with his spurs on at least.

"I must say, while the added tonnage was a bit of a surprise, your new *South Dakota* vessels have certainly made nice gifts for Admiral Godfrey," Farmer observed.

Jacob kept his face passive as the British officer's biting tone. Vice Admiral Godfrey had been expecting a routine tanking operation after departing Madagascar's vicinity. Instead, a significant portion of the United States Navy's Atlantic Fleet had shown up at the rendezvous point.

Then again, Rear Admiral Lee did defer to Gordon's experience and place his vessel's under the man's command, Jacob thought. *That probably helped smooth the waters.*

"Here's to hoping we get a chance to see who did a better job packing a battleship into treaty tonnage," Jacob replied. "

God help us that we're at the point we don't feel comfortable telling our own allies what vessels the Navy is bringing to a fight, His sealed orders had been delivered by breeches buoy from one of the destroyers that had accompanied the *Massachusetts*. The young lieutenant carrying them had indicated the Office of Naval Intelligence had some concerns regarding the upper levels of the Royal Navy in the Battle of Iceland's aftermath.

Some folks are categorically unable to accept that maybe, just maybe, the Krauts might know what they're doing.

Unlike some of his comrades, Jacob could accept the possibility that, yes, the Nazis had somehow turned a senior officer or perhaps an aide in the Commonwealth fleet. However, having had to increase his own respect of the Japanese despite prewar misconceptions, Jacob was willing to accept that the Germans might have become quick learners with regards to modern naval warfare.

"Sir, the *Massachusetts* is vectoring fighters towards the enemy aircraft," one of his talkers reported.

Jacob nodded, still sweeping his eyes around the formation to make sure the *Houston* was not going to collide with anyone. Satisfied the Officer of the Deck was keeping suitable station, Jacob brought up his own binoculars and again swept the sky in the bearing of the reported aircraft.

There it is. The distant dot was swelling rapidly through the binoculars. It took a full thirty seconds before one of the lookouts also sighted the aircraft, and Jacob made a note to have a word with Commander Sloan about their training.

"Looks like one of the Italians' flying boats," Farmer observed, then narrowed his eyes. "Or actually, one of ours."

Jacob couldn't resist throwing a jab.

"One of 'yours?'" he asked, raising an eyebrow and dropping his binoculars slightly. Commander Farmer dropped his binoculars and gave the *Houston*'s captain a brief, unhappy glare before recovering his military bearing.

"A *Sunderland*, sir," the man said, voice clipped. Jacob nodded, then brought his binoculars up again.

That was cheap, but so is bitching about Vice Admiral Fletcher not dropping everything to run off and defend a colonial possession, Jacob justified.

"Hmm, he appears to be coming closer," Farmer observed. "Awfully brave of him; he must have different orders than the Mediterranean Fleet always did."

"Which were?"

"Simply to make and maintain contact," Farmer replied. "Let the next aircraft up get closer, then set about trying to figure out the force's composition."

"He might be trying to make a good report so they can figure out whether they should give battle or just run," Jacob noted. "Then again, I can't imagine *not* coming out to fight given all the damage we've been doing to convoys."

"There are limits to most navies' aggressiveness, Captain Morton," Farmer observed. "I seem to recall not even yours ventured out that much in the face of a massive blockade during our nations' most recent disagreement."

Jacob grunted at that point as the *Sunderland* banked just outside of anti-aircraft range. It made one complete circle before suddenly straightening out its turn and heading west. The reason for the pilot's change of course was easy to ascertain as smaller, faster dots closed with the *Sunderland* as it ducked into a cloud bank.

The ensuing combat's outcome was certain, even if not as one-sided as Jacob would have expected. Judging from the one missing and one smoking fighter out of the flight of four that flew back over *Houston*, the *Sunderland* had died hard. The black finger reaching towards the sky on the western horizon, however, indicated the *Sunderland* had indeed died.

"What's the report from the *Massachusetts*?" Jacob asked, stepping back onto the bridge with Commander Farmer.

"Splash one flying boat, sir," Lieutenant Ness, the Officer of the Deck, reported. "However, it appears one of our fighters crashed."

"Do we need to ready to launch our seaplane for rescue?" Jacob asked.

I'm pretty sure I know the answer, but I want to see if the good lieutenant thought to ask. Seeing the look on the young officer's face, he could tell Ness had not.

"See that we inquire at your convenience," Jacob said. "Tell the XO I'd like to see him in my day cabin, please."

Ness visibly swallowed at the last statement, and Jacob's expression softened.

"Lieutenant Ness, I assure you, we didn't even have aircraft when I was in your billet. So I'd be slightly hypocritical for expecting you to inherently remember to ask, no?"

Lieutenant Ness looked at Jacob nervously as he considered his options.

The problem with Ness is he's not instinctual enough, Jacob thought. *Which reminds me, I also need to tell Commander Sloan fitness reports are apparently due.*

JAMES YOUNG

"Yes, sir," Ness replied finally. Jacob nodded.

"File it away for next time," he said, then nodded at Commander Farmer and headed for his day cabin.

I do love the fact that BuPers was kind enough to send along my naughty note for not doing fitness reports with the **Massachusetts***, yet somehow no one back in Australia can get our mail forwarded. Maybe I'll write Josephine a letter before lunch.*

As he sat down at his desk, he glanced at his daughter's picture.

"I do wonder what in the heck you're up to right now, young lady," he muttered aloud. "With apparently half the Japanese Navy here in the Indian Ocean, I guess I don't have to worry about Hawaii getting invaded."

Jacob paused to look down at the half-finished letter to one Lieutenant Eric Cobb also sitting on his desk.

"Or, for that matter, that fly boy of yours being less than a gentlemen."

U.S.S. YORKTOWN
0615 LOCAL (2315 EASTERN)
INDIAN OCEAN

"PILOTS MAN YOUR PLANES," THE LOUDSPEAKER CRACKLED ABOVE Eric's head, jerking him from a cat nap. Shaking the cobwebs away, he grabbed his plotting board.

"Little early, isn't it?" Lieutenant Ramage stated, looking at the clock. "I didn't think we were launching for another hour."

"We weren't," Lieutenant Commander Brigante said as he stepped into the ready room. "Plans changed once the surface folks got themselves sighted by a flying boat. I think Vice Admiral Fletcher wants to try to catch the Italians as they're preparing a strike."

If he wanted to do that, we probably should have done a predawn launch. Oh well, I'm not a staff officer.

"I need to see section leaders when we get topside," Brigante called behind him.

The noise of an aircraft rolling down the flight deck briefly filled the ready room.

That sounds like we're getting some of our fighters launched, Eric thought. *Which means they're strengthening the CAP either in anticipation of something getting flown back at us or sending more fighters out towards the surface folks.*

It was a short walk up and out onto the *Yorktown*'s flight deck. The carrier's strike was arrayed aft, engines starting to turn over as crews made the final pre-flight checks. A *Wildcat* trundled down the flight deck, then soared off to join the other three stubby fighters in its flight.

"Helluva way to earn our pay, ain't it?" Lieutenant Ramage shouted, the wind over the *Yorktown*'s bow causing his Mae West to flap in the wind.

The big carrier's deck vibrated underneath them as she steamed at near full speed, her wake broad and white behind her. As he walked over towards the island where Lieutenant Commander Brigante knelt with a mapboard in front of him, Eric turned to look over the rest of the formation. With just a pair of light cruisers and four destroyers around her, the *Yorktown* was sailing along with the smallest escort she'd had since the start of the war.

I'd feel a little exposed if I didn't know there was a surface group less than three hours away. Less than that if we steam towards one another.

"Okay guys, here's the dope," Lieutenant Brigante began in his strong Brooklyn accent. "The wind's being cooperative for operations, so *Yorktown*'s going to continue to steam towards the Italian port until we return. CAG believes as long as we keep behind the surface bubbas, no need to worry about the Italian bombers flying all the way out here to hit us."

Well that seems a bit optimistic, Eric thought.

"We're going with Plan Able from last night," Brigante said. "Vice Admiral Fletcher figures even if the battleship and carriers come out to fight, they're going to need fuel afterwards to go anywhere. Our job is to make sure the tankers that are allegedly in harbor don't make it back out."

Gotta wonder how many tankers the Italians are going to have after this, Eric mused. *We've sank quite a few.*

"The torpeckers are going to go plaster what intelligence indicates is one of only two airfields capable of handling bombers," Brigante went on. "That's the only change from Plan Able."

Eric wasn't the only one who looked back in surprise at the *Avengers*.

"Yeah, I guess that's a wrinkle that got slipped in while we were sleeping, and the ordnance boys had a long night of it swapping stuff out," Brigante observed.

Wonder if Vice Admiral Fletcher is trying to conserve torpedoes? It was a long, long way to an American depot, and scuttlebutt from the replenishment was that the *Lassen* had been long on bombs, short on torpedoes.

I wonder if the rumors are true about BuOrd recalling a bunch of tin fish for testing? Eric thought. Nick had told him about the submariners' problems. Several of VT-8's survivors had also sworn they should have gotten at least one hit on the damaged Japanese carrier that had escaped during the Battle of Hawaii. Other incidents from the Dutch East Indies and the Battle of Iceland had increased the tension between BuOrd and the active fleet.

"Now, there's a possibility that we might run into some British aircraft," Brigante said, consulting his notes. "Besides the birds carried on the escort carriers intel says are in port, apparently our black shoe brethren were sighted by a British flying boat."

You know, for all the complaining people were making about not doing this with the Royal Navy carriers as well, I think I'm glad to know any British aircraft I see are enemy.

"Rendezvous points are as follows," Brigante said, then began rattling off the respective latitudes and longitudes. Consulting his notes one last time and seemingly satisfied, Brigante tucked the piece of paper away.

"Let's go make our mothers proud, gentlemen," he said. "See you guys back here in a couple of hours."

The flight towards Mogadishu seemed longer than it actually was. With VB-11 and VS-11 both flying the strike at almost full strength while the *Enterprise* acted as the duty carrier, the *Yorktown*'s "Sunday Punch" was almost fifty aircraft strong. Puttering along behind and below the twenty-four dive bombers, the carrier's twelve *Avenger* torpedo bombers each lugged a 2,000-lb bomb while twelve F4Fs weaved protectively overhead.

"Isn't it kind of strange that the torpecker pilots aren't carrying any of their tin fish?" Radioman 1c Brown asked.

"Vice Admiral Fletcher wants to make sure we wreck the harbor," Eric replied. "If we destroy the facilities, the ships can't come across the Indian Ocean after us while we're fighting the Japanese."

There was a long pause.

"I'm no admiral, but doesn't putting a hole in their side keep the vessels from chasing us just as well?" Brown asked.

Yes, but you're assuming their torpedoes would work.

"A whole lot easier to hit a building than a ship, Brown," he said aloud. "Plus if the British are right, this harbor has horrible defenses."

"Pardon me if I'm not all that eager to take the opinion of a bunch of people whose carriers are rushing east," Brown replied, disgusted.

"Careful Brown, you'll get both of us banned from their rum if you keep up that attitude," Eric said with a smile.

"Sir, I don't get to eat all the...*bogeys, four o'clock high!*"

Eric had just enough time to look up and to his left before the flight of *Spitfires* dove on the combined dive bomber flight. The rattle of machine guns and cannon fire came even as Eric sideslipped his *Dauntless*. Out of the corner of his eye, he saw three *Wildcat*s falling, their pilots dead before the fighters had a chance to jettison their wing fuel tanks.

Dammit, looks like they were expecting us!

Brown fired away with his twin guns as another flight of *Spitfires* slanted in. This group made the mistake of swinging in slow and directly astern, the two leaders each picking a VB-11 *Dauntless* as their prey. Unfortunately for the two RAF pilots, the twenty-four .30-caliber guns were more than enough to see one *Spitfire* off and severely maul the other. In exchange, one *Dauntless* spiraled away in flames and another was forced to jettison its bomb into Mogadishu below.

"What in the hell are the *Wildcats* doing?" Brown asked, taking a snapshot as a *Spitfire* flashed by on a beam run.

"Dying," Eric snapped back as he watched two of the F4Fs plummet as flaming comets. Just as the victorious *Spitfire* began to circle around to try and draw a beam on the bombers, it exploded as four dark blue and grey shapes hurtled down on it from altitude. Two more *Spitfires*, similarly focused on the *Avengers*, also paid the price for failing to maintain eternal vigilance as they also were shot down by a group of gull-winged aircraft.

Those are friendly planes! Eric realized belatedly as defending aircraft were engaged by more of the newcomers. Turning to look south, Eric saw a large gaggle of aircraft approaching from that direction. Bringing up his binoculars, he saw all of these aircraft were also a uniform dark blue.

Where did they come from? The sharp *crack!* of exploding anti-aircraft fire and the *Dauntless* jostling brought him back to the task at hand.

"Cobb, take your boys after that tanker there by the pier!" Lieutenant Commander Brigante ordered.

Eric saw the ship in question, realizing there was a reason the squadron commander was pointing the target out. The large vessel was just starting to back away from the oil refueling terminal, froth underneath its stern indicative of full power.

"Red One, Blue One, roger!" Eric replied, looking left and right to see that his two wingmen had heard the conversation. Both young officers were staring at him, with Ensign Strange's eyes seemingly as wide as dinner plates. As the rest of VB- and VS-11 opened their dive flaps and dove towards the fuel tanks below, Eric circled to his left above the long ship. Another volley of flak shook his bomber, the bursts far too close for comfort.

Those are some damn accurate gunners, Eric noted, lining up from the tanker's stern. Reaching forward he grabbed the dive brake lever and pulled, feeling the *Dauntless*'s drag immediately increase. The subsequent movements were by rote, Eric feeling a grim familiarity with the process.

It was only when they nosed over that the routine was suddenly, irrevocably changed. Brown's cry and the rattle of machine guns was something Eric forced himself to ignore. What broke his concentration, albeit briefly, was the bright flash and sudden fireball of Ensign Strange's *Dauntless* exploding as a hurtling *Spitfire* shot it down.

Fucking asshole!

Rage burned through Eric's chest, and his eyes briefly burned before he regained control of his emotions.

Lacking dive brakes of its own, the British fighter kept going at high speed after killing Strange and his gunner. Blue Two fired his machine guns after the *Spit* more in anger and frustration than any hopes of getting a hit. The utterly futile burst came nowhere near hitting the *Spitfire*, but the trigger-happy 20mm gun crew on the tanker's bow had a much better angle. Eric whooped without shame as the British fighter was hit just as it started pulling out, its port wing fluttering away just before the remaining wreckage smashed into the water of Mogadishu harbor.

"Five thousand!" Brown shouted.

Shit, might want to actually aim this thing, Eric thought, putting his eyes to the sight. The tanker was not stationary, but was certainly just a bare step above helpless. As tracers flashed into this field of view, Eric depressed the button on his twin machine guns. Not sure if returning fire did any good, he concentrated on the task at hand.

"Three thousand!"

The *Dauntless* shook violently as *something* exploded with a thunderous roar roughly a half mile away.

"Holy shit, someone must have hit an ammo dump!" Brown shouted.

"*Altitude!*" Eric screamed, the tanker's deck incredibly large in his sight.

"Two thousand!" Brown replied, panicked at having been distracted. "Nineteen hundred!"

Dear Lord, please do not be full of avgas. Despite the terror that suddenly gripped him at that possibility, Eric pulled the release without hesitation. There was the familiar vibration as the trapeze swung into the airstream, then the *Dauntless* shifting upwards as the half-ton bomb left from underneath. Eric braced himself and pulled back on the stick, the dirty brown water of Mogadishu harbor receding away from his field of view as darkness rushed in.

"Hit!" Brown grunted, just before the *Dauntless* was struck by metal debris from their bomb exploding.

Looking back, Eric could see flames shooting up from the tanker's forward hold just as Blue Two's bomb landed close alongside alongside. Scanning for his wingman, Eric saw the dark blue *Dauntless* at his eleven o'clock. Blue Two suddenly skidded, at which point Eric belatedly noted the long-nosed Italian that had elicited the maneuver. For his part, the Italian pilot barely managed to avoid smacking into the harbor, the tip of its wing dragging a briefly.

You son-of-a-bitch, Eric thought, cursing his inability to remember what the long-nosed Italian aircraft were called. Then it came to him: *Folgore*.

"Hold on," Eric snapped, then put his own *Dauntless* into a tight turn to intersect the circling Italian's. Smoke was pouring from the *Folgore*'s nose as its pilot added power to avoid stalling as he stalked Blue Two.

"Uh, si–" Brown started to say, then grunted as he was thrown into his belt.

He doesn't even see us, Eric thought, dismissing Brown's concerns.

As if to prove his point, the Italian fighter half-rolled to draw a bead on Blue Two, exposing his belly towards Eric. Gritting his teeth, Eric squeezed the trigger as he applied lead.

While he wasn't either of his brothers, Eric had spent just as many years bird hunting with their father as they had. Whether the Italian pilot inadvertently jerked or was incapacitated by the stream of bullets erupting through his cockpit floor, the *Folgore* suddenly tightened its turn, went into a spin, and then cartwheeled forward in a cloud of spray.

"Blue Two, you owe me a drink when we get back to port!" Eric shouted into the cacophony of the squadron net. His hands were shaking with adrenaline as he pulled up alongside. His exultation died in his mouth as he looked over at the other *Dauntless*, Van Horn's gunner slumped lifeless in a shattered cockpit.

Dammit. Van Horn looked over at him and gave a signal indicating that he was all right, and Eric led them out towards the rendezvous point. Brown was strangely silent as they began climbing.

"Brown, you okay?" Eric asked finally as several other *Dauntlesses*, as well as a couple of larger dive bombers in USN colors that he did not recognize, reached the rendezvous point.

"Sir, have you ever considered that maybe I want to fucking survive this war?" Brown snapped angrily.

I guess I asked for that, Eric thought. *Still*.

"That makes two of us, Radioman," Eric snapped back.

"Well you sure don't need me back here if you're going to go looking for trouble, *sir*," Brown replied.

"What would you have had me do, Brown? Let the damn fighter shoot Blue Two into the water?"

There was a long silence from the back cockpit. For several horrified seconds, Eric wondered if his tail gunner had actually *wanted* him to let Blue Two die so that they didn't attract the fighter's attention. Then the man spoke.

"My apologies, sir," he said sincerely. "It's just...it's kind of hard being back here, helpless, while you get to decide what in the hell we're going to get into."

Eric considered Brown's point.

"I understand," he replied. "I really do. We've been through a lot of shit together, though. Have I ever done something reckless?"

"No sir," Brown answered without hesitation. "But you do seem to have a way of attracting trouble."

"My last gunner thought so too," Eric said somberly. "That's why he's now sitting the war out. So did my fiancée, and that's why she ended our relationship."

Eric swallowed as he continued, sliding their *Dauntless* into a gaggle of VS-11 and VB-11 aircraft heading back towards *Yorktown*.

"So if you want to switch planes and fly with someone else, or even put in for a transfer, I'll understand."

I mean, if everyone else in my life is leaving me, I guess I shouldn't be surprised you do as well, Eric thought.

"Sir, knowing my luck, they'd stick me with Lieutenant (j.g.) Read,"

JAMES YOUNG

Brown said after a long pause. "If there's one person who is unluckier than you..."

"You know he's dating my sister, right?" Eric asked.

"Sir, a man hitting a jackpot just before his brakes fail is still unlucky," Brown replied without missing a beat.

"Did you just compare my sister to a jackpot, Brown?"

The two of them were interrupted by a series of Morse code coming over the radio. Eric stopped talking so Brown could work on transcribing the report, as it sounded like a USN scouting code.

"What's the word?" he asked after a few moments.

"Looks like the Italian surface fleet headed south," Brown replied. "Also, did you know that we apparently had additional carriers in the area? The pilot is claiming to be from the U.S.S. *Bonhomme Richard*."

Eric smiled at that.

"They mentioned something about don't be alarmed if there's a strange squadron making reports during the briefing last night," Eric replied. "I wasn't expecting John Paul Jones' ghost, though."

"Explains the other dive bombers," Brown noted.

"Also the other fighters, although I just thought they were dark-painted *Wildcats*," Eric replied. "Although if they're new carriers, they must be Atlantic Fleet, which makes me wonder who is minding the store on the East Coast."

"Not my problem, but I assume we're going back out?" Brown said.

"Yes, I imagine so," Eric replied with resignation. "Unless the surface ships catch them. However, think they're going to need help with that."

*R*ATMALANA *A*IRFIELD
1130 L*OCAL* (*0200* E*ASTERN*)
C*OLOMBO*, C*EYLON*
5 A*UGUST*

"S*IR*! S*IR*! W*AKE UP*!"

The furious pounding on his door was not how Russell would have preferred to be awakened. Indeed, for a brief moment anger washed over him as he swung his feet out of bed, then strode toward the door. It was only after he'd had a moment to recognize the panic in Pilot Officer Elliot's voice that he stopped to get his temper in check.

The man sounds positively manic, Russell mused, casting his eye at where his sidearm remained hanging next to his life jacket. Russell listened and did not hear any sounds of gunfire, explosions, or voices shouting in Japanese.

Right then. He opened the door just as Elliot began another furious round of knocking.

"Pilot Officer Elliot, I can only assume that Oliver Cromwell himself has appeared in the middle of the runway," Russell drily observed. "To, no doubt, state he will not speak with anyone other than me with regards to dealing with the current menace inhabiting Buckingham Palace?"

Elliot stopped, looking at Russell in utter befuddlement.

"In other words, there better be a bloody good reason you're knocking on my door, in that manner, less than six hours after I finally fell asleep."

Elliot looked sheepish, opening then closing his mouth. For a moment Russell feared he'd so disrupted the young officer that the teenager had forgotten his urgent mission. Thankfully, the man quickly recovered.

"Sorry sir, but Wing Commander Hains stated it was of utmost importance that all, and he repeated, *all* officers report immediately to the tower."

"The tower?" Russell confirmed. "Why the bloody...wait, nevermind."

Forgot about the typhoon taking the roof off of wing headquarters, he recalled grimly. *Thankfully they're focusing on fixing the radar shack and hangars before getting around to nonessential buildings*. Russell was thankful that it wasn't any of his aircraft lost in the storm. A couple of the *Spitfire* squadrons had not been as lucky.

"All right, I'm on my way," Russell said.

. . .

"Looks like going to a nocturnal schedule's not working out all that well, eh?" Bellingsley noted as they walked.

"There's a reason I only shifted Baron Flight," Russell replied sourly. "Bloody Japanese don't have squadrons of 110s floating around in the dark, at least not off their carriers."

"Take a right idiot to try and fly at night off a flattop," Bellingsley replied. "I remember a few of their blokes did it back in the Indies, but I'd love to know how many of them crashed because of it."

"Not enough," Russell replied grimly. He noted that Wing Commander Hains stood atop one of the airfield's 5-ton lorries. A *Spitfire* driver by trade, Hains had flown some missions in North Africa during the first phase of the war. From an upper class family, Hairns was surprisingly egalitarian in his treatment of the officers under his care.

Man looks like someone has shot his dog, Russell thought.

"Squadron leaders, do we have everyone?" Hairns called. Russell cursed inwardly, looking for his flight leaders.

"Gratham present!" Flight Lieutenant Badcocke called from somewhere to his left. That started a bedlam of other flight leaders following the man's lead. Thankfully, most of 505 Squadron was near Russell.

"Jersey's here, sir," Flight Lieutenant Hibbert said, his distinctive Scottish accent setting him apart from many of the other voices.

"Baron Squadron present, sir," Russell called.

The other fighter squadrons chimed in, and Hairns nodded grimly. Taking a deep breath, he looked over the gathered group.

"Gentlemen…" he began, then stopped to gather himself. "Gentlemen, it is with deep regret that I report Lord Winston Churchill died of his wounds approximately an hour ago in New York."

There was a ripple of shock and anger that went through the gathered group. Russell himself had trouble taking a breath, swallowing past the bile that rose in his throat.

"I apologize for having to deliver you this news in this manner, but I wanted to make sure all of you heard things directly from me," Hairns continued.

Churchill is dead. The Lion has laid down his burdens indeed. Although he had not been keen on politics, Churchill had been a presence in English society for his entire life. Russell's father had served in the Royal Navy throughout the entirety of World War I. A great uncle had fought in the Boer War. Both men had held Churchill in high regard, and the man's ability to recognize the Nazi threat for what it was had always been appreciated by the Wolford family.

Hairns let the men have their moments, many of the younger pilots openly sobbing or crying in response to the news. After about five minutes, the Wing Commander gestured for the men's attention.

"I am afraid that we must carry on," Hairns stated. "For the other news is that the Imperial Japanese Navy has been sighted in strength at various locations entering the Indian Ocean."

This statement brought a response of a totally different sort from the gathered men. Suddenly the group became silent and pensive, looking at one another.

"Gentlemen, I do not believe I need to tell you what this news means," Hairns said. "I can only assure you that *all* of our services shall be involved in making a concerted effort to keep Ceylon free."

I think he just informed us that the Navy is taking steps to come meet the Japanese, Russell thought.

"I will need to speak with all squadron leaders after this," Hairns finished. "I have spoken with the quartermaster and headquarters. Other than designated alert pilots, all duties for today are cancelled and the first round of drinks is on me. For the Queen!"

"For Her Majesty!" the gathered men thundered back before dispersing. Russell was headed for the Wing Commander Hairns when the unit adjutant intercepted him.

"Sir, mail for you," the man said, handing over several wrapped letters. Russell recognized the scent on them even before he turned the envelopes over to see Maggie's neat cursive.

This will have to wait. He tucked the post away as he headed for where Hairns clambered down off the truck. Russell watched the man struggle with his own emotions before adopting a closed expression. It took ten minutes, but eventually the five fighter squadron leaders stood alone before Hairns and his adjutant.

"The Navy liaison has informed me our old friend Ozawa is

bringing his larger, angrier brother Vice Admiral Yamaguchi with him," Hairns stated.

I guess we get our chance to see what the Japanese fleet carriers can do. I'm sure the Americans will be thrilled to find out that the Japanese decided Ceylon was more important than Hawaii.

He listened as Hairns detailed what they were facing. Five, perhaps six, carriers between the invasion force sighted leaving Staring Bay and striking element that had transited the Straits of Malacca. Likely accompanied by four battleships. The troops on transports were, at that point, a discussion of overkill.

"I will be frank," Hairns said, grimacing. "The governor considered evacuation of all military forces before the Japanese get here."

Russell bared his teeth in anger at that. Hairns nodded as he continued.

"Then Governor Sampson recalled 'we were men charged with maintaining Her Majesty's possessions.' Furthermore, 'he'd be damned if he was going to have to explain his actions to King George upon reaching the Pearly Gates.'"

There was a smattering of laughter at that.

"The expectation is that the Japanese will be here within a week," Hairns said. "The Americans will, if they move expeditiously, arrive roughly two days after that. Our orders are to inflict as many losses as possible to the Japanese carrier groups in order to support the battle that will ensue."

Hairns looked at the gathered group.

"I intend to do this by forming up into a wing before attacking the incoming enemy group."

Have you gone bloody mad? Russell marveled. The First Battle of Britain had seen a very vigorous debate between proponents of wearing down the German escorts by attacking as squadrons came available and those who believed a large mass of interceptors did more damage than dribs and drabs. The Second Battle of Britain had put paid to the latter argument, as the Germans had turned their own escorts loose to hunt their British counterparts.

This is how one runs into a buzz saw of Japanese fighters and never gets near their bombers, Russell thought.

"Sir, does that include Baron Squadron?" he asked. There was a moment's silence as everyone turned to look at him.

"No, it does not, Russell," Hairns replied. "In talking with Air Marshal D'Albiac, the intent is to hold Baron Squadron back as a long range strike asset against the Japanese."

Don't fancy our odds if we have to attack during the day, Russell thought. The *Mosquito*'s primary advantage was that it was fast, with the ability to carry a large bombload a close second. Neither of those would matter one bit in a general melee.

"Understood, sir," he replied.

"I will not lie to you gentlemen," Hairns said. "None of the senior leaders expect us to survive this fight. But we will make the Japanese pay dearly for this island."

4

THE FEINTING GARGOYLE...

Let your plans be dark and impenetrable as the night, and when you move fall like a thunderbolt

— SUN TZU

U.S.S. HOUSTON
1000 LOCAL (0300 EASTERN)
5 AUGUST

WAS WONDERING *when enemy aircraft were going to show up*, Jacob thought as the *Houston* began accelerating. TF 25, for its part, was rushing south after the Axis fleet flushed from harbor. Radar had detected a large blip approaching from the northwest, roughly in line from Mogadishu.

I am sure someday history will reveal whether the Italians were tipped off to our presence or they had just happened to be leaving Mogadishu for Mombasa when our strike showed up.

The fleet had been sighted by a scout from the *Bonhomme Richard* roughly fifty miles south of Mogadishu heading towards Mombasa at fifteen knots two hours before. The joint British-Italian force had immediately sped up once it had realized TF 25 was coming south in full pursuit. Now, even as the *Houston* vibrated in a way that gave Jacob a great deal of concern, TF 25 wasn't closing the gap very much.

"When you said that Vice Admiral Godfrey would chase the Italians all the way to Mombasa, I did not think we'd get a practical demonstration," Jacob noted to Commander Farmer.

"It's why I find it quite amusing the Italians have some Usurper vessels with them," Farmer replied. "They built their own ships fast so they could always get away from the Royal Navy if it came to a fight."

I don't blame them for running, Jacob thought. *If I'd had four carriers launch that strike against my harbor, I'd probably try to fight another day as well. Especially with the wind out of the south letting **their** carriers get aircraft off as they run.*

"*Massachusetts* estimates the northern group at approximately thirty aircraft," the talker reported.

"Understood," Jacob replied.

"I guess your strike didn't suppress the airfields as much as they'd hoped," Commander Farmer observed grimly.

"Hard for four carriers to tie down an entire base complex," Jacob replied. "I don't know how your vessels ever attempted it with those flight decks and smaller hangars."

"We usually stayed within range of our land-based aircraft."

"Kind of hard to do that without colonies, but I take your point," Jacob said, then changed topic. "If it's British birds, any insights you'd like to give us?"

Commander Farmer pursed his lips.

"Well, I am already surprised that your lads ran into *Spitfires* and *Hurricanes* as well as Italian fighters. So it could be anything from *Beauforts* to some big bombers. Nothing specific though, no."

"Sir, the *Tallahassee* is reporting additional radar contacts from the south," one of the talkers interrupted. "Range approximately seventy miles."

That would be the British carriers' contribution to things. I am concerned at how well they've coordinated with the Italians. Admiral Hart's forces had greatly improved since fighting in the Indies. They also had not started out the war bitter enemies. *Could get rather, as the British say, 'sporting' the next time we come into the Indian Ocean.*

"Time for steel pots, gentlemen," Jacob stated, very obviously putting on his helmet. The warm breeze from the *Houston*'s passage swirled around the vessel's bridge, and he immediately felt like it was twenty degrees warmer inside the structure. Turning, Jacob looked towards starboard, keeping a keen eye on the *Houston*'s position relative to the *Massachusetts* and *Indiana*.

Guess we'll figure out how well those new ships handle. Well aware that his force had not had a chance to work together, Vice Admiral Godfrey had ordered a very loose circular formation in the face of the imminent attack.

"Port ten degrees rudder," he ordered the helmsman. "We're already bow on to the folks from the south, but it looks like the folks from Mogadishu are going to get here first."

"Not surprising," Farmer said. "The folks from the south are probably coming in biplanes."

That's right, I forgot your navy hadn't joined the modern world with regards to carrier aircraft, Jacob thought. *Which is why our boys had to keep flying older models while Roosevelt gave you the newer production.*

"So, about the insights?" Jacob pressed. Farmer looked embarrassed.

"Sorry, I was just thinking about my perverse joy at the RAF utterly gelding our Fleet Air Arm between the wars," he replied. "This far out, this soon, it's probably *Beauforts* if it's our chaps. Tough birds, but not all that maneuverable and not something I'd want to press an attack in given your navy's habit of bolting anti-aircraft guns to every horizontal surface."

Have you observed your old friends the Japanese lately? Jacob thought sarcastically.

"In any case, they'll probably ignore us and go for the battleships," Farmer said. "They'll try to fly past us and engage from the bow, makes for a better run. Textbook says you can't drop a torpedo at over one hundred fifty knots, one hundred is preferred if that helps your gunners any."

"OOD, pass that last bit of info to Guns," Jacob said. "Thank you, Commander Farmer."

"You're welcome, sir," Farmer said. "May we not kill anyone I know too terribly well."

"Combat Air Patrol is being vectored to the planes coming from the north."

JAMES YOUNG

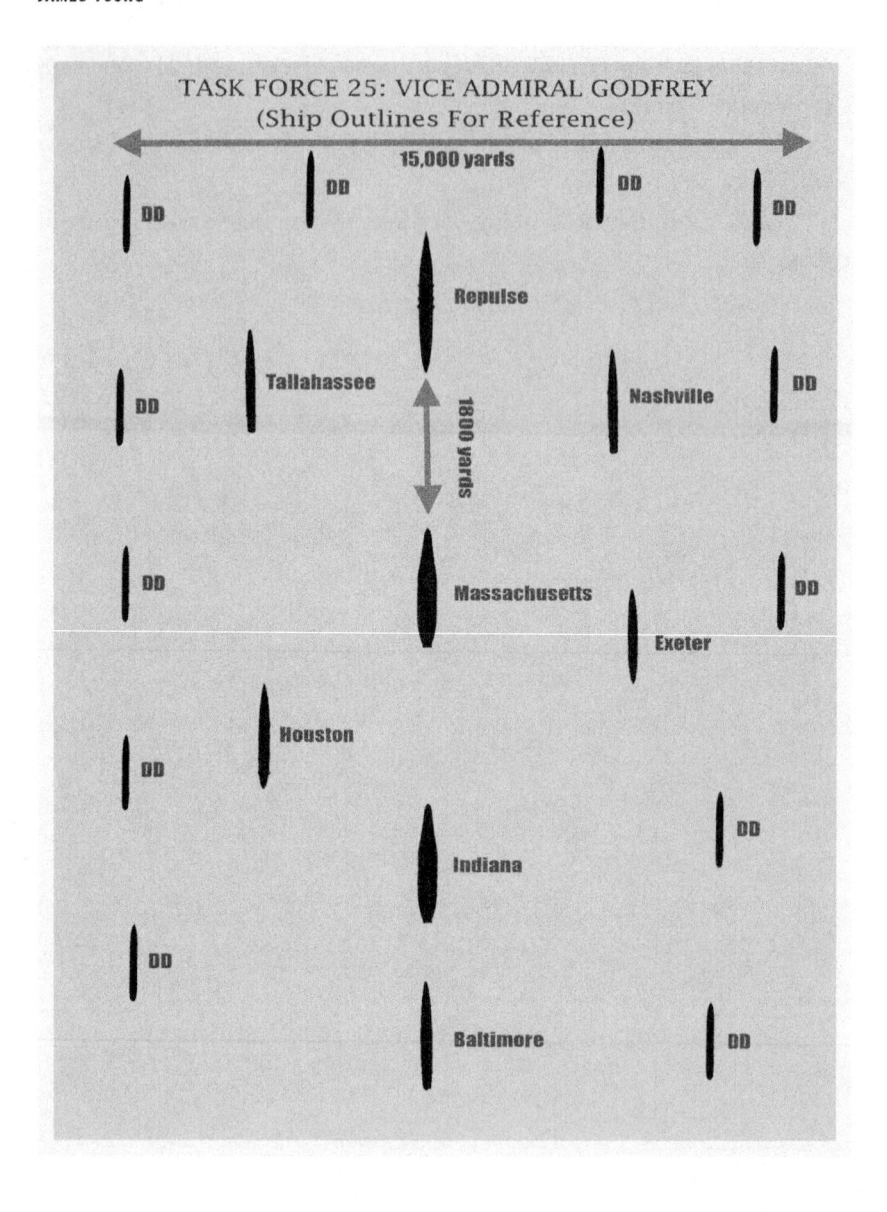

Commander Farmer would have been joyful if he'd realized the group attacking from the north was, in fact, Italian. Escorted by ten *Folgore* fighters operating at the extreme limit of their range, the fifteen *Sparviero* torpedo bombers had been cobbled together from the survivors of the Allied carrier strike that morning. Despite a lack of familiarity with one another, the Italians managed to maintain a steady formation right up until the radar vectored CAP descended upon them thirty miles short of the surface group.

Looking more at their fuel gauges than their surroundings, the ten *Folgores* completely missed the mixed bag of F4Fs and *Hellcats* sent to intercept them. As a result, the twelve Grumman fighters executed a perfect bounce, coming in from upsun and above. Two of the *Folgore* pilots paid an immediate price for their inattentiveness, their fighters arcing down into the Indian Ocean below. They were joined by two of their charges, the *Sparviero* leader among them.

The American CAP converted their speed back into altitude, the eight *Hellcats* separating away from the four *Wildcats* as they did so. As a result, the *Folgores* had a brief advantage in numbers as they sought revenge. Unfortunately for the Italians, the flight of VF-3 *Wildcats* was led by Commander Jimmy Thach himself. In a demonstration of artful deflection shooting followed by excellent teamwork, the four *Wildcats* managed to avoid loss while picking off the lead *Folgore* and damaging another. Then the two flights of *Bonhomme Richard* fighters rejoined the fray, finishing the cripple and downing two more *Folgores* before the battered Italians broke off.

Gaining local air superiority was relatively pointless however, as it allowed the *Sparvieros* to continue unmolested towards TF 25. Descending rapidly, the bombers raced down either side of TF 25's formation at twelve miles range with the two senior surviving officers hurriedly marking targets.

"Well, looks like it's going to be Italians," Commander Farmer observed from *Houston*'s bridge wing. The TF's destroyers were already making smoke, the black obscuration pouring from their stacks as they surged forward through the placid Indian Ocean swells. Jacob turned to look at *Repulse*, the battlecruiser now in the van of the advancing formation. *Houston*'s 8-inch turrets were swung out and at the ready, Lieutenant Commander Willoughby prepared to try and splash the onrushing bombers with salvoes in their path.

You know, now that I think about it, we might need those shells if we catch the surface fleet, Jacob considered. *Didn't work in the Indies, probably not going to work here.*

"Tell Guns to hold fire with the main battery," he ordered. The talker at the bridge's rear spoke rapidly, and the *Houston*'s forward turrets returned to the centerline. Jacob watched as the bombers finished swinging wide then turned more or less as one in towards the Allied formation.

There was no overt order to open fire. One moment the only sound was that of the cruiser's engines pounding along and the rush of the wind. The next first the destroyers, then the cruisers, and finally the capital ships at the formation's center began blazing away at the incoming Italians. The *Houston*'s 5-inch guns selected a group of three *Sparviero* charging in a vee from the port bow. The bomber's goal was apparently the *Massachusetts*, their bombardiers not even concerned with attempting to reduce the battleship's screen.

Come on then, you bastards, Jacob thought, the tri-motored *Sparviero*'s swelling in size as they crossed the danger zone. Initially the screen's fire appeared to be behind the big bombers, but quickly corrected as the range closed down to 15,000 yards. At 10,000 yards from *Houston*, either one of the cruiser's 5-inch shells or that from the destroyer *Guest* burst just beneath the starboard bomber in the vee.

Trailing smoke from the damaged engine, the *Sparviero* lagged behind its brethren. Ten seconds later, the H.M.C.S. *Garland* hit the bomber with fire from a Bofors 40mm gun just as the U.S.S. *Hudson* blew the leader's cockpit in with 20mm fire. Both bombers slapped into the water, their crews dying as the hunchbacked aircraft disintegrated.

Let's see how brave the last one is. He had his answer a moment later as the approaching bomber skidded to line up on the *Tallahassee* then hastily dropped its weapon.

Her captain is going to want to comb that track.

"Port thirty degrees," Jacob said calmly as the weapon splashed into the water.

"Port rudder thirty degrees, aye aye," the helmsman replied, spinning *Houston*'s helm. As the heavy cruiser's bow heeled over, Jacob watched the torpedo start to make its run for the *Tallahassee*. The light cruiser's guns continued to fire at both its assailant and a flight of three *Sparviero*'s streaking from starboard to port on their way out of the Allied formation post-drop. Despite the ferocity of fire, the trio of escaping Italians made it through the formation seemingly without significant damage.

THE ITALIAN PILOTS' BRAVERY WAS NOT MATCHED BY ACCURACY, AS their attack yielded no hits. What it did do, however, was remove the American CAP from the equation while the strike from the carriers *Dasher* and *Battler* bore in. Rather than slaughtering the incoming Fairey *Albacores*, the *Wildcat*s and *Hellcat*s either turned for home or chased the departing nine *Sparviero*'s respectively. All but forgotten, the twelve Fairey *Albacore* biplanes continued determinedly towards where bursts of flak, smoke screens, and rising smoke columns from destroyed Italian aircraft marked the Allied formation. Their advance was lost in the confusion of the Italian attack.

"AIRCRAFT, BEARING TWO NINE OH!"

The lookout's cry brought Jacob's head around from where he was trying to regain station behind the *Tallahassee*. For a moment Jacob thought himself hallucinating, the dozen biplanes approaching online like something out of a matinee movie on World War I.

"Bloody hell, *Albacores*!" Farmer shouted, recognizing the aircraft. As if his shout spurred cognition throughout the screen, the entire left side of the Allied formation, then all ships that could bear, opened fire.

Where did they come from? Jacob thought, then remembered the earlier report and kicked himself. *We lost track of them in all the chaos.*

"Hard to port!" he barked.

"Hard to port, aye aye!" the helmsman replied, spinning the wheel rapidly so the *Houston* could begin to turn her bow onto the approaching torpedo bombers. The range was already at 7,000 yards, the approaching aircraft having made good use of the lingering smoke from the earlier *Sparviero* attack. Jacob realized two of the *Albacores* had picked the *Houston* as a target, with his last minute turn foiling their best angle. Still, the biplanes bore in.

Brave men, he allowed grudgingly, the vessel's 5-inch guns banging away at the slowly advancing British aircraft. He forced himself to turn and look around *Houston*, making sure the heavy cruiser wasn't about to run into an accompanying destroyer or other vessel in the screen. The destroyer *Phelps* had cut inside the *Houston*'s turn and was steaming forward, smoke pouring from her stacks and fire shooting from her guns.

It was over in moments. Both *Albacores* managed to drop, but only one survived the storm of fire thrown at it by *Houston*, *Phelps*, and several other vessels in range. Jacob was alarmed by several shell splashes that surrounded the *Houston* as other vessels engaged their own assailants, but fortunately none hit the heavy cruiser. The *Hudson* was not as fortunate, and Jacob winced when he saw several 40mm shell impacts walk down the destroyer's side.

Friendly fire is a problem with a formation this size. Then his mind turned back to the torpedoes, and he saw with relief that both tracks were going to miss the *Houston*.

"Ah hell, they hit the *Nashville*," someone muttered. Jacob brought up his binoculars and looked to where a long column of water was falling back from the light cruiser's bow.

"Dammit," he muttered, drawing a sympathetic nod from Farmer.

The strike on the *Nashville* was the only success the British torpedo bombers could claim despite near total surprise. In return, only six *Albacores* managed to stagger away from the Allied force.

The *Nashville* was fortunate in where she caught the tin fish. The TORPEX warhead vented its fury on the light cruiser's narrow bow, blasting a large hole in the structure. The forward bulkheads just managed to hold as the vessel's bridge crew brought her to a slow stop, two destroyers circling nervously. The remainder of TF 25 began to turn once more into formation, the *Repulse* leading the way south towards the fleeing Axis fleet.

Jacob read the *Massachusetts* signal as the big vessel regained station behind the *Repulse* once the latter had dodged two torpedoes.

ALL VESSELS, CONTINUE TO PURSUE

"Well, I hope our flyboys manage to make that the last strike those carriers launch," Jacob muttered.

"I do not think that there was much that returned," Farmer observed. "But yes, hopefully your pilots will land a fortunate hit on our prey."

Blue One
1130 Local (0430 Eastern)

Too long, Eric fumed. That strike took way too long to spot, way too long to launch, and now we're going to be lucky if we catch this enemy formation.

The *Yorktown* and *Enterprise* had finally joined up with the two Atlantic Fleet carriers. In retrospect, the added efficiency in joining the four carriers under one loose screen had been more than outweighed by the clumsiness of trying to coordinate four different air groups' Sunday Punch. On one hand, Eric was glad the lull had given *Yorktown*'s plane handlers a chance to look over his aircraft and repair where a 20mm shell had apparently clipped his rudder. On the other, a hasty repair was not worth the apparent gains the Axis force was making in its movement south.

About three more hours and they'll be in range of long-range fighters from

Mombasa, Eric calculated with disgust as he looked down at his plotting board. VB-11 was fifth in a string of dive bomber squadrons that stretched back for miles like a long daisy chain of woe. He could only imagine what would happen if British, German, or Italian fighters showed up.

If anyone had asked me, I'd think we would be better off with just heading for the target as we were ready like doctrine says. I don't exactly know how we're going to coordinate almost fifty dive bombers over the target anyway, but I hope we at least get the anti-aircraft fire reduced for the torpeckers.

"Sir, Ensign Stratmore is slipping back again," Brown stated contemptuously. Eric looked over to his right and saw that the new Blue Two was, indeed, drifting back in the formation.

"I'll cut the man some slack," Eric said. "He hasn't flown formation in at least a month."

Brown snorted at that one. Ensign Stratmore, the new Blue Two, had been one of the spare / utility pilots carried by the *Yorktown*. Normally condemned to flying antisubmarine polls, the spare pilots were expected to man the additional aircraft carried lashed to the roof of the hangar deck in anticipation of losses. In order to keep these men somewhat proficient in their aircraft, they were often assigned antisubmarine patrol duties or messenger aircraft flights.

I also imagine knowing he's stepped into a dead man's spot probably isn't helping any, Eric left unsaid.

"Smoke ahead," Lieutenant Commander Brigante stated. "Looks like we've found our friends."

Eric immediately raised his eyes and scanned the surrounding area. Somewhat mollified by the two flights of *Corsair* fighters he found circling over their heads, Eric looked back forward.

A whole lot easier to concentrate on the task at hand when I know that someone will at least occupy the enemy's fighters, Eric thought as he listened to radio cross chatter between the squadron leaders and Commander Montgomery, *Yorktown*'s CAG.

"We're going to keep pushing south," Eric said over the intercom. "The torpeckers are taking on the battleships."

"Without dive bombers to split the fire?" Brown asked.

"They're taking the Atlantic dive bombers with them."

Brown was silent, and Eric had the feeling the gun of splitting the group. Waggling their wings, the *Bonor Independence*'s air groups turned towards the smoke sighted. Air Group Six and Eleven, for their part, set finally sighting the carriers just as Eric was beginning to be concerned regarding his fuel state.

"Two escort carriers," Commander Montgomery stated. "We'll take the far one, *Enterprise* and her group have the near one. VB-11, standby to see if you're going after carriers or double back to hit the BBs."

I think I'd rather hit the—

"Fighters, fighters inbound one o'clock!"

There's our welcome committee. Eric listened as Brown cocked the twin machine guns, then watched the American fighters turn to engage.

As Combat Air Patrols went, the dozen *Sea Hurricanes* launched by H.M.S. *Dasher* and H.M.S. *Battler* could easily have qualified as "paltry." Along with the six of their fellows that had been hastily scrambled to circle over the surface vessels ten miles away, the twelve obsolescent fighters were the best that the two carriers could do. It was far from enough, as there were 14 F4U *Corsairs* from *Bonhomme Richard* accompanying the dive bombers alone.

Eric listened as Commander Montgomery smoothly directed targets. The two carriers had a pair of cruisers and four destroyers in attendance, and Montgomery ensured that the four larger vessels would all receive attention.

Those carriers look like that former merchie Sam and David nearly got killed on, Eric realized. *I can understand why Montgomery is holding us back, as I don't think it's going to take more than one or two bombs apiece to finish them off.*

. . .

As Eric looked on, VS-6, VS-11, and VB-6 all stooped down from their perches to dive on the small carriers. Facing anti-aircraft fire from the pair of AA cruisers and four destroyers that comprised the vessels' screen, the three squadrons lost four SBDs. In exchange, the twenty-eight *Dauntlesses* that had pitched over scored four hits on *Dasher*, and then three on *Battler*. The 1,000-lb. bombs, designed for far larger prey, easily penetrated to both carriers' vitals. The small flattops were wracked with secondary explosions from bow to stern as the *Dauntlesses* egressed at low altitude.

The H.M.S. *Dido* and H.M.S. *Argonaut*, sister ships designed to combat the very menace that had befallen their small task force, were fortunate in that only twelve SBDs were allotted to their destruction. Although failing to protect their charges, the *Argonaut* and *Dido* managed to claim another pair of the *Dauntlesses* attacking them before pullout. The remaining bombs were split almost evenly between them, and *Argonaut* managed to avoid the quintet aimed for her. With only slight flooding from a VS-6 near miss, the light cruiser remained capable of continuing further action even as the escort carriers burned nearby.

Dido was almost as lucky, then terribly unfortunate. The last VB-6 section, led by Lieutenant Richard Best, was able to put one bomb into the adroitly maneuvering vessel. The half-ton bomb slammed into the cruiser's amidships, knocking out half of her propulsion and starting a major fire. Briefly surrounded by a cloud of steam, the damaged cruiser came to a stop while her crew began damage control procedures.

"Jesus," Eric said, looking at the burning pair of escort carriers as VB-11 turned back to the north.

"Pretty sure that's the work of a fallen angel, not the savior, sir," Brown replied, his voice raspy.

"I can't argue with you there," Eric agreed. He could only imagine what it was like aboard both of the doomed vessels, with fire and smoke probably clogging all of the passageways belowdecks.

Not a whole lot of men getting off of either of them. Hell of a way to go.

"Almost wish the torpeckers had been here to make it quicker," Brown said. He had just barely finished speaking when the *Dasher*'s own torpedo magazines went in a massive explosion that briefly obscured the vessel's stern. Eric turned away, stomach churning. What he saw in front of him was not much better.

Some vessel has had a bad day. A black pillar of smoke was rising to the heavens amongst all the flak bursts. He listened as Commander Montgomery had another discussion with his counterparts from *Enterprise, Independence,* and *Bonhomme Richard.*

"Damn torpedo planes," he muttered angrily. It appeared that the only vessels the *Avengers* had managed to hit was a British heavy cruiser and an Italian destroyer. The dive bombers had scored several punishing hits on the two Italian battleships in turn. However, unless VB-11 got lucky with a hit to something vital, both vessels were likely going to evade TF 25's clutches.

This is just going to be more grist for the mill that there's something wrong with the damn tin fish, Eric thought. *At this point we might as well ask the British if we can use some of theirs.*

"Listen up Haymakers," Lieutenant Commander Brigante said. "We're going to hit one of those big bastards so the surface boys can catch her. The *Richard*'s boys claim they put four into the smaller one, so we're going to try and see if we can match that."

"I got ten bucks says we make five," someone muttered over the net.

"Hell, I'll take odds on seven," came another response.

"Clear the net," Brigante said, his voice stern. "It's a three day pass if we get eight."

There were several incredulous whoops over the radio net. Eric shook his head.

Even if we had VS-11 helping us, there's no way we'd hit eight. Eric picked up his binoculars to look over the stopped vessel. The British heavy cruiser resembled the high-sided, three-funneled vessels they'd all seen in Australia. Eric was about to suggest that at least one section should make sure of that vessel, then reconsidered.

Unlike the late Lieutenant Commander Hitchcock, Brigante actually knows what he's doing. He secured his binoculars so they didn't fly up and hit him in the face during the dive. *The surface boys are only three hours away and there's plenty of daylight left. If they can't catch and finish a cripple, that's not our problem.*

"Wind's out of the south at about fifteen knots," Brigante noted as VB-11 finished circling and began boring in. Anti-aircraft bursts reached up towards them as the ships below opened fire and went into evasive maneuvers. Eric watched Red section reach its pushover point and once more went through the steps to prepare his own *Dauntless*.

Just as he finished extending the dive brakes, a shell burst off their port wing. The *thumps* of fragments slamming into the SBD's side was accompanied by a curse from Brown, then it was too late to pay attention to anything else. Pushing over, Eric saw the battleship's superstructure alive with flashes, its graceful lines already marred by two areas where bombs had hit her.

"You okay, Brown?" he asked, pushing his head forward to the bomb sight.

"Yes!" Brown replied, voice pained.

Ahead of them, Red Two disintegrated, some sort of shell touching off the SBD's bomb. The sight caused Eric's bladder to loosen, and he had a brief flashback to the death of his squadron leader off *Ranger*. Screaming, he forced the image from his mind and bore down on the target.

"Sir?"

"I'm fine!" Eric snapped. "Altitude!"

"Six thousand!"

We're almost becoming experts at this, Eric exulted. There was a bright flash on the target as Lieutenant Commander Brigante's bomb struck the forward turret. The explosion was spectacular, but Eric bet that the thick roof armor meant no real damage would be done. Tracers shot by their SBD, and Eric resolutely held his position. Then they were past two thousand feet and he was releasing, counting to two, then stomping rudder and pulling back hard on the stick. He heard Brown's machine guns firing as the tail gunner sent some love messages back at the battleship's gunners.

"Missed sir, close to port," Brown said in between bursts.

Dammit. Eric picked a path out through the screen at just over five hundred feet. An Italian destroyer fired on him briefly, the medium AA gun's shell exploding four lengths behind. Then they were through, and Eric was putting the *Dauntless* into a shallow climb to clear the area.

"Talk to me Brown," Eric said, turning around in his seat.

"Just a fragment wound, sir," Brown said. "I'm not even really bleeding."

Eric put the *Dauntless* in a gentle turn and scanned for his wingmen. Both had managed to stay fairly close to Eric as he egressed, and rejoining was easy. With both ensigns gathered, Eric turned to look back at VB-11's collective handiwork.

She's going to spend some time in the yard, but she's far from lamed, Eric thought. The vessel appeared to be of the *Cavour*-class, which meant she was the *Giulio Cesare* as the *Conte di Cavour* lay on the bottom of Gibraltar harbor. A major fire raged amidships, with a smaller blaze near her bridge, but she continued to steam south at near full speed.

Long day of chase for little gain, Eric mused, then grimaced as he looked south where two floating pyres burned. *I doubt those carrier crewmen would agree that little was accomplished today.*

IN THE END, VICE ADMIRAL FLETCHER STOPPED TF 25'S PURSUIT TO the south due to fuel concerns. The *Dido* would live to see another day. The battered *Sussex* would not. With her machinery spaces holed and power knocked out by the rare event of functioning American torpedoes, the heavy cruiser had no means to stop the progressive flooding in her hull. Two hours after TF 24's air groups had departed, her amidships' bulkheads finally gave way due to inexorable pressure. As she rolled over, what Vice Admiral Godfrey dubbed "The Action of 4 August" and his Italian counterparts named "The Battle of Mogadishu" ended with a desultory whimper rather than a fleet action.

MORTON RESIDENCE
1200 LOCAL (1700 EASTERN)
6 AUGUST

The knock on the door startled Josephine just as she was starting to slice into the tomato she was cutting for her lunch sandwich. The sharp sting from the fruit's juice spilling on her finger was confirmation she had cut the digit, and Josephine took a moment to loudly curse her roommate.

*Why, why, **WHY** must every knife in this house be so keen that chickens not even born yet are already bleeding in anticipation?* Jo grabbed the nearby dish towel to staunch the wound.

It was a short walk to the front door, which explained some of Jo's annoyance when the knock came again. That emotion disappeared as she looked through the front window to see a Navy commander and a pair of Marine noncommissioned officers standing in the doorway. The officer was in whites and his companions were in khakis, with the enlisted men bearing sidearms.

What in the Hell is this? Jo wondered after the momentary panic had passed. Casualty notifications, especially for officers' families, were not done by enlisted men. That much she knew from recent, dark experience.

It seems like half this neighborhood got a visit after the Battle of Hawaii. It was an exaggeration, but not much of once. Pausing before she opened the door, Jo studied the men in front of her. The officer was very pale, the fairness of his skin causing his freckles to stand out even more. Jo noted that the man's hair was a red so dark it was almost brown, yet his blue eyes were almost luminescent. Although she was quite taken by a certain dive bomber pilot, she could acknowledge that the combination was striking and memorable with his patrician features.

Well, guess I can't make them stand out there forever, she realized. Taking a breath to steady herself, she opened the door.

"Can I help you, Commander?" she asked, clenching the finger tighter involuntarily.

"Pardon me, but are you Miss Morton or Miss Cobb?" the officer replied.

"I am certain that your mother told you it was impolite to answer a question with a question, Commander…" Jo began, then obviously looked at the officer's nametag, "…Tannehill."

The officer nodded, blushing slightly as he checked his notes.

"You are right, Miss Morton," he said after a moment. Jo raised an eyebrow at the action, seeing both Marines looking at the officer as if he were an idiot.

"Please tell me the note did not say, 'if she gives you sass, it's Josephine,'" Jo stated. "Because there are numerous individuals, all of whom we are related to, who may have *mistakenly* wrote that down in a note."

The officer's blush deepened, and stammered over his words.

"N-n-no, Miss Morton, the notes actually say that you're the one with a strong northeastern accent. It comes out a great deal when you're...uh..."

Jo crossed her arms, then remembered her finger was still bleeding.

"Goddammit," she said, then realized apparently the pressure had worked. She looked up at Tannehill giving her a faint look of disapproval, even as the two noncoms starting to smile somewhat. Both Marines were broad-shouldered men of average height, their features so nondescript that Jo wondered if she could have picked them out of a line up if they'd actually meant her harm. The one with light, blonde hair was a sergeant whose nametag read Blaesa. The other man, a gunnery sergeant with black hair, was apparently named Longstreet.

"Look, if you're going to judge me for taking the Lord's name in vain, you need to hurry up and say whatever you're going to do and get on your way, Commander," she snapped. "I assure you, I am a sailor's daughter, and my father was not exactly the best at raising me in good graces."

Commander Tannehill almost took a step back before steadying himself.

"Well, I'll cut to the chase," he replied. "Would you like to come work for my department at Pearl Harbor?"

Jo raised an eyebrow.

"I'm sorry, Commander Tannehill, but your department?"

"Yes, Miss Morton, my department," he replied. "I assure you it's nothing sinister, but I am not at liberty to discuss it here standing on your porch."

So you expect me to let three strange men into my house in the middle of the day? Jo mulled, even as she fought to keep her face serene. *Hmm, maybe I should have kept that knife in my hand.*

"Josephine, is there something wrong?" Alf Olrik, Patricia and her's neighbor, asked. The dock worker had come out to stand on his front porch in his overalls, half-eaten sandwich in one hand, a large wrench held oh-so-casually in the other. The two Marine noncoms both noticed the tool and took steps back from behind Commander Tannehill. For his part, Commander Tannehill was looking at Olaf as if a walking, talking bear had just appeared in front of him.

If you think Olaf is big, just wait until you meet either Sam or David. That would require a long plane or boat ride, but still.

"No Alf," she said. "I believe Commander Tannehill was asking me if I was still interested in working in the stenography section at Pearl Harbor."

Alf nodded, taking another bite of his sandwich.

"Very good," he said. "Niole has some cookies coming out of the oven. Since you have guests, perhaps it'll be better if she brings a batch by in about ten minutes?"

I love my neighbors.

"That sounds lovely," she replied. "I'm sure Commander Tannehill and his men would love some as well."

"Actually I'm allergic to–" Commander Tannehill started to mutter.

"I'm not allergic to a thing, Miss Morton," one of the NCOs interrupted him, smiling and nodding at Alf.

Alf gave one more smile and waved the hand full of sandwich at the men, then stepped back inside his house.

You'd all be very scared if you realized he's left handed, Jo thought. *Sure from what I've seen when he's helped us around the house the man is actually ambidextrous, but Alf had every intention of smashing some skulls when he came out here.*

"Well, looks like you've got ten minutes to explain this work to me, commander," Jo stated, her voice airy.

. . .

Okay, we're all very lucky that I'm sitting down, or Alf might have come over to find me passed out in the kitchen from shock, Jo thought. She chewed slowly on her sandwich, mulling things over.

"So just to make sure I completely understand, you have out of the blue decided to ask me to work on a very secret project copying information from broken codes? Of which you are also going to go ask my roommate?"

"This is actually hardly out of the blue, Miss Morton," Commander Tannehill responded. "It should come as no surprise to you that both Miss Cobb and yourself are known to many of the officers on post."

Jo once more gave Commander Tannehill a look that was best described as suspicious, and once more the officer began growing flustered.

I know most redheads look ten years younger than they actually are, but he really does seem way too inexperienced for his rank.

"What I mean is, when I began asking around for possible nominees for these positions, your names came up several times," Commander Tannehill said.

"Why us?"

Commander Tannehill was about to answer when there was a knock at the kitchen door. Turning, Jo didn't immediately see anyone, then looked down and saw a child's head just barely poking above the window.

"Excuse me for a moment, but I believe those are cookies," Jo stated. She opened the door to reveal Anya, the youngest Olrik daughter. The precocious five-year-old was holding a plate of what appeared to be chocolate chip cookies, and immediately began speaking with great urgency.

"Mama said to come over here and hand you these cookies," the little girl said. "I was also supposed to make sure no one was hurting you."

Jo heard Gunnery Sergeant Longstreet guffaw behind her as she too began to smile. Leaning down, she took the cookies and kneeled down to look Anya in the face.

"I don't think you were supposed to tell me the last part," she whispered. Anya's eyes grew wide as Jo held her finger up to her mouth in a shushing motion.

"Tell your mother I'll be over for dinner later, and thank you for the cookies," Jo said, then took the plate. Patting Anya on the shoulder, Jo barely avoided letting out a giggle. "I'll see you later, and I'll bring a book with me."

Anya's eyes brightened at that, and she quickly tore off back towards her house.

"You certainly seem to have a good relationship with your neighbors," Commander Tannehill observed.

"You have no idea," Jo said, grinning as she put the cookie plate down on the table. "They're really good kids, and Niole brings them by the library all the time."

Longstreet stepped forward and took a cookie, and her mental attention switched back to the matter at hand.

"So, again, why us?" she asked. "I'd hardly think we have some magical powers."

"Actually, we have found that women make better codebreakers than men," Commander Tannehill replied. "For some reason, women are very good at picking out patterns and rhythms, and that's what's necessary for good cryptography."

"Are you married, Commander Tannehill?" Jo asked conversationally. Tannehill looked at her, quite startled, as Longstreet and Blaesa both chuckled.

"I'm not propositioning you," Jo said, face reddening. "I just find it odd that women's ability to pick out patterns and rhythms, as you put it, is mysterious to you."

"No, I am not married," Tannehill said quickly. "I've never really had much luck with women."

"Interesting," Jo said, noting that both Longstreet and Blaesa were entirely too happy with watching Commander Tannehill squirm.

"I wouldn't get too amused, gentlemen," she said, turning to look at them. "If we're to be working together, I'm pretty sure I'll have opportunities to ask you embarrassing questions as well."

Gunnery Sergeant Longstreet had the decency to looked

nonplussed at her idle threat. Blaesa met her eyes briefly as she turned back to Tannehill.

"When do you need me to start?" Jo asked. "I've already worked today and I'd like to give my bosses at least a day's notice. Does Monday work?"

Tannehill was still flustered as he considered the proposed timeline.

"Yes, that will do well," he said.

"Where will I be going to?" Jo asked. "I am guessing I can't just show up at the gates to Pearl Harbor and say, 'I'm looking for the super secret facility with the single redhead commander,' can I?"

Tannehill's blush returned.

"No, you cannot," he said hurriedly. "But if you ask for the Smithsonian Ferry Company, the front gate guards know who to call."

That doesn't sound fishy at all.

"When are you going to ask Patricia?"

"I was hoping to catch you both home for lunch, but I see that was futile."

"Toots is probably contemplating homicide against her boss somewhere in the Navy Yard," Jo said. "She would likely appreciate the interruption."

THE SMELL OF FRANCES' COLOGNE HUNG IN THE DRAFT ROOM LIKE an oppressive cloud. Patricia had trouble deciding which she hated worse, the man's general scent or the midday bourbon on his breath.

"Miss Cobb, I must commend you once more on your fine work," he said, pressing closely into her left side.

Oh God, I really hope that is his flask that is pressing into my hip, she thought, nausea swimming over her. Frances had become more... brazen in the past few days. Patricia worried it was a vicious cycle of the increased work in drafting modernization plans driving Frances to drink. His inebriation, in turn, made him more amorous towards the small coterie of young women in Patricia's office. Although she would not have necessarily considered herself of sterner stuff than her colleagues, many of them had taken sick days in the aftermath of having Frances press himself on them.

Or maybe it's just that I realize everything I'm doing is bringing Charles closer to coming home. Wherever he may happen to be.

Frances studied the U.S.S. *Northampton*'s lines on the drafting table in front of Patricia. Anticipating his next maneuver, she twisted out of reach of the hand beneath the table's edge that would have landed squarely on her posterior if she'd not adroitly dodged.

I would smack you if I believed it would make any difference, Patricia thought, heart racing. One of the women had complained to Commander Evanston, the officer in charge, a week prior. That woman had soon found herself reassigned to the stenographer's pool and another local woman in her place. Patricia didn't think someone needed a degree in hieroglyphics to make the connection.

"Sir, when do they think the *Northampton* will begin these modifications?" Patricia asked, attempting to distract Frances.

"You'd have to talk to the dock draftsmen," Frances said. "I just know that we have far too many plans coming in here for copying or modification over the last couple of days."

Why, you'd almost think there was a war on. The Pacific Fleet was only just now finally catching up with all the damage from the Battle of Hawaii. In a macabre way, it was fortunate the Japanese had sunk the *California*, *Long Island*, and *Archer* outright. Many more vessels returning to Oahu would have resulted in more ships being sent back to the West Coast.

"Excuse me, Frances, I have to go to the ladies room," Patricia said, stepping away from the table. When she returned fifteen minutes later, Frances had moved on to harassing another one of her coworkers in the office.

Saints be praised, she exalted, then bit her lip guiltily as she took her chair.

It was an uneventful following three hours for Patricia. Unfortunately, as the workday was drawing to a close, Patricia could slowly see Frances making his way back around to her side of the table. Looking at the clock, she pondered if it was time for another trip to the powder room while the man was still on the far side of the room.

Trying hard not to stare, Patricia saw one of her newest coworkers visibly lurch, nausea clearly running over the woman's face.

There are days I wish I'd taken up knitting, she thought, mulling over her options. *Mother always stated a knitting needle to the thigh calmed the most amorous of pursuers.* For the first time in her life, Patricia realized her mother may have meant "thigh" as a euphemism.

Then again, maybe it's for the best I don't stab my boss in the privates. The sound of footsteps coming down the stairs was a relief for Patricia. Frances stopped approaching her and turned towards the door, clearly perturbed at the interruption. A moment later, Commander Evanston was entering the room with a redheaded officer followed by two Marines.

"Miss Cobb, Commander Tannehill would like to have a word with you," Evanston said, nodding towards the redheaded officer behind him.

"What is this regarding?" Frances interjected, stepping in front of Patricia.

"Official business," one of the Marines, a gunnery sergeant, stated bluntly.

"Miss Cobb is my subordinate, Gunnery Sergeant," Frances said, his eyes narrowing as he stepped past the edge of the drafting table. "A very important one, I might add."

"Understood sir," the gunnery sergeant said, neatly stepping forward another step and blocking Frances' path towards the door.

Well this can't be good. Butterflies starting to flit in her stomach.

"I was told to assure you, Miss Cobb, that I am not with the chaplain's office," Commander Tannehill said easily. "The woman who gave me that instruction also said, and I quote, 'stop sharpening the knives, the animals are already dead when the butcher sells them to us.'"

That last comment brought a titter of laughter from several of the women present. Patricia rolled her eyes, as only one person would make that complaint.

"I take it someone cut herself making lunch again?" Patricia said evenly as she stepped towards the door.

"Miss Cobb, I expect you back in ten minutes," Frances said, starting to press past the gunnery sergeant. The look in the Marine's eyes made the civilian reconsider.

"Miss Cobb will return when Commander Tannehill is done speaking with her," Evanston said, fixing Frances with a firm look.

I wonder what has the Marine so cross with Frances? Patricia thought as she walked out the door into the hallway.

"Miss Morton said I should probably cut to the chase," Commander Tannehill said after looking around to make sure no one was in earshot.

"I cannot imagine that Josephine would give such advice," Patricia replied deadpan. Tannehill stopped, then clearly realized Patricia was joking. With a look that bespoke a great deal of exasperation, the Navy officer began his pitch.

"Would you like to work in a different office environment helping the war effort? Effective tomorrow?"

Patricia looked at him, furrowing her brow.

"Doing what?" she asked.

"Not having to deal with lecherous bosses who wear entirely too much perfume," the gunnery sergeant stated, joining them.

"I think it's called cologne on a man," Patricia corrected.

"If half of what I've heard about Mr. Carter is true," the gunnery sergeant said, "he's no man. My platoon sergeant's daughter was working here up until a few days ago."

Patricia looked at the gunnery sergeant, then looked at Tannehill, then back towards the doorway.

"Commander Evanston told me he could not spare you," Commander Tannehill stated. "I informed him that, based on your ability to draw diagrams and familiarity with geometry, he could spare you now or after I informed Vice Admiral Halsey himself about Mr. Carter's predilection for preying on patriotic young women."

"I have to admit, sir, I wasn't expecting that out of you," the gunnery sergeant stated.

"Miss Morton is correct in that I have yet to marry," Tannehill stated. "That does not mean I do not have a sense of decency. In any case, would you like to come work for me?"

Patricia looked back and forth between the two men.

I feel like I've stepped into act three of a play as the lead actress, yet no one felt the need to give me my lines. She looked back towards the closed door.

"On one condition," she stated at last.

I'll not just leave those other poor women to suffer that fool's hands.

"Mr. Carter will not be working here at the end of the day," Tannehill replied evenly.

Why Old Scratch, you look quite differently than I expected, Patricia thought wildly. *I always expected to meet you at a different locale.*

"I am surprised that you are confident in that amount of power," Patricia observed.

"The man smells of bourbon, is harassing women, and was sent out here from Mare Island with already two strikes against him," Tannehill replied. "I did my homework before we came to talk to you. I'm also a man of my word."

"Then yes," Patricia replied. "Whatever you're asking me to do, yes."

U.S.S. Chenango
1745 Local (2345 Eastern)
7 August

Whomever said this was "just like riding a bike" has either never rode a bike or landed on a bobbing cork in the middle of the ocean, Adam reflected bitterly as he took the wave off. The FM-2's engine roared as he advanced the throttle and began to circle out of the landing pattern. It was his third waveoff in as many days. The fact the rest of the squadron was even worse at carrier landings than he was did little to mollify his mood.

We're extremely fortunate we haven't inadvertently splashed any birds from fuel starvation. The Marines had managed to bend two of their FM-2s in hard landings, but the *Chenango* had sailed with four spares lashed to the vessel's hangar deck ceiling. Still, both of the young lieutenants involved had been grounded by the *Chenango*'s captain, and Adam didn't blame the man.

The LSO is God of landing, and thine shall obey his will when waved off. 2nd Lieutenant Greenwood had panicked due to the carrier being close to entering a squall. 1st Lieutenant Silverstein had simply ignored the wave off and come barreling onto the small vessel, just barely managing to avoid jumping the barrier and ending up into the aircraft parked forward.

At least I have a great view up here. Just wonderful scenery to possible die in. The *Chenango* and her two escorts seemed to be the only ships on the ocean. Adam had deep respect for Captain Damon and his command of the small task force. The two destroyer escorts had started the voyage being visibly lackadaisical about their duties. Adam had been on the *Chenango*'s bridge when Captain Damon had prepared and sent the signal about *that*.

"Red One, Home Base," his radio crackled as he got ready to settle back into the landing groove.

Uh oh. Adam squinted into the setting sun, then looked around worriedly. Something significant had to be occurring for the *Chenango* to break radio silence.

"This is Red One, over," he replied.

This is what I get for always letting the rest of the flight land first. Adam had always been very good at fuel conservation, and as an experienced flight leader always knew his wingmen used far more fuel than he did. It was only prudent to put them back aboard the deck first. Now, as he looked at the setting sun, he pondered whether that was about get him killed.

"State fuel," the carrier's bridge replied.

"I'm roughly fifteen minutes from being into reserve," he replied.

"Radar has a contact at bearing oh one zero true, estimated range forty-five miles, altitude probably angels seven, closing with our current position." *Chenango* replied. "Do you feel it is safe to investigate?"

I will never cease to be amazed at people who ask dumb questions, Adam thought. *It's about to be dark in probably a half hour or so, there's no air sea rescue capability aboard this carrier, and you're asking if it's **safe**? No, it most certainly isn't **safe**, but I'll go anyway.*

"On my way towards contact," Adam said. "Please provide vector when within fifteen miles."

There was a long pause, his instructions apparently causing some concern on the carrier's bridge.

Just in case someone on the receiving end of those radar beams has our frequency open and speaks English, I'd rather see him first than be seen. A prudent man only had to get bounced by opposing aircraft eavesdropping on the fighter control radio network a single time to learn that lesson. Unfortunately, Adam had flown with some dense flight commanders during the Second Battle of Britain.

"Understand, will give you vector at fifteen miles."

Adam put the *Wildcat* into a climbing trim and advanced his throttle. Looking out over the wings, he gave a heavy sigh and jettisoned the two empty drop tanks.

We're going to Pearl, he thought. *If this is what I think it might be, two less drop tanks won't be a problem.* The *Wildcat*, even the new FM-2, wasn't the best climber in the world and Adam wanted to get to angels ten as quickly as he could.

That the hostile contact was heading directly towards the task force helped the relative closure rate immensely. A little over ten minutes and one additional radio call later, Adam found himself slightly below and off the port quarter of a single-engined, dual float aircraft.

"Red One, do you have the bogey in sight?" *Chenango* asked. Adam ignored the call, gradually closing on the enemy from below with the other aircraft outlined against the darkening sky. As he got within one hundred yards, the bright red circle on the dark green fuselage became visible.

"Red One, this is Home Plate, please respond," *Chenango* stated.

Oh, I'm about to respond. He charged his four .50-caliber machine guns and took a deep breath then pulled up. It was only when the floatplane's wings filled his reflect sight from end to end that Adam squeezed his trigger. It was a 3-second burst, and the Yokosuka E14Y's crew probably never knew what hit them. The four streams of thumb-sized bullets sliced upwards through the fuselage, through the cockpit, and finally into the fuel tanks. The lightly built *Glen* burst into a fireball, the flames bright against the darkened ocean below as the aircraft fell towards the water.

Adam immediately threw his *Wildcat* into a reversal and cleared his own tail just in case his victim had a friend.

Can't imagine a submarine carrying two of those things, but I'm betting that poor bastard wasn't expecting someone to sneak up on him either.

"Home Base, Red One, scratch one bandit," Adam stated tersely. "I am returning towards base."

"Roger Red One, good job," the *Chenango* replied. "Be advised we are changing course, come to heading one nine oh true from your current position."

You know what's harder than landing on a postage stamp in the middle of the ocean? Adam belatedly realized twenty minutes later, bile raising in his stomach. *Finding that postage stamp in the dark.* At his altitude, the sun was still a faint disc on the edge of the horizon. However, the surface of the ocean was dark, and he realized that perhaps it might have been prudent to pay a bit more attention during the impromptu ship search class held by the *Dauntless* squadron aboard *Chenango*.

"Red One, look to your five o'clock," his headset crackled, and he recognized Sam Cobb's voice. Rotating in his seat, Adam strained to see into the darkness.

There, he thought, his heart in his throat. It was only now, as he saw the carrier's wake, that Adam realized just how much he'd been sweating in fear. As he turned around to get in the groove, he made sure to keep his eyes on his instruments rather than attempting to view things through his canopy. Once straight and level, he risked looking up.

Oh shit! He stabbed the electrical gear button and lowering his arrester hook. The *Chenango* was barely two miles ahead of him, the dark outline now just visible in the last vestiges of nautical twilight. He advanced the throttle slightly to account for the increased drag as the *Wildcat* got mushy with its gear coming down. Quick, furtive movements saw to his trim.

Thank goodness Eastern's engineers didn't do anything to mess with the low speed handling. The flight deck swelling as he closed. It was only as he was making his last adjustments and about to land on the deck that his mind clued him in to the lack of a LSO. Then the *Wildcat* was hitting the deck...and snagging the first wire as he chopped his throttle.

Okay, and people do this on a permanent basis?! he marveled, panting wildly in the cockpit. He was reaching forward to kill the engine when the *Wildcat*'s engine just died on its own.

"No more of this bullshit, Adam," he muttered. "Nope, gonna change that flight roster right out."

"Sir, you okay?" one of the *Chenango*'s plane handlers asked him. Adam hadn't even heard the man clamber up on the wing.

"Oh, I'm wonderful," he replied, short of breath. "I face the thought of dying from exposure every day."

"Sir, captain would like to see you," Sam drawled drily from the other side. "Something about apparently being blind as a bat."

"Bats can see at night," Adam replied as he levered himself out of his seat. "I think we have irrefutable evidence, however, that *I*, nor any other sane person, should be expected to land on a flight deck in the dark."

It was a short walk to the *Chenango*'s blacked out bridge.

"Fine bit of flying there, Major Haynes," Captain Damon said as Adam made his way into the compartment. The Navy officer extended his hand and Adam took it, hoping that his still sweaty palms weren't too clammy.

"Thank you, sir," Adam said. "It was a single seater, which means there's either a cruiser or a carrier out there somewhere."

"Probably neither, actually," Captain Damon said, then continued. "The Japanese have submarines with seaplanes, and I'm wondering if this one was supposed to keep tabs on who is coming and going to Pearl Harbor."

"Well, they're going to need a new set of eyes," Adam replied. "I'm pretty sure I got him."

"Lookouts saw the flamer," Damon replied with a smile. "How many does that make for you?"

Adam had to think about that one.

*Clearly it's been too long since my **Spitfire** days*, he realized. Having a long line of kills was part of what helped him maintain the confidence necessary to go up day after day during the Second Battle of Britain .

"Depends on who you ask, sir," Adam replied honestly. "But that's twenty-six confirmed."

Damon looked at him, face breaking into a broad grin.

"Well you just tied Eddie Rickenbacker, Major Haynes!" he said, clapping Adam on the shoulder.

Oh crap, I guess I did, Adam thought as Damon grabbed the microphone for the *Chenango*'s intercom.

"Attention all hands, attention all hands, we have all just been part of a momentous moment…" Captain Damon began.

"You know this means they'll probably send you back home, right?" Sam muttered from behind him.

Adam turned and looked at the man.

"God, I hope not."

Ratmalana Airfield
2300 Local (1330 Eastern)
Colombo, Ceylon
8 August

"Well, that tears it," Russell muttered, looking at the signal. "Go wake the rest of the squadron."

"Yes sir," Pilot Officer Len Hatheway, Baron Four, stated. He grabbed Pilot Officer Gil Perkins, Baron Two, then ducked out of the blacked out ready hut at a fast trot. Russell waited until the man left, then turned to look at Flying Officer Peterson.

"Looks like you're about to be a rich man," Russell said, gesturing at the squadron board chalkboard. Next to the alert rosters, there was a column listing the time and date that it was expected the Japanese would be sighted. Scrawled next to 8 August, 2300-0100, was Peterson's name.

"Dammit, if only the *Lancaster* had radioed in ten minutes ago," Bellingsley snapped.

"It's a pittance," Russell said, goading his pilot.

"One hundred pounds is nothing to sneeze at!" Bellingsley snapped, then realized both who he was talking to and the tone he'd used. "Sorry Sir."

"Help Rhett plot where we're going tonight while I walk down to the tower," Russell replied with a smile. "Best make sure that plans haven't changed in the last hour or so."

"Yes sir," Bellingsley said, heading towards the map. Russell passed through the double blackout doors and into the humid Ceylon night, once more feeling as if he was walking into a sauna.

More than one reason I miss England. A mosquito alighting on his neck drew swift retribution. *That would be another.* With a pang of anger, his thoughts turned to the letter in his pocket.

Not that I have a home and hearth waiting for me really anymore, he considered, face narrowing. *Either because my former wife no longer loves me or because the Usurper's government is so in bed with the Nazis that they need to ensure the populace lets the occupier do the same.* Maggie had apparently found solace in the arms of a Luftwaffe pilot, and the man had put her in the family way. She apologized, but just couldn't face the nights alone anymore without him. The local magistrate had agreed, and as of two weeks before, Russell was divorced.

In some ways you'd think the censor would have simply decided I didn't need to see this. The arc of his marriage's destruction had been plain as day in the ten letters he'd received, starting with the resumption of hostilities. If it *was* a Nazi or Usurper plot to gradually sap the morale, Russell didn't know whether to be angry or in awe of the opposition's thoroughness.

"Halt! Who goes there?" came the call from the machine gun post now placed one hundred yards to the tower's north.

"Baron Leader," he replied.

"Please advance to be recognized," came the reply. Russell strode forward, and a bright light shone in his face.

"You know, putting a torch into the eyes of a man getting ready to take off is bloody stupid," he snarled.

"Sorry sir, orders!" came the reply. Russell could tell the sergeant was genuinely remorseful and waved it off.

"Might want to have a word with the officer of the guard for tomorrow," Russell said. He moved forward and into the darkened tower, the heat only slightly less oppressive and the insects much more aggressive.

"You'd think we had the garrison's blood supply in here, the damn mosquitoes are so thick," Wing Leader Hairns said. "I had the signal dropped by here as well. The bomber lads are waiting until dawn provided the *Lancasters* and *Sunderlands* can stay in contact. Do you wish to do the same?"

Russell considered the pros and cons briefly.

"Sir, if I'm going to be attacking fleet carriers, best to do it when their fighters aren't thick as flies," he said, then slapped his arm. "Or mosquitoes."

"The irony," Hairns observed, drawing a chuckle from Russell.

"Indeed, sir," Russell replied. "The Japanese are four hundred fifty miles out, so we might as well get our licks in and see if we can level the playing field."

"Yes, taking one of their flight decks out of the equation would be appreciated," Hairns replied. "Especially as this probably means we can expect trade tomorrow."

"Sir, do you expect the Navy to make their appearance tomorrow as well?" Russell asked.

"Vice Admiral Cunningham is personally commanding the fleet," Hairns said. "I've only met the chap a couple of times, but he seems to be almost as cagey as Somerville was."

Well, we all know what that got him, Russell recalled. *Although he took at least one Japanese carrier down with him. Maybe if the Americans ever get around to deciding to risk their fleet before the Japanese gobble up the Empire, that exchange rate will start to matter.*

"I never believed I'd be back out this way," Hairns mused, looking out the window. "I'd done my bit flying in Palestine and figured No. 11 Group was where my flying days would end, one way or the other."

"If you'd told me I'd be leading a Mossie squadron against the Japanese from Ceylon two years ago, I'd have thought someone was quite mad," Russell agreed. "In any case, we'll be off in ten minutes once I brief the men."

Hairns nodded, then extended his hand.

"Hurt them, Squadron Leader Wolford," he said. "Hurt them dearly."

"That's why we have the bombs, sir," Russell replied cheerfully. He hoped his smile was a lot more confident than he actually felt.

THE NEXT TWO AND A HALF HOURS SEEMED ALMOST SURREAL. To Russell's pleasant surprise, Baron Squadron managed to get into the air without incident. After much discussion with his flight leaders, Russell had decided to vary Baron Squadron's armament. Gratham Flight, as befitting Flight Lieutenant Badcocke's former career with Coastal Command, would lead the squadron towards their Japanese target. His four *Mosquitoes* carried a battery of underwing rockets and a single 500-lb. bomb, as they would spend most of the night dropping flares for the other flights to see their targets. Jersey Flight was similarly equipped, and Russell hoped that both could manage to alternate attacking escorts so that Baron could get in and hit home with their pair of 1,000-lb. bombs.

"This lot seems a lot less keen than their friends in the Indies," Bellingsley observed. Baron Squadron had just received another report from the *Sunderland* that had taken over shadowing the Japanese group from the departing *Lancaster*. The Japanese force had turned away from Ceylon, and was now roughly four hundred and fifty miles southeast of the island's southern tip.

They turn much further out we're going to have an interesting flight home.

"In the Indies they had a lot more support from land-based fighters," he stated out loud. "I don't blame them for deciding to see what came out to greet them in the dark far as possible from our airfields."

"Glad to know we made an impression on them," Bellingsley replied.

"Thank you, Portal Leader, we have the targets," Flight Lieutenant Badcocke replied. "Multiple targets bearing one six five true, range twenty-five miles."

Russell turned to look into his scope. Not two minutes later, he too picked up the target group.

Well if this lot has radar, I suppose the **Lancaster** *or* **Sunderland** *would have figured it out by now. At least, I hope that's it, and not that they only decided to launch fighters once they saw multiple blips.* Russell shrugged off his paranoia and turned to running his squadron's attack.

"All right Gratham, Jersey, let's be about it," he ordered. The eight *Mosquito*s accelerated into their descent, breaking through the intermittent cloud at 10,000 feet towards the Indian Ocean below. The sea's surface reflected the waxing moon breaking through the clouds, and Russell's experienced eye picked out the numerous wakes of enemy vessels below.

"Ten miles," Badcocke said.

"Baron Leader, Jersey One, I have airborne trade bearing oh two oh, range five miles."

Well, looks like they've got cats eyes fighters up, Russell noted with a bit of concern. He looked off towards their right front and saw the brief glint of moonlight on canopy.

"All right lads, I see at least one bloke coming in for a look see, two o'clock!" he said into the radio. "If there's one, there's going to be more of them."

Russell was correct in his summation that there would be multiple fighters airborne. Vice Admiral Ozawa's Second Carrier Fleet, while not as well-known as the *Kido Butai*, was a tough, experienced force that had benefited from several of its vessels being sent back to Japan for repairs and refit in the previous three months after the DEI campaign. The cruiser *Nachi*, having been severely damaged by Allied surface vessels in the Battle of the South China Sea, had received a radar during her time in the yard. A British air search set captured from the Germans then transferred to the Japanese, the Type 281 was an early example of that type. Still, it had been been far in advance of anything the IJN had fielded in 1942, and was quite functional despite having been used for extensive experimentation.

Nachi had detected Baron Squadron at a little over one hundred miles. That had been more than enough time for the carriers *Ryujo*, *Ryuho*, and *Chitose* to each launch a single *chutai* of *Zero* fighters.

Utterly lacking in radar, what each aircraft did have was a functional radio from which to receive general headings and altitude towards Baron Squadron.

In the end, the system worked about as well as could be expected, which was to say hardly at all. The *Ryuho*'s *chutai*, confused in the darkness, was horribly out of position as Jersey and Gratham Flight began their ingress. *Chitose*'s trio of fighters flew a reciprocal heading to the one they were given, then only realized their mistake as the *Nachi*'s radar operator began screaming invectives at them. This left *Ryujo*'s fighters, led by a veteran of that carrier's grievous wounding during the Dutch East Indies campaign, to attempt the intercept of twelve fast, heavily armed *Mosquitoes*.

Gratham One, seeing the *Zeroes* turning in towards his flight, elected to rely on the *Mosquitoes*' speed to see them through. As planned, Badcocke and his wingman began passing over the Japanese formation at roughly 5,000 feet. As they reached the outer ring of escorts, Vice Admiral Ozawa angrily issued the order to open fire due to his fighters' ineffectiveness. As if a switch was thrown, tracer fire stabbed upwards towards Gratham One and Two. Both *Mosquitoes* were unscathed, a string of flares opening behind them and descending towards the ocean below.

Gratham Three and Four, coming forward into maelstrom, targeted the light cruiser *Noshiro* at the left front of the formation. Squeezing one eye shut to protect from the flash of their rockets, both *Mosquitoes* fired their the 3-inch devices at three hundred yards, then followed up with strafing as they dropped their bombs in a shallow glide attack. The light cruiser's upper works were whipped with fragments as four of the rockets hit, killing many of the anti-aircraft gunners at their posts. Unfortunately for the two *Mosquitoes*, a last minute turn caused both bombs to miss without real effect.

Jersey Flight, attacking a few moments behind Gratham, attempted to repeat their attack on the *Nachi*. The big heavy cruiser's anti-aircraft guns managed to score a lucky hit, the burst of 25mm fire striking Jersey Two as it was in the midst of putting in flares. With a scarlet flare of flame, the port engine caught ablaze, then exploded in a brilliant pyrotechnic display. Flying Officer Wash had just enough time to scream over Baron's radio net before he and his observer both disappeared in a plume of spray off the *Nachi*'s starboard quarter.

Jersey Three and Four, already committed to the attack, opened fire with their rockets. They did better than Gratham Flight, managing to put six projectiles into the heavy cruiser's superstructure. Unfortunately for both aircraft, the *Nachi* and her accompanying destroyers were much better at shooting than their counterparts aboard the *Noshiro*. Jersey Three's bomb was wide as Flight Lieutenant Desmarais, its pilot, broke off his run early. The Greek expatriate had barely ten seconds to be angry about this drop, as a heavy anti-aircraft shell obliterated the *Mosquito*'s cockpit. Jersey Four's weapon was also wide and forward of the *Nachi*, its pilot having waited just a few moments too long.

Still, both flights had achieved their purpose, so distracting the Japanese gunners that Baron Flight was able to dive on the *Chitose*.

"THOSE AREN'T FLEET CARRIERS!" RUSSELL SAID AS BELLINGSLEY arrowed towards the illuminated flight deck in front of them. "That's a goddamn escort carrier!"

"Well we're not bloody well circling around to look for the right vessels," Bellingsley shouted, a stream of 25mm fire passing just over their fighter. The run in towards the *Chitose* was tense, the carrier starting to turn away from the approaching fighter bombers into a tight circle.

Come on, come on, come on.

There was a cry over the radio, and a brief flare of fire to their left rear as Baron Two was struck. Russell turned and saw the *Mosquito* wreathed in flames, but still trying to get push on.

"Sir!" Bellingsley said, jolting Russell back to where his mind needed to be. He bent to the bombsight, the *Chitose* swelling as he aimed.

"Wait...wait...*now!*" Russell said.

The pair of 1,000-lb. bombs separated cleanly, the *Mosquito* leaping into the air. Doing a quick, loud two count, Bellingsley yanked back on the yoke, the *Mosquito* leveling off before shuddering with the blast of their ordnance impacting. Looking back, Russell saw that both bombs had just missed the carrier close aboard.

Dammit. A sudden wave of helplessness and anger washed over him. *Jersey Two didn't–*

His thoughts were interrupted by first one, then two flashes suddenly erupting from the *Chitose*'s flight deck. There was a brief glimpse of Baron Three's outline in the explosions, tracers reaching out toward the *Mosquito*. Baron Four's bombs missed long, their blasts barely shaking the now burning carrier.

Well at least we got two hits on her, Russell observed with brusque satisfaction. A pair of secondary explosions increased the size of the sizeable blaze on the Japanese carrier..

"Baron Leader, this is Jersey One, we're going to have another go at that light cruiser," Flight Lieutenant Hibbert reported.

"Jersey One, give me a second and I'll illuminate, then Gratham Three can assist."

"Right on, we'll stand by."

"We need to call Ratmalana and let them know this is not the bloody main force," Russell said. "Get us up to altitude and let's start heading back."

"Roger," Bellingsley said, pulling back on the yolk. Russell turned just in time to see Jersey and Gratham's remaining aircraft with ordnance have another go at the *Noshiro*. The string of flares outlined the Japanese light cruiser once more, and again anti-aircraft fire reached up towards the descending British aircraft.

Come on lads, get a lick in.

"Sir, what hea–"

Suddenly the inside of the *Mosquito* was alive with flashes and several loud bangs. Pain stabbed sharply in his legs, his abdomen, right arm, and chest. Bellingsley screamed as the *Mosquito* tumbled to the right, throwing Russell against his straps, then forward into the radar screen with a teeth-jarring *crunch*! that sent the world into a brilliant white for a moment.

What...wha– He attempted to grab his seat straps as the world continued to go topsy turvy. There was the sound of ripping wood, then debris was flying all around him. Russell threw up his hand to cover his face, then realized what swung up into his field of view seemed to be a bit of meat attached to his arm by strings of sinew rather than a hand.

Russell was still in shock and trying to figure out what had happened to his arm when the *Mosquito*'s front half tumbled into the Pacific. The *Chitose Zero* that had shot Bellingsley and he down, satisfied with the will, turned to claw back to altitude. To the Japanese pilot's disappointment, there was no more prey to find in the darkness.

The remainder of Baron Squadron, egressing at high speed, did not realize they had faced the Second Carrier Fleet, not the *Kido Butai*. As the senior surviving officer, Flight Officer Badcocke was responsible for providing an action report to Wing Leader Hairns. Upon his return to Ratmalana, Badcocke would state that the *Mosquitoes* had engaged and set ablaze a *Hiryu*-class carrier. The report would be made in total and complete earnestness.

Badcocke's case of misidentification would have grievous consequences.

5

...WITH A STRIKING CASTLE

"When we are near, we must make the enemy believe we are far away; when far away, we must make him believe we are near."

— **SUN TZU**

MORTON RESIDENCE
2236 LOCAL (0436 EASTERN)
HAWAII
8 AUGUST (9 AUGUST)

"I SWEAR by all that's holy, someone is going to die," Patricia drawled as the knocking on their *kitchen* door continued. She had just finished brushing her teeth and slipping into her night robe for a last bit of reading before bed. Now someone, undoubtedly either confused, drunk, or both was quietly, but insistently, tapping.

"Violently," Jo agreed as Patricia stepped into the hallway. Patricia stopped stock still, bringing her hand up to her mouth in shock, as she regarded her diminutive roommate.

"Where in the *hell* did you get a shotgun?" Patricia asked, her voice rising in concern.

"How about you don't announce to the whole world we're armed?" Jo snapped. She stopped, eyes narrowing as she turned towards the kitchen.

"What is..."

"Shush for a second," Jo said, clearly concentrating. "That sounds like Morse code."

Listening for a few more knocks, Jo's eyes flew wide, then she rushed towards the kitchen door making joyful noises. Stopping in her head long rush, Jo leaned the pump shotgun up against the wall before entering the kitchen.

What in the hell? Patricia asked, following along behind at a much more sedate pace. Before she was halfway through the house, she heard Jo give a whooping scream and throw the door open.

"*Sam!*" Jo shouted, jumping through the door and into the open arms of one Samuel Cobb.

Oh my God! Patricia thought, tears suddenly welling up in her eyes as David stepped past his brother and into her kitchen. She rushed forward, throwing her arms around him and embracing him.

"Does she realize she's only wearing a night shirt?" David whispered as he squeezed his sister.

"Shush you!" Patricia sobbed into his shoulder. "You know they've always had a weird friendship."

"Who has always had a weird friendship?" Jo asked, wiping tears away from her eyes as she led Sam by the hand inside.

If by weird you mean just this side of presentable, perhaps the woman holding the wrong brother's hand as she leads him into the house.

"I need to get changed, Sam," Jo said. You don't go *anywhere*."

"What am I, chopped liver?" David asked in faux indignation.

"I'll give you your hug when I get decent," Jo tossed over her shoulder.

Both Sam and David turned to watch her go.

That's it, I'm giving you both a piece of my mind, Patricia bristled. *Yes, Eric did not depart here on the best of terms and neither of us have heard from him or Charles in **weeks**, but there is no excuse for Sam to be flirting with Jo.*

Patricia glared at both her brothers, rattling her fingers on the table until they belatedly turned to look at her. Both men took a simultaneous, clearly involuntary step backwards just as she opened her mouth. The movement stopped her for a second, eyes narrowing.

"Yes, I know, I look like Mom," she almost hissed.

"It's uncanny, Toots," Sam said, his voice somewhat shaken.

"Maybe you should consider *why* I look like her," Patricia replied. "Could it be that you're looking at my roommate like she's a mutton chop and you're a wolf?"

David smirked at that comment, causing Patricia to whirl towards him.

"Is there something amusing, David? I know Sam and you have always been thick as thieves, but I didn't think you'd literally help him steal your other brother's girl."

"Point of order," Jo said coolly from the kitchen doorway. "I'm no one's 'girl.' Not that it's any of your business."

Patricia's cheeks felt positively ablaze as she looked towards Jo. The shorter woman's face was calm, almost serene, as she stepped into the room and gave David a huge hug.

"God I missed you both," Jo said. Patricia could hear the tears almost ready to flow again in her roommate's voice. Fighting down her own emotions, she turned to Sam.

"Did you both forget how to write? We haven't heard from either of you in weeks."

Both Sam and David looked at one another, then at the two women with mutually wide eyes.

"I wrote every day before we came out here," Sam said. "Hell, I've got letters for you both back at the squadron."

"You're the first people Sadie and I wrote with the news," David said.

"What news?" Patricia asked, looking at them both.

Sam started laughing.

"Sadie and I are pregnant," David said. "You're going to be an aunt, Patricia."

Patricia looked at her brother.

An aunt? I'm too young to be an...wait, really?

Her face broke into a slight smile, then a broad grin as David looked goofily back at her.

"Sorry Jo, you'll just have to be an 'aunt,'" Sam stated, making air quotations that led to a dirty look from both Patricia and Jo.

"Has it ever crossed your mind that I might enjoy just being the person who buys this child random gifts during the year?" Jo replied, voice dripping in sarcasm. "Aunt sounds so stuffy, so formal."

Patricia rolled her eyes as she sat down at the table.

"Don't rain on my parade, Josephine Morton," she chided happily. "So are you guys going to actually sit down or just look in our kitchen?"

Sam and David looked at each other.

"Actually we'll stand," they both said in unison.

"Stop it," Jo said, her smile belying any indication that she may be actually annoyed. "You know I hate it when you two do that."

Both men smiled mischievously.

"Anyway, why are you even here?" Patricia asked. "I thought you were both being forced to convince people to pay for the war?"

"We were," Sam said, making the face of someone who had just been reminded of an unpleasant chore.

"Then *someone* here asked a random officer to get us assigned to his squadron," David said. "Three guesses as to who would do something like that."

Jo looked at Sam with worry on her face.

"You mean, you had a chance to spend a few weeks not getting shot at and you *talked your way out of it?*"

Patricia saw a number of emotions cross over Sam's face as Jo continued to glare at him.

"It wasn't like that exactly..." Sam began, holding up his hands defensively.

"That is a lie, Sam Cobb," David snapped. "Major Haynes was enjoying a nice dinner with Nora and you completely invited yourself to their date."

"You make it sound like I stepped right up and just started taking food off their plates, David," Sam said. "I merely asked him if he could use a pair of experienced pilots."

Patricia watched Jo's face throughout the entire exchange.

I've only read about volcanoes in books. But if Vesuvius looked the day before the eruption like Jo looks right now, every single one of those people in

Pompeii deserved to die for not paying attention. Patricia leaned forward in nervous anticipation of what was coming.

"Do you ever think of anyone besides yourself, Sam?" Jo asked, her tone clipped. "Just kinda, maybe, sorta consider the feelings of people around you rather than whatever impulse just pops into your fool head?"

Sam looked at Jo, his expression hard.

"In case you haven't heard, there's a war on," he said lowly.

"Hadn't noticed," Jo replied, adopting an expression of mock shock. "Oh, wait, there's a lieutenant who your sister's been pining over that hasn't been around for a few weeks. So, yeah, I guess I remember something about a war being on."

Uh oh. The vein in Sam's temple was starting to throb.

"I was thinking the dead bodies piling up amongst our friends might be a clue as well," Sam replied coldly. "Or has your Uncle K and Peter been by since we've been gone?"

There was a stunned silence in the kitchen. Patricia stood from where she'd sat down.

That was utterly unacceptable.

Patricia saw Jo's mouth working but nothing coming out.

"Get out, Sam," Patricia snapped.

"You're going to kick your own brother out, Patricia?" David asked.

"Yes. I believe I've done it before."

"Jo started it," David said evenly. "I didn't agree with what Sam just said, but I understand why he did it."

"And why was that, David?" Jo asked angrily. "Wanted to make Sadie a rich widow?"

David glared at Jo, then turned back to Patricia as if to say '*See?!*'

"We were going crazy on the tour. Did you really want us to have to relearn how to fly after the Navy decided we'd made them enough money?"

"I mean, our squadron commander is only the deadliest American pilot in history," Sam chimed. "Not like we just decided to fly with some random bunch of yahoos."

"Wait, what?" Jo asked.

"Major Haynes tied Rickenbacker's kill total a couple nights ago," David explained.

"How in the Hell did he tie Rickenbacker's record?" Jo asked. "Did you guys take a side tour to Tokyo over the last couple of days or something?"

"That's not important," Sam said, brushing aside the question. "The fact of the matter is, we both agreed that if anyone has a chance to get out of this war alive, it's Major Haynes."

"Even if he can't find a carrier," David muttered, causing Sam to shake his head.

"So no, neither one of us are glory hounds or bounty seekers," Sam continued. "We're trying to figure out how to get onboard with the best man possible."

"Plus he's not going to try to split us up like seemingly everyone else wants to," David added.

"That's called safety, David," Patricia said. "Safety, you know the kind of thing you guys should try out once in awhile."

"How is it safe to split us up?" David asked. "We're both the best wingman the other one has ever had and ever will have."

"Look, there's no safe place in this war," Sam broke in. "Hell, for all we know, the Japanese could show back up here tomorrow."

Actually, two of us in this room can tell you that's highly unlikely.

Patricia fought hard not to look over at Jo.

"Yes, but they're a lot less likely to show up in *Seattle*, Sam," Jo retorted.

Patricia sighed, causing them all to turn to her.

"Enough arguing," she stated. "What's done is done, and I don't think you guys came to visit us to get read the riot act. How long are you on liberty?"

"Two days," Sam and David said in unison.

"We have to work tomorrow," Patricia said. "You both know how the foldout couch works, and I promise I'll make you Mom's pancakes when you get up."

. . .

PATRICIA COULD TELL FROM THE LONG, STRAINED SILENCE OF THE first fifteen minutes of their walk to work that something was eating at Jo. The *click clack* of their heels on the sidewalk seemed to beat a steady increasing pressure.

I can't take it anymore.

"Why is it that you and I are thick as thieves for weeks, months even," she began, "but the minute my brothers show up, we're at each other's throats?"

"Because for some unknown reason you seem utterly convinced you have any say in which of your brothers, if any, I fuck," Jo snapped.

Patricia gasped at Jo's directness.

"Then there's the fact you also try to mother the shit out of them," Jo continued, her swearing drawing a disapproving look from a woman walking past them.

"I don't think swearing is necessary, Jo," Patricia said angrily.

"I also think you must have a very low opinion of me if you think I'm going to complicate your family by having sex with Sam," Jo replied. "For God's sake Patricia, he and I are friends. *Friends*"

"But..."

"But we flirt? Talk to each other like a couple? Are utterly comfortable with one another in a way that most husbands and wives never achieve?"

Well, I see that I've struck a nerve.

"Yes, all true," her roommate continued. "But I'm smart enough to know that Sam, out of all your brothers, is an absolute coward when it comes to commitment."

"What?" Patricia asked, aghast.

"I did not stutter," Jo replied. "If you asked that man to fly to Tokyo *right now*, he'd do it. If you asked him to run into a blazing building to pull out women and children, same."

Oh dear, she's crying, Patricia realized, seeing the glistening in Jo's eyes.

"But boy howdy, ask him to put in the work that people have to in order to really make a relationship work, and he turns more yellow than a bunch of bananas," Jo observed bitterly. "This is known, and I realized it a long time ago before you even came out here."

They made the last turn toward the back access gate and Jo stopped for a moment to dig in her purse for a handkerchief. Quickly dabbing her eyes and checking her appearance, Jo then looked at Patricia.

"So please, for the sake of our friendship, don't think that I'm going to sneak out to the damn couch, grab your brother, and seduce him," Jo said. "Quite frankly, even though we haven't gotten mail in forever, I *think* I care about Eric too much to do that to him. I *know* I love you and the rest of your family like the one I never had."

Wait, what?

Jo had been so matter-of-fact about her emotions that Patricia wasn't sure she heard her correctly. The other woman plowed on, not even pausing.

"With God as my witness, I will deny ever saying any of this if you tell another living soul. I will also kick you out of our house so fast it will make your head spin."

Oh Josephine Morton, you know how to keep people off balance.

"I don't know what to say, Jo."

"You can start with, 'I'm sorry,' as Sam was scared to even hug me goodbye this morning," Jo replied. "I miss that man's hugs."

Patricia shook her head.

"I don't think my mother would know what to do with you if you did marry one of my brothers," she observed.

"Judging from what you do with the kitchen knives, she'd probably try to stab me," Jo stated. Then once again Patricia could tell the wheels were working.

"So last night we established that the boys have been writing us, but we haven't gotten any of their letters," Jo said. "Now that I think about it, when was the last time you heard from your mother?"

Going to have to think about that one, Patricia realized.

"No matter, let's get inside and see what puzzles await us today," Jo stated.

The two of them passed through the access gate, making small talk with the guards as always. Commander Tannehill had informed them the side gate was only for a few select personnel, the better to avoid getting caught in the crush of humanity that was the coming and goings of various vessel crews. The departure of the *Rodney*, *Nelson*, and *Maryland* along with a couple of escort carriers had reduced the sheer number of personnel on Oahu, but Pearl Harbor was still a very crowded place dominated by young men. Patricia was well aware of the eyes that followed her and Jo as they walked towards their work, just as she appreciated the shore patrol that very conspicuously walked thirty yards behind them.

Been a few weeks since some idiot groped an admiral's daughter. While I think that was a one off, the shore patrol putting a couple people in the hospital afterwards sure has retaught some manners.

"Good morning, ladies," Gunnery Sergeant Longstreet said as they came through the door. He stood up to make a perfunctory check of their identification, eyes narrowing as he saw Jo's puffy eyes.

That man is entirely too observant.

Longstreet did not say anything, however, as he turned and pulled a keychain from around his neck. Pressing the intercom buzzer, he spoke into the speaker.

"Two on their way down," he stated. "The Songbirds."

I will never understand why Commander Tannehill is so paranoid about security. Jo and she had very pointedly *not* told either Sam or David that they were no longer working at their previous jobs. It seemed such a silly thing, but Commander Tannehill had been quite adamant that *no one* could know what they did.

I mean, anyone telling my brothers we're known as 'songbirds' will have them both wondering if we're operating without 'visible means of support.'

The idiocy of that concern elicited a nervous titter from her that caused Longstreet and Jo to both give her a look.

"I'm not cracking up," she said, then explained her thought. Longstreet guffawed while Jo just shook her head with a smile.

"Whether or not your marbles are about to roll down this hallway is up for debate," Jo replied, stepping into the car. The doors closed behind them, the elevator descending rapidly into the bunker below.

"God I hate the smell of new paint," Jo muttered. The entire facility, at least according to Commander Tannehill, was brand spanking new. When Great Britain had fallen, the Germans, and thus the Japanese, had become aware that the United States had broken their codes. Although almost certainly the flight of paranoia, this had caused the previous Pacific Fleet G-2 to recommend the codebreaking section and most other intelligence functions be moved to a different building. Everyone had laughed at the man, right up until the Japanese had shown up and kicked the Pacific Fleet's ass back in March.

*Too bad he apparently died on the **Arizona**. He appeared to have a better grasp of the Japanese than just about anyone else.*

The doors opened to reveal Commander Tannehill standing waiting for them.

Are we late?

Patricia looked towards the clock on the far side of the room.

"I need to ask if either of you are prone to fainting spells or bouts of hysteria," Commander Tannehill said crisply without preamble.

"Well good morning to you as well, sir," Jo replied with a wave. The officer's severe countenance did not waiver as he turned to look at her, then Patricia.

"I do not think I will require a couch or sedative anytime soon, no," Patricia replied cautiously. "Why are you concerned?"

Tannehill sighed in relief.

"The map in the next room has been updated," he replied. "I know from both of your files that the Indian Ocean has suddenly become of interest to you."

With that, he led them through the doorway into the Pacific Fleet G-2's main mapboard.

"Well shit," Jo said, looking up at the board. Patricia looked also, seeing a "FLETCHER" pinned on an arrow that appeared to be several hundred miles east of Africa. Another, this one painted in British blue and labeled CUNNINGHAM seemed to be in the middle of the Indian Ocean pointed north.

"It's unbecoming of a lady to swear, Josephine," Commander Tannehill said.

"Commander, my father has not broken me of the habit despite the aggressive use of a soap bar when I was seventeen," Jo replied. "My roommate has not had any success despite attempting to be the mother I haven't had in over a decade."

Tannehill sighed.

"I suppose reminding you I am your superior and boss will merely earn myself a further demonstration of your vulgar vocabulary, won't it?"

"Make you a deal," Jo said, looking at the map with obvious concern on her face. "You tell us what that scarlet arrow labeled 'KB' south of Ceylon is, and I'll never swear in *this* office again."

She's lying. Or at the very least, hedging her bets.

Patricia was unsurprised that Tannehill, but not Longstreet, missed out on Jo's obvious gambit.

"That is what the Japanese have termed the *Kido Butai*, their name for what we'd call the First Air Fleet."

"Uh, sir…" an ensign said, whipping his head around.

"Yes, Ensign Moldavus, clearly the fact Miss Morton and Miss Cobb have been here for two days means they are so dire a threat to security I cannot say the words *Kido Butai* in front of them," Tannehill snapped. "A name that has been being trumpeted by radio broadcasts from our friends in Tokyo for almost five months now, I might add."

The younger officer stiffened at the rebuke, but wisely turned back to his task.

Horribly nervous around women, damn near overbearing with subordinates. Commander Tannehill is somewhat of an enigma.

"In any case, as I believe it will help you with your pattern analysis, the British believe their aircraft on Ceylon engaged the Japanese fleet yesterday," Tannehill said. "They are also certain that the aircraft in question damaged one of the Japanese carriers."

"This is good news," Jo observed. "Why would we faint at good news?"

"Because if that is the main Japanese fleet, it means Vice Admiral Fletcher is about to engage them in two days." Tannehill replied, his tone funereal. "It also means the British had better not tarry where they've been refueling in the south, or he'll do so facing four carriers with his two."

Jo visibly swallowed, and Patricia felt her own stomach do a flip flop. Her roommate took a step back from the map, nervously clasping her hands together like she'd seen a horrible specter.

"Are you okay, Miss Morton?" Tannehill asked. Patricia could see that her friend was just shaken, but could understand why Tannehill would be worried.

I'm certain I look like the finest white sheet bleach can buy myself. So it's understandable Jo looks there's a possible tie between her breakfast ending up in that trash can or her running shrieking to the lady's room.

"Can..." Jo asked thickly, then swallowed hard. "Can Vice Admiral Fletcher wait for the British?"

"Depends on how attached Admiral Hart feels he should be to Ceylon," Tannehill replied. "I don't know that I'd consider a crown possession, even one that was responsible for so much rubber, worth *Enterprise* and *Yorktown*."

I.J.N.S. Akagi
1000 Local (0030 Eastern)
400 Miles Northeast of Addu Atoll
Indian Ocean
9 August

THE *KIDO BUTAI*, THREE HUNDRED MILES SOUTHWEST OF WHERE A misguided American intelligence officer believed it to be, was about to spring an elaborate trap.

"Sir, *Tone* No. 4 reports a contact."

Vice Admiral Yamaguchi continued to stare serenely out the *Akagi*'s bridge window as his staff sprang into action at the report.

So it begins.

"I do not think that it would be prudent for you to ever be alone in a room with The Gargoyle again," Rear Admiral Kaku noted as he walked up behind him. "It appears, however, that his feint has flushed the prey."

"*Vice Admiral Ozawa,*" Yamaguchi stated, "is an Imperial officer loyal to the Emperor. He is performing his duty."

Kaku stiffened at the rebuke entailed by the dual emphasis on name and title. Vice Admiral Ozawa was known as "The Gargoyle" due to his large stature, less than handsome visage and, at least according to the *Kido Butai* staff, surly nature. All of these things were true, but

Yamaguchi was well aware that the man was having to stand in and absorb British blows off Ceylon so that his force might see off the Far Eastern Fleet.

I will give him due deference even if I am also tired of his squalling like a spanked child about Admiral Yamamoto's orders..

"Launch the strike," he ordered simply. "I am sure you are going to tell me what the *Tone*'s aircraft has seen."

Kaku bowed, then turned and barked orders at the signal staff. Yamaguchi stepped out onto the bridge wing, the din of the decked park aircraft loud once he was through the hatch. The *Akagi*'s crew had spotted the aircraft on deck over the last hour and a half in anticipation of his moment.

It is a risk you are taking, Tamon, Yamaguchi chided himself. *But it beats the original plan.* Rear Admirals Hara and Kaku had, as he directed, developed a new plan. The revision had required the approval of IJN Headquarters in Tokyo, with which communication had required several relays of seaplanes to avoid breaking radio silence. Vice Admiral Ozawa, as Rear Admiral Kaku had alluded to, had been less than pleased at being relegated to suppressing Ceylon's airfields rather than keeping them down once the *Kido Butai* passed through. This was, however, necessary to trigger the British into believing that the Japanese were going to immediately suppress Ceylon. Judging from the initial and continued reaction to Ozawa's presence, the Ceylon garrison firmly believed his carriers to be the *Kido Butai*.

His fighter pilots are feasting on the heavy bombers, from all accounts. This "radar" is indeed a war changer.

He stared back at the *Taiho*, the large radar aerial prominent on her island. The purloined electronics were vastly superior to the primitive, native Japanese sets on *Shokaku* and *Kirishima*.

Alas, it cuts both ways. The British will undoubtedly see this strike coming in time to scramble fighters off their carriers. Which is why we're throwing everything possible in two waves.

Unlike their Western counterparts, Japanese carrier strikes revolved around divisions of two vessels, not each carrier's air group. In the case of the *Akagi*'s first strike, this meant that her dive bombers and fighters would join the *Kaga*'s torpedo bombers as one strike package. Roughly thirty minutes from now, once the aircraft were spotted, the *Akagi*'s torpedo bombers would then join the *Kaga*'s dive bombers and fighters. Each evolution would be mirrored by *Soryu* and *Hiryu*, while the *Shokaku* and *Taiho* were only contributing dive bombers and torpedo bombers to the first strike in order to maintain a CAP.

If the CAP is necessary, of course we are doomed. The beauty of the plan was to catch Vice Admiral Cunningham's carriers almost a full day before they were expecting to make contact with the "*Kido Butai*," a.k.a. Ozawa's feint. This in and of itself was also the culmination of several months of subterfuge. Officially, the Japanese Navy had never acknowledged the well-developed Royal Navy anchorage at Addu Atoll in the Maldives. When the British had been forced to cede Singapore to Japan way back in 1942, their staff had been thorough in destroying all mention of the base's ability to sustain a large fleet such as Cunningham's. Unfortunately, that hadn't done anything about the paperwork back in the Admiralty in London.

Of course, the Germans became privy to many 'secrets' after the Treaty of Kent. I am sure we have not been told all of them, even as those smiling racists call us friends.

Unlike his counterparts in the Army, back when those idiots had been in charge, Yamaguchi had never been under any illusions as to how the Germans regarded Japan. Indeed, his preference would have been to figure out some way to make common cause with the United States after several years of residence there as an attaché and student.

*Alas, while not as overt as the Germans, it is clear the Americans have their own problems with us, as we do with them. Which is why we must inflict so great a defeat here in the Indian Ocean that **both** Great Britain and the United States turn to focus on our friends in Berlin.*

"Sir, the *Hiryu* and *Soryu* report that they are launching," Rear Admiral Kaku stated. Yamaguchi signaled his understanding.

"Has the *Taiho* picked up *any* contacts?" he asked.

"No sir," Kaku replied.

The first *Shiden* rolled down the *Akagi*'s deck. Rear Admiral Yamaguchi was pleasantly surprised at how cooperative the weather had been. Most of the cloud cover being thin and intermittent, and the wind was conveniently blowing out of southwest. This allowed the carriers to continue closing the range as they launched, rather than having to come about.

I have no desire to engage in a surface action with Cunningham.

Yamaguchi cast his eyes towards the *Kirishima* and *Hiei*. *I need him to go away, not strive for total annihilation.* He looked at his watch as the *Akagi*'s strike continued to launch.

In a little over three hours, I will have either won a great victory or doomed our nation, the *Kido Butai*'s commander thought. *Now I wait.*

U.S.S. PLUNGER
2036 LOCAL (0236 EASTERN)
PEARL HARBOR
8 AUGUST (9 AUGUST)

IT WAS RARE FOR A SUBMARINE TO RISK ENTRY INTO PEARL HARBOR during the night. However, as if the battered vessel herself had wanted to prove Nick and Chief McLaughlin's point, the *Plunger* had suffered a catastrophic failure in her forward engine room roughly two days out of Midway.

I wonder if they can smell burnt oil ashore, Nick wondered idly as the submarine eased up to the pier. *Because that stench will be all over us until we get our clothes laundered.*

"Well, looks like we're not going to be totally neglected," Commander Emerson sneered, gesturing towards the dock.

You, sir, have been damn near insufferable.

It did not help that, upon further evaluation, the folks on Midway had agreed *Plunger* needed to have a refit, if not a full dry dock period, before going back out against the Japanese. The *Fulton*'s divers had found further dings in the submarine's hull forward. These had been invisible unless one swam completely underneath the submarine, evidence of a couple of ash cans exploding lower than the keel.

Given the late hour and it being dark, I can understand if no one had met us at all. Not like there's a war on or anything.

JAMES YOUNG

"I'm going below to grab the log, XO," Commander Emerson stated. "I will meet you on the dock momentarily."

Nick nodded, hoping against hope that Commander Emerson would retrieve his log before the *Plunger* put down her gangway. It was not to be, and Nick greeted Rear Admiral Graham as the senior officer stepped onto *Plunger*'s deck.

"Welcome aboard, sir," Nick said as the bosun's pipe sounded. Graham wrinkled his nose as the wind shifted.

"Smells like you gentlemen had some trouble," the senior officer said, returning Nick's salute then extending his hand. Nick shook if just as Commander Emerson returned to the bridge.

"Nothing a little yard time won't fix, admiral," Commander Emerson said breathlessly. He handed over the *Plunger*'s log.

I don't know why Graham started the custom of the log being turned over. Other than the morbid rumor he wants there to be some permanent record of past events if the ship gets lost on patrol.

The Pearl submarines had been relatively lucky, having lost only three boats since the war had started. Allegedly the Asiatic Fleet, by contrast, had lost seven vessels to all causes.

Just because three of their losses were old 'Sugar'-boats doesn't make that any less scary. It had been confirmed that several acquaintances and classmates had been aboard the lost subs.

"Lieutenant Cobb, if you could go to my car and retrieve my briefcase," Rear Admiral Graham said. Nick looked at the man in surprise, then at his aide. Coming to attention, he saluted and moved smartly off the *Plunger*'s gangplank towards Graham's vehicle.

That was a little strange, he thought, walking up to the Packard. *Why wouldn't he send his aide?*

As the got closer, the door opened and a familiar figure stepped out of the vehicle.

"Agnes," he said, starting to run forward before his lover held her finger up to her lips.

"I am not here if you ever want to see me alive again," Agnes replied, her tone and smile belying the seriousness of her statement. "There are many, many officers' wives who have asked to meet the boats at the dock."

Nick stopped short and took the proffered briefcase. Agnes smiled at the pained expression on his face as he maintained professional decorum. Looking forward, Nick saw Rear Admiral Graham's driver struggling to hide a smile.

"You know, there's a word for this," he said crossly.

"Yes, it is patience," Agnes said with a lilt. "I'm not planning on dying in the next two hours or so, and it appears neither are you."

"No, no I am not," Nick replied. "Although let's not tempt the fates."

"I would not dream of tempting fate with you, Nicholas Cobb," Agnes replied. "Now, hurry back, and without a, how you say, 'shit eating grin.'"

I will never tire of hearing her saying American aphorisms in a Portuguese accent. It was a long story how Agnes had ended up in Hawaii as the admiral's secretary. Nick was well aware of the chain of consequences that had led to him ending up with her, and Death's recurring presence in both their lives suddenly gave him a sense of urgency.

I need to make an honest woman of her. The thought was almost as quick as his steps back to the gathered officers. *If these were ordinary times I'd want Mom and Dad to meet her first, to meet her folks, and do all the things we're supposed to. But this ain't ordinary times.*

"Thank you, Lieutenant Cobb," Rear Admiral Graham said as Nick returned. "I expect you to be with Commander Emerson in two days when he gives me his report. Until then, I've already informed him that the *Plunger* crew is to be given a week's liberty while we figure out what to do with the sub, and with *you*."

Another reason for Agnes and I to find a priest. Because they won't let her go back to the Mainland with me unless she's a spouse.

"Aye aye, sir," Nick replied.

"You have all done amazing work," Rear Admiral Graham said. "The *Plunger* has been a Stirling example of how one conducts a submarine war. It will be unfortunate if we have to send you back to Mare Island for repair, but I don't think I'm going to get you into drydock with all the other damaged ships."

"Understood, sir," Commander Emerson said. "Is there any possibility of us falling in on a new vessel?"

Nick did not miss the look that crossed Rear Admiral Graham's face as he seemed to ponder Emerson's question.

That man just decided the skipper needs some time on the beach. Which now almost certainly means I'm about to be out of Hawaii.

Nick's hands began to go clammy. Over Emerson's shoulder, Chief McClaughlin shook his head, then mouthed an apology.

I'm sorry too, Chief. But sorry beats being dead any day of the week. Even if it means that I'll be stuck stateside while my brothers are trying to win a war.

A<small>KAGI</small> F<small>IGHTER</small> C<small>HUTAI</small> #2
1312 L<small>OCAL</small> (0312 E<small>ASTERN</small>)
I<small>NDIAN</small> O<small>CEAN</small>
9 A<small>UGUST</small>

T<small>HE RAIN POUNDING AGAINST HIS CANOPY MATCHED THE RAPID PACE</small> of Isoro Honda's heart.

The weather was so beautiful when we left, he thought, fighting against the *Shiden* trying to throw itself about in the squall's moderate updrafts. *Now I can't even see my hand in front of my face and there's dozens of aircraft all around me.*

Isoro fought the urge to look around, focusing steadily on his instruments. His radio remained silent, and part of him wondered whether the troublesome device had just ceased working or the strike's discipline was actually holding that well.

We should have heard something from the **Tone**'s *search plane at least. It would have been nice if the bastard had told us about the developing front.*

Isoro gritted his teeth at the search plane's delinquency. The weather was going to certainly make it harder to acquire the British vessels. Even worse, it would be next to impossible to detect the CAP that would almost certainly be at altitude, if not higher than the Japanese strike group when it came out of the clouds. If the intelligence reports were true, the *Kido Butai*'s blow would likely face variants of the *Spitfire*, *Hurricane*, and some of the Americans' Grumman *Wildcats*. Isoro counted all of the types among his twenty-eight confirmed kills. Ergo, like most fighter pilots, he was not concerned about the opposition...provided he saw them.

This is madness. We should be almost over—

Like a curtain suddenly ripped apart, the clouds parted before the *Akagi*'s nine *Shiden*...to reveal a sky full of enemy aircraft slashing in towards them. Isoro immediately pulled back on his stick as the two groups passed through each other so rapidly no one had time for shooting. The violent sound of aircraft colliding behind him told him some had not even had time to react before they and their opponents were smashed into oblivion.

Spitfires. Isoro's mind belatedly recognized the trademark elliptical wing of the enemy aircraft as the fight spilled out into the clear sky. Checking quickly to make sure Warrant Officer Oda and Petty Officer Takahashi had survived the literal merger, Isoro finished his Immelmann turn then immediately stood on the rudder to turn towards a pair of grey British aircraft. Out of the corner of his eye, he saw the *Kido Butai*'s strike aircraft spilling out into the daylight, olive green fuselage paint glistening from their transition through the storm.

Also Grummans.

The familiar stocky shapes were flashing towards the torpedo bombers, but Isoro had no time for them with the *Spitfires* much closer. He chose his prey, a pair of British fighters fixated on the *chutai* of dive bombers they'd chosen. The *Shiden* closed quicker than Isoro had expected from the *Spitfires* he'd fought in the Dutch East Indies, but he adjusted all the same.

The trail fighter saw him at the last moment, its wings starting to come up in an evasive maneuver before Isoro squeezed his trigger. The British fighter staggered, then burst into flames as the four 20mm cannon pierced its fuel tank.

Realizing the danger, the British leader broke right in a tight turn. Isoro continued past, rolling his fighter to the left to cover Oda as the latter cut across the *Spitfire*'s turn to fire a snap shot. The burst scored several hits, the *Spitfire*'s nose losing a piece of the engine cowling and streaming glycol as its pilot desperately dived away.

"Leader look out!" Isoro's radio crackled with Takahashi's desperate warning. He didn't attempt to see what the man was calling about, throwing his *Shiden* into a snap roll. There were several impact sounds from behind him in the fuselage, and he saw a dark gray Grumman hurtle past his tail, wingman behind him.

That fighter looked...strange.

Instead of attempting to get around to pursue the Grumman, Isoro leveled his wings and advanced his throttle while looking for more prey. He saw that Oda had disappeared somewhere and the radio net was total chaos. Anti-aircraft fire bursts were roughly twenty miles to the south, meaning that the *Kido Butai*'s first strike had found something.

In a manner that had become far too familiar in the last six months, the skies immediately around them had suddenly become devoid of aircraft. Isoro signaled for Takahashi to follow him and began climbing towards the flak.

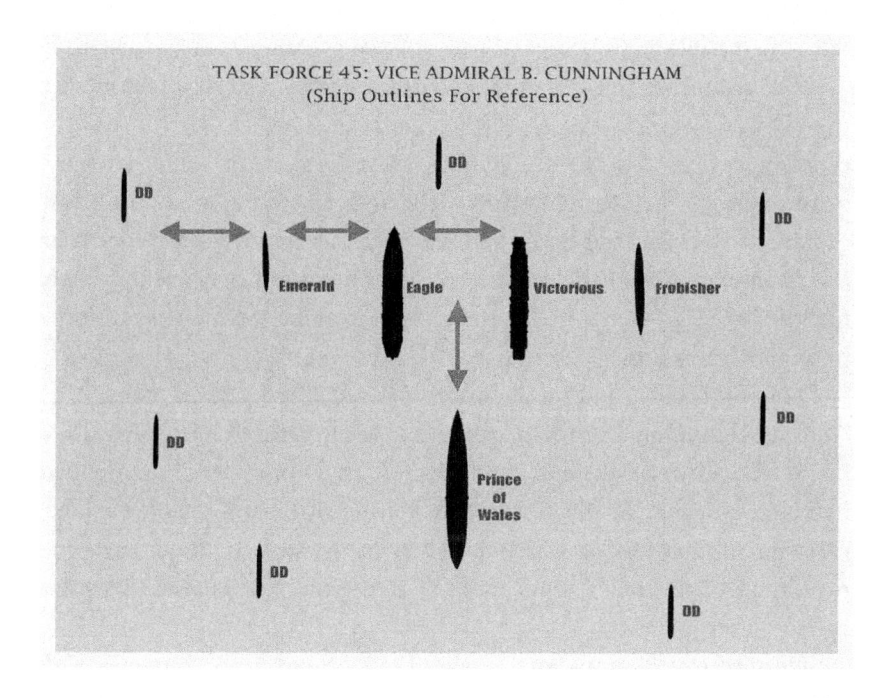

TASK FORCE 45: VICE ADMIRAL B. CUNNINGHAM
(Ship Outlines For Reference)

DD | DD | DD
Emerald | Eagle | Victorious | Frobisher
DD | DD
Prince of Wales
DD | DD

INDEED THE FIRST STRIKE HAD FOUND SOMETHING: PREY.

Vice Admiral Cunningham had sortied north from Addu Atoll with the H.M.C.S. *Ark Royal, Eagle, Illustrious,* and *Victorious* as the centerpiece of his fleet. Unlike their American and Japanese counterparts, the Royal Navy had anticipated combat in close proximity to both land bases and opposing surface vessels rather than the open expanses of the Pacific Ocean. Therefore, the Fleet Air Arm had made design tradeoffs for their carriers and doctrine that resulted in smaller air groups.

The detection and destruction of *Tone* No. 4 had cued Vice Admiral Cunningham that his force had been detected. Unfortunately, his staff had believed the lone aircraft and another of its fellows detected on radar to be launched from one of Japan's many seaplane-carrying submarines. It was only when the first *Kido Butai* wave was detected at just under two hundred miles that the four carriers had realized their danger.

Despite excellent radar placement, the clouds and thirty-six *Kido Butai* fighters had mostly served to neutralize the CAP. With the exception of a pair of *Tenzan* and a solitary *Suisei* dive bomber, Commander Fuchida found himself directing the entire *Kido Butai*'s strike at the *Victorious* and *Eagle* as the *Ark Royal* and *Illustrious* disappeared into the squall line.

The two British carriers were escorted by the *Prince of Wales*, heavy cruiser *Frobisher*, light cruiser *Emerald*, and seven destroyers. Fuchida, quickly assessing the situation, allocated his forty-seven dive bombers and fifty-five torpedo bombers among the thirteen vessels. As the British formation opened to allow the capital ships room to maneuver, first the heavy, then medium, then finally, desperately, light AA guns blazed aways at the Japanese force.

In ten minutes it was over. In accordance with their doctrine, the dive bombers went in slightly ahead of the torpedo bombers to reduce enemy fire. Having just transitioned to the *Suisei* from the slower *Val*, the *Kido Butai*'s timing was slightly off. Several bombers nearly collided as they pushed over, pilots from separate squadrons screaming at other even as British tracer fire and shell bursts reached up towards them. The dense flak claimed six of the dive bombers before they released, with another eight or so being damaged enough to affect their drops.

The thirty or so remaining aircraft more than accomplished their task of suppressing defenses. *Emerald* was the first to suffer, her captain avoiding four bombs only to catch three in rapid succession. The elderly cruiser, laid down in the waning days of World War II, was no more suited for that level of abuse than a grandmother was for a heavyweight boxing match. Each 1,000-lb. bomb was, in effect, a body blow to an already frail frame, with the bridge, then the amidships engineering spaces, and finally the rudder and stern being blasted into ruin. Horribly maimed, with steam and smoke gushing from her midsection, the light cruiser coasted to a stop then began to list.

On the opposite side of the *Victorious* and *Eagle*, the heavy cruiser *Frobisher* was more fortunate than her lighter counterpart. Like *Emerald*, her captain ably maneuvered the vessel to dodge the first *chutai*. The second was similarly thwarted despite each *Suisei* releasing two 500-lb. bombs apiece rather than the heavier half-ton weapons.

It was a sole *Shokaku Suisei*, pressing in close, that manage to put a pair of 500-lb. bombs on the cruiser's stern. Catching a burst of 1.1-inch pom poms to the cockpit for his perfidy, the Japanese pilot did not see that only one of his weapons detonated. Still, the blow managed to sever the *Frobisher*'s rudder controls, sending the heavy cruiser careening in a circle towards the H.M.C.S. *Catterick*, a destroyer in the screen. Fortunately for both ships, the bridge crew of the latter were alert and managed to get their smaller vessel out of their larger companion's way.

Lieutenant Commander Maki led the *Akagi*'s dive bombers down towards the *Victorious*'s deck. Unlike the unfortunate *Shokaku* dive bomber who had hit the *Frobisher*, Lieutenant Commander Maki did not suffer a burst of fire into the canopy. Instead, a bursting shell from the *Victorious*'s heavy anti-aircraft battery turned his dive bomber into its namesake. Whether by design or due to the chaos inherent of finding oneself in the center of a blazing "comet," Lieutenant Commander Maki's attack dive terminated in the center of the *Victorious*'s flight deck. His two wingmen, realizing their leader's distress too late, released their weapons too low and had their bombers damaged by their own hits as well as the *Victorious*'s guns. Slightly less determined, the twelve other dive bombers attacking Vice Admiral Cunningham's flagship only managed to put one more bomb onto the flight deck and three more close enough to damage *Victorious*'s hull.

If the *Victorious* had been an American or Japanese carrier, the damage would have been enough to see her off. Instead, the vessel's armored flight deck reduced the severity, even as serious fires broke out and crew casualties were immense. With smoke pouring from her flight and hangar decks, the carrier's bridge crew scanned frantically for the torpedo bombers they knew were approaching through their escorts' smoke screen.

Eagle was nowhere near as fortunate as her younger, more modern cohort. Built on the hull of an intended battleship, still nursing the repaired wounds suffered during the Dutch East Indies campaign, and less ably handled by her new captain, the *Eagle* absorbed three 1,000-lb. bomb hits. Unlike *Victorious*, *Eagle*'s flight deck was not heavily armored. This did not stop the first weapon from detonating just as it passed the hangar deck roof, causing a massive bulge forward. The next weapon detonated in the forward crew spaces, killing twenty-five men in a damage control party there and starting a roaring fire. The final bomb also started a fierce blaze, this one in the carrier's stern from the ready ammo for the 6-inch guns.

The remainder of the Japanese dive bombers missed due to a combination of factors. The aircraft had just barely cleared their drops when the *Tenzan*s began the final phases of their runs. The sixteen bombers that targeted the *Prince of Wales* had their attack disrupted by a late launched *Seafire*. Piloted by Flying Officer Eric Brown, the British fighter downed the *Soryu* leader with a quick burst, then caused another torpedo bomber to dip its wing into the ocean before reaching the drop point. With one half of the hammer and anvil attack disrupted, the *Prince of Wales* was able to narrowly turn to starboard and comb the tracks from that direction.

Unfortunately for the *Eagle* and *Victorious*, their large companion's turn to starboard took her light anti-aircraft battery out of protective range. Despite the valiant effort of the remaining destroyers, there were far too few guns to prevent both flattops getting caught in the classic bracket attack. The carriers' own anti-aircraft guns made their assailants pay dearly, with the *Eagle* shooting down three and the *Victorious* six of their attackers.

In response, both carriers were hit by two of the *Sandaburo* warheads. *Victorious*' first torpedo struck the No. 1 fire room's forward bulkhead. Whipping the carrier her entire length, the blow killed every man in the compartment as well as knocked many of the crew off their feet. Oil bunkerage fell back onto the already burning hangar deck, adding to the fires there.

The vessel had barely finished whipsawing from the first hit when the second weapon hit just below the carrier's avgas storage. Although not as instantaneously fatal as such hits had already proven in the war, the torpedo did immediately ignite a massive fire. Now with her aft third fully engulfed, *Victorious* hove to an immediate stop as her crew set to work attempting to save their vessel.

H.M.C.S. *Eagle*'s damage was both less and worse than *Victorious*'. The first torpedo struck her starboard prop shaft, blowing the propeller off the hull. Even as water rushed through the glands around the shaft and into the hull, the second torpedo ripped open the carrier's No. 2 engine and fire room. The shock from the damage tripped the vessel's electrical system, and in an instant the *Eagle* was left in darkness belowdecks and without means to fight the myriad fires visible to her escorts.

With two carriers burning behind them, the battered survivors of the first wave initiated their egress back to the Japanese carriers. Commander Fuchida, making one last circuit with a pair of *Shiden*, quickly determined that the *Victorious* and *Eagle* were no longer a threat. Looking towards the rain squall that *Ark Royal* and *Illustrious* had slipped away into, Fuchida made his report back to the *Kido Butai*. It was clear that the British Far Eastern Fleet would need another strike beyond the one already on its way. The question would be how quickly the *Kido Butai* could land, refuel, spot, and relaunch it.

LOOKING BEHIND HIS FIGHTER, ISORO COULD SAW THE COLUMNS OF smoke that indicated the *Kido Butai* had landed a strong blow.

But at what cost?

The *Kido Butai*'s formations were ragged as they staggered back to the rendezvous point. A *Kaga Shiden* had joined up with him and Petty Officer Takahashi. Warrant Officer Oda remained nowhere to be found, and Isoro was beginning to think the man had perished.

Unless he is very good at navigation, he will not make it back to the carriers alone.

Isoro made one last weave around the rendezvous point, then joined up with the two squadrons' worth of bombers just starting to stake out their own formations. Although every one of the IJN fighter pilots could navigate, their aircraft lacked the homing radios in their bomber counterparts. The vastness of the Indian Ocean, plus the increasingly poor weather, could kill a lost pilot just as well as a British fighter aircraft.

I'd much prefer that had been the Americans, Isoro thought. The Royal Navy had been Japan's ally for many years, but their home island's subjugation by Germany meant they were no longer a major threat to his country. The Americans, on the other hand, were Japan's mortal enemy.

Better to kill them here, far away from their homes, than fighting them on the way to Japan. However, I have to wonder who is guarding things in the Pacific while we fight the enemy here?

U.S.S. YORKTOWN
1400 LOCAL (0400 EASTERN)
NORTHERN INDIAN OCEAN
9 AUGUST

"YOU KNOW, PEOPLE ARE GOING TO START TO WONDER ABOUT ANY man who lays about next to the island while a war's on," Lieutenant Charles Read said, plopping down next to Eric.

Well it's about time we actually got to see one another, Eric thought, grinning as he extended his hand. Charles took it with a nod, the section leader and his former wingman both having a moment to appreciate each other still being alive.

"I think, at this point, it's just generally accepted I've lost my mind," Eric said, holding up the letter in his left hand. "Especially according to my sister and Jo both."

"I'm just glad our damn mail finally caught up to us," Charles replied. "Who knew it would take the slow boat to Australia, then an even slower boat out to get to the ship?"

Eric shrugged, looking out over the ocean.

Makes me wonder if they just waited for enough of it to accumulate before sending it or just realized a lack of contact with what we're fighting for is how mutinies happen. Still missing about three weeks of letters and clearly none of ours have arrived back in Hawaii.

"The powers that be, apparently," Eric replied. The two of them were momentarily interrupted by *Yorktown* launching a *Bonhomme Richard* TBF for anti-submarine patrol. The two men watched as the ungainly looking torpedo bomber rumbled down the flight deck with its three-man crew.

That's one bad thing about having so large a force: The poor bastards doing sub hunting and other things are having to cover a lot of ground. He looked astern of *Yorktown* to the large battleship trailing her, then out to her starboard quarter where the U.S.S. *Houston* also kept station.

At least the surface boys rejoined back up temporarily. I'll have to tell Jo that I "saw" her father finally.

"Another fine mess we find ourselves in, I have to say," Charles said after the noise had passed. "I think the Japanese have sent everyone and their brother to conquer Ceylon."

*Going to be one hell of a surprise for those bastards **and** the British when we show up with two extra carriers.*

"Who knew that rubber was that damn important to them?" Eric quipped. "I mean, with all the fuss out this way, it makes you wonder why they even started a fight with us. Pretty sure we would have let them take the Queen's rubber."

Charles raised an eyebrow at that.

"I thought the Queen and you were friends," Charles joked.

"I would never presume to believe in royal friendship," Eric replied. "The 'we' in question was America, however."

"It does seem like an awful lot of folks President Roosevelt has us brawling with," Charles said. "Although the British appear to have sent a lot of help our way. More at Hawaii if you read between the lines of Patricia's letter."

It's a little unnerving to talk with someone who knows my sister's subtle comments that well. Not that I can say anything. His former fiancée had been one of Patricia's good friends. Eric was surprised to realize Joyce Cotner had not crossed his mind in almost a month.

Maybe there is something to time heals all wounds. Eric mused. *Or maybe I've just developed a better taste in women. Even if I made a mess of things with the one I want.*

"You look lost in your head there for a second, Eric," Charles said, snapping him back to the present.

"Thinking about how nice it will be to rejoin up with Admiral Cunningham's force before we go north," Eric lied easily. "The thought of—"

"Pilots report to the ready room," the radio crackled. "I say again, all pilots report to their ready room."

Eric and Charles looked at each other, then heard the shouts and bustle of the *Yorktown*'s plane crews beginning to grow quite agitated.

Well, that's not a good sign. Looks like something is going to Hell in a handbasket.

"Gentlemen, approximately one hour ago, the Japanese launched an attack on the British Far Eastern Fleet here."

Commander Montgomery's finger rested on a point on the map roughly six hundred miles to *Yorktown*'s southeast. *Yorktown*'s CAG had decided to personally brief VB-11 rather than having Lieutenant Commander Brigante do so.

I know the CAG was going to choose one of the squadrons to sit in on. It does seem like he chooses us an awful lot for these sort of things though.

Brigante seemed nonplussed at Montgomery giving the briefing, sitting front and center in the first row.

"The Japanese have hit the *Victorious* and *Eagle* along with some other ships," Montgomery continued. "It is unknown how many Japanese carriers there are, but judging from the reports it would appear that their main striking fleet has come to the south of Ceylon."

Eric looked at the map, squinting.

"Lieutenant Cobb, you look perplexed," Commander Montgomery said.

"Sir, the last intelligence report stated that the Japanese fleet carriers were east of Ceylon," Eric said. "I'm no mathematician, but I don't think there's been enough time for them to sail that far south, has there?"

"It would appear that the intelligence reports were incorrect," Commander Montgomery said. "This thing seems to happen quite often when the Japanese carriers are involved."

That brought a grim chuckle from several in the room.

"The British have sent a general azimuth the enemy aircraft returned towards, but they have no firm information as to the location of the enemy fleet."

So our friends could literally just be over the horizon and not expecting us, or about to do to us what they apparently did to the British. That's just peachy.

"Don't they have any flying boats in the Maldives?" someone asked, looking at the map.

I'm more concerned we have to pass in that narrow area between the uppermost Maldives and Ceylon.

"The British sent all their flying boats north to Ceylon for reinforcements," Commander Montgomery stated.

The men looked at him, eyes wide in wonder, until he continued.

"The British gave Vice Admiral Fletcher a copy of their operational plan to better affect combining our fleets."

*Then we went and sank a bunch of **other** British sailors and smacked around some Italians. On top of that, we refueled yet again, delaying us another day. I can see this discussion in the history books now.*

"Are the torpecker pilots going to get any tin fish that work?" someone asked sotto voce.

That drew a baleful glare from Commander Montgomery.

"You gentlemen let me worry about VT-11, thank you very much," he snapped.

As much as the torpedo idiots go on about theirs is the only sure way to sink a ship rather than just let the air in, it's a valid question. I don't envy their job on the best of days, but getting shot down delivering weapons that don't work has to be a huge problem.

"In any case, VS-11 will be launching within the hour to conduct a search to our east," Commander Montgomery continued. "We'll ready a strike just in case they find something."

Eric looked at the clock on the bulkhead behind Montgomery.

*That's going to be downright interesting. I'm not sure there's enough time for a search **and** a strike.*

Eric sighed in relief as he realized the *Bonhomme Richard* was the duty carrier for the day, meaning that no *Yorktown* aircraft should be stuck possibly poking a *Hornet*'s nest of Japanese carrier planes.

*Then again, if there's a force this far north **and** one where they'd have to be to hit the British carriers? Well, we might as well all just slit our wrists and jump overboard now.*

"If the search finds anything, the plan is to conduct an attack even if it means we have to return in the darkness, gentlemen," Montgomery said. There was sudden dead silence in the room.

"The last report from the British was dire," Montgomery said. "They had another strike inbound, and had not fully refueled their surviving CAP from the attack which hit the *Victorious* and *Eagle*."

This news was also greeted with somber silence.

A carrier without her CAP is meat on the table, Eric thought. *Makes you wonder how many Japanese flattops are out there. If there's any consolation, the fact that the British don't know about **Bonhomme Richard** and **Independence**, it means our friends from the Rising Sun won't know either.*

Strangely, the thought didn't give Eric as much comfort as it might have before the news. If the British were getting pummeled *and* carriers were around Ceylon, it didn't take a strategic genius to see the IJN was indeed taking things seriously.

What in the Hell are the surface boys back and Pearl doing?

"All right gents, I'll be getting with the squadron leaders after this," Montgomery said. "They're serving sandwiches in the wardrooms. I suggest everyone get a meal, as we might be launching before dinner."

I.J.N.S. Akagi
1800 Local (0830 Eastern)
400 Miles Northeast of Addu Atoll
Indian Ocean
9 August

"Sir, all carriers have have recovered their aircraft," Rear Admiral Kaku stated.

Vice Admiral Yamaguchi turned to look inside the island, ignoring the drama on the flight deck. The final *Akagi* aircraft, Commander Fuchida's *Tenzan*, had just crash landed after the force's third strike. The CAG's aircraft had been damaged in some action.

His survival caps a long, strenuous day. But a victorious one.

Yamaguchi took a moment to smile at his inadvertent pun given the British losses on the day.

*We'll see what Ozawa-san has to say about my ability to manage the **Kido Butai** next time he sees Admiral Yamamoto.*

"Thank you, Rear Admiral Kaku. Compile the results from the other carriers and have the staff prepare to brief me in thirty minutes."

"Hai, sir," Kaku said. "Do we need to prepare a plan for strikes on Addu Atoll?"

Yamaguchi smiled at his subordinate's aggressiveness.

Better to have to rein in a tiger than prod a donkey into battle.

"I think we have done enough for His Majesty in this section of the Indian Ocean. We need to return to Ceylon and the reason we came here before Vice Admiral Ozawa runs out of aircraft."

Kaku bowed at that, then left the flag bridge.

*Or for that matter, before **we** run out of aircraft,*

Not for the first time, he was glad that the IJN had transitioned to sturdier, more modern aircraft based on the lessons the Germans and British had learned in Europe. The losses, at least what the staff had informed him of so far, had been troubling.

Roughly thirty aircraft shot down with another twenty or so damaged. Yes, we have spares, but I hate to lose so many pilots. Especially the ones we will just have to abandon to their fates.

In a perfect world, Yamaguchi would have had enough aircraft or ships to go search for the twenty or so aircrew from aircraft who had ditched on the way back to the *Kido Butai*. In reality, the best he'd been able to do was send a request back through Combined Fleet Headquarters to have Fifth Fleet's submarines in the area attempt to find the proverbial needles in the haystack.

"Sir, would you like to have your meal brought to you?" his steward asked. As if on cue from the inquiry, Vice Admiral Yamaguchi felt the first pangs of hunger he'd had all day.

It does neither me nor this force any good to pass out on this bridge, Vice Admiral Yamaguchi realized.

"I will take the meal in my cabin," he said. "It will have to be fast, I will be meeting with the staff shortly."

"YOU ARE CERTAIN?" YAMAGUCHI ASKED COMMANDER FUCHIDA forty-five minutes later.

Fuchida looks like hell. He cannot fly tomorrow.

The CAG had apparently been jumped by an expertly flown *Seafire*. It was only through pure fate that the *Tenzan*'s pilot had started a turn just as the British fighter opened fire. As a result, it was only Fuchida's arm in a sling and his tailgunner's blood all over his uniform rather than the man dead somewhere in the Indian Ocean.

"*Hai*, Admiral," Fuchida said, wincing. "I saw the *Victorious* explode myself from the second strike's torpedoes, and *Eagle* could not have survived the three more hits."

Those were certainly low numbers given both vessels crippled condition, but should be enough, yes.

"The third strike also scored at least two torpedo hits on what we believe to be *Ark Royal*, and another four on the *Malaya* or *Warspite*, two on the other battleship."

"Then you saw one of the battleships capsize before the British fighter attacked you?"

Fuchida nodded.

"She rolled onto her beam ends, then her magazines exploded," Fuchida said. "It is why the pilot banked."

Yamaguchi stood for a moment, contemplating his options.

Perhaps Kaku is right, I could continue to head south. We lack the ability to seize the Maldives, but if we can finish off the last two carriers then perhaps that would persuade the British to seek terms with us at least.

The *Ark Royal* and *Illustrious* were, if *Victorious*'s demise were correct, the last two modern carriers Queen Elizabeth's commonwealth possessed. If the former was as badly damaged as Fuchida claimed, then that left only *Illustrious*.

"Where is Fletcher?" he asked, looking across the table at the staff. "Do we have *any* word?"

"No, sir, none," Rear Admiral Kaku replied.

"Well, we do know he did not chase the Italians all the way to Mombasa," Vice Admiral Yamaguchi said. "But other than that, do we believe the Italian claims to have damaged a battleship?"

There was silence from the staff.

I do not want to insult Fuchida-san publicly, but aviators are known to exaggerate. I would take a grave risk with this force, especially as we do not know what is at Addu Atoll.

"In the morning, we will continue to have the *Tone* and *Chikuma* handle search operations," Yamaguchi said. "We will reinforce their search with aircraft from the *Kirishima* and *Hiei*. All sectors will have double the aircraft, and the entire Second Division will provide a CAP."

As he searched his staff's faces, Yamaguchi could see that his decision was not popular with Fuchida and a couple others.

I am sure they will tell me I am being far too cautious and that a strong CAP will hurt any strike we launch. Still, Fletcher has only two carriers, so a strong CAP prevents his blow from landing while ours will almost certainly get through.

"Let me know what our aircraft strength is within the hour," Yamaguchi finished. "But it is past time we get back to Ceylon in case Fletcher has decided to head *there* rather than attempt to rendezvous with the British first here in the south. In his shoes, given the reports Vice Admiral Ozawa has hopefully generated, it is what I would do."

With that, Yamaguchi nodded at the staff to dismiss them. To a man, the group bowed in his direction, then immediately set about their tasks.

I cannot help but think I am failing to see something. If only there was a way to speak with our British and Italian allies directly.

Yamaguchi looked at the map, mentally measuring the distance from Mogadishu to Mambasa. It was a long way to run with a fleet. Especially after apparently mauling an Italian force so thoroughly it had ran away rather than fight.

Something must have made a man with multiple battleships and two carriers, albeit small ones, flee like he was being chased by a pack of wolves, Yamaguchi pondered. *What was it?*

U.S.S. HOUSTON
2006 LOCAL (1036 EASTERN)
INDIAN OCEAN
9 AUGUST

THE KNOCK ON HIS HATCH WAS NOT UNEXPECTED, EVEN IF JACOB wished the visit was unnecessary.

Might as well pull this scab off the hard way. Sighing, he braced himself. "Enter!" he barked.

The hatch swung open to reveal Commander Farmer. The British officer's face was set in a hard line, his eyes fixed upon the bulkhead behind Jacob. Lieutenant Commander O'Malley, the *Houston*'s chaplain, followed along behind the British officer.

Guess I get to find out what O'Malley's made of, Jacob thought. He'd been very impressed with Lieutenant Commander Mulcahy, the vessel's former chaplain. Unfortunately, so had

"Close the hatch please, chaplain," Jacob said, standing and moving from behind his desk.

"Well sir, now I know there's bloody bad news," Farmer said, his voice wavering slightly. Jacob went to clasp the man on the shoulder, then stopped as the British officer stiffened.

"I'd rather not, sir," Farmer said, his voice clipped. "It's my brother, isn't it?"

"Yes, Commander, it is," Jacob replied simply.

"When?"

"This afternoon. The *Victorious* was lost when her bomb magazines exploded. Your brother was last seen belowdecks attempting to fight the fire."

"Thank you, sir."

Vice Admiral Godfrey sends his regrets, and has passed along that if there's anything he can do for you, do not hesitate to ask."

Jacob paused.

"I echo that sentiment, Commander.".

"Permission to speak freely, sir?" Farmer asked, the last part coming out almost as a sob.

"Yes, Commander, you've earned it," Jacob replied.

"I hope you fucking Yanks decide whether or not you want to be a part of this bloody war," Farmer spat venomously. "My brother might goddamn be alive now if your bloody Admiral had not had his dick up his arse with all the fueling and dawdling."

"Commander Farmer, that's not helpful," Chaplain O'Malley snapped.

"Let him speak," Jacob countermanded, waving the chaplain down.

Farmer looked at him, his mouth working but nothing coming out. Stopping, he swallowed hard.

"That's all I had to say, sir." Farmer stated, then came to attention. "Permission to return to my cabin."

"Permission granted, and I am sorry for your loss," Jacob replied. "What was said will remain in this room."

Farmer gave a short nod, saluted, then quickly moved out of Jacob's day cabin.

I hope this never becomes routine for me.

"Sir, how did word get to us so quickly?" O'Malley asked.

"Commander Farmer used to be Vice Admiral Cunningham's aide," Jacob replied. "I understand that the reason he was assigned to the *Repulse* was that his brother had just became the *Victorious*' executive officer, and Vice Admiral Cunningham didn't want them both in the same vessel."

Jacob looked at the map of the Indian Ocean hanging on the bulkhead behind his desk.

"Vice Admiral Cunningham apparently didn't make it off the

Victorious either," he continued. "The British appear to lose an admiral every time they fight Japanese carriers."

"It's been a bad last six months for their senior leaders any way you slice it," Chaplain O'Malley observed. "Phillips, Somerville, and now Cunningham."

"How is the crew's morale?" Jacob asked. "I assume scuttlebutt is running rampant."

"Can't keep many secrets aboard this ship, sir," O'Malley replied. "But the crew is ready to scrap with the Japanese again. Having the two big boys along helps with that."

Jacob chuckled.

"They do certainly look impressive. Let's hope that translates into them actually *being* impressive."

6

CHAOS DAWN

It is an invariable axiom of war to secure your own flanks and rear and endeavour to turn those of your enemy.

——**KING FREDERICK II, PRUSSIA**

MORTON RESIDENCE
0600 LOCAL (1200 EASTERN)
9 AUGUST

ONCE MORE, someone was knocking on their kitchen door.

"This sort of thing has *got* to stop," Patricia said as Jo stepped out of her bedroom.

"We are in violent agreement about that," Jo replied running her hand through her hair.

We were both up way too late last night. Especially for people who have to keep secrets. They'd sat up with Sam and David as the twins caught them up on everything that had happened in the last few months. The whole time, Jo had been distracted on what was likely happening out in the Indian Ocean. It had been a very sleepless night.

"Were you guys expecting company?" Sam asked lowly as he slid off of the couch bed and sauntered towards the kitchen.

It's kind of scary that a man that big can move that quietly. Patricia wondered why I asked who won hide and seek in her family. If she wasn't used to it, she'd know how weird it is that all of her brothers move like Injuns, with Sam the chief.

"No, we're not," Patricia answered, looking at Jo speculatively.

"I figure anything that Sam and David can't handle just might shrug off a shotgun," Jo said, then stopped.

Goddammit, she thought, relieved when Sam and David both started smiling. Patricia looked at all of them with a questioning glance.

"You want to get the door, Sam?" Jo asked with a giggle.

"Why yes, yes I think I will," Sam said, walking into the kitchen. She watched as the eldest Cobb threw the door open to look down at his younger brother.

"Didn't Mom teach you to *call ahead?*" Sam asked, dragging Nick Cobb into a giant bear hug.

"Agnes!" he said with a surprised smile as Nick's girlfriend walked into the Morton residence.

"Nick!" Patricia said simultaneously, rushing forward to hug her brother as well.

"What the hell? Is Eric going to show up tomorrow?" David asked, smiling as he also embraced his brother.

I notice he's not in his khakis, which means he didn't just get here. Jo met Agnes' eyes from behind all the embracing Cobbs and gave the secretary a knowing smile. The Portuguese woman just gave a slight smile and shrugged back.

"Well, there's no more room for anyone else to sleep here, so you guys better start looking for a place to stay," Patricia said, her smile belying her words.

"I assure you, we'll find room," Jo said. "Although it would be very amusing if my father found out I'd turned this into a boarding home."

"Amusing isn't the word I think would apply," Patricia said. "Let me get some coffee started."

. . .

"So now I'm in limbo," Nick said a few moments later. He glanced over at Agnes before continuing. "There's apparently been some big shake up at BuPers, which means that the previous order got rescinded."

Sam and David looked at one another, then at Nick.

"You know about Admiral King, right?" Sam asked.

"I've heard rumors that he's not in charge anymore, but no one's said anything directly," Nick said, drawing a startled gasp from Agnes.

"I'm sorry, I thought for sure Commander Emerson told you," she said. "Nick, Admiral King has been dead for almost two weeks."

Nick looked at her, thunderstruck.

"What?"

"Dropped dead of a heart attack," Sam said. "Scuttlebutt is in mid-argument with Secretary Knox."

"That explains why there's been some changes at BuPers, as I imagine whomever is going to replace him probably wants his own folks in charge," Nick said, eyes still wider than normal.

"Why would someone change out people in charge during a war?" Patricia asked. "That doesn't seem to make a lot of sense."

"The war is going badly," Jo stated flatly. "So I can imagine that will lead to changes of leadership. Especially since they've got a carrier admiral in Halsey who is *not* someone you chain to a desk."

"I can't believe Admiral Jensen's replacement still hasn't been named," Sam said. "I thought for sure that would have been done already."

"Might have happened and we just don't know it yet," Nick said, then took a pull of coffee. "Holy shit, I still can't believe King is dead though."

"Language, Nick," Sam stated lowly.

"Yeah, best watch your fucking mouth," Jo responded without a moment's hesitation, drawing a titter from Agnes and a glare from Sam.

"Anyway," David said, "do you guys care if we bring Major Haynes over for dinner tonight? We'd like you all to meet him."

Clearly this is a man who has gotten their respect, Jo noted. As well as their friendship.

"Where is Major Haynes from?" Patricia asked. "If we need to make something special for him, I can try and scrounge up some food."

"Upstate New York," Sam said. "He was born into money."

"What kind of money?" Patricia asked, genuinely curious. "Vanderbilt money?"

"He's kind of reticent to talk about it," David said. "Doesn't throw it around, but other people in the squadron said he's the sole heir to an optics fortune."

"I bet his family's just thrilled he's out here," Nick said "I imagine his Mom is like ours, just on steroids and with money to interfere."

Sam and David shared a pained look.

"His mother's dead, actually," David replied. "It's a story he's best able to tell."

Patricia, Sam, and Nick all swiveled their eyes towards David with various degrees of shock, then looked at Jo.

I can't believe he just said that, Jo thought as she grimaced. David at least had the decency to look briefly pained before Jo twisted the rhetorical knife.

"Oh, hello Major Haynes. Glad to meet you. Why don't we quiz you about what is probably the worst thing to ever happen to you?" Jo said sarcastically. "Let me tell you, I'm always happy when people ask me *that* question."

Self-consciously, Jo touched the burn scar on her arm. Sam reached over and patted her leg in a comforting way.

"Sorry Jo," Sam said, glaring at his twin. "His mother actually died of cancer last year. Major Haynes was in the Dutch East Indies."

"What took him to the Dutch East Indies?" Patricia asked.

"Killing Japanese," Sam replied.

Now I'm starting to understand what you guys see in him as a leader.

Jo reached down slowly so as not to draw attention to her movements. Finding Sam's hand on her leg, she squeezed it once to let him know it had stayed on her knee too long. He squeezed back, then took his arm away.

*Goddammit Sam, I hate the way you make me feel sometimes. I don't **think** you mean to, but Jesus.*

Looking across the table, Jo saw Agnes looking at Sam and her speculatively. Before Agnes could say anything, Jo's alarm clock went off.

"Well, Patricia, if you don't mind starting breakfast, I'm going to get a shower," Jo said.

"Wait," Sam stated, standing up.

"Wait *what*, Sam?" Patricia asked, then stopped and covered her mouth in horror.

"Wait I have to go use the restroom and don't think Jo wants to get scalded?" Sam replied. Before his sister could answer, he left. Jo gave him a moment, then followed.

I think that Eric needs to hurry up and get back here. There's something ... different about Sam and I.

A few minutes later, as she was finishing setting out her clothes, there was a knock on the door. She opened it to find Agnes.

This is a surprise.

Jo gestured for the other woman to come in, then closed the door behind her.

"I guess I can ask you—has always been as much a busybody as her brothers claim?" Agnes asked quietly, startling Jo.

"Uh..." Jo started, pondering the best way to answer. Agnes smiled.

"I will take that as a yes."

"I don't think she's a busy body per se," Jo said. "More she hasn't gotten punched in the face by life yet."

I mean, there was poor Peter, but that relationship hadn't really taken off.

A shadow seemed to cross Agnes' face.

"I don't' think you and I have that problem," Jo continued evenly.

"Yes, like you, I have suffered tragedy," Agnes said simply. "My father died when I was young, my mother a couple of years ago."

Oh my God, I cannot imagine. With a chill, her mind turned to where her father was. *I might not have to **imagine** soon.*

"I'm sorry, I have reminded you of something untoward," Agnes said, starting to turn to go.

"No, please, stop," Jo said. "I was just thinking about my father is all."

"Yes, I remember you mentioned he was in the Navy as well when we first met," Agnes said.

"Yes," Jo replied. "That seems like ages ago. But yes, you and I have both seen different things than Patricia."

"I think it makes both of us much more direct and less demure than what the Cobbs are used to," Agnes said. She then looked back at the closed door, raising an eyebrow as her gaze met Jo's.

"It's solid enough to block sound and the board outside squeaks. We're alone."

"I know where you and Patricia work now," Agnes said lowly.

"I don't know what you are talking about," Jo replied without a second's hesitation.

She turned back to the closet to compose herself, then realized that grabbing a dress when one was already on the bed was a dead giveaway of guilt.

Smooth Jo, really smooth. To attempt to salvage her gambit, she put the other dress back.

Have to remember to wear the padded bra, she thought, looking at the garment. *It's a little cold in that basement.*

"I am happy to see you are the soul of discretion," Agnes replied with a smile.

Yep, totally busted.

"I'm like a vault," Jo replied simply.

"Nick and I are getting married tonight."

Jo nearly dropped the dress and the slip that was going to go under it. She took two steps towards Agnes, causing the other woman to step back as if expecting an attack. Jo waved her concerns away, even as she spoke in a fierce whisper.

"I'm sorry, I swear I just heard you say you want to meet the vengeful spirit of Alma Cobb, matriarch of the Cobb family, in some dark alley," Jo said.

"What?" Agnes asked. "Nick's mother is…"

"I say vengeful spirit, because that woman will most certainly have a heart attack at the idea of one of her sons getting married without her meeting the bride in question," Jo said, her eyes wide in genuine terror.

Agnes covered her mouth and fought hard not to laugh.

"I'm serious," Jo said, her smile indicating she could at least see some of the humor. "I will not be an accomplice to murder nor sign my own death warrant in the form of Nick Cobb's marriage license."

"I was more worried about Patricia," Agnes said. "That she'll feel like I'm preying on her brother."

Jo smiled at that.

"Out of all the boys, Nick is the least afraid to tell Patricia to mind her own business," Jo said. "Just as long as this isn't a shotgun wedding, you'll be fine."

Agnes giggled.

"We are careful," she replied. "I have no desire to become pregnant and lose my job."

Jo nodded at that.

Stupid customs that arise from stupid men.

"Do I need to make sure his brothers are there?" Jo asked.

"No, just Patricia," Agnes said. "One of Sam and David's classmates owed me a favor. I have already arranged for the brothers to be told after they get to Ewa."

"Remind me to never cross an admiral's secretary."

"That is always a wise decision," Agnes replied.

"Compared to what you've already done, Patricia will be child's play. But, I need to get ready for work."

Agnes nodded, turned towards the door, then stopped to ask a question.

"Do you love Sam?"

"I don't know," Jo replied honestly and rapidly. "I'm not sure if I love Sam, or I love Eric and Sam's just the one who's here."

That was probably a bit of oversharing.

Agnes reached out a hand to touch Jo's arm, smiling sadly.

"When my fiancée died," Agnes said, "there was one night with his brother, too much wine, and things we'd both like to forget. I understand."

"Eric's not dead," Jo said quietly. "Nor are he and I officially an item."

"There is a reason some Catholics believe purgatory is worse than Hell," Agnes responded with a shrug. "It is much worse not knowing. Both about a relationship and whether someone is okay."

"There were...some unfortunate words passed," Jo replied.

"It is unfortunate that you need to get ready for work," Agnes said. "I am curious as to why you are not, as you say, an item?"

"Pride and stubbornness," Jo said. "Both of them mine. Plus a fear of loss."

"God knows the number of the hairs on our head and days in our lives," Agnes said. "Both are unknowable to us, so we should enjoy each day like it is our last."

"I lived each day like it was my last once," Jo said with a wistful smile. "It led to my father nearly putting me in a convent and a young man getting sent to the Philippines."

"Was he skillful at least?" Agnes asked. Jo looked at the other woman in shock, feeling her face warm.

Quite, thank you very much.

"Then not all was lost," Agnes said with a wicked look.

I am never playing poker with this woman. Oh Jesus Nick, are you really ready for her?

Before Jo could respond, Agnes opened the door, stepped into the hallway, and was gone.

Then again, ready or not, she'll be a very nice addition to the family.

Jo smiled, not feeling the least bit of guilt at her next thought.

Not the least because Patricia won't know what to do with her.

As if summoned, Patricia opened Jo's door and slipped in.

"You know, for someone who is concerned about her brothers seeing me in a state of undress, you sure don't care about knocking."

"My brothers are all on their way out to Ewa," Patricia said. "Apparently that's where Sam and David's squadron is temporarily staying."

"They just left Agnes?" Jo asked in a fierce whisper.

"Yes," Patricia replied.

"So *maybe* one of us should go keep her company?" Jo said.

Patricia took a deep breath.

"I'm not sure how I feel about that woman," Patricia replied. "I think Nick might have gotten in last night and stayed at her place."

Jo really hoped that her expression didn't match her internal ruminations.

You know, I think maybe I should just let it rip.

"I'm sure they did," Jo replied evenly. "And I hope it was amazing for Nick as long as he's been at sea."

Patricia looked at Jo, her eyes wide in shock.

"Josephine!"

"There's a war on, genius," Jo replied. "I doubt you sent the good Lieutenant Read out of here with just a familial hug."

If Patricia had been shocked before, Jo had a moment where she wondered if her roommate was going to lose consciousness.

You opened this dance 'Toots,' and we've been roommates long enough you should know better.

"But you know what's more important?" she continued, pressing her advantage. "I don't care, because if the last thought he has of you on this world is whatever happened in your bedroom, then at least he'll die knowing someone loved him."

Patricia's face sobered.

Good job, Jo. You may not have said 'unlike Peter,' but damn if Patricia didn't hear it.

Before Patricia could speak, Jo held up her dress and undergarments.

"Now if you want a shower, you'll go out and be a good hostess," Jo continued. "Or I'm going to go be a good hostess and wonder if I'm giving off a stench all day. That will not make me happy, especially if we're entertaining tonight."

"Fine, I'll go sit with her," Patricia said.

"Try not channeling your mother for about thirty seconds," Jo said. "While I've never met the woman, I'm pretty sure you'll get along a lot better with your brother's girlfriend."

Patricia rolled her eyes, but left.

I swear to God, someday I'll meet the famous Mrs. Cobb. I just hope she doesn't make me want to grab and give her a shake like Patricia does at times. I can see that going poorly for me.

Jo looked at the clock and cursed under her breath

Going to be a quick shower unless I just want to put my hair up. I think Commander Tannehill believes I have enough mannish habits already, I really don't need to start looking like one.

The sound of laughter from the kitchen made her smile as she slipped into the bathroom. It was Patricia's deep, surprised laugh that indicated Agnes had apparently said something quite witty.

I guess she took my advice to heart. Or maybe I just misunderstand her sometimes.

As she put her clothes on the vanity, she noticed the corner of a piece of paper sticking out from her jewelry drawer.

Well that's a little odd, she thought, pulling the drawer open. There was a folded up note inside. She pulled it out and recognized Sam's handwriting. It was quick read, and Jo made sure to pass over it twice to make sure it was not misunderstood.

That complicates things. That complicates things a lot.

Taking a deep breath to fight down rising panic, Jo put the note back in the drawer and began getting ready for the day.

Gonna suck when I tell Patricia that her brother went looking for us first at the library, then at the shipyard.

For a moment, Jo indulged herself in a fantasy of Sam meeting Patricia's former boss.

Probably fortunate for that handsy asshole he got reassigned to sanitation.

U.S.S. Yorktown
0400 Local (1800 Eastern)
350 Miles Southwest of Colombo
10 August (9 August)

"Sir, Lieutenant Commander Brigante would like to see all section leaders in the ready room."

"Thank you, I am awake," Eric said.

Actually I've been awake for the last half hour. But what's a lack of sleep between all us boys?

The sailor nodded from the hatchway, but only moved off once Eric actually swung his legs out from his bunk. He rubbed his eyes then looked at his watch.

Well, glad we both dodged the bullet of a dusk strike and possibly getting jumped in narrow waters. Now let's see what fresh hell awaits us this morning.

"I swear to God, I am never bunking with another one of you damn dive bomber pilots again," Lieutenant (j.g.) Adam Seward of VT-11 stated. The two men had been shuffled together in the most recent shift in bunking after the Battle of Mogadishu.

I get that the CAG thinks having people sleep alone after their roommate gets whacked is a morale issue, but I'm about to stab this son of a bitch while he's out, Eric thought.

"Well, the way this war's been going for torpedo pilots, I think one or the other of us won't have to worry about that problem after today," he returned angrily.

Seward rolled over and fixed Eric with a hard glare.

"Before you say a single word, I want you to consider who started this conversation," Eric snapped, buttoning up his shirt. "I don't like getting up early any more than you do."

Now that he was fully awake, Eric could hear the sounds of planes being moved about on the hangar deck. The bustle had a definite air of urgency.

*Something big is in the offing. Maybe I'll get a chance to avenge those 'lads' on the **Victorious** soon after all.*

"Quite frankly, you might as well get up," Eric said. "Beat the line to the head."

"Go to Hell," Seward said, rolling back over.

Suit yourself. He quickly visited the head to brush his teeth and do his morning business, then headed up to VB-11's ready room. To his surprise, he was the first section leader to arrive.

Brigante looks like he hasn't slept a wink.

The ashtray next to the squadron commander already had several butts in it, and Eric was reasonably sure that was not the first cup of coffee Brigante had consumed since lights out the previous night.

"Grab your plotting board," Brigante said by way of greeting. He pulled out his battered pack of Lucky Strikes and offered one to Eric.

"No thank you, sir," Eric said.

"You sure?" Brigante asked, fishing out his own cigarette. "I feel like now would be when I point out a condemned man should smoke them if he's got them."

"I'll wait until I see who's in the firing squad, sir," Eric replied. "Maybe they're all cross eyed."

Brigante gave him a small smile at that as the other sections leaders filed in.

"We can only hope to be so lucky," Brigante said, then turned to the gathered foursome.

"I've been up since oh two thirty," Brigante stated to the gathered group. "I intend to be sleeping warm in my bunk by fourteen hundred after a good day's work. I hope that you will all be doing the same."

With that, Brigante put his plotting board on the table in front of him.

Holy shit.

Eric noted that there were a series of locations moving inexorably northwards for most of the night. The positions then suddenly turned eastward away from *Yorktown*, then back southwards as it grew closer towards dawn.

If we keep coming southeast at our current speed, we'll stay barely two hundred miles apart when the sun comes up.

He did the math in his head again as he realized *Yorktown* and her compatriots had sped up over the last six hours.

No, we won't even be two hundred miles. Barely one hundred and fifty.

"It appears whomever is left in charge of the British fleet remnants is either a fool or has a noisy walk from his brass balls clapping together," Brigante said. "These position reports have been broadcast in the clear, followed by authentication in code, for the last eight hours."

"What?" Lieutenant Ramage and Lieutenant Dale Connors, White One, both asked simultaneously.

"Radar, gentlemen," Brigante replied after checking the hatch was closed. "The British have fully embraced it, and it appears the *Illustrious* has been keeping a steady relay of aircraft in contact with the Japanese using it."

Brigante took a puff of his cigarette.

"Which means, more than likely, they are going to die today," he continued. "Since as you can tell from the last position report, the Japanese have turned to swat the mosquitos behind them. I suspect they intend to launch a strike as soon as they figure out where the British force that's chasing them is located."

*The British are insane. Unless the **Ark Royal** is in better shape than the scuttlebutt said, it's **Illustrious** versus four Japanese carriers.*

"Kinda like chasing the gang that burned your house down and murdered your family into the night, isn't it?" Lieutenant Connors noted.

"With a lantern and while screaming at the top of your lungs," Eric replied with a grimace. "What has Admiral Fletcher's staff decided we're going to do?"

"It will be a predawn launch," Brigante replied. "We're throwing everything into the punch in the hopes we'll catch them looking south at the British carrier rather than at us."

"Are we forming up with the rest of the carriers?" Eric asked.

"Staff thinks that will be too hard in the darkness," Brigante replied. "So no, we're all going to go as we launch."

"Helluva a penalty for whomever's the quickest carrier," Lieutenant Ramage observed.

Before Brigante could reply, the *Yorktown*'s loudspeakers blared with reveille.

Hope Seward enjoyed his twenty extra minutes. Might be the last night's sleep he ever gets.

"I just pray the boys from the Atlantic Fleet haven't changed doctrine since we came out here," Brigante observed. "From what I understand talking to Vice Admiral Fletcher's staff, their little kerfuffle with what Admiral Kimmel calls the Usurper's Navy led to some second thoughts about how to do business."

This could get chaotic over the Japanese fleet. There won't be all that time to coordinate like there was over the Italian one.

The Pacific Fleet had developed certain rules for potential carrier battles for just such a situation as this. Things like which air groups attacked which targets, the priority of ship types, and rendezvous points had been discussed several times prewar.

Well, too late now. We got to the fight with whatever we have right now.

"Scouting Eleven will be carrying 1,000-lb. bombs as well," Brigante said.

"I hope they account for the different weight when they figure out their flight plan," Lieutenant Drake responded.

"It's going to be under two hundred miles by the time we launch," Eric said. "I don't think fuel is going to be our problem."

"Are the *Wildcats* going to actually be able to fly as escort?" Lieutenant Connors asked. "Not for all the good they'll do against the Japanese fighters, but more targets increases our odds."

"Pretty sure Commander Thach would slap you in the mouth for saying that," Brigante said. "The *Wildcats* have held their own, they've just been outnumbered every time we've gotten into a fight."

"Holding their own ain't saving our ass any," Connors snapped back.

"There's a reason those two Atlantic carriers have double the fighters," Brigante replied, his patience wearing thin. "When you get back, you can add those *opinions* to *your* after action report."

The rest of VB-11 began filing in, ending the discussion. Eric took his customary seat near a ventilation outlet, as he was sure it was about to get almost fog like with cigarette smoke.

Only thing I like about when we go to General Quarters: The damn smoking lamp gets turned off.

He looked at the plotting points on the map once more, noting where the *Victorious* had apparently gone down.

Commander Martin, I'll get a hit for you chaps.

Eric felt a slight burning in his eyes as he thought of the gathered British flyers, then blinked it away.

Least I can do for a shot of rum and some mail.

EWA FIELD MARINE CORPS AIR STATION
1200 LOCAL (1800 EASTERN)
9 AUGUST

"WELL I DON'T KNOW, GENTLEMEN, I MIGHT HAVE HAD OTHER plans tonight," Adam said airily as he looked at the three Cobb brothers. "I mean, it being my first time in Hawaii and all."

"Sir, the Royal Hawaiian has a hell of a spread," Sam replied earnestly.

Man looks a bit nervous, like there's some reason he really wants me at the Royal Hawaiian.

"Plus while our sister's kind of taken, her roommate Jo is available," Nick said.

Oh man, if you had eyes in the back of your head.

Sam's face had gone from exasperated to homicidal in a flash. David reached out and shoved his twin in the arm, causing the man to nearly swing at him.

"Lieutenant Cobb, I assure you that *I* am quite taken by an amazing woman," Adam said with a smile. "Although I'm sure Miss Morton would appreciate your efforts."

"I wouldn't bet on that with anything you enjoy owning," Sam rumbled. Once again, David swatted his brother.

You three must have been fascinating to have in the same house. There are definitely times I wish I hadn't been an only child.

The thought of his upbringing and associated memories of his mother triggered a brief wave of melancholy. Shaking himself out of it, Adam was about to say something when there was the sound of an aircraft in the distance. All three aviators stiffened and turned towards the noise.

"Didn't you say no one was flying out of here today?" Sam asked Adam, his tone worried.

"No one was," Adam replied. He stopped for a second, listening more intently. "That's some sort of large bird, like a *Fortress*."

"Transport," David said, pointing. Following his finger, Adam saw the aircraft after a few moments as well.

"What the hell, I don't see a damn thing," Nick said.

"Which is why you ride in a ship that sinks itself on purpose," Sam replied. After a moment, he relaxed.

"Looks like one of those Douglas transports."

"DC-3," Adam said. "Or whatever the Navy calls it."

That brought a chuckle from both Sam and David, eliciting a puzzled look from Nick.

"Major Haynes hasn't been a Marine for long," Sam said. "It shows itself from time to time."

They watched as the transport plane, in Navy colors, did a circle around the station, then lined up to come in for a landing.

"Huh, brave pilot trying to put that thing down on this runway," Sam noted. His voice held a slight bit of professional concern.

"Has to be some reason he's setting down here instead of Barber's Point or Ford Island," David agreed.

"Can't think of a good one, especially if he wants to take back off again," Adam replied. "Good thing you tore yourself away from headquarters to join us, Nick. You might be about to see a Grade A fuck up."

Regardless of the pilots' professional opinion, the transport flared in for Ewa's short runway. Touching down at the very end, the pilot managed to bring the transport to a stop with room to spare.

"Well here comes the welcoming committee," Sam noted, pointing at the cars rushing over from Barber's Point.

I'm thinking that this is someone who is both important and also not a fan of pomp and circumstance.

"Boss, you sure we want to still be hanging around?" Sam asked, seeing the transport starting to taxi towards their hangar.

"We'd look kind of suspicious running away from a transport, wouldn't we?"Adam replied, then turned and looked around the hangar.

"Heads up folks, we may have some sort of bigwig walking in here in a few seconds," he shouted to the enlisted Marines all working on aircraft. "Keep doing what you're doing, there's a damn war on."

"Roger sir," Master Sergeant Bolan, VMF-21's chief maintenance NCO, shouted back. He and the rest of the squadron's mechanics were giving each of the FM-2's a once over prior to reembarking on the *Chenango*. With the next stop likely being a distant island garrison, it was the best time to figure out any maintenance shortcomings.

The transport actually slowed to a stop a hundred and fifty feet short of the hangar, the twin engines loud even inside of the structure. After another couple of minutes, the pilot shut down first the port, then the starboard radial. The sound of rapidly approaching cars grew louder in the sudden silence.

Kind of crazy to throw a monkey wrench at the welcome party like that.

"I suppose we're about to meet someone important," David muttered.

"Last guy who surprised us on an airfield was an asshole," Sam replied. "Of course, he got burnt to a crisp later, so there's some balance in the world."

Adam didn't ask for an explanation as he watched the transport's door open.

Whomever it is, clearly they know how to make an entrance.

THE WHOMEVER IN QUESTION, ONE ADMIRAL THOMAS DUNLAP, DID indeed know 'how to make an entrance.' With a briefcase full of operational plans and communications tightly in his hand as the Douglas' exit hatch opened, Dunlap spared a moment to think of the long, insane path to this point.

Well Ernest, you son-of-a-bitch, I hope you're seeing this front and center from your spit in Hell. Looks like this "elephant" not only came back from the graveyard, but is about to go out and try to win this damn war.

"Sir, I really wish you'd let me actually be your aide," Commander Frederick Powers observed. Like his admiral, Commander Powers was dressed in spotless, starched whites, his submariner's dolphins gleaming as the two men stepped onto the tarmac. The tall, gangly man's blue eyes met his admiral's green ones.

"God gave me two hands so I could carry my own briefcase, Fred," Admiral Dunlap replied. He glanced over to the hangar in front of them, seeing a group of officers standing around a dark blue FM-2 *Wildcat*. Glancing to his right, Admiral Dunlap saw a group of four cars pull onto the edge of the runway then start racing towards them.

"I don't think Vice Admiral Halsey is going to be happy with you," Commander Powers observed.

"Bill Halsey is about to have the weight of an entire theater lifted off his shoulders," Dunlap replied. "I'll be lucky if he doesn't try to kiss me like a long lost bride."

"Thank you, sir, for that truly terrifying visual," Powers replied.

"Let's go talk to some Marines, shall we?"

With the rhetorical question, Dunlap set off for the hangar. He watched as the group of officers first stared at him in shock, then looked at the balding, stout officer they were all standing around. As he got closer, Dunlap realized the middle officer was not actually short, he just appeared that way standing next to the two hulking men on either side of him.

Is it just me or do three of these men look related?

"Group attention!" the senior officer said. Something about his face seemed familiar.

"Good afternoon gentlemen," Dunlap said, returning the Marine major's salute. "What unit is this?"

"VMF-21, sir," the major replied. "I'm the squadron commander, Major Haynes."

That's how I know him. He's the squadron commander that busted Bowles' kid in the chops for screwing another officer's wife.

"Well you're a long way from Pensacola, major," Dunlap observed, smiling and extending his hand. He could see that Major Haynes looked confused as to how Dunlap knew who he was or why there was a four-star admiral inside of his hangar.

"I go where the Marines send me, sir," Major Haynes stated as he shook the admiral's hand, then gestured at his companions. "Sir, this is Captain Sam Cobb, his brother David, and his younger brother Lieutenant Nick Cobb,"

*So they are **all** related.*

"Your poor mother must be worried sick," Admiral Dunlap observed as he looked the three men over. "Are there any of you left back home?"

A brief moment of worry crossed all three men's faces.

"No, sir," David replied. "Our brother Eric is aboard *Yorktown* and our sister works for the library downtown."

Dunlap saw the other Captain Cobb give his brother a sideways glance, like he knew something that Sam did not. Before Dunlap could ask any more questions, however, they were interrupted by rapidly approaching footsteps.

"Admiral Dunlap, sir, I think your pilot can't read a map," Vice Admiral Halsey said as he came walking up. The man's craggy face was split into a cautious smile, and he saluted Dunlap as the man turned around.

"My pilot can read a map just fine, Bill," Dunlap replied with a broad grin. "You know I hate pomp and circumstance."

"And love surprises," Vice Admiral Halsey replied, his face also breaking into a grin. "Which, sir, you might want to come with me, as it appears Vice Admiral Fletcher is about to spring one."

The three Cobb brothers' expressions all perked at Halsey's comment.

This isn't the place to have a conversation if we don't word spreading from here to Honolulu by nightfall.

"We can talk on the way back to headquarters, Bill," Dunlap said. "Commander Powers, get Major Haynes' and these men's information. They're cordially invited to dinner tonight at my quarters."

There were various degrees of concern on the three Cobb brothers' faces, while Major Haynes looked nonplussed. Indeed, if Dunlap didn't know better, he would have sworn the youngest Cobb brother looked almost panic stricken.

I feel like I'm missing something, but Commander Powers can figure it out, Dunlap thought. *I don't expect to get blown off by some lieutenant unless he's literally getting married.*

As Commander Powers started taking down the requisite information, Admiral Dunlap turned and walked towards Vice Admiral Halsey's waiting vehicle. Halsey's aide stood by as the two flag officers slipped into the Packard, then closed the door behind them.

"I suppose there's a good reason you wanted me to land out here, Bill?" Dunlap said once they started to pull away. "Because my pilot isn't looking forward to getting back out."

Vice Admiral Halsey's face dropped the façade of optimism it had borne previously.

"I think ol' Black Jack has dropped the ball out in the Indian Ocean," Halsey said, fists clenched and eyes narrowed.

"Is that because he has actually done something wrong or because you want to be out there instead of him, Bill?" Dunlap asked quietly. Halsey, clearly set to launch into a tirade of Fletcher's sins, stopped.

"Before I left Washington, Secretary Knox let me in on the orders he had Admiral Stark dispatch along with the *Bonhomme Richard* and *Independence*," Admiral Dunlap said. "Given the damage to the *Essex*, *Wasp*, and *Ranger* at the Battle of Iceland, he was not comfortable with basically denuding the Atlantic Fleet of its operational carriers."

Dunlap watched as shock, understanding, then sorrow crossed Halsey's face while he continued.

"Sir, I thought the *Essex*, *Wasp*, and *Ranger* suffered no damage!" Halsey stated.

"Well, that's what we told the public," Dunlap replied. "The *Essex* took a torpedo, while the *Wasp* and *Ranger* each caught one of those new German glide bombs."

"Jesus," Halsey said, his face paling. "And we thought the Senate was in an uproar over what they were told."

"Especially given that the Krauts and *their* Limeys smacked the living crap out of the *Washington*, *North Carolina*, and *South Dakota*," Dunlap responded.

"When is the public going to be informed on how heavy the losses were?" Halsey asked. "Bad news doesn't get better with age, and the man in the street still believes we lost some transports and old battleships."

We're lucky we "just lost some transports." When Secretary Knox had briefed him on the war to date upon his recall to active duty, Dunlap had nearly vomited.

"Once there's a victory to overshadow what happened," Dunlap stated. "Which Vice Admiral Fletcher has delivered part of one."

"What were his orders, if I may ask?" Halsey inquired.

He recovers from bad news quickly, at least.

"At no point was Vice Admiral Fletcher to allow the *Bonhomme Richard*, *Independence*, *Massachusetts*, or *Indiana* to drop below enough fuel to be able to make it past the Cape of Good Hope and into the Central Atlantic," Admiral Dunlap stated.

"Here I figured ol' Black Jack was channeling his uncle," Halsey replied, tone somber. "This is the situation so far."

Dunlap had a sensation akin to falling off a tall building as Halsey succinctly recounted what had been happening in the Indian Ocean.

Mother of God.

"I'm glad I'm not in Washington right now, as Admiral Tovey was already fit to be tied," Dunlap observed somberly. "I imagine he's positively apoplectic at this point, especially if Vice Admiral Cunningham is confirmed dead. Who did you say was in charge of *Illustrious?*"

"Rear Admiral Philip Vian," Halsey replied. "He's the senior surviving officer with the British fleet. Vice Admiral Cunningham's deputy was also killed aboard the *Malaya.*"

"The Japanese seem to be very good at killing admirals," Dunlap said, pursing his lips. "Let's hope they're not going to add Jack Fletcher to the list."

Halsey glanced at his watch.

"Jack should be in contact with them right about now."

Dunlap shook his head angrily.

"I truly hope I'm not taking command of a fleet just in time for my carriers to get sunk an ocean away," he remarked. "When this is over, we're bringing *Yorktown* and *Enterprise* back to Pearl."

Halsey nodded as Dunlap continued, looking out the window towards the Ford Island.

"I had already anticipated those orders, sir," Halsey said. "They were just awaiting the arrival of whomever took over from me. I don't think the British will be happy about it, though."

"Our navy has worked on the same warplan for over twenty-five years, Bill," Dunlap stated. "The British can either help us execute it or not, but I'm not losing any more vessels trying to hold on to someone else's colonies."

"Sir, you sound like you don't think Jack is going to win."

"Jack is outnumbered six to four, and that's before you count that second carrier force that's apparently up near Ceylon," Dunlap replied. "My best hope is that he knows when to call it a day. Unlike this Vian fellow."

"Oh, Vian is being very cagey," Halsey said, holding up a hand as warding off an attack. "When we were testing night operations off Canada back in March, the British developed a way to maintain contact with our *Avengers*."

Dunlap raised an eyebrow as they passed through Pearl Harbor's main gate. He returned the sentry's salute, noting that the Marines manning the machine gun never left their weapon's mount.

On one hand, I would think that's a bit of paranoia. On the other hand, I'd feel awfully stupid if a Japanese Fifth Columnist showed up in my office to put two in my head.

"Sir?"

"Sorry Bill, I got distracted," Dunlap said. "Run that by me again."

Halsey nodded.

"The Brits figured out a way to put a bigger ferry tank in the *Avenger*'s bomb bay," Halsey said. "Whole plane would go up like a roman candle if anyone shot it, but it added another hundred and fifty miles to the range."

"Could they put any bombs under the wings?" Dunlap asked, intrigued.

"Not much point in doing that, sir," Halsey replied. "The important thing is keeping contact with your opponent so you *or someone else* can smack him at dawn the next day."

He has a point. This isn't like a gunnery battle where both sides are going to stand toe to toe until someone gets tired or scared.

Further discussion was interrupted by the car coming to a stop.

"I will need someone on your staff to bring me up to speed on carriers, Bill," Dunlap said.

"Sir?"

"I've been on the beach for almost ten years, Bill," Dunlap said. "My predecessor clearly didn't understand what carriers could do and it got him killed. I want to make sure I don't make the same mistakes."

"Rear Admiral Towers is a good man to talk to, sir," Halsey replied after a moment. "He's on his way back from Florida."

"What was he doing in Florida?" Dunlap asked.

"We're planning a surprise for the Emperor," Halsey said. "He has an idea using some B-25s and a carrier. Needed to go to Eglin Field to try it out."

Let's hope I have carriers left, Dunlap thought grimly, looking at his watch. *Going to be a long day of waiting.*

I.J.N.S. A*KAGI*
0435 L*OCAL* (*1835* E*ASTERN*)
N*ORTHERN* I*NDIAN* O*CEAN*
10 A*UGUST* (*9* A*UGUST*)

"S*IR, WE ARE READY TO LAUNCH THE COMBAT AIR PATROL,*" R*EAR* Admiral Kaku said. "As per your orders, we have made First Division the duty carriers today."

Vice Admiral Yamaguchi turned his bleary eyes towards the man. The two officers were in the vice admiral's day cabin, Yamaguchi having finally retreated there after a night of poor rest thanks to what he assumed was the *Illustrious'* air group.

"Thank you, Kaku-san," Yamaguchi replied. "Has the weather improved any?"

"We still have the low hanging cloud and squalls from last night, sir," Kaku replied. "But the *Chikuma*'s scouts report that the weather is clearing to the south."

"How long ago did they launch?" Yamaguchi asked, trying to clear the fog from his head.

I need tea, badly.

"Thirty minutes," Kaku replied. "Given the losses yesterday and the need to cover more area than expected, I countermanded your orders to double up on scouts but did narrow the sectors. Given the weather, I thought it was prudent."

"Very well," Yamaguchi stated, rubbing his eyes and nodding. "I do not know how the British were able to fly in that crap. "I would like to have not been harassed the entire night."

"I am sure we can properly thank our friends for our sleeplessness before lunch," Kaku said, eyes narrowing.

"How long as it been since the last British aircraft departed?" Yamaguchi asked.

"An hour, sir," Kaku replied. "We began spotting our strike immediately after they left the *Taiho*'s radar screen."

That is not nearly enough sleep for me or the pilots. There will be accidents.

"We should have determined they were merely feinting sooner," the vice admiral said aloud. "It would have been a miracle for them to hit in those conditions."

Kaku shrugged.

"They managed to damage one of Ozawa-san's carriers in the darkness," his chief of staff replied. "Our opponents seem desperate."

Yamaguchi grunted at that.

"Cornered rats, my friend," he replied. "You and I both know the Army will take no prisoners once they storm the island."

Kaku nodded, his face passive. Yamaguchi was aware his chief of staff believed such a course of action was proper given the extended supply lines.

It is unfortunately he cannot see what it does to the enemy's willingness to fight. None of the zealots can.

"Do you still wish to hold back a second strike, sir?" Kaku asked, politely changing the topic.

"Yes," Yamaguchi snapped, then caught himself. "If Fuchida is correct, there is only the *Illustrious* to our south. I still want to have something to throw at Fletcher when he makes his appearance."

I can only imagine how complicated this would be if we also had to account for land attacks from Ceylon or suppress the island's garrison.

Yamaguchi once more ran through the timing in his head.

*At least this way we can immediately begin preparing our second strike in anticipation of Fletcher being sighted **or** the need to hit the British again. Torpedoes and bombs do not care what flag a warship is flying, after all.*

Thinking of torpedoes made Yamaguchi consider another factor.

"How many *Sandaburo* torpedoes do we have left?" he asked.

"The first strike will have the last of the weapons," Kaku replied.

"I hope that damn American submarine captain hit a mine on the way home," Yamaguchi snarled.

"It is unfortunate our pilots were so zealous in going after the battleships as well as the carriers," Kaku stated.

"Fuchida-san said the *Illustrious* was still on the edge of a squall," Yamaguchi replied, defending the *Akagi*'s CAG. "*Warspite* and *Malaya* are old, but I will take either of them being destroyed rather than a continued threat."

"I hope the weather gods do not smile as fortuitously on *Illustrious* today," Kaku observed.

"The weather gods can smile on whom they please at this point," Yamaguchi replied. "Unless she's underneath a hurricane, we will sink her with the first strike or the second."

As if on cue, there was the sound of rain falling on the *Akagi*'s flight deck. Yamaguchi fought the urge to head up towards the bridge and look out at the squall

If I go up to the bridge, the staff will feel the need to wake up. I need them fresh, if only for another hour.

"Do not have the pilots man their planes until the rain stops," Yamaguchi ordered. "Turn us back northward to buy us some time."

"Yes admiral," Kaku said. "This will also give the searchers more time to find the *Illustrious*."

Yamaguchi could have kicked himself.

I am tired and not thinking clearly.

"I do not think Fletcher would be in range yet," he said aloud. "However, better to be safe about it. Tell the staff good work for not becoming overly focused like their admiral did."

"Yes sir," Kaku replied with a small bow. "Due to our losses, the staff believed it prudent to only use the seaplanes and maximize our strikes."

U.S.S. HOUSTON
0535 LOCAL (1920 EASTERN)
NORTHERN INDIAN OCEAN
10 AUGUST (9 AUGUST)

I wish I was in Hawaii right now, Jacob thought as he completed his circuit of the *Houston*'s deck. *Probably a wonderful afternoon to sit on the back porch with Jo and just read something from the library.*

He moved aside in the predawn gloom as one of the heavy cruiser's damage control parties passed aft.

"Morning captain," the chief petty officer in charge greeted him.

"Morning chief," Jacob replied, then quickly added, "Carry on."

Wonder what they're doing? He wondered briefly, then cleared the question from his mind. Damage control was not his job anymore, fighting the *Houston* was.

If the XO and Lieutenant Haven have a plan, best to leave them to it.

Haven, the *Houston*'s damage control officer, had been one of the wardroom's replacements after the Dutch East Indies. Trained at the school only established in November '42 to take advantage of what the Royal Navy had shared, the young officer had relentlessly trained the heavy cruiser's damage control parties.

*Here's to hoping that man has **no** opportunity to put theory into practice.*

Jacob climbed the ladder to the bridge, took a deep breath, and stepped into the structure.

"Captain on the bridge!"

"At ease," Jacob said. "What's the latest from the *Yorktown*?"

I hope I sound way more rested than I actually am.

He'd had a terrible night's sleep, especially given the last signal from the *Repulse*.

Not sure if I like the idea of being a forward picket, but we'll see how that works out for us. When the *Yorktown* turned south into the wind, the *Massachusetts*, *Repulse*, *Houston*, and four destroyers were going to continue moving to the east. They'd join the *Indiana*, *Exeter*, and four more destroyers to reform TF 25. Ostensibly their mission was to be prepared to close with the suspected enemy carrier force and finish off what the air strike did not kill. However, Jacob strongly suspected their real purpose was to be so tempting a target that the Japanese split their own return strike.

Bait. We're about to be freakin' bait.

"The last signal from *Yorktown* is that she will be conducting launch operations in ten minutes," Lieutenant Ness reported crisply. "The XO left strict instructions to go to General Quarters at that time, but no sooner."

Which is why Commander Sloan is probably one of the best XOs this vessel has ever had. Myself included.

"Commander Sloan also left instructions to inform you we are ready in all respects for a surface action," Lieutenant Ness stated. "Barring your countermanding orders, he has directed the main battery to load armor-piercing."

"Well, I think that will certainly work against carriers if the flyboys get lucky and cripple one," Jacob said.

Too bad our secondaries are loaded with those fancy new shells that were sent over from the **Mauna Loa**.

The new ammunition's mechanism was apparently secret, with a the manual on its use restricted to Jacob, Commander Sloan, and Lieutenant Commander Willoughby's eyes only. Called the "variable time" fuse, the new shells apparently used radio signals to detonate in close proximity to attacking bombers rather than at a set altitude. Only available in 5-inch shells, it was supposed to make the *Houston*'s secondary guns more lethal.

I'll believe it when I see it. It also makes the shells quite useless against enemy surface vessels, so here's to hoping we and everyone else have time to change out fuses if the enemy's closer than we think.

"Looks like there's a fair bit of weather developing to our east," Commander Farmer observed as she stepped onto the *Houston*'s bridge. The man's voice was calm and he appeared back to his unflappable self on a quick examination. It was only when he met Jacob's gaze that the façade flickered for a moment.

"Indeed," Jacob replied. "I hope the flyboys don't get lost."

"Well, the American flyboys, that is," Farmer replied grimly. "If it keeps the Japanese from finding us, that's a bonus."

"Sir, signal from the *Massachusetts*," the talker said. "Prepare to execute separation."

"I'm not familiar with how your aircraft carriers conduct operations, sir," Farmer stated. "What exactly are you blokes doing?"

"Usually its searchers first, then a strike at whatever they find,"

Jacob replied. "But apparently your snoopers' positions were considered accurate enough to swing at."

"I hope the staff aren't wrong," Farmer replied.

"Sir, the *Massachusetts* is coming about," the OOD reported, pointing. Jacob nodded, seeing the signal coming from the big battleship a few moments later.

"That tears it then," he said, then quickly issued orders to the helm. As the *Houston*'s own bow swung to the new heading, he spared a glance towards the *Yorktown*.

There are a bunch of young men getting ready to go die aboard that flight deck. That is madness. Give me broadsides any day of the week.

"Sir! The *Massachusetts* reports a radar contact, bearing oh eight oh true, just at the edge of her scope."

Jacob turned to the talker even as he tried to do the geometry in his head.

*Good on the **Massachusetts** using a true bearing as we're all turning in this formation.*

"That's got to be a searcher," Farmer observed. "Which means either they launched very early this morning..."

"Or we're even closer than we think," Jacob replied, lips pressed in a thin line.

I need to visualize this on a map.

"Lieutenant Ness, you have the conn," he barked after a moment. He quickly walked to the *Houston*'s tactical plot, Farmer close behind him. The group that had been maintaining the hasty bridge plot parted, and he looked down at the map.

"If that aircraft is coming directly from his carriers, they turned sometime in the last hour," Jacob said after a few moments. "If he's not on the outward leg, then we have serious problems."

"That or the Japanese are running a ridiculously short search arc," Farmer noted.

"Sir, the *Independence* is vectoring CAP towards the bogey," the talker reported.

Jacob noted it was slowly getting lighter outside the *Houston*'s bridge. Even so, he did not envy the fighters attempting to find and shoot down the Japanese search aircraft.

Only good thing about that is we're going to be hard to see before the fighters get to him. First thing he'll see is wakes.

"What is the *Yorktown* doing?" he asked.

"Continuing to launch, sir," the talker reported back after a moment. "No signals reported from her."

"Sir, the *Massachusetts* is signaling twenty-five knots," Lieutenant Ness reported.

"She's rather fast for a large lady," Farmer muttered.

"We've got places to be, looks like," Jacob remarked, feeling the *Houston*'s own engines starting to grow louder. The cruiser's deck vibrated beneath his feet as she began gathering speed.

We're going to need a long refit after this cruise. While we haven't taken any damage yet, we've been driving the old girl hard.

It was a tense twenty minutes as the CAP began to head towards the still closing contact. The swirling colors of dawn were readily apparent as the pair of F6Fs off of the *Independence* finally found the Japanese aircraft. Less than two minutes after that, the Japanese aircraft was falling to the Indian Ocean...just as another contact was reported.

"I think our opponents are going to figure out very fast that we're here and what direction we are approaching," Farmer said. "Search planes disappearing in a given area is a sure sign of enemy action."

Only if their staff is on the ball.

The sound of several aircraft flying overhead was audible even over the *Houston*'s own engines. Jacob quickly walked out to the starboard bridge wing just in time to see the receding group of planes in the brightening sky.

Godspeed men, he thought, once more cognizant that he was seeing pilots heading to their own executions. It was impossible to confirm in the poor light, but a look at the paint scheme led him to believe the aircraft were the *Bonhomme Richard*'s. Bringing his gaze down to sea level, Jacob realized he could now easily make out the other vessels of TF 25 in the gloom.

"Going to be a long day, sir," Farmer said, standing beside him.

"Very long indeed," Jacob replied.

7

THE NEUTRALITY OF ELECTRONS

The art of war on land is an art of genius, of inspiration. In that of the sea there is nothing of genius or inspiration. The general of the sea has need of only one science, that of navigation. The one on land has need of them all."

— **NAPOLEON BONAPARTE**

AKAGI COMBAT AIR PATROL
0710 LOCAL (2140 EASTERN)
NORTHERN INDIAN OCEAN
10 AUGUST (9 AUGUST)

ISORO SHOOK HIMSELF VIOLENTLY, fighting the fatigue that had once more caused his head to droop downwards. Taking one hand off the throttle, Isoro smacked his leg several times, attempting to get his blood flowing faster.

This CAP has just begun, he thought angrily.

Looking down, Isoro briefly considered the stimulant pills in his flight suit pocket before deciding against them.

I will need them if enemy aircraft show up. They make me jittery anyway.

Isoro took a deep breath as he brought the stick over into a gentle turn. The *Kido Butai* was laid out in its usual box formation ten thousand feet below him, both line of carriers slowly curving back to the east after spending a little over an hour steaming south into the wind.

Part of me wishes I was flying with that strike.

He looked down as he crossed over the , crossing over the *Hiei* and *Kirishima*. The two veteran battleships' turrets were swinging back and forth as their gunnery officers conducted final checks.

Then again, there cannot be that many enemy fighters left after yesterday.

Allegedly the staff had changed the duty carrier roster from *Hiryu* and *Soryu* because the Second Division had more available strike aircraft after the previous day's efforts. Isoro could believe it having seen how many of the First Division's dive and torpedo bombers had staggered back from the third strike.

Even more frightening is how many would have been lost without the modifications to the fuel tanks and pilot armor. I wonder how **Soryu** *and* **Hiryu**'s *fighter squadrons fared yesterday with the old* **Zeros**.

His radio crackled, jerking him out of his his distraction. Looking around, Isoro sheepishly realized his *chutai* had flown ten miles further south than he'd planned.

Dammit, maybe I should take some of those pills... he had time to think before his blood ran cold.

"Attention! Attention! Many enemy aircraft inbound, two eight oh true!"

As the *Akagi* repeated the warning, Isoro brought his *Shiden*'s nose around and started to climb. Once the fighter was trimmed and rising, he snapped his oxygen mask closed and ensured that he had a good flow. Belatedly, he remembered the pills. Once more, he reconsidered whether he needed them, then laughed at his stupidity. It was quick work unsnapping his mask, gulping down the two pills, then resnapping.

Well I guess we have found the Americans.

Isoro looked left and right for other *chutai* to join up on. Below, the

Kido Butai began turning once more into the wind, black smoke pouring from funnels as the vessels accelerated.

They're coming from the slightly northwest. At least the carriers can both open the distance and launch reinforcements.

Roughly ten thousand feet below and twenty-five miles away from Isoro, Vice Admiral Yamaguchi was looking at the map in front of him as the *Kido Butai*'s staff reacted with near panic.

"One at a time!" Rear Admiral Kaku roared at the staff. His shout brought a momentary calm to the *Akagi*'s flag spaces.

"First, what was the response from the *Kirishima* regarding her search aircraft?" Kaku asked.

"They cannot raise three of their scouts," a harried commander replied, the man's skin almost pale. "They simply believed the aircraft were maintaining radio silence."

*If we survive the next hour, we must figure out a way to make sure **that** never happens again. Or a way for the aircraft to know that it is being detected by radar.*

He dimly recalled their German allies mentioning some sort of countermeasure device aboard their submarines, but pushed the thought away as unimportant at the moment.

"How long until the Second and Third divisions can launch?" Yamaguchi asked, still looking out the bridge windows.

"The Second Division reports they will be able to launch as soon as we finish coming back into the wind," Kaku replied, turning from the staff. "Third Division had not warmed up their aircraft and will need more time."

That is not a sufficient time!

"Have all carriers launch what aircraft they have available." Yamaguchi ordered. "They will land and recover after the American strike. Fighters will augment the combat air patrol as they launch."

"Sir?" Kaku asked, his eyes wide.

"Fletcher has launched an attack against us from two flight decks," Yamaguchi said, his face saturnine as he regarded his chief of staff. "*Wildcats* lack range to escort, so our CAP will have an advantage if they launch now. We cannot get *Shokaku* or *Taiho*'s strike aircraft warmed up and launched in time, so we must take this first attack."

"Understood," Kaku said, then quickly bowed. "Sorry Vice Admiral." With that, the Chief of Staff turned and began issuing Yamaguchi's orders over the din of *Akagi* starting to launch her emergency CAP.

I need to know where Fletcher is, right now, Yamaguchi realized.

"Have the Second Division set aside two *chutai* of *Zero*es and one of torpedo bombers to follow the American strike home after they strike," Yamaguchi said.

"Yes sir," Kaku replied.

They will also likely die getting me the information we need. At least coming in behind a returning strike they will be harder to sort out as hostile.

A runner burst into the compartment just as Kaku was beginning to issue Yamaguchi's orders.

"*Haruna* #3 reported it was under attack before going off the air," the breathless ensign reported.

"Where, you idiot?!" Kaku exploded. Yamaguchi walked the ensign's face fall briefly, then brighten as he remembered the sheet of paper in his hand. Before he could respond, a commander snatched the paper from him and cuffed him on the head, shouting at the man to learn to report properly before striding over to the map.

"Listen to *me*, you fools," Kaku barked at the two men he'd been speaking with. Yamaguchi ignored his chief of staff, moving to consult the chart as the commander hurriedly plotted the position report.

Well at least one thing is going correctly.

The crew of *Haruna* #3, almost certainly dead, had provided a very important last service for the Emperor.

"If only they had been twenty minutes earlier, we could have just launched our second strike at that position to get it off our decks," Kaku said, his fingers white as they pressed on the chart table.

"I do not think that we will have that much extra time, Kaku-san," Vice Admiral Yamaguchi said.

He stepped outside onto the bridge wing, the stiff breeze and *Akagi*'s maximum speed combining to nearly knock him off his feet. Bracing himself against the wind, Yamaguchi raised his binoculars and looked aft at the other two divisions. The *Kido Butai*'s escort vessels were starting to assume protective positions for anti-aircraft defense, smoke belching from the destroyers' funnels as they moved to their respective places.

*The **Taiho**'s radar saved us. We will have time to take some measures, to get some ordnance back into the magazines. Heaven help us if the strike had arrived unannounced.*

For an instant, his mind's eye saw the *Soryu* and *Hiryu* ablaze, caught with their hangars full of armed and fueled aircraft.

I would have lost the war in five minutes.

Yamaguchi pursed his lips.

I still may lose it. But at least now I have a chance.

Once more, the sound of running feet announced a message from the *Akagi*'s radio room.

"Sir, our fighters are engaging!"

THE BLOOD DRAINED FROM ISORO'S HEAD AS THE *SHIDEN* CAME around in a tight turn. He could see tracers arcing behind him as the strange, gull-winged American fighter attempted to bring its long nose around to pull lead.

Where...are...my...wingmen? Isoro wondered, cold prickles of fear creeping into his mind. His consciousness attempted to slip away, but Isoro bore down harder in his abdomen and legs to keep the blood in his head.

This is how it—

He never had time to finish the thought. The dark gray American fighter suddenly erupted in 20mm shell hits and staggering out of its turn. Even as Isoro lightened his touch on his own maneuver before the *Shiden* stalled, he saw another *Shiden* arc past the now blazing American.

Thank you, friend.

Isoro waggled his wings then leveled off and trying to gain speed while looking wildly around.

The sky was chaos. One moment, Isoro and roughly twenty other fighters had been forming up to turn towards the incoming American raid. They'd been close enough to see *Wildcats* climbing towards them, light-colored fuel tanks falling away like rain drops. Then there'd been a frenzied cry of alarm followed by screaming as the new, more capable, American fighters had bounced the Japanese CAP.

There!

A gaggle of American bombers was heading for the *Kido Butai*. His companion waggled his wings and slid in to cover Isoro's tail as the latter turned towards the descending Americans. From a distance, the bombers looked like *Wildcats*. Then Isoro realized that they were still out of firing range and growing in size.

Must be the new American torpedo bombers. The one they call the **Avenger**.

Tightening his turn, Isoro aimed for the rearmost pair of the bombers, drawing lead with almost full deflection. As his finger squeezed the trigger, he noted several of the bombers' bulbous turrets swing towards him. Then the *Shiden* was shaking as his cannon spat a quick burst towards the light gray target. The tracers passed in front of the larger aircraft.

Too much lead.

The Japanese ace had just enough time to correct and fire again before he had to avoid a collision by rolling away. The *Shiden*'s shuddering and several impacts told him he had not gotten away unscathed, the tail gunners managing to put several rounds into his fighter's belly and under surfaces. Seeing the tracers falling away behind him, Isoro started to pull up into a loop to assess the situation.

That's not good.

The *Shiden* was reacting sluggishly. Isoro turned to look back towards his tail. No sooner had his eyes fallen on his elevator than, with a loud *snap*, his port elevator tumbled away from his fighter. Reacting quickly, Isoro pushed the stick forward to get back to level flight. The *Shiden* once more reacted as if it was drunk, yawing towards a spin.

Stupid tail gunners!

Isoro's pulse raced, and he swore he could hear the blood in this ears. A quick look around and the blossoming of flak near the American aircraft now receding to his starboard told him he was close to the *Kido Butai*'s screen. Very gingerly moving his rudder, he brought the fighter's nose around towards the group of ships.

If I go into there now, I will get shot down.

It was only as he thought about getting shot down that Isoro realized his fighter was severely damaged. The *Shiden*'s engine's pitch and sound was far rougher than it had been only a few moments before. The instrument panel told him that his flight was perhaps about to become abbreviated regardless of intent, as the radial's temperature was beginning to rise. Isoro cursed, then took his head back out of his cockpit to look around.

The scene before him blossomed into total bedlam as the American strike caught the Third Division at last.

I of course assume that there will be someone left to search for me, Isoro thought with great despair.

ISORO'S PESSIMISM WAS NOT QUITE WELL-DESERVED. BY DINT OF their faster cruising speed, the *Bonhomme Richard*'s air group and the accompanying *Independence*'s torpedo squadron had arrived a few minutes earlier than the *Yorktown* and *Enterprise*'s strike. Thus, the former had been severely disrupted by the *Kido Butai*'s CAP before the additional escorting *Wildcats* had decisively tilted the numbers in USN's favor.

Still, the *Bonhomme Richard*'s CAG had died at the front of his SB2Cs, dispatched by a *Shiden* off *Akagi*. The knock on effect of his loss was that all twenty-five of the SB2Cs that made it to push over initially concentrated on the *Taiho* rather than dividing their attacks and the anti-aircraft fire. From the Japanese perspective, the *Helldivers* resembled a falling tidal wave of light gray aircraft. The voluminous Japanese anti-aircraft fire claimed another three SB2Cs on the way down before they could release. Four more more fell into the ocean as they began their pullout.

In return for the high butcher's bill, the *Bonhomme Richard*'s dive bombing squadrons put only two bombs onto the *Taiho*. Like her British counterparts, the Japanese carrier was built with an armored, enclosed flight deck to mitigate the damage from just such an assault.

This made the first bomb's point of impact all that more ironic, as the weapon pierced through the new radar aerial atop the island, penetrated into the structure, then completed the annihilation of the *Kido Butai*'s most potent sensor by detonating in the radar flat. The resultant fragments and explosions rippled through the flag and navigational bridges, decapitating the vessel's captain and cleaving the helmsman in two.

The second 1,000-lb. bomb hit after three successive near misses holed the large carrier's starboard side. Like the trio of weapons before it, the big half-ton warhead was off the point of aim, piercing the starboard flight deck edge at an angle. This delayed the weapon's detonation while simultaneously clipping an aviation fuel line that had not been drained. In a horrible, roiling instant, *Taiho*'s forward hangar deck became a cauldron fed by spraying aviation gas. The resulting fireball ignited several of the fully fueled aircraft that had been intended for a strike on Fletcher's carrier force once that group was found. While the weapons aboard the *Suisei*'s and *Tenzan*'s had been stricken below thanks to the warning provided by the *Taiho*'s now defunct radar, the intense cauldron almost immediately began warping the carrier's forward flight deck.

Even with the resultant major fires, the *Taiho*'s damage was not fatal in and of itself. It was what the two bombs facilitated that wrecked the IJN's newest vessel. Even as the big carrier was continuing sharply into the tight turn initiated by a dead man, the *Bonhomme Richard* and *Independence*'s *Avengers* were beginning their run through fire and flame. Belatedly sighted by gunners who had been tracking *Helldivers* through their weapons' deliveries, the large Grumman aircraft set up on the *Taiho*'s bows in a classic anvil attack pattern.

If the SB2C's had paid a butcher's bill, the torpedo bombers went through the equivalent of buying an entire stockyard. The *Independence*'s squadron, their numbers depleted by Isoro and Hiroyoshi Nishizawa, began their attack from *Taiho*'s starboard side with eight TBFs. *Bonhomme Richard*'s squadron struck from port with eighteen more Grummans. Of these, only thirteen would survive to begin their egress back towards Task Force 24.

With her bridge destroyed, it was only through dumb fate that *Taiho* turned into the *Bonhomme Richard*'s squadron. The twelve weapons dropped resulted in zero hits with two of the weapons bracketing the carrier by less than thirty feet on either side. In avoiding the more lethal threat, however, the *Taiho* turned her entire length to the five *Avengers* that managed to drop from starboard. *Independence*'s squadron commander, in an act of professional bravery he did not survive to reap the fruits of, had ordered the magnetic pistols removed from the weapons. The late lieutenant commander had then doubled down by having the torpedoes depths set five feet shallower than the targeting directives called for.

Rather than a court-martial, the man's act led to *Taiho* suffering three major wounds. First the carrier's No. 1 engine room was struck, with the blast and fragments also damaging a fuel pump. Scarcely had her hull stopped shaking from that strike when two more torpedoes struck Fire Room and Engine Room No. 4. The whipsaw from the dual blows knocked out several of the carrier's circuits and a dynamo, with the resultant electrical cascades killing two dozen men at their post. More ominously, the rolling brownout cut power to both the firefighting apparatus and the carrier's pumps. Burning, listing, and leaderless, the *Taiho* began coasting to a stop as the *Bonhomme Richard* and *Independence*'s air crews fled for their lives.

Blue One
Northern Indian Ocean
0800 Local (2230 Eastern)

"Holy shit, look at that bitch burn!" a shocked voice said over the VB-11 radio net.

"Cut the damn chatter!" Lieutenant Commander Brigante barked. "Red Section, fo..."

VB-11's squadron commander was cut off by the strident notes of a trumpet and the muffled sounds of anti-aircraft guns. Indistinguishable yelling and banging on metal shortly followed, as an unknown Japanese transmitter continued to jam the VB-11 net.

Well that's as annoying as it is effective.

The sky was suddenly alive with flak bursts, the *crack*! and smell of acrid smoke taking him briefly back to a different sky half a world away. Biting his tongue and shaking his head, Eric forced the memories of his former squadron's leader's death from his mind as he began seeking targets.

Damn Atlantic boys concentrated on the same carrier. That's not helpful when there are at least two more here than we were briefed about.

Looking forward, Eric saw Brigante furiously waggling his wings. A moment later, a red flare shot out to port from the tailgunner, followed a moment later by a green one to starboard.

Well, glad I paid attention during the briefing.

The signal was for section leaders to hunt their own carriers. With the Japanese interference a constant din in his ears, Eric looked for a target. VS-11 was pushing over on the closest carrier even as VT-11 was arrowing in on the same ship far below.

Have to put as many holes in flight decks as we can. These are the same bastards that hurt the **Hornet**. *I don't feel like going through survivor's reissue again.*

"We're going after the next two carriers," Eric said over the intercom. "Scouting Eleven's got that one in hand."

"Why in the hell are *Enterprise*'s air group going after the battleships?!" Brown asked incredulously. Eric turned and saw that his gunner was right, some of *Enterprise*'s air group was attacking the two *Kongo*-class vessels that were close at hand rather than going for the two additional Japanese carriers a little over ten miles away.

Those battleships aren't going to fly back and hit us! We could hit at least one more flattop!

"Don't know, but keep your eye out for fighters!" Eric said, seeing several dark shapes rising from below. Their *Dauntless* was shaking from the roaring engine, and he briefly scanned his instruments as the flak continued to burst all around them. He watched as a section of *Wildcats* turned towards the approaching Japanese fighters, then cursed as White Three disappeared in a puff of all too familiar brown smoke.

Then finally, *finally*, his section was at the pushover point. Their target circled tightly beneath them, her flight deck edges aflame as the guns attempted to simultaneously engage Eric, the remnants of Yellow flight now sliding in behind him, and a group of six *Avengers* attempting to hit the carrier.

***Soryu* or *Hiryu*,** *I believe.*

For a brief moment he tried to remember the distinguishing features that might tell him which carrier it was, then realized this was utterly unimportant. Extending his dive flaps, pulling back his throttle, and doing one last check to make sure his weapon was actually armed, Eric Melville Cobb began his date with destiny.

Oh shit, he thought, pressing his eyes to the bombsight. The carrier's deck was suddenly large, the red rising sun symbol bright against the yellow deck. As he watched, an aircraft rolled down the long wooden expanse, a fighter by the looks of it. Despite the sudden bile in his throat, Eric didn't flinch, imparting very gentle changes to the rudder to adjust for the carrier's turn. Time slowed, the tracers from the 25mm AAA floating by as he flashed through 10,000 feet... then 8,000 feet...then 7,000 feet.

"Goddammit!" he heard Brown shout, then the chatter of the twin guns. With a roaring sound, a gray Japanese fighter flashed in front of the *Dauntless*, Eric briefly noting its ailerons as the Japanese pilot skidded to avoid flying in front of the SBD's twin machine guns. Putting the *Zero* from his mind, Eric added a little more rudder, anticipating where the Japanese flattop was going to be in a few moments when he pressed the release.

"Three thousand!" Brown shouted.

So soon? Shit...gotta...no, I'm going to be on target any second now.

Eric's patience was rewarded as Brown sang out two thousand feet. The large rising sun was suddenly in the middle of his sight picture, and he pressed the bomb release. Waiting...waiting...and he felt the bomb separate from the end of its trapeze, safely on its path.

"*Seventeen hundred!*" Brown screamed, terror in his voice even as Eric hauled back hard on the stick.

The *Dauntless* creaked, the engine screaming as he fed it throttle. Eric's vision dimmed, his eyes briefly registering the aft end of the flight deck, then suddenly the blue water frighteningly close as their bomber leveled off. Then the *Dauntless* was being pelted by debris, chunks of wood and metal slamming into his wings and fuselage as Brown let off a wild scream and long machine gun burst back towards the Japanese carrier.

I hope that I got a hit. More pressing problems though!

As if summoned, the angry Japanese fighter that had overshot began a run in from his starboard front. Eric skidded the *Dauntless* and mashed his own trigger as the Japanese pilot fired simultaneously. Sparks flew from the front of the fuselage as the 7.7mm machine guns started to walk backwards, but a spray of glass told Eric his own machine guns had gone right through the *Zero*'s canopy. The gray fighter seemed to barely clear the *Dauntless* before splashing astern.

"Sir! Sir! You're supposed to drop the bombs, *I'm* supposed to do the shooting!" Brown shouted, his voice several octaves higher than normal.

Eric laughed as he quickly began heading through the Japanese task group, trumpets interspersed with screaming still sounding in his headphones. There was one more burning carrier, a *Shokaku*-class if his eyes didn't deceive him. Looking around, he saw only one other *Dauntless* with him, and it was not either of his wingmen.

Oh God, I hope I didn't lose them both.

"Did we hit her?" Eric asked.

"Did we...sir, you nearly fucking landed on that bitch," Brown replied, his voice incredulous. "Once again, I've got a piece of a damn ship back here with me and the guns."

I've got to stop doing that.

Suddenly he was nauseous, the adrenaline starting to ebb as he winged his way northwest towards the rendezvous point. His head on constant swivel, Eric put the *Dauntless* into a shallow right turn and craned his neck around. He counted three columns of smoke, two larger than the one over the carrier he had attacked.

*Guess **Enterprise**'s gang got some licks in after all. There's still three carriers left, though, and they're going to be **pissed** about what just happened.*

Looking at his fuel gauge, then doing one more scan for threats, Eric did a gentle circle orbit back towards the Japanese task force as Brown banged around with something in the rear cockpit. After a few minutes, his gunner looked out and saw which way they were heading.

"Sir, if you don't mind me asking," Brown began, "*what the fuck are we doing?*"

"Taking a quick note," Eric replied, jotting down some things on his plotting board. Satisfied, he reversed the *Dauntless*' course, still checking behind and above him for any enemy fighters.

"I'm also checking to see what happened to Two and Three," Eric continued. "But I'm not going to hang around the scene of the crime until the cops arrive because the rest of the bank robbers stopped to take a piss."

"That sounds good to me, sir!"

U.S.S. Houston
0900 Local (2330 Eastern)
Northern Indian Ocean
10 August (9 August)

"Massachusetts reports many contacts, bearing one six oh true, range seven oh miles."

"Here's to hoping those are friendly, or we're about to have a very bad day," Jacob observed, glancing at the plot before him. "Let me know when they're down to twenty miles."

"Aye aye, sir," the talker replied.

"Now, explain Rear Admiral Vian's plan again?" Jacob said, looking over at Commander Farmer. The British officer looked down at the scribbled notes he'd just made from the very long signal passed via semaphore lamp from H.M.C.S. *Repulse*.

"Rear Admiral Vian employed aircraft fitted with long-range tanks to keep tabs on the Japanese task force," Commander Farmer said. "That's why your blokes were able to launch before dawn."

"Understood," Jacob said. "But you lost me when you started talking about unicorns."

The British officer's lips pressed into a thin line.

Not my fault you people have weird names for your ships. I know my way around mythology, but I've never had the urge to name a ship after it.

"The *Unicorn* is an aircraft repair vessel," Farmer stated. "She's got a flight deck and she was in the process of ferrying two squadrons of your new P-47s and P-38s to Addu Atoll. Rear Admiral Vian ordered her north to cover the *Ark Royal*'s retreat and provide an additional flight deck for fighters to land on if necessary."

*Case in point. Why would someone name a carrier the **Ark Royal**?*

"So he's basically serving as bait?" Jacob asked, incredulous at yet another force being offered up as a sacrifice.

"Not quite, apparently," Farmer replied. "Admiral Vian believed he would be at extreme range from the Japanese carriers this morning and that they would not launch until they found him."

Farmer looked at the map, visibly overcome by emotion.

"It would appear that we were quite wrong about Japanese capabilities," he stated after gathering himself. "However, the P-47s joined some P-38s and *Beaufighters* from Addu and ambushed the strike just as they were getting close to the task force."

About time something broke our way.

"There were still casualties among the fleet," Farmer stated, killing Jacob's smile.

"How bad?" Jacob asked.

"The *Unicorn* took four torpedoes and is likely a loss," Farmer said. "The *Illustrious* took another. But they report heavy losses among the Japanese strike, and the extra hundred miles they had to fly probably means some of the damaged aircraft aren't going to make it home."

Jacob nodded.

"Hopefully our boys made it so there's not a lot of flight decks for the Japanese to land on anyway."

Farmer looked at his watch.

"Unless your pilots are extremely accurate or we caught them by surprise, I'm certain the Japanese will be sending a counterattack in this direction," Farmer said. "Their commander would have to be criminally negligent if he sent everything south after only *Illustrious* knowing **this** force was about in the Indian Ocean."

Jacob nodded.

"Of course, considering *I* wasn't even aware of the two extra carriers and battleships until they hove over the horizon," Farmer noted, his bitterness very thinly veiled, "I wouldn't blame them for turning and running."

"Or alternatively calling down whatever carriers are up by Ceylon," Jacob mused. "I really hope it doesn't come to that."

Farmer laughed bitterly.

"Sir, the returning aircraft are twenty miles out," Lieutenant Ness stated.

"Thank you, Lieutenant," Jacob replied. He turned to Farmer and asked, "What's so funny?"

"When speaking of battlecruisers before World War I, some wag stated they were 'eggshells running around with triphammers,'" Farmer said. "I wonder what that man would say about bloody aircraft carriers, as it seems like things just come down to who gets their bolt off first."

"You might be onto something," Jacob said after a moment's contemplation. "The Japanese had it all their own way at Hawaii, then again at..."

"*Aircraft attack!*"

The lookout's cry was followed shortly by one of the heavy machine guns mounted amidships opening fire. It was joined a moment later by every other light anti-aircraft weapon on the *Houston*, then several other ships in the task force as a trio of olive green aircraft came swooping in from the heavy cruiser's port quarter. All three aircraft arrowed towards the nearby *Repulse*, the red rising suns on their fuselage and wings leaving no doubt about their nationality.

"Bloody hell," Farmer said just as the leader, then the two wingmen, released their weapons. It was the former's last act, several 40mm guns combining to blow the Japanese torpedo bomber out of the sky. The remaining two torpedo bombers turned hard away, streaking towards the rear of TF 25's formation. Jacob couldn't be sure, but he swore he saw a pair of impacts on the torpedo bomber's fuselage before the aircraft was out of sight.

"Where in the hell are the fighters?" Jacob asked, voice rising.

"Sir, *Massachusetts* is reporting that the CAP got bounced by enemy fighters," the talker replied.

"Probably busy trying to count heads of the returning flight," Farmer said quietly.

Well, I can't say I blame them. Probably worried about friends coming back.

Jacob watched the *Repulse*'s bow came around in a tight turn to comb the torpedo tracks. He did some quick mental math on where the battlecruiser was likely going to end up and didn't like the answer.

"Port ten degrees," Jacob barked.

Whether those torps hit her or not, we don't need to be that close.

There were several anxious moments as the *Houston*'s bridge crew collectively watched the torpedoes close with the *Repulse*'s path. The exhalation of breath was audible as the British vessel cleared, furiously signaling to the vessels beyond her about the weapons passing through.

"Going to be very interesting here in about an hour," Farmer stated.

"I agree," Jacob replied. "It might have been a mistake to put us out here, as the carriers can't maintain a CAP over both us and them."

"I don't envy that Japanese admiral right now," Farmer stated. "Those two planes that survived are probably warning him he's also got a surface group heading towards him."

Jacob chewed on the inside of his cheek.

"Depending on whether he has any cripples, we just became priority target number one."

Just as Vice Admiral Fletcher intended. I sure hope the carrier boys make it worth it.

ROYAL HAWAIIAN HOTEL
OAHU
1800 LOCAL (2330 EASTERN)
9 AUGUST

"THERE BETTER BE A VERY GOOD REASON FOR THIS, JO," PATRICIA Cobb seethed. "I was looking forward to actually *going home* to start cooking, not heading off to some dance or whatever it is you're dragging me to."

"I promise this will be totally worth it," Jo replied, doing her best to keep her voice civil while paying the taxi driver.

"Perhaps I'd be a bit more trusting if you'd tell me what 'it' is,"

Patricia replied archly as the two women turned towards the massive pink façade of the Royal Hawaiian.

I could strangle you sometimes, Patricia.

Jo thanked the doorman as the two of them walked in. She glanced over at Patricia and felt a mild pang of guilt.

*Okay, fine, the fact that your brother **and** the man you love could both be dead as we speak means I should give some allowances.*

"Blame your brothers," Jo said, looking once more at the message a runner had brought her. "They're the ones who said dinner plans have been changed and we were to meet them here."

More correctly, it was Nick who told me that the wedding had been moved up two hours. He's lucky that I got the message.

Agnes and Nick's plan for notification had apparently started going awry as soon as she'd gotten into the office. Which had led to Nick having to hot foot it out to Ewa and the three brothers getting invited to a higher priority gathering.

I really hope Agnes is right and Rear Admiral Graham will smooth things over for Nick.

Jo almost smacked herself at that thought.

Then again, Nick is a submariner. What is Admiral Dunlap going to do, send him someplace he might get shot at?

A passing contingent of submariners leered at Jo and Patricia as they walked past. Jo looked back over her shoulder and gave the pair of ensigns fixated on Patricia's backside a withering glare. Both junior officers colored and immediately swept their eyes forward to the amusement of the lieutenant (j.g.) that was shepherding them.

Men. Or more correctly, men who need to understand there's a difference between a lady and 'lady of the evening.'

Jo was certain the majority of the local women present were just doing what they considered their patriotic duty to entertain men who might be dead within a month. She was also quite confident that a large number of pros were actually working the establishment.

I know Vice Admiral Halsey has bigger fish to fry, but one would think the last thing he'd want was submariners with the clap on patrol.

Jo stopped at an intersection to look at the hallway signs. Reading quickly, she turned and headed off towards to their destination.

"Why are we headed *away* from the restaurant, Jo?" Patricia asked, suspicion hanging off every word. They rounded the corner before Jo could answer, and Patricia's surprised yelp told Jo the vision before them had answered her question.

Oh my god, Agnes, you are beautiful.

The bride-to-be stood in a resplendent white gown, her face covered in a pale veil that was obviously a family heirloom of some age. Standing beside her in his dress whites, Rear Admiral Graham had a slightly bemused smile on his face.

"I take it this would be the Maid of Honor and your future sister-in-law?" he said, seeing the smile crossing Agnes' face.

"Yes, sir, it is," Agnes replied, her smile growing warmer as Jo stepped forward to take the ring from her. Jo turned back around to see a stricken Patricia still standing with her mouth open, color rising in her cheeks.

"You've got about five minutes to make a scene, breathe, or get inside, Toots," Sam said, coming up behind them in what was obviously a borrowed dress uniform.

He looks like some Banana Republic dictator who gets sewn into his uniform. But hail to the chief indeed...

"You...you...you *knew*?" Patricia said, looking at her older brother. She was about to say something else, then closed her eyes and took a deep breath.

Oh shit.

Patricia, to Jo's surprised, opened her eyes and gave a gracious smile.

"Agnes, let me apologize for my brothers' behavior," Patricia said slowly, her drawl deep as she stepped forward. "This is no proper way to throw you a wedding."

Rear Admiral Graham, looking confused, stepped to the side as Patricia continued to embrace Agnes.

"Welcome to the family," Patricia continued. "I assure you, this is *not* how we usually do things in the Cobbs."

"These are not normal times," Agnes replied, holding the embrace. "Thank you, and I am sorry for the short notice."

Patricia nodded, stepping back to glare first at Sam, and then

David, who had stepped out of the ballroom in a set of dress whites a half size too small.

"Mother clearly didn't spend any time training these idiots, as you can see," Patricia stated. "You're marrying the best of the lot, and I look forward to not being as outnumbered. I hope that we will have more time to talk after your vows."

"I look forward to it," Agnes replied.

That...that went better than I expected. Not sure they're not both lying through their teeth, but either way that was polished all around.

"Thank you, Rear Admiral Graham, for doing this," Patricia said, her tone deferential. Jo was shocked to see her roommate's eyes glistening. "I'm going to go take a seat before I make a mess of myself or the bride."

With that, Patricia walked inside, leaving Sam and David looking at each other, then at their receding sister.

"I see that her reputation for throwing curveballs is well deserved," Agnes said quietly.

"You have no idea," Jo stated, then looked at Sam. The eldest Cobb looked like a man who was expecting the tornado to double back and hit his house any second.

Yep, that tells me we haven't heard the last of this, she's just not going to ruin her brother's wedding day, Jo thought.

"Let's get this started, gentlemen," Rear Admiral Graham said, smiling. "I think the bride and groom deserve to have as much time as possible together."

That sounded ominous. I'll have to ask Nick what happened during the maid of honor and groom dance.

"Aye aye, sir," Sam said, stepping in and making a signal.

As she walked up the aisle arm and arm with Sam, Jo was pleasantly surprised at the Royal Hawaiian staff members playing of Beethoven. Standing at the front of the ballroom, Nick watched as Jo and his brother moved carefully up the aisle. The room was rather full with members of COMSUBPAC staff, the *Plunger*'s wardroom, and several other officers, sailors, and Marines that Jo did not recognize.

"I'm about to split a seam," Sam muttered.

"I was going to ask if maybe you'd had a little too much milk this morning, Sam," Jo chided gently.

"Ha ha ha," Sam said, patting her arm as they separated.

It's also his sense of sarcasm that I missed.

Jo nodded at the unfamiliar, older chaplain standing ready to perform the ceremony. In contrast to most everyone else present, the man was wearing the blue service dress uniform rather than whites. He gave Jo a small smile and looked as though he was about to speak right as the small brass ensemble started into the "Wedding March."

Oh, the look on Nick's face.

Her stomach was full of butterflies as the youngest Cobb was riveted staring toward the ballroom's open doors. Turning to look herself, Jo watched a group of passing officers look on in awe as Agnes stepped into the room. Glancing over at Sam, Jo was also pleased to see the best man's awestruck expression.

Every woman deserves to be regarded as a goddess on her wedding day.

The exchange of vows was relatively quick. Jo recognized the standard Protestant ceremony from the Navy's manual. As the rings were exchanged, she looked past Sam and saw David wiping at his eyes for a brief moment. That started her own burning, as she thought about the last time the Cobb children had all been gathered.

At this point, Sadie would have been better off just staying here.

"You may kiss the bride."

The phrase jolted Jo back to the present, and she watched as Nick leaned in to give Agnes a rather chaste kiss. To the youngest Cobb's shock, his new bride was having none of that, and the room erupted in cheers and catcalls as she dragged him in for a proper kiss.

"That's just a downpayment for tonight, Mr. Cobb," Agnes whispered fiercely. Jo fought to keep a smirk off her face as Nick grew flush with embarrassment. That brought about a few catcalls from the *Plunger*'s gathered contingent. Scanning their faces, Jo realized something.

Where is Nick's commander?

Even with the apparent bad blood from *Plunger*'s return, it seemed odd for Commander Emerson to be missing.

"Ladies and gentlemen, I present to you Lieutenant and Mrs. Nicholas Cobb."

As the last of the guests finished moving through the receiving line and were ushered out of the room by Royal Hawaiian staff, Jo finally had a moment to turn and look sideways at the rest of the wedding party. Taking a last glance around the room to make sure no one was in ear shot, Jo waited until Patricia came back in the room to ask the question that was on everyone's mind.

"So, what gives on the time change?"

Nick and Agnes looked at each other, then back at them.

"I've got orders again," Nick said. "The *Amberjack*'s XO came down with blood clots and word got to headquarters this afternoon. I leave via plane for Midway in three days."

"That sounds like a good reason," David said, eyes wide.

"Try not to break this submarine," Sam added.

"Thanks guys, I love you too," Nick said, rolling his eyes. He glanced at his watch. "I'd love to stay and chat, but we have to be out of this room in ten minutes or they're going to fine Rear Admiral Graham."

"Wait, what?" Jo asked.

"He told them to treat him no different than they would anyone else asking to borrow the room," Agnes said with a laugh. "So they didn't remind him that it was his own Chief of Staff who had rented it for the next two weeks."

Jo saw Nick and Agnes share a moment's look.

I think someone is wanting to hurry up and get the wedding night started. I don't blame them.

"I guess we better get out of here also," Sam said, glancing at his watch as well. "We managed to beg out of dinner with a four star, but were told to arrive for an officer's call no later than twenty hundred."

"Wait, four-star?" Patricia asked, realizing that no one else seemed surprised. "What are you talking about?"

I am so freakin' dead.

"We had the pleasure of making the new fleet commander's

acquaintance this morning," David said. He quickly ran through what had transpired at Ewa field.

"That's where Major Haynes is right now," Sam finished.

"Well, if you'll excuse us," Nick said, squeezing Agnes' hand and gesturing at a tall, thin civilian standing in the doorway with a clip board. "I'm not going to be responsible for our boss losing $75, and I believe I owe my wife a dance."

Mattress dancing, maybe. Jo tried to ignore the slight bit of jealousy behind the thought.

The gathered group quickly moved out of the room, Patricia and Jo both giving Agnes and Nick one last embrace before the couple rushed off. Patricia then hugged both of the twins, the pair looking particularly nervous at how well their sister was taking things. Giving one last anxious look at Jo, the two men moved off to get changed back into their khakis.

"Am I really so terrible?" Patricia asked quietly as soon as her brothers were out of sight. Jo turned to look at her roommate. Before she could speak, Patricia continued. "I mean, it appears everyone knew that my brother was getting married except for me."

Jo's stomach flip flopped at the bitterness in Patricia's voice.

"Patricia, you are not terrible," she said simply. "I've only known since this morning."

As soon as the words left her mouth, Jo realized the mistake she had made.

"Oh. Just this morning," Patricia said quietly, lip quivering. "I think, Jo, I shall be going home to read."

"Patricia, I..."

"Don't wait up for me at the cab," Patricia stated. "I need some time to think, and a walk to clear my head.

"Patricia!" Jo protested, but the other woman was already turning to leave.

I better let her cool off before I go home.

She considered the Cobb family's current living arrangements and winced.

It's going to be even worse when Sam and David get away from the officer call back at Pearl.

I.J.N.S. Akagi
0945 Local (0015 Eastern)
Northern Indian Ocean
10 August

Vice Admiral Yamaguchi wanted to both vomit and wildly punch the hatch leading back into the *Akagi*'s bridge as Rear Admiral Kaku spoke.

"Sir, our strike reports they struck the *Illustrious*...and another British carrier," Rear Admiral Kaku continued with his report.

I must get control of my emotions.

His hands still shook in helpless rage as he studied the two massive columns of smoke to the *Akagi*'s west. The one receding into the distance was basically a grave marker for the *Taiho*, as it was clear the IJN's newest carrier was going to succumb to the massive fires raging in her hangars. *Shokaku*, on the other hand, was somehow keeping pace with the formation despite her own flames and occasional secondary explosions.

There is still a battle to be run.

Closing his eyes, he forced himself to regain his calm. After a long two minutes of having indulged his rage, The *Kido Butai*'s commander turned back to Kaku and nodded his understanding.

"How soon until the strike returns?" Yamaguchi asked, stepping back into the island. He squared his shoulders and looking at the clock on the flag bridge's aft bulkhead.

"It will be another forty-five minutes to an hour," Kaku replied. Yamaguchi did some fast math in his head.

"Why so long?"

"The British were further south than we believed, sir," Kaku stated. "Roughly one hundred miles."

This morning gets better and better. We will be lucky to get the fighters back, and will certainly lose most of the damaged aircraft.

The Chief of Staff seemed to have still more news.

"Out with it," Yamaguchi seethed, then stopped to calm himself.

If I lose my head, everyone else will start to lose theirs.

"There were land-based fighters," Kaku said stiffly. "American and British two-engined models and very large single-engined planes."

"*Thunderbolts* and *Lightnings*, sir," a staff commander interjected. This drew a glare from Kaku, and the man bowed in apology then moved back to arranging the plot.

"Sir!"

Vice Admiral Yamaguchi turned to where the same messenger from earlier stood in the hatch attempting to get his attention. The man gave both of the admirals a neck bow, clearly waiting permission to speak.

"I assume this message is important?" Kaku asked, his tone clearly promising dire consequences if it was not.

"The *Soryu*'s search aircraft have reported finding and attacking an enemy task force," the young officer stated. "The squadron commander perished, but his wingmen stated he managed to torpedo a *Renown*-class battlecruiser."

Well, there's only one vessel that could be after Java Sea. Guess we have found Vice Admiral Godfrey.

"What else?"

"They reported at least three American battleships, *South Dakota* or *Idaho*-class," the man stated. Bowing apologetically again, he pulled the message flimsy back out of his pocket and read the coordinates, his hands shaking.

"Did they say there were carriers?" Yamaguchi asked archly, striding to the map. A chill ran down his spine.

*Those battleships will catch the **Soryu** before nightfall if we do nothing. If we have any more cripples, they'll catch those too.*

"No, Vice Admiral," the ensign replied.

How did we get our intelligence so wrong? Fleet intelligence said that there should only be two American carriers out there, but surely that many planes means three. Now there's additional battleships. Likely modern, fast ones.

Another report interrupted his ruminations.

"Sir, signal from the *Soryu*."

Yamaguchi considered that the ensign was starting to look drenched in sweat from running up and down the stairs.

"What is it?" he asked.

"Divers have cut away her number two prop," the young man replied. "Her fires are out, and she will be able to make twenty knots shortly. Captain Yanigamoto reports the pumps are staying ahead of the flooding, but just barely."

"How many torpedoes did she take?" Rear Admiral Kaku asked incredulously.

"Three, and three bombs also," the ensign replied.

"That should have sank her!" Kaku said, taking a step back in horror.

"Clearly the American torpedoes leave something to be desired," Yamaguchi said. "Or more likely, she was extremely lucky."

"Probably the latter given the bombs that hit her as well," Kaku stated. "If all three had detonated in her hangar deck, she'd look like *Shokaku*."

The ensign looked nervously between the two officers, not sure how to react to the senior officer's comment.

"Thank you, Ensign Takara," Yamaguchi said. The ensign beamed at being recognized by his task force commander, then saluted and left.

"*Shokaku* is basically a beacon pointing directly at the task force," Kaku said grimly.

"Are you advocating we scuttle her along with *Taiho*?" Yamaguchi asked. "I am not prepared to write off a carrier that can still steam, even if she is having difficulty with her fires."

Kaku nodded, making his face blank.

"Speak freely, Kaku-san," Yamaguchi said. "But we have already paid a dire price today, and I do not think the Americans will have difficulty finding us again regardless given *Soryu*'s reduced speed and the oil she is trailing."

"We need to ask for help from Vice Admiral Ozawa," Kaku said, his tone making the words sound like bitter poison.

"I am sure that Vice Admiral Ozawa is already taking steps to send us aid," Yamaguchi said. "In case the enemy is monitoring our communications, I do not want to remind them that they have several carriers to their northeast."

Kaku pursed his lips, but nodded.

"Ozawa would not be in range until late this afternoon at the earliest," Yamaguchi continued, looking at the map. "We know the Americans are in range, the only question is whether they will continue to close."

Yamaguchi pondered for a few moments, his state akin to a man who suddenly had a knife pressed against his spine.

"The battleships *are* their plan to close with us," he stated aloud.

"Sir?" Kaku said, his expression confused.

"If it was Halsey, I would worry about him rushing in to finish the job," Yamaguchi said, thinking of the intelligence dossiers he'd reviewed in the previous months. "He'd attack us without question, without respite, and Ozawa be damned."

Yamaguchi joined his hands, thinking through the geometry.

Having Nagumo-san go to England after the Treaty of Kent continues to pay dividends. Who could have thought that the Royal Navy's evaluations of flag admirals would come in so handy? I wonder what mine said?

Pushing that thought from his head, Yamaguchi continued to mull over what he remembered about Fletcher. Suddenly it was so apparent to him what Vice Admiral Fletcher was attempting to carry out, and what had to be done to stop it.

I must make Kaku and the staff understand. Especially with our limited assets.

"Fletcher is a cautious, studious man," Yamaguchi began. "In some ways, he reminds me of Vice Admiral Nagumo."

That brought a chuckle from Kaku which stopped as soon as Yamaguchi looked at him.

"The difference is Fletcher's caution is probably based on his unfamiliarity with carrier operations," Yamaguchi said. "Unlike Nagumo, he will not dither and consider things over and over again. No, he will now await our strike while constantly glancing over his shoulder to make sure Ozawa is not going to surprise him."

There is only one way out of this trap if I want to save any portion of this force, Yamaguchi realized.

"Thus, we must give Fletcher a reason to be cautious, with or without Ozawa. Prepare to strike the force that the *Soryu*'s torpedo bomber found."

"But sir, that means Fletcher will attack us again," Kaku said, aghast.

"We do not know where he is, and we are rapidly running out of aircraft," Yamaguchi snapped. "If we are able to damage his battleships while we still have the *Kirishima* and *Hiei*, he will break off pursuit."

Kaku considered arguing then thought better of it.

"Unless you can think of a way to figure out where the Americans are in the next thirty minutes, carry out my orders," Yamaguchi said.

Kaku looked over at his intelligence officer, then back to Yamaguchi.

"We may have something yet, sir," Kaku stated. "The destroyers have picked up several Americans from their rafts."

"Can you get me the information before the strikes are ready to launch?" Yamaguchi asked. Kaku and the intelligence officer looked at one another.

"Unlikely," Kaku said finally.

"Then begin spotting the attack against the battleship," Yamaguchi stated, his tone brooking no argument.

"Hai," Kaku said, bowing.

"Kaku-san, I want to find the carriers as much as you do," Yamaguchi stated. "However, two modern battleships and a British battlecruiser are a threat to annihilate this entire force. We must get Fletcher to slow down, if for no other reason than to make it easier for Ozawa to hit him."

8
A DIMINISHED RIPOSTE

Whether I float as a corpse under the waters,
  Or sink beneath the grasses of the mountainside,
I willingly die for the Emperor

— —JAPANESE WARRIOR CHANT, 1932

SHUTTLE BUS #5
OAHU
1830 LOCAL (0030 EASTERN)
9 AUGUST (10 AUGUST)

"PATRICIA? PATRICIA COBB?"

The feminine voice that called her from the back of the bus sounded familiar, but for the life of her Patricia could not place it.

Wonderful, someone else who probably thinks I'm an insufferable bitch.

Patricia forced her face into a study of politeness as she looked past the sailors at the short, brown-haired woman in a nurse's uniform. The sandy-haired doctor sitting next to her promptly stood, offering his seat. Patricia nodded appreciatively as the soldiers, sailors, Marines, and pair of civilians standing in the bus's center aisle parted like the

JAMES YOUNG

Red Sea. She took a seat beside the woman, then noted the pair of sailors in front of them had stopped their conversation. The darker-haired of the duo seemed to be the most befuddled until his straw-haired companion elbowed him in the ribs.

Well at least the blonde one has some sense.

"Thank you, uh..." Patricia started, suddenly drawing a blank at the familiar woman's name. The nurse smiled.

"Jennifer," the woman replied. "Jennifer Zempel. I helped in your brother Eric's ward."

Patricia's exhaled, embarrassed.

She was such a nice woman, I cannot believe I forgot her name!

"I'm so sorry," Patricia said, holding out her hand. "I feel as if it's been ages."

Jennifer shrugged with a smile.

"Well, I certainly feel as if I've been aging in dog years," the woman replied as the bus began pulling away from the station. For a moment, an expression of pain and grief passed over Jennifer's visage. "At least we had our last patient leave the ward three weeks ago."

Patricia sensed the doctor shift beside her, then diplomatically clear his throat.

Oh you silly man. I'm pretty sure the Japanese are well aware that they haven't attacked Hawaii in five months.

That thought turned her mind to Charles and Eric's current location. Her eyes started to burn, and suddenly she was fighting against tears.

Goddammit, I feel so ridiculous.

"Are you all right?" Jennifer asked quietly, reaching into the handbag beside her before Patricia could reach into her own clutch purse.

"I'm fine," Patricia replied, taking the offered tissue. Jennifer gave her a skeptical look.

"Right," Jennifer said, her voice carrying much more than she probably realized. "I believe that as much as I believe the last woman who said it to me just thirty minutes ago."

Patricia thought the doctor accompanying Jennifer was going to have a stroke. Patricia looked up at him, smiling, and he quickly turned away.

"Captain Morrison doesn't like to talk about what we've gotten ordered to do," Jennifer whispered conspiratorially. "He's a bit of a prude. Probably that Catholic upbringing."

I'm going to regret asking this, I'm sure. But with a lead in like that...

"Just what exactly have you been ordered to do?" she asked slowly.

Jennifer made sure the two sailors in front of them were still locked in an animated conversation about the relative superiority of Flash Gordon vs. Buck Rodgers.

It's like the universe has set out to remind me of my siblings at every turn.

"We've been doing health and welfare checks on the working girls in the Vice District," Jennifer answered, her smile impish.

"What?" Patricia asked, aghast.

"You know, the 'Patriotutes?'" Jennifer clarified, deadpan.

"Oh, I know," Patricia whispered fiercely. "I'm just shocked that the Navy sends a doctor and a nurse down to check on them!"

Jennifer shrugged.

"Well, it's either have us check them or have some working girl put an entire destroyer out of commission," Jennifer stated. "Hell, the woman I was mentioning who was 'fine' was lucky we didn't take her word for it."

Patricia was at a loss for words, something that caused Jennifer to actually giggle.

"Sorry, I shouldn't laugh," the nurse said. "But the look on your face right now is priceless."

Patricia suppressed a sneer, or at least attempted to. Jennifer looked at her knowingly.

"We're trapped on an island with thousands of men who are afraid they're about to die," Jennifer observed. "I, for one, am glad that the authorities have provided an 'outlet' for their urges."

She may have a point, but I don't have to like it.

"You don't have four brothers and a fiancée here on the island, Jennifer," Patricia returned, her tone somewhat icy.

"With the exception of the fiancée, I don't think I would particularly care what my brothers did."

Patricia looked at the nurse in shock as Jennifer continued.

"The whole 'maybe possibly dying' thing. Plus let's be honest: everyone here is someone's son, father, or brother. Doesn't make their needs less valid."

Patricia opened her mouth to speak, closed it, and just as suddenly her tears started anew..

"Oh my gosh," Jennifer said, her voice suddenly panicked as she pulled out more tissues. "Did something happen to your brothers?"

Patricia laughed bitterly.

"Yes, but not what you might think," she replied, then proceeded to talk about her night. The words came out in a rushed whisper, her shoulders shaking as she sobbed quietly. To her surprise, Jennifer put her arm around her shoulders in a side hug about halfway through.

"So, yes, I guess I *am* just that stuck up bitch no one likes to have around because her nose is in other people's business," Patricia observed.

"I know it might not be much consolation, but I think your brothers are all capable of figuring out a way you didn't have to be there tonight," Jennifer observed. "They clearly wanted you to be there."

"Yeah, they just didn't want me to interfere," Patricia seethed.

"Well, would you have if you'd known?" Jennifer asked.

Patricia opened her mouth to protest, then thought about it.

"I...I honestly don't know," she said. "I feel like Nick was rushing horribly into things and hardly knows the woman. Who apparently has been engaged before, and Lord knows mother and father won't approve of that when they find out."

Patricia realized how manic she was sounding when there was a bit of silence in their corner of the bus. Jennifer turned from regarding her with a slight smile to the two men in front of them, both of whom had stopped talking and were clearly listening to Patricia ramble.

I have the urge to scream.

Looking at Jennifer and making a shushing motion, Patricia glared at the back of the sailors' heads. Watching the light haired one start to blush, Patricia had an idea.

"Dale Arden," Patricia said brightly, her countenance in no way reflecting the homicidal rage she could feel rising.

"Excuse me?" the dark haired sailor asked, whipping around before he realized his mistake. He looked sheepish for an instant, and Patricia pressed her advantage.

"Well, I of course figured if you were going to be nosy about our conversation we should actually join yours," Patricia continued sweetly. "So Wilma Deering is, by far, the superior heroine to Dale Arden, if for no other reason than Ms. Deering actually does something besides go, 'Oh Flash, save me!'"

"Wait a second, that's not..." the blonde sailor started to say, then stopped as he too realized he'd made an error. Patricia, having already noted his drawl, recognized a fellow Alabaman when she heard one.

"Well, while I cannot account for your friend's upbringing, I can tell from your accent that you were *certainly* raised better," Patricia stated.

It was only when she saw half the bus turn and look that Patricia realized about how loud she'd inadvertently become.

No matter, this young man is going to get the scolding of his life.

"So, I trust that you will now *mind your own business* and leave me and my friend to continue our conversation like your mother taught you some manners."

"No, I can't see why your brothers were scared at all," Jennifer muttered lowly as the chastised sailor brushed to the roots of his hair. Thankfully, the bus began slowing to a stop as the bus driver called out the next destination.

"Pearl Harbor!" the man shouted. "All off for Pearl Harbor!"

The bus began to empty in short order.

You know, improving shuttle bus system was one of the few smart things that idiot Admiral Jensen did.

Jennifer and Patricia were the last to step off.

"Well Nurse Zempel, I don't need you for anything else," Dr. Morrison said. "Sorry that took longer than expected."

"I'm just trying to figure out where the houses seem to be getting these new women," Jennifer replied. "I thought there was a moratorium on new mouths to feed coming to the island?"

Morrison shrugged.

"General Short's been more focused on getting troops to Australia than he has been dealing with some of the administrative stuff here," Morrison said. Belatedly realizing he'd said too much, he looked at Patricia.

"I assure you, Doctor, if I'm a spy then I'm very poor at my job," Patricia said drily. "Mata Hari is surely not rolling in her grave at my powers of perception or garnering of intelligence."

"In any case, since President Roosevelt has forbidden the imposition of martial law there's not a whole lot he can do about civilians coming and going," Morrison continued. "It's the same reason the blackout and curfew weren't vigorously enforced after the first month."

Patricia shook her head.

I suppose there's no real fear of the Japanese swooping down upon us given all the fighting has been on the other side of the Pacific.

"In any case, I'm going home to take a hot shower in disinfectant," Morrison said. Patricia looked at him in shock as he turned to leave.

"I swear that man is scared of women," Jennifer said, shaking her head. She then turned to Patricia. "I've got a fifth of Scotch back at my place and my roommates are both out with their boyfriends if you want to talk about it."

Patricia was about to protest about the time, then thought better of it.

Let my brothers worry about me for a change. I'm off tomorrow.

"That sounds like a splendid idea," Patricia replied. "If I hurry, I can probably make it to my place and then meet you at yours?"

"Excellent plan," Jennifer said. She reached in her purse and pulled out some paper, then scribbled an address.

I.J.N.S. AKIGUMO
1015 LOCAL (0045 EASTERN)
NORTHERN INDIAN OCEAN
10 AUGUST

Isoro finished hauling himself, dripping, up onto the I.J.N.S. *Akigumo*'s deck.

"Ah, the *great* Isoro Honda, ace of aces," a sarcastic officer said, standing at the top of the line Isoro had just finished climbing from his dinghy. Isoro squinted, the sting of saltwater in his eyes making him momentarily regret that decision, before his face broke into a wide grin.

"Yuta Nomiya, you swine!" Isoro said, stepping forward towards his Eta Jima classmate before both legs swiftly reminded the pilot of the last hour's exertions. Two ratings quickly stepped forward and grabbed Isoro before he completely fell to the deck. Yuta let a brief moment of concern cross his face before once again adopting a faux haughty expression.

"Once more you have cost me a couple dozen yen due to a bad bet," Yuta said, shaking his head. "As it was at Kure, here it is again far from home."

Isoro's grin grew wider.

Give some man bad advice on a horse race and he never forgets. I blame the sake.

For a moment, he basked in the memory of a far more peaceful time.

"I bet our captain we'd haul more Americans than Japanese out of the sea today," Yuta continued, gesturing towards the destroyer's stern. "You would have been American number six."

Isoro looked over at his classmate, surprised.

"Just how many Japanese have you pulled out of the water?" he asked.

"There are a couple more of you fighter pilots down in the wardroom," Yuta replied. "The captain ordered we give them warm tea and some food. After we're done talking to the Americans, you can go below and liven up the place a bit."

Isora was about to respond when a low *BOOM* brought both of their attention towards the *Akigumo*'s starboard side. Approximately eight miles away, a massive mushroom cloud was erupting from the burning *Taiho*.

"Could be worse," Yuta observed grimly. "We could be involved in that goat screw."

"They need to just scuttle her and be done with it," Isoro said bitterly. "In about two hours she's going to be a nice, big arrow pointing the way to the task force."

Yuta turned and pointed astern, in the direction of the sailing away *Kido Butai*. Smoke from the *Shokaku* could be seen on the horizon, billowing up like an accusatory finger.

"I do not think we're going to be hard to find," the destroyerman replied. "Plus that sounded like her magazines, which means she won't be around much longer.

Both men braced themselves as the *Akigumo* began to get under way, lookouts scanning the water to see if there were any more dinghies.

There are a lot of men from both sides who are going to die alone and in the middle of this damn ocean. I was lucky I ditched within sight of the destroyer.

"But, anyway, I'm glad you're aboard," Yuta said. "You can help me question our American friends."

Why do I get the feeling this is not going to be conducted over a nice cup of tea? Isoro thought, feeling a slight wave of apprehension.

"Come, let us not tarry," Yuta stated, gesturing aft towards the destroyer's fantail. The vessel was starting to accelerate, smoke pouring from her twin stacks. With the wind starting to freshen from the southwest, the destroyer was starting to pitch slightly in the gathering swells. Isoro felt a chill, and was unsure if it had anything to do with the breeze hitting his wet clothing.

"After our questioning during Hawaii," Yuta began, his tone as if he was discussing a new recipe, "I realized that we were rather inefficient in questioning the two men from *Hornet*. There were so many more things we should have asked them."

"Two men from *Hornet*?" Isoro asked, not understanding Yuta's reference.

"Yes, the two aviators from *Hornet* that we captured," Yuta replied proudly. "How do you think you aviators knew where to strike off Hawaii? Divine intervention?"

Isoro moved past several of the destroyer's crew scrubbing down her deck. The red-tinged water and visible bullet impacts told him all he needed to know about what had likely happened.

"I didn't give it much thought, to be honest," Isoro replied. "That was...that was a busy day. Much like this one. What happened there?"

"One of the American fighters strafed us," Yuta replied angrily. "Killed most of a gun crew and our torpedo officer. We were too busy trying to stop the torpedo bombers attack *Soryu* to get the fighter."

The duo reached the *Akigumo*'s fantail before Isoro could respond. The feeling of nausea in his stomach increased as he looked at the five standing men surrounded by several glowering members of the *Akigumo*'s crew. All five men had clearly been beaten, and the largest of them was being held up by one of the men next to him. Looking at the insignia, Isoro noted that two of the men were ensigns, two were enlisted, and the large man wore the silver oak leaves of a commander.

"Good morning, gentlemen," Yuta said, his words slow as he tried to remember his years of English. "I am Lieutenant junior grade Nomiya, gunnery officer of the destroyer *Akigumo*."

One of the two enlisted men glared at Yuta, then slowly and deliberately spat upon the *Akigumo*'s deck in his general direction. A chief petty officer stepped forward to deliver a blow to the man's face.

"Stop!" Yuta barked in Japanese. The petty officer immediately followed orders, turning towards the lieutenant with a questioning look on his face. It was an error, as the American chose that moment to spit again directly into the man's face. Enraged, the Japanese NCO immediately turned to strike the American once again, then remembered his orders.

"Your monkey's pretty well trained," American enlisted man sneered.

Yuta ignored the man, looking at the commander.

"I have demonstrated that I will control my men," Yuta said conversationally. "Will you do the same courtesy, commander..?"

The senior American officer started to crack a smile, but the pain of moving his visibly bruised jaw stopped the gesture. Instead, he opted to shake his head.

"Sure, complain about a little spit in the face after your sailors worked us all over," the man replied angrily.

He has a point. Still, it is dishonorable to allow oneself to be captured. The man should not be surprised at his treatment.

A runner came rushing back from the *Akigumo*'s bridge and bowed to Yuta, then approached to talk lowly. The officer nodded grimly twice, then spoke rapidly in response to whatever he'd been told. The petty officer bowed, and turned to move back towards the destroyer's bridge.

"Well, commander, it would appear that the time for niceties is over," Yuta said apologetically. "Vice Admiral Yamaguchi is demanding we obtain information regarding your forces."

Isoro watched as the American officer's eyes narrowed. Behind him, the man who had spat in the petty officer's face sneered in contempt, even as the other three Americans began to look on in apprehension.

"Commander Joshua Jacobs, service number 724..."

The man's recital of his name, rank, and service number was interrupted by a sudden, violent punch to the kidneys. In moments, the scene on the *Akigumo*'s stern was bedlam, as the two enlisted Americans immediately attacked the nearest Japanese sailor and one of the ensigns screamed in terror.

What kind of men are we?

The sick taste in bile in his mouth increased as he watched the spat upon petty officer kick his assailant repeatedly in the groin. The American shrieked, clutching himself as he fell to the deck with a two burly sailors grabbed his shoulders.

"Bind them this time!" Yuta shouted angrily.

Isoro stomach turned as the petty officer took a step back then savagely kicked his target again, causing the other man to begin vomiting. Even as rope was brought forward, the petty officer produced a pair of pliers from his pocket.

What are you doing?

Isoro watched in horror as the man grabbed the American gunner's hair and pulled his head back. Before he even realized it, Isoro strode forward and punched the petty officer hard in the face, stopping him from whatever he was doing. The man flew backward in shock, eyes wild as he began to step forward then suddenly realized what he was about to do. Coming to attention, he quickly bowed to Isoro.

"The man is no good to us if you rip his tongue out," Isoro snapped. Even as the words left his mouth, he considered his justification.

Yes, what a brave samurai I am.

"I see you have a knack for this," Yuta said from behind him.

Isoro tried to ignore the sound of the youngest ensign sobbing uncontrollably in fear as it carried across the stern. Several of the Japanese sailors chuckled at the man, his flight suit obviously soiled from where he had wet himself and eyes wide with fear.

"What is your name?" Isoro asked, his English halting.

"Sir, don't tell them shit," the man lying on the deck in front of them gasped. "Let the little yellow bastards figure it out."

Before Isoro could reply, Yuta gestured with a grunt. The petty officer he had struck nodded, dropped the pliers, and produced a small knife. Before Isoro's horrified eyes, the petty officer sawed off the enlisted sailor's pinky. The American let out a hoarse gasp, then to Isoro's amazement started laughing.

No one will mistake that for humor.

Seeing blood start to pour from the man's hand, Isoro looked away so that he did not vomit.

"Fuck you, you little Jap bastards! *Fuck you!*" the man screamed before someone shoved a gag into his mouth.

"M-m-my name is Ensign Stan Van Horn," the soiled officer said, his voice quiet. The man licked his lips as he looked at where Commander Jacobs lay prone.

I hope he is not dead, or this was an exercise in futility.

A Japanese sailor came rushing from belowdecks with a pail attached to a rope. Isoro watched the man throw the metal bucket into the *Akigumo*'s wake, only to have the object yanked from his hands by the water pressure from the destroyer's passage. A nearby petty officer screamed at the sailor, striking him with an open slap across the face that made Ensign Van Horn jump.

"Will you stop hurting these men if I tell you what you want to know?" Van Horn asked, looking at where one of the other ensigns was attempting to scream past his own gag. The two sailors gleefully attempting to dislocate his shoulder seemed focused on their task, and Isoro was surprised that Van Horn's accosters were not similarly attempting to harm him.

Wait, they are deferring to me.

"Yes, yes we will," Isoro said.

I am now not just a bystander, but an accomplice.

"But only if you are quick about it."

"There are four carriers," Van Horn began.

"Yuta, stop your men!" Isoro shouted in Japanese, then turned back to Van Horn.

"Go on," he said as the destroyer officer came over. The American sailor who had lost his pinky attempted to yell something past his gag, but was immediately silenced by the knife being placed next to his eye.

"Go on," Isoro repeated quietly, using the tone one would to calm a scared child. He locked eyes with the petty officer holding the gunner's head.

Over the next five minutes, Isoro quickly came to realize just how grave the *Kido Butai*'s danger was. Quickly explaining the important things to Yuta, he questioned Van Horn with a level tone, double checking the ensign's answers by asking things a slightly different way. Even as Commander Jacobs was brought back to consciousness from the contents of a second pail, Isoro realized there was really nothing more they needed from the men.

"Let us go talk," Isoro said calmly to Yuta. "Thank you, Ensign Van Horn."

"Remember, you promised not to hurt me or my companions anymore," Van Horn said nervously, seeing the feral looks that several of the Japanese sailors were giving him.

"You have my word, Ensign Van Horn," Isoro replied.

"Do not do anything while we are gone," Yuta said in Japanese. "Do you understand?"

"Hai," the senior petty officer said. "We will only gag them, nothing more."

"See that is so," Yuta replied, motioning for Isoro to follow him towards the destroyer's nearby superstructure.

"You must signal the *Akagi* quickly," Isoro said, fear coursing through him as they stood in the aft turret's shadow. "The Americans will have a second wave ready by midday, and there are not nearly enough fighters remaining to deal with a second strike."

Yuta looked at him, realization starting to dawn.

"But how can there not be enough fighters?" he asked.

"Because they caught us by surprise," Isoro replied, then gestured at the *Taiho* and *Shokaku*'s smoke plumes. "Two carriers are out of action."

"Three," Yuta said grimly.

"What?"

"Three," the destroyerman repeated, then pointed off to the *Akigumo*'s starboard side. Isoro turned to follow his finger and felt a brief pain in his chest. The *Soryu*, with two of the *Akigumo*'s fellows in attendance, was visible several thousand yards away. Now that he was focused on the carrier, Isoro could also *smell* the bunker oil that visibly trailed the vessel like a blood trail. Wordlessly, Yuta handed over his binoculars.

She's smoking heavily from her stacks. Isoro wordlessly scanned the vessel. *But it looks like the smoke is mainly damage to the stacks, not the engine room on fire.*

"Can she fly off any aircraft?" Yuta asked.

"There are men working on the holes in the flight deck," Isoro answered. "With her flight deck canted like that, even if the managed to repair the holes, *Soryu* will have trouble conducting flight operations."

"I imagine they'll have to counterflood," Yuta replied.

Isoro shrugged as he handed the binoculars back.

"I am not a damage control expert," Isoro said simply. "But if she cannot get off her aircraft and she cannot steam, she's as good as dead when the Americans return."

The sound of aircraft engines caused both men to turn and look skyward in alarm. Their fear was eased a moment later as they both realized the large gaggle of aircraft was heading east to west.

Looks like the three remaining carriers have launched their strike. It was a mixed blessing that the Americans caught the vessels that had already sent a strike south.

As he counted the aircraft, Isoro gave a grim nod.

"We launched everything," he said.

"Hmm?" Yuta asked, puzzled.

"We did not split our strike between the carriers as we normally do," Isoro said. "I suspect so we would have decks free to handle the strike we launched against the British."

Isoro could tell that the destroyer officer only partially understood what was being said. Both men turned as a runner came down from the bridge.

"Sir, the captain has ordered us to execute the prisoners," the petty officer said.

Isoro looked at the man in shock.

"I'll need the standard work party," Yuta said without missing a beat. "Please have Petty Officer Harikawa fetch me my sword."

Isoro looked from the petty officer to his friend.

"I gave the ensign my word we would not harm him or the group any further!" Isoro shouted, causing several nearby sailors to look at him. Yuta gave the men a withering look, and they immediately turned back to their work.

"You were serious?" Yuta asked, incredulous.

"Why wouldn't I be serious?" Isoro snapped. Yuta raised an eyebrow.

"He is a coward," Yuta replied. "You saw him, he was literally wetting himself rather than trying to resist. This is the man you would argue with the captain for?"

Isoro picked up the subtle warning in his friend's tone.

A captain is absolute master of his vessel during time of war.

Isoro was despondent at the thought. While it was not likely, it was entirely possible the *Akigumo*'s skipper would have him killed alongside the Americans for having the temerity to question a direct order. Moreover, by the IJN's regulations and discipline, no one would question it.

The 'great' Isoro Honda's head split like a melon for some stupid Americans. No one would remember it was a question of honor.

A junior petty officer, one who Isoro could only assume was the aforementioned Harikawa, returned with a silk wrapped bundle. The man bowed deeply, extending his arms with the rolled package in hands while still casting his eyes downward. Yuta bowed slightly in return, then took the item and unwrapped it.

We are ritualizing murder! This is not the way of Bushido!

"Isoro-san, thank you for your help," Yuta said as he solemnly buckled the sword to his uniform. "You may go below."

How dare you? I will not be dismissed like some rating.

"I will not," Isoro replied firmly. "If you are going to murder a man who I have promised to protect, I may as well be looking at him when you do so."

The petty officer briefly glanced at Isoro, then back down at the deck. Yuta looked as if he was going to say something, then stopped. Impassive, he simply nodded, then began proceeding toward the *Akigumo*'s stern. Isoro followed along behind, his chest growing tighter with every step.

The Americans were all on their knees, facing the destroyer's stern. Isoro felt the wind from the destroyer's passage blowing onto his back, but noted that a stiffening cross breeze was swirling the smoke drifting astern. Thunderheads were starting to form in the far distance. He also noted that the smoke from the *Taiho*'s direction was starting to dissipate, indicating that vessel had finally succumbed to her wounds.

*The weather is starting to muddle things again. Maybe the Americans won't find us so easily after all, now that **Taiho** has finally sank.*

Bringing his eyes lower, Isoro was horrified to see a pair of dorsal fins threading along behind the *Akigumo*.

Ensign Van Horn looked up as Isoro came back. The two men gripping him by his shoulders stiffened but allowed the motion. Gagged, the young man looked like he was trying to say something, but was stopped as Yuta's voice rang out over the destroyer's stern.

"Gentlemen, the captain has directed that you are to be executed as enemies of His Majesty," Yuta stated simply. Even as the words were registering, the Yuta's katana was drawn in a flashing arc from its scabbard. Isoro saw that the sword looked like a true ancestral weapon, not the mass produced swords issued to Imperial officers upon their commissioning.

I hope your ancestors are looking upon you with shame and anger right now.

Van Horn looked at Yuta's blade, then back at Isoro, his eyes wide as he tried to scream something past the gag in his mouth. Yuta, giving one last glance at Isoro, gestured to the two men behind the young officer. For a brief moment, the American's eyes met Isoro's, then the man was bent over double and the sword was flashing downwards.

For all of his faults, at least he is a decent swordsman, Isoro noted.

The ace felt a strange sense of detachment as Ensign Van Horn's head rolled across the deck. Hoping it was only a trick of his mind, Isoro swore he saw the American's eyes blink once. Then one of the *Akigumo*'s sailors kicked his skull into the ocean. The young man's body followed shortly thereafter.

The remaining executions only took a matter of minutes. Only one American, the pinky-less gunner, struggled. For his troubles, Yuta eviscerated the gunner rather than option for decapitation. Even gutted, the man attempted to loop his leg around that of one of his captors as they hurled him over the side.

That is a man I hope none of us see in the afterlife. For he will truly walk through the entirety of Hell to challenge us all again.

The last to die was Commander Jacobs, his lips moving in prayer. Unlike the others, his body was not immediately tossed over the side so that Yuta could wipe his blade on the dead man's uniform. That clean up done, he gestured and had Jacobs' body committed to the gathered sharks behind the vessel.

"Damn fish are probably going to be ungrateful if we end up in the water later," Yuta observed haughtily, a slight sweat on his brow. Isoro did not respond, watching as the *Akigumo*'s crew began to swab the blood off the deck.

"You are displeased, Isoro," Yuta stated.

"That was unnecessary," Isoro replied, barely restraining his anger.

"So was pulling you out of the water," Yuta said ominously. "But we did it just the same."

Isoro considered his classmate for a moment.

"Tell me, is it because I question your actions that you equate rescuing me with murder," Isoro asked. "Or because you lack the opportunity for honorable combat and it bothers you a great deal?"

Yuta's face paled, and Isoro saw him grip his sword handle tightly.

"Come now, what's one more unarmed man to add to your tally?" Isoro asked, not even bothering to lower his voice. "What an amazing warrior your men must think you are."

"Perhaps you should go below, Honda," Yuta replied. "We will notify you when we are about to rendezvous with the *Akagi*."

I have pressed my luck far enough.

Not bothering to bow, he turned to a nearby sailor.

"Could you please show me to the wardroom?" he asked, noting several eyes upon him.

"At once, sir," the sailor replied, bowing. As he walked forward, Isoro peered at the cloud of smoke from *Shokaku*.

It appears to be lightening. And getting thinner. Is she putting her fires out? Will that matter?

The size and ferocity of a fire that gave off that much smoke almost certainly meant *Shokaku*'s flight deck had been severely burned and damaged. If the carrier could not fly aircraft, she was little more than a target.

Still, a target that causes the Americans to split their fire has its purposes.

He pushed such thoughts from his head as he entered the *Akigumo*'s small wardroom. The other rescued fighter pilots engaged in animated conversation. They all stopped and looked at him, and Isoro realized he didn't recognize a single one of them.

Attrition is grinding us to dust.

His still sodden flight gear and life jacket seemed to double in weight.

"Lieutenant Honda, please join us," one of the sitting pilots stated reverently. Isoro nodded and started forward into the compartment. It was only he who realized each step felt as if it was leading to a last communal meal before the gallows.

BLUE ONE
1035 LOCAL (0105 EASTERN)

"For the love of God, hurry up and land you stupid motherfuckers!" Brown shouted from the *Dauntless'* rear seat.

While he was not as vocal (or blasphemous) in his anger as Brown was, Eric could feel his own pulse starting to throb in his temples.

Man, I would hate to see what would be happening right now if we'd made this strike at extended range

Eric put the dive bomber into a gentle turn, beginning yet another wide orbit around the *Yorktown*. His fuel situation wasn't horrid, but it certainly wasn't getting any better the longer they waited.

"Sir, do you know why we're taking aboard the *Bonhomme Richard*'s dive bombers?" Brown asked, his voice incredulous. Eric shrugged, then realized his gunner couldn't see the gesture.

I'm more punch drunk than I thought.

"I don't know what the hell the staff has planned," Eric said. "I just know that the fighters seem to all be heading for *Independence* and *Bonhomme Richard* while the dive bombers and torps are splitting between us and *Enterprise*."

Probably didn't help this recovery cycle when the torpedo bombers have crash landings. They got the shit shot out of them.

Brown and he had watched three additional *Avengers* land, get assessed, then be immediately shoved over the *Yorktown*'s side alone. Judging from the signaling and chatter, at least one or two more had also fouled *Enterprise*'s deck. Litter crews moving to and fro had also seemed to cause some issues as far as handling went.

"Wonder if the boys off the Atlantic carriers are going to get lost trying to move around Old Yorky?" Brown mused, using the *Yorktown*'s nickname.

"I imagine the *Bonhomme Richard* folks shouldn't be too confused," Eric replied. "She just looks like a bigger sister."

"Like the ugly one you hope your buddy will date so you can actually talk to the cute one," Brown agreed, drawing a chuckle from Eric.

"You're lucky I only have one sister, Brown," Eric replied. Thinking of Patricia made him once more examine the other *Dauntlesses* still in formation.

Come on Charles, you don't need to break my sister's heart.

"It's entirely possible Lieutenant headed for the *Richard*, sir," Brown stated, startling Eric.

"That obvious?" Eric asked.

"The plane always wobbles when you start trying to look at something," Brown replied easily. "Can't think of any other reason you'd be checking out *Dauntlesses*."

"Well I still haven't seen Stratmore or Van Horn, so there's that," Eric noted.

The silence over the intercom was deafening.

Brown isn't usually this quiet. He needs to get out with i—

"I didn't want to tell you until we got down, sir," Brown said finally. "But I'm pretty sure Ensign Van Horn would have had to ditch."

Eric closed his eyes, feeling hot pain behind them.

"Roger," he choked out.

"Wasn't your fault, sir," Brown said. "He started smoking during his dive. He pulled out, but if he made it more than five miles I'd be surprised."

Eric swallowed to clear the lump in his throat.

"Thanks Brown," he rasped.

"Yes, sir," Brown replied. "I didn't see what happened to Ensign Stratmore. Got kind of busy shooting back at those assholes trying to kill us."

Eric didn't reply, the hot tears finally starting to roll down his cheeks.

That's one of my men definitely dead, one a Japanese prisoner.

Once more Eric flashed back to Strange's *Dauntless* engulfed in flames.

If the Japanese are even taking prisoners.

It seemed as though their time in Australia had passed in the blink of an eye, but there had been several opportunities for the *Yorktown*'s crew to talk to their counterparts who had survived the Dutch East Indies maelstrom. The men who had escaped and evaded back to Australia had talked about how the Japanese Army had treated men they'd captured. It had made Eric resolve to never be captured alive.

It's not like we would have left those escorts in a sunny disposition either.

I'm pretty sure at least two of those carriers are done for. Nothing smokes like that and survives.

He had plenty of time to think about what he'd tell the task force's intelligence officer over the next fifteen minutes. Just as Eric's bladder was convincing him he might wish to consider using the relief tube again, the *Yorktown* signaled for him to begin his approach.

"Are we literally the last dive bomber up here?" Brown asked.

"It would appear that way," Eric noted in disbelief. "Guess we shouldn't have let that *Helldiver* off of *Bonhomme Richard* cut in front of us."

"Kinda says something when the replacements for ol' 'Slow But Deadly' can't wait in line properly," Brown noted with disgust.

"I'm just glad he didn't foul the deck," Eric noted as he descended astern of the *Yorktown*. He could see smoke pouring from the plane guard destroyer's stack as the tin can attempted to keep up.

Hmm. Fletcher's probably not such an idiot as we all thought given how much fuel all the escorts must be using.

The *Dauntless* shuddered slightly as he dropped the gear, the controls getting mushy for a second.

"Hey sir, we're streaming something," Brown said from the tail gunner slot. "Looks like hydraulic fluid."

Well that's just peachy.

Eric gritted his teeth and dropped the SBD's tail hook.

I hope whatever just came loose to start that leak isn't so bad the controls fail.

Ignoring the problem, he glanced forward and watched the LSO's paddles. After what looked like a few moments hesitation, the lieutenant on the paddles began signaling that he was slightly high. Making the correction, Eric settled down into a comfortable approach and dropped his hook.

"Shit," Brown said behind him. "Sir, we got smoke."

Eric didn't even both looking back, still focusing on the LSO.

We're landing. I don't care if we turn into a flaming comet.

Once more it looked like the LSO was considering waving them off, but reconsidered at the last moment. With a plume of white behind his aircraft, Eric dropped the hook and took the cut signal, thudding down hard onto *Yorktown*'s deck as his controls became slightly mushy. The impact slammed him hard against his restraints, knocking the breath from his lungs as the arrester hook did its job. Quickly chopping the throttle and cutting off fuel to his now heavily smoking engine, Eric began unstrapping himself from the SBD.

What in the hell caught fire?

Looking up, Eric saw the men rushing forward with fire extinguishers and unrolling the hose from the island. The men in different jerseys began clambering up the bomber's side to assist him in getting out.

"Sir, you injured?!" a corpsman asked, already looking Eric over.

"No corpsman, I am not," Eric said quickly. "Just getting my damn map."

"Fuck the map, sir, we have to get you off the deck!" a chief shouted from the wing. Eric shook his head vehemently.

"I've got information on that map," he snapped, the mapboard free. Something snagged on his flight gloves, and he looked down to see a jagged slash down the board's underside. Taking a further look around his cockpit from the standing position, he noticed a couple other holes in the floor.

Holy shit, I guess we did get nicked up by something. Eric started to move off when his head snapped back. Cursing, he realized that he had not disconnected his helmet's leads. Water from the firefighting crew sprayed in his face as he reached back for the wire, giving it a sharp tug that caused it to come loose from the dive bomber. Hopping down off the bomber, Eric saw that Brown was already by the island, looking back at him with some anxiety. The gunner seemed to be holding an oversized plot board as Eric started to rush over towards him.

Not dying today.

Despite his adrenaline surge, Eric was surprised he was unable to run at anything approaching full speed. His legs were like rubber from the long time in the cockpit, his breath seeming to come raggedly.

Wait, that's no plot board. Holy shit, that's a piece of wood!

The charred edges and red paint barely visible towards the item's bottom half was an indicator of where the material had come from.

Brown started to grin, then winced in pain as he pushed the wood towards Eric.

"When they ask you if you got a hit, you give them this, sir!" the gunner said proudly, voice shaking with emotion. Eric's eyes once again burned he grabbed the wood carefully with his gloved hands, then set it on top of his plotting board.

"Thank you, Brown," he bit out.

"You're welcome, sir," Brown replied, then looked behind Eric. "Well shit."

Eric turned around just in time to see the work party shoving his damaged and still smoldering plane over the side.

"Guess we'll never know what started the fire," Eric said, disgusted.

"Last *Dauntless* pilot, report to the flag bridge," the 1MC crackled. "I say again, last *Dauntless* pilot, report to the flag bridge."

Well shit.

He was about to say something when someone nearly tackled him from behind with a whoop.

"You son-of-a-bitch!" Charles bellowed, letting him go after a second. "I thought you were dead!"

Eric didn't know whether to belt his future brother-in-law or hug him. He settled for a hard embrace back.

"Hell of a way to talk about your future mother-in-law," he muttered, shoving Charles forcefully back and giving him a once over. "I am so fucking glad to see you."

Charles laughed at that.

"Sweet Jesus, Charles, you know Patricia would have killed whichever one of us made it back, right?"

The younger officer laughed at that one.

"Yeah, well, the day is young," Charles replied. "But I heard you have an appointment with the old man, so best get going."

"You need to tell me what the hell happened to you when I get done here."

"You know where our ready room is."

With that, Eric turned and headed up the *Yorktown*'s island

Thank God.

Relief gave him some of his energy back as he moved up the stairs.

He passed two men in flight suits he did not recognize as he entered the structure. Both looked at him, then down at the object in his hands with confused looks on their faces. Eric nodded at both of them but kept moving through the narrow passageway, noting that one was a lieutenant commander.

*Wonder if he's a torpedo or dive bomber pilot? Must be off the **Bonhomme Richard**, as I know all of **Enterprise's** squadron commanders.*

Eric put the man out of his mind as he passed the *Yorktown*'s conning tower. Captain Kiefer was calmly giving orders to the helmsman as the carrier turned out of the wind. Seeing Eric in the hatchway, Captain Kiefer turned over the conn to the officer of the deck and headed over.

"What in the hell do you have there?" Kiefer asked, gesturing towards Eric's hands.

"Piece of a Japanese carrier, sir," Eric replied with a grin. "Appears I may have been a little low pulling out from my drop."

Kiefer's eyes widened as he looked at Eric's hands.

"Well, guess we better get upstairs to see Vice Admiral Fletcher then," *Yorktown*'s skipper replied. "There's been some dispute as to just how many carriers got hit. Lieutenant Commander Fairborn from *Bonhomme Richard* swears we got four."

"Three, sir," Eric said. "My gunner and I saw three. How many did Commander Montgomery say we got?"

Captain Kiefer looked left and right, then leaned in.

"Commander Montgomery didn't make it," Kiefer said. "He was last seen leaving the carriers with two Japanese fighters on his tail."

Shit, Eric thought, feeling as if a ton of bricks had landed on him.

"I was heading back up to the main bridge," Captain Kiefer said, not giving Eric a chance to think about the information. "I'll walk with you to the flag plot." Eric followed his captain up the *Yorktown*'s island towards flag country, looking up to see a glowering commander was waiting outside the hatch. The man looked ready to say something to Eric, but stopped at the hard glare Captain Kiefer gave him. For his pat, Eric looked right at the superior officer as if daring him to say something.

Yes, I know I didn't come right here like I was some nugget at your beck and *call I just got through watching my friends die and killing Japanese. What have **you** done this morning, asshole?*

"Sir, I still don't think the Japs know where we are," a voice was saying from inside the compartment.

"I know Aubrey," a second man Eric recognized as Vice Admiral Fletcher's replied. "But we're going to concentrate on getting the fighters turned around before I even think about a second strike. Even if the aviators are right and they bagged four carriers, that apparently leaves two."

Well, that must be Rear Admiral Fitch. Always fun to walk into a room full of stars fresh off the flight deck.

"Even so, most of their strike went south to hit the British," Rear Admiral Fitch pressed. "They'll have to recover that strike before they can hit us. Given the range at which they had to hit the British, that's going to be awhile. We can bag them, sir."

There was a long silence.

"You know what our orders are, Aubrey," Fletcher said. "I know you want me to turn a blind eye to them, but there's a lot of war left to fight. Half the Japanese fleet must be out here given what happened to Vice Admiral Cunningham *and* Ceylon."

The man has a point, especially with what we saw today.

"We've taken a big bite out of what we've found, but I don't want to be sitting here with full flight decks only to have the rest then hit us. We stick with the original plan."

"Aye aye, sir," Rear Admiral Fitch replied, his tone sorrowful.

Does it make me yellow to be so concerned with not going for another swim that I agree with Fletcher?

It had been weeks since he'd had a *Hornet* nightmare, but that didn't mean the carrier's loss didn't haunt him. Eric imagined it was ten times worse having been in command when the *Saratoga*, *Lexington*, and *Hornet* had all been lost.

*Even if he was not technically commanding our task group, he was still the senior carrier officer when the **Hornet** went down.*

"Sir, Lieutenant Cobb," Captain Kiefer stated, stepping past the commander into the flag plot. He gestured for Eric to step forward, freezing the commander in place with another glare. "He's brought something I think you'll want to see."

Well, if that doesn't put me on the spot.

Eric shoved his nerves away.

"Sir, compliments of VB-11," Eric said, walking to an open corner of the map and sliding the charred wood from *Soryu* onto the map.

"What in the hell is that, Lieutenant Cobb?!" the commander asked from behind him.

"It's a piece of a Japanese carrier's flight deck, sir," Eric responded levelly, not even bothering to look at the man. "It landed in my gunner's cockpit."

"I imagine it nearly took his poor head off," Captain Kiefer observed.

Oh shit.

It was he first time he considered just how small the rear cockpit was in relation to the piece of debris' size.

I need to buy Brown a beer when we get back to civilization. Hell, maybe even a whole night in the vice district.

"How many carriers did you see hit, son?" Vice Admiral Fletcher asked.

"Three sir," Eric replied. He quickly laid out what he had observed during his attack. Swallowing hard, he also recounted what Brown had seen during the egress. Finally, pointing out his plotting board, he estimated where he estimated the Japanese would be if they'd continued on their course.

"I drew this circle of how far I thought the *Hiryu*-class ship I hit might get," Eric continued. "But I'm pretty sure that at least one *Hiryu*-class and what looked like two larger carriers were still functional."

"Gentlemen, I'm returning to the bridge," Captain Kiefer stated. "I'll have my air officer provide you with how many functional aircraft we have remaining."

"Thank you, Captain Kiefer," Vice Admiral Fletcher said. He turned once again to look at his flag map with Eric's information as Captain Kiefer left. A runner nearly ran into *Yorktown*'s master in the hatchway, quickly ducking back to let the senior officer pass before handing a message flimsy to the glowering commander standing by the flag plot's aft bulkhead.

"The *Independence* reports she's launching the first batch of returned fighters to bolster the CAP," the commander said. He brought the flimsy over to Vice Admiral Fletcher.

"Thank you, Commander Babin," Fletcher replied, then read the message. His brow furrowed.

"How many more fighters on the *Bonhomme Richard?*" he asked.

"They report roughly twelve *Corsairs* and ten *Hellcats* are available right now," Babin replied. "In another two hours they'll probably have four and eight more, respectively, repaired or brought down from the spares."

"Jesus," Fitch muttered.

"Perils of weighting the strike force with them," Fletcher replied. "This just further reinforces what we've said about needing more fighters even if it means we cut some of the dive bombers."

"I can only hope our opponents have the same problem," Fitch stated. "If not..."

"Sir!" one of the talkers spoke up. "The *Massachusetts* reports a large raid bearing oh nine seven true, estimated range seventy miles!"

"Well, looks like we have our answer on how many planes the enemy sent south," Fletcher said. "Scramble the emergency CAP. How many fighters do we have over Vice Admiral Godfrey's force?"

"Eight sir," Commander Babin said, his face pale. "Eight more on the way."

"How did that happen?!" Fletcher asked.

"We withdrew sixteen to cover the carriers during landing operations, sir," Rear Admiral Fitch said. "The last thing we wanted to happen was us getting caught from another direction."

Vice Admiral Fletcher looked at the map.

"Let's hope those new anti-aircraft shells work," he said, his tone forlorn.

Better the surface forces than us, Eric thought, then immediately regretted it.

"Lieutenant Cobb, you look like you've seen a ghost," Rear Admiral Fitch said, concerned.

Just how do I explain what Jo is to me?

Eric mulled for a moment, then hedged his bet.

"My friend's father is the *Houston*'s captain," Eric said, realizing his tone and demeanor was that of a plebe caught in the middle of a mistake. Thankfully no one pressed the issue.

"The *Houston*'s a good ship," Fletcher said. "I haven't had much interaction with Captain Morton, but I'm sure she'll be fine and so will he."

"Thank you, sir," Eric replied.

There's plenty of other big targets out there for the Japanese to try and hit. What are the odds they'll decide to waste bombs on the **Houston**?

U.S.S. Houston
1115 Local (0145 Eastern)

Here goes nothing, Jacob thought.

The *Houston* was pushing through the gathering swells as TF 25 continued its rush southeast after the reported Japanese cripples. The wind from the cruiser's passage blew in his face as he stood atop her pilot house. The binoculars around his neck felt as if they were three times their weight from the fear he was doing his best not to show.

Why do air attacks always seem so much worse than a gunnery fight? he pondered, briefly glancing at Commander Farmer. The man stood with his own glasses to his eyes, looking towards the east over the port side. It was Farmer who had *strenuously* suggested that, in the face of the large carrier raid heading towards them, Jacob give heading and course directions from a position where his view upwards would be unimpeded.

Part of me thinks he's fucking crazy. But I've also never been had to deal with this many dive bombers at once.

During the fight for the Dutch East Indies, it had been land-based torpedo bombers that were the bane of the Allied surface vessels. Farmer had been quite adamant that handling attacks from small dive bombers was a different kettle of fish.

"I don't think those thunderheads are going to make your combat air patrol's job any easier," Farmer observed grimly, then suddenly tensed. "And it seems like the game's afoot."

"Sir, *Massachusetts* is ordering a heading change," the talker behind Jacob shouted. He looked across at the massive battleship, her bow wave and wake raised behind her as she began to accelerate.

*She's doing at least twenty-five knots. Almost as fast as **Repulse** while packing a much heavier right hook.*

"Understood," Jacob said, watching the flagship's signal mast.

"Looks like the CAP has begun their work," Farmer said, pointing. Jacob glanced quickly over and felt his heart stop at the numerous dots now approaching, having just exited the thunderheads roughly thirty-five miles away. Farmer was correct in that *someone* had to be dying, as there were numerous plumes of smoke starting to fall from the sky.

I just hope it's not that many of ours.

Hope, or more correctly Ares, was not in the mood to succor the *Houston*'s captain. With Vice Admiral Fletcher having so heavily weighed his strike's fighter escort, albeit with good effect, there had only been so many *Hellcats* and *Wildcats* to go around. The air staff had believed radar and good fighter direction would give them time to shift their forces to cover either TF 25 or TF 24. What they had not foreseen was the long time it would take to recover their strike and attempt to respot for CAP operations. Nor had they planned for the massive line of thunderstorms that played havoc with TF 25's radar sets.

As a result, the first eight reinforcements for TF 25's CAP were still 20 miles away when the *Kido Butai*'s riposte pierced the wall of squalls to the east. Having done so, it took ten minutes for Lieutenant Commander Takahashi Sadamu, *Kaga*'s CAG, to corral some of his wayward charges. In that time, the escorting *Shiden* and *Zeroes* summarily dealt with the four *Hellcats* and equal number of *Wildcats* orbiting over TF 25, then moved on to engage the approaching eight *Hellcats* from the *Bonhomme Richard*. The melee that followed was pitched, but only conclusive in that it cleared the way for the Japanese strike force to descend upon TF 25.

AGAINST THE TIDE IMPERIAL

Surveying his prey, Sadamu quickly identified the *Massachusetts*, *Indiana*, and *Repulse*. Giving rapid orders over the radio, he assigned twelve *Tenzan* apiece to each of the large vessels, then ordered the remaining two *chutai* to concentrate on the *Baltimore*. That done, Sadamu then sent the *Suisei* to attack the *Houston*, *Exeter*, and *Tallahassee* before descending to lead the assault on *Repulse*.

"Well, looks like the CAP wasn't quite strong enough," Farmer observed grimly. The task force had quickly shifted into its circular anti-aircraft formation as the Japanese began screaming in towards them. Jacob watched with professional detachment as the wave seemed to shift like a swarm of bees.

*The single-engine jobs definitely seem to be **a lot** more nimble than the land ones*, Jacob thought, watching as the Japanese swung wide. Then it was bedlam as the outer screen opened fire.

"Port twenty degrees," Jacob called calmly, seeing the *Massachusetts* starting to come about. The *Houston*'s anti-aircraft guns began to fire as Japanese dive bombers turned towards their target. Jacob felt the deck starting to lean to starboard as the bow was swung around to the left. Looking up, he saw three of the Japanese bombers clearly angling for the *Houston* as the others chose their target.

"Increase rudder to forty-five degrees!" Jacob barked, hearing the talker relaying the command. The *Houston* heeled even further over, and Jacob risked a quick glance along the heavy cruiser's path. The *Hudson* was heading on a collision course, but Jacob could see the destroyer's bow already starting to come around.

We should clear the...

"Sir look out!" someone screamed. The next instant Jacob was getting tackled as suddenly 20mm shells were exploding all around open platform. The two offending *Shiden* fighters roared past, the sounds of men screaming from just below telling him that there were casualties among the anti-aircraft guns.

Jacob had barely processed that before there was the sound of another aircraft engine just above the *Houston*'s mast, followed immediately by an explosion right off her starboard side. The near miss shook the cruiser violently, and was followed immediately by another just astern.

"Missed us, you f–" a talker began to shout.

The man was cut off as the final *Suisei*'s bomb struck the *Houston* just aft of her forward stack. Passing inboard of the starboard catapult, the 1,000-lb. bomb easily penetrated the heavy cruiser's thin deck armor, its fuze finally activating just above the forward boiler room. The resultant explosion immediately killed every man in the compartment beneath, either through storm of fragments or flesh stripping effects of superheated steam. The *Houston*'s starboard catapult was blasted from its mountings as the cruiser's hull moved buckled upwards and whipped from the blast's effects.

Atop the pilot house, the vertical shearing movement bounced Jacob's head hard off the deck with a hollow *thunk*. Seeing stars, Jacob dimly heard and felt the passage of splinters all around him, accompanied by screams of wounded from below as scalding steam billowed upwards from the cruiser's hull. Shaking his head to clear the cobwebs, Jacob registered the sounds of fire and smells of burning flesh as the *Houston* continued to vibrate hard from the impact. The rising wails to aft were abruptly stopped, with various crewmen starting to cry out in alarm.

"Man overboard!"

"Oh Jesus, he jumped!"

This is starting to become a goddamn trend.

Jacob's hands shook as he tried to stand. It was only then that he belatedly realized something had his legs pinned. He quickly slithered out from under the dead weight, looking down to see the decapitated body of one of *Houston*'s lookouts. Scanning the pilot house roof, Jacob saw that Commander Farmer was calmly speaking into a sound powered telephone, the *Houston*'s movements indicating she was still under control.

Have to fight the ship, Jacob!

With that, he shook off the momentary fear that was causing his hands to tremble.

"Tell the OOD to get me a damage report!" Jacob called to Farmer, hoping the man heard him over the bedlam of the cruiser's guns. The

British officer waved acknowledgment, then repeated the order into the phone.

Dammit, we're really ablaze.

Pushing hard on the corpse's shoulders in front of him, Jacob struggled from under the dead lookout. His trousers were soaked in the young man's blood, the coppery smell mixing with the stench of burning oil and gunpowder in a noxious mixture. As he got to one knee, the roar of engines made him turn to port.

Oh shit.

A trio of bombers was approaching from port, their rising suns standing out starkly against their dark green fuselages. The *Houston's* guns knocked pieces off one of the dark green bombers as they passed in front of the heavy cruiser. Turning back to port, Jacob saw no more Japanese aircraft coming. He whirled back to starboard just in time to to see one of the trio burst into flames and fall into the water before it could release its torpedo.

"What the hell happened to the *Massachusetts?!*" he asked Farmer, seeing the battleship wreathed in fire. A second later that Jacob realized it was the BB's own guns that were the source of most of the flame, but not all of it. Unfortunately, the vigorous AA only clipped the *chutai* leader after the Japanese pilot and his wingman released their ordnance towards the battleship's port side.

Why is she turning to give them a broader...shit, nevermind, Jacob thought as another trio of Japanese aircraft flashed past the battleship's bow towards *Houston. They anviled her.*

JACOB'S GUESS WAS MORE OR LESS RIGHT. LIKE THEIR AMERICAN counterparts several hours before, the Japanese torpedo pilots had drawn the most dangerous task of their attack. Resolute, and well-disciplined, they pressed into the cauldron of fire that surrounded the three Allied capital ships in the finest tradition of *bushido*.

Unfortunately, much like their ideological forebears had found at Shiroyama, *bushido* did not make up for a marked difference in technology. The simultaneous attacks of the *Suisei* initially managed to distract and divide the Allied anti-aircraft fire. However, as the thirty-four *Tenzan* covered the final thousands of yards to their drop point, gunners aboard multiple vessels switched to engage the far more dangerous threat.

Twenty-nine of the torpedo bombers made it past the outer screen and a lone *Hellcat* that managed to evade the escorts long enough to splash two Japanese attackers. Another four bombers cartwheeled or plunged into the Indian Ocean's depths before they could release. Two *chutai* broke from the intense fire, either launching their weapons far out of range or diverting to attack the *Exeter*.

It was the assault of the remaining bombers that Jacob witnessed. The *Massachusetts* had suffered significant damage before the torpedo bombers had managed to trap her with their attacks on two axes. However, a jammed No. 3 turret, cleared her auxiliary bridge, and a hangar fire were hardly fatal. What they did do was distract the "Big Mamie's" captain, which in turn led to his misjudgment of the attackers' speed and timing. Although faster and vastly nimbler than her older compatriots that had fought at the Battle of Hawaii, the mistake meant *Massachusetts* could not avoid intersecting with three torpedoes.

The first of these weapons, dropped at comparatively long range as the battleship heeled away, came in at an awkward angle. Rather than detonating against the vessel's armor, the *sandaburo* warhead exploded prematurely from the sheer water pressure exerted by a 36,000-ton battleship moving at twenty-seven knots. Other than shaking the *Massachusetts*' black gang, the weapon had no effect.

The two *Tenzans* from starboard, on the other hand, had far better luck. Led by Lieutenant Tomonaga off *Hiryu*, the duo braved the Big Mamie's prolific fire to almost point blank range. His aircraft burning, blood pulsing from a massive chest wound, Tomonaga dropped his weapon barely a football field's length outside of minimum range. A moment later, Tomonaga's wingman followed suit, then was immediately blotted out of the sky by a VT shell from the *Massachusett*'s secondary battery. Another shell from the barrage ignited Tomonaga's fuel tanks and simultaneously killed his tail gunner. Surrounded in flames and screaming his loyalty to the Emperor,

Tomonaga continued on to crash into Big Mamie's superstructure in a bright gout of flame.

Other than immediately killing twenty-five of the battleship's crew, the suicide crash had little impact on the big vessel's fighting ability. On the other hand, the two torpedoes that impacted a little over a minute proceeded to maim the vessel in a horrific way. Tomonaga's weapon, running deep, hit just forward of the juncture of the engine rooms one and two. Normally, the weapon's 660-lb. warhead would have been well-contained by the battleship's torpedo defense system. Unfortunately for the Americans, the *sandaburo* explosive was one and a half times more powerful than its high-explosive counterpart. The influx of fragments and water was not immediately fatal for all of engine room 1's occupants, but sufficient for the survivors to begin heading for the escape trunks.

Most of the crew had just began this journey when the second torpedo hit barely ten feet aft of the first. In a demonstration of effectiveness that would have upset every American torpedo bomber pilot, the second warhead also performed exactly as designed. With the anti-torpedo bulkheads already weakened, almost the entire explosive force scythed across engine room number two in a bow wave of spall and gases. What men the metal and heated air did not rend or dismember, the Indian Ocean drowned. More importantly, in a fury of arcing electricity, smoke, and screams, much of the *Massachusett*'s electrical power was knocked out due to the explosive vibrations. In the chaos and the darkness, the survivors of engine room #1 heard the screech of plating being torn back from water pressure as the battleship continued forward.

JACOB WATCHED AS *MASSACHUSETTS* CONTINUED HER TURN TO starboard, away from *Houston*. Oil trailed in the battleship's wake, and Jacob could see her starting to list to port from the two torpedo hits. Smoke poured from her superstructure as her guns gradually fell silent, the Japanese strike fleeing east.

That Jap bastard didn't even flinch.

Looking down, Jacob saw his hands were shaking once more.

Clasping them, he turned to look over the rest of the formation. The *Indiana* was also burning, but did not appear to have taken any severe damage. *Repulse*, on the other hand, was burning profusely forward and noticeably down by the stern.

We did not come out of this well. Looks like Vice Admiral Fletcher's bait plan worked all too well.

"Sir, the XO is asking for us to come about and cut speed!"

The replacement talker's words yanked Jacob out of his bitter thoughts.

"Slow her to one third ahead," Jacob ordered. "Then signal the *Hudson* or any other available DD to please help us by maintaining an anti-submarine watch."

"Aye aye, sir," the talker replied.

We're no longer venting steam. She's still handling okay, so I'm going to assume that we still have steerage.

"Commander Farmer, I think it's time we returned to the bridge," Jacob said, stepping aside as a casualty detail began taking the dead off the top of the pilot house.

"Yes, sir, that's probably a good plan," Farmer replied, his voice pained. Jacob looked closer and saw the man's left arm was quite obviously broken.

"You need to see the surgeon," Jacob stated.

"I'll be all right sir," Farmer replied. "I think you've got far worse casualties to worry about."

"Wasn't a request, Commander," Jacob stated firmly. "Get to the sick bay. I don't want to see you back without a sling."

Farmer briefly looked as if he wanted to argue, then gave a curt nod.

"Thank you, Commander," Jacob stated. "For your actions during the fight as well."

This time the nod was one of respect.

"You fought a fine ship, sir," Farmer replied, then headed for the ladder. Jacob watched as the man very gingerly made his way down into the superstructure. A few moments later he followed and stepped onto *Houston's* bridge, only to nearly slip in a pool of blood.

"Sorry sir," Lieutenant Ness said apologetically, then looked around for some means to clean up the mess.

"We've got it, sir," a petty officer called out, stepping onto the bridge with a bucket. Jacob watched as the man began covering the spot with it. As the adrenaline wore off, Jacob became more aware of his own injuries.

My head is fucking killing me. I will never have to be talked into a steel helmet again.

"Have the department heads provide me with a casualty report," Jacob ordered. "I need to speak with Lieutenant Haven."

"Sir, Lieutenant Haven is dead," Ensign O'Rourke, the *Houston*'s assistant damage control officer, reported from the port bridge hatch. The man's chest was heaving from exertion. "The XO respectfully requests that we come to a halt so that we can shore up bulkheads, otherwise we may lose the forward engine room due to progressive flooding from the hit forward."

I don't have to like it, but I'm going to have to do it.

"Hoist the Mike flag," Jacob ordered, referring to the signal that would inform surrounding ships the *Houston* was adrift but not disabled. "Helm, full stop."

As the crew began carrying out his orders, Jacob reached for his binoculars.

"Goddammit," he said, feeling a sharp pain that caused him to release them. Looking down, Jacob saw that the left binocular tube had been gouged open by either a fragment or a passing shell. The tube was empty of everything but a few stubborn shards.

"Sir, you're bleeding," Lieutenant Ness the man said, as he reached into his pocket and pulled out a handkerchief. Jacob gave his thanks and took it, pulling the binoculars over his head and depositing them atop the rubbish bin in the bridge corner. By the time he turned around, Ness was handing over his own binoculars.

"No, you need those," Jacob stated, then turned to the still waiting Ensign O'Rourke. The officer's face looked a little less ruddy as he was regaining his breath.

"Okay, how bad are we hit?" Jacob asked, listening to the sound of crackling flames and shouts for hoses.

"Sir, I don't know the full extent," O'Rourke said. "But there's no passage down the deck due to the blaze, the bulkhead between fireroom number and engine room number one is seeping fuel oil and water."

"What happened to Lieutenant Haven?" Jacob asked.

"He was with the damage control party in the compartment the bomb exploded in," O'Rourke said. "We still have sound powered telephone communication with Battle Two and the black gang are receiving the bridge's telegraph inputs."

Jacob winced.

I don't even want to know what the casualty report already looks like. But so far it seems like we can still talk and still fight if we have to.

"Go aft to Battle Two and tell Commander Sloan his priority is that fire," Jacob said. "We don't need to be a signpost in case there's another wave of Japanese."

"Aye aye, sir," O'Rourke responded, turning and quickly making his way down to the main deck.

Jacob turned to Lieutenant Ness. "OOD, you have the conn, I'm going to radio to figure out what in the hell is going on with the rest of the task force."

"Yes sir," Ness replied. The deck below their feet vibrated, and Jacob looked out to see the main battery first elevating, then the turrets rotating.

Yes, indeed, we can fight her if it comes to that.

Once more, he looked to the *Massachusetts*, now stopped with her list visibly increasing.

Which might be better than that big lady is doing.

I.J.N.S. AKAGI
1245 LOCAL (0315 EASTERN)

"SIR, THE STRIKE WILL BE RETURNING IN TWENTY MINUTES," REAR Admiral Kaku said.

Vice Admiral Yamaguchi turned from watching the destroyer

Akigumo transfer pilots via breeches buoy across to the *Kido Butai*'s flagship.

Lucky men, every one of them. Even luckier that Fletcher nor a submarine interrupted us mid-transfer.

The breeches buoy required both ships to steam in a straight line, in parallel, while the occupants were passed between the vessels. A submarine or strike would have meant an immediate and likely fatal separation between the two ships. Watching the *Akigumo* bob next to the *Akagi*, Yamaguchi hoped the men involved had iron stomachs.

"Have someone go wake Commander Fuchida," Yamaguchi stated wearily.

"Already done, sir," Kaku stated solemnly.

He too knows how badly Fuchida's strike was mauled

A wave of nausea passed over Yamaguchi as he thought about the casualty report.

*Three quarters of the **Shidens** lost due to fuel exhaustion. Half the **Suiseis**. Half the **Tenzans**.*

Yamaguchi would have admired his British counterpart's masterful trap had it not all but emasculated his force's striking power. Instead, he struggled to control his rage lest it lead to him doing something foolish.

It is most fortunate for that man, whomever he may be, that the Americans are bearing down on me. I would love nothing more than to take the aircraft remaining from my strike at Fletcher to truly end the Royal Navy's presence in the Indian Ocean.

His temples started to throw to throb as he considered his current impotence.

"Sir, Vice Admiral Ozawa has responded to our message," Kaku stated. "He cannot come south more than 100 miles. The damnable army is behind on their timelines, as the British are resisting almost fanatically."

Gee, perhaps our treatment of prisoners in the Dutch East Indies has something to do with that? Or maybe the fact those Army barbarians raped almost every woman under sixty in the Chinese quarter of Singapore, so the natives on Ceylon have no idea what to expect?

Allegedly Admiral Yamamoto had personally told the Imperial

Army General Staff that the Navy would leave their troops to rot on Ceylon if similar atrocities took place. While that might have been apocryphal, Yamaguchi doubted the British had received the memo.

"Then we will fight Fletcher as best we can with what we have remaining," Yamaguchi said, hoping his words conveyed more confidence than fatalism.

"Hai," Kaku responded.

Regardless, we will die like samurai. If only we had a report from the strike against Fletcher's surface vessels. Commander Sadamu's last transmission had been that he was initiating an attack and that the escorting fighters had eliminated the CAP over the battleships. The ominous silence led Yamaguchi to believe that *Hiryu* would need a new commander air group.

"Sir!" one of the staff officers shouted, rushing in. "The *Shokaku*! Her fires are out!"

"What?" Yamaguchi asked, looking at Kaku. The two men both rushed outside to look towards the *Akagi*'s stern. In the distance, they could see that the report was mostly correct. Defying all odds, the *Shokaku* continued to stream only a slight bit of white smoke rather than the dark stream that had been pouring from her almost non-stop for several hours. Yamaguchi brought up his binoculars to further assess the carrier's damage.

Her deck is a ruin. But she continues to sail, thankfully.

"If the American torpedoes worked..." Kaku began.

"If the American torpedoes worked, *Shokaku* would have died with her sister at Hawaii," Yamaguchi cut him off. "Let us hope they never fix those problems."

"Sir, you asked to see me?" a familiar, if much frailer, voice said from the compartment's hatch.

Yamaguchi turned to look at the *Akagi*'s CAG, fighting to keep a frown off of his face.

Fuchida must rest if we survive this. I should have stuck with my original thought there was no way he should be flying today.

The *Akagi*'s CAG had insisted he should fly to coordinate the *Kido Butai*'s strike. The man was pale from blood loss, an evasive maneuver and flak having reopened his wounds. He had required an emergency transfusion upon landing on the *Akagi* and been confined to the sick bay until summoned."

"Yes," Yamaguchi said. "Someone find Commander Fuchida a chair."

The staff sprang to his orders, and Fuchida sunk into the furniture without protest.

The fact Fuchida is willing to accept a chair tells me just how badly hurt he is.

"Sir, when will we launch our strike against the American carriers?" Fuchida asked, his voice just loud enough for Yamaguchi to hear.

"You will not be leading it, Commander," Yamaguchi stated, his tone brooking no argument. "We will assess what damage we've done to their battleships first."

Fuchida looked like he wanted to argue, but lacked sufficient energy.

"The strike group is in sight!"

Kaku and Yamaguchi looked at one another, then moved as one to the bridge wing once more. Both men braced themselves as the *Akagi* began to turn into the wind.

Captain Aoki is apparently trying to minimize the carrier's predictability, Yamaguchi thought, struggling to retain his footing as the *Akagi* heeled over. He reflexively glanced to where the *Akigumo* had been and was relieved to see the destroyer had already begun transitioning to a station on the outside of the *Kido Butai*'s screen.

*The destroyers will have to refuel. Especially with the screen spread...***shit***.

"Rear Admiral Kaku, what vessels did we leave with the *Soryu*?" Yamaguchi asked, narrowing his eyes as he quickly swiveled around the screen.

"The *Agano, Chikuma*, and four destroyers," Kaku stated. The *Chikuma* is preparing to launch her next search to try and find the American carriers."

Yamaguchi nodded, then brought up his binoculars.

"Well, looks like some of the squadrons are coming back sooner than others," he stated. Kaku murmured his agreement, also scanning the returning group.

It was only after fifteen minutes passed that Yamaguchi's pulse began to race. As the first *Tenzan* lined up "into the slot," he turned to Kaku. His chief of staff's face reflected the worry that was almost surely on his own.

"Where is the rest of the strike force?" he asked. "Did *Soryu* recover some aircraft?"

"We will find out immediately," Kaku said, his voice strained. He strode into the bridge, shouting as Yamaguchi turned back to watch the torpedo bomber, slightly weaving, line up on the *Akagi*'s deck lights.

He's too low.

The shouts from other observers on *Akagi*'s island told Yamaguchi several others shared in his assessment. As the landing officer began screaming below, the *Tenzan* pilot made a radical correction and just barely slammed his bomber down onto the *Akagi*'s deck. The bomber's arrester hook caught, but the engine continued to roar before it was belatedly cut.

By the gods...

The torpedo's rear cockpit was shattered, with the savaged remains of the tail gunner still holding what was left of the rear gun. The observer was nowhere to be found, but the bloodstained fuselage and peppered empennage didn't bode well for his survival either.

"What is the matter with that idiot?!" Kaku asked, then cursed as he too realized what had happened to the aircraft. As the crews rushed forward, the pilot ripped his seat belt off and stood up, screaming and flinging his helmet at the *Akagi*'s bridge. The first crew chief to reach him attempted to render assistance and collected a blow to the head for his troubles. The crazed man continued to scream expletives, his eyes wild as he began ripping off his life jacket, then threw his navigational chart at another member of the deck crew.

"He's gone mad," Kaku noted. Clearly that opinion was shared by several others, as a contingent of crew rushed towards the pilot and tackled him. It took five or six men to finally drag the inconsolate man down, the sound of his screams drowned out as the next *Tenzan* roared low over the *Akagi*'s deck.

"I want the senior surviving officer to report to me immediately,"

Yamaguchi ordered. "I also want a report on how many aircraft the *Soryu* recovered. I will be in my flag cabin."

As he turned to walk away, Yamaguchi hoped no one realized how close he was to vomiting. Nodding to the orderly outside his hatch, he stepped through it and closed the entry behind him. Only then did he allow his knees to buckle as he dropped to the deck.

We are lost.

Bile rose in his throat as he considered what had apparently happened, his doubt frantic. It was only through the greatest effort that he prevented himself from vomiting as he stood, then staggered to his desk. Dropping into his chair, Yamaguchi put his face into his hands. For several long minutes, he gave into his despair, shoulders shaking as he drew quaking breaths.

The victor of Hawaii. Undone by his arrogance and stupidity.

Even as he berated himself, Yamaguchi realized he was being an idiot.

Think how to get out of the trap, Tamon. Nothing else is important.

Once more, Yamaguchi considered what factors were involved. His pilots had savaged the Royal Navy. The majority of his force could continue to steam at high speed. Even with his four carriers untouched, Fletcher's air groups had not come through the morning unscathed. Ozawa was to his north, and as humiliating as it was, the *Kido Butai* would have to flee towards him.

*I will likely lose the **Soryu**, but I do not need to sacrifice cruisers with her. Especially given the Vinson bill and what is coming.*

Yamaguchi's thoughts turned to the shipyards he had seen during his assignment to the United States.

It is fortunate indeed the Germans forced the British to provide fleet assets in the Atlantic. If we had to fight the USN solely by ourselves, we would drown in an overwhelming tide.

The knock on the hatch broke him out of those dour ruminations. Taking a moment to compose himself, Yamaguchi sat up straighter at his desk.

"Enter!" he barked.

That the strike's senior survivor was a lieutenant whom he did not recognize nearly sent Yamaguchi back into a tailspin of despair. The young man looked shell shocked, as if he had watched his comrades eaten by some great monster. Nearly staggering as he came forward, the lieutenant regained his equilibrium, came to attention, and saluted.

"Lieutenant Minase reporting, sir," the man said. Kaku walked in behind the young officer just in time for Minase to mutter a curse, turn, and suddenly vomit on the chief of staff's shoes. The rear admiral looked at the man in shock, even as the lieutenant stepped back in horror and bowed while muttering apologies.

"You idiot!" Kaku began.

"It's all right Lieutenant Minase," Yamaguchi said, standing up and motioning for his chief of staff to back away. "Orderly, have the surgeon get some sake for this man."

Ten minutes later, as sailors scrubbed where Minase had lost his lunch and the surgeon was handing him a second glass of sake, Yamaguchi gently prodded him to start talking. After a few moments, the dive bomber pilot started his account.

"The escorts cleared the enemy fighters," Minase said, shaking. "It appeared that it would be like Hawaii all over again."

Yamaguchi saw tears starting to form in the man's eyes.

"We went in first, to clear the way for the *Tenzans*..."

As Minase recounted the attack on the Allied fleet, Yamaguchi began to make mental notes.

I wish there was some way we could have sent a camera.

The *Kido Butai* had correspondents, but most of them had gone to document the first strike on the British. Seeing the attack unfold would have told him a great deal about the American defenses.

"Thank you, lieutenant," Yamaguchi said when Minase was done. The junior officer nodded, finished his sake, then bowed. Yamaguchi watched him go, then waited until the orderlies and his flag lieutenant left also, the latter closing the hatch behind him.

"Order the *Chikuma* to detach from the *Soryu*," Yamaguchi ordered.

"Sir?" Kaku asked, aghast.

"She cannot keep up with the rest of the force," Yamaguchi stated. "I cannot launch another strike, not in the face of those defenses."

"Sir, we can..."

"We can what, Kaku?" Yamaguchi snapped. "Throw more pilots we can't replace into a cauldron? *This* battle is over, and we must save what we can."

Kaku continued to look at him, shock clearly on his face.

"I have no trouble with dying as a samurai," Yamaguchi continued. "I will *not* throw these men as snowballs into a furnace."

Kaku looked like he was about to argue, then bowed.

"Admiral Yamamoto can countermand my orders if he thinks they are improper," Yamaguchi continued. "Have a signal prepared for the *Soryu* to send."

It only took a moment for Kaku to realize what Yamaguchi's orders meant.

"Sir..." Kaku said.

"The time for pleasantries is past," Yamaguchi replied. "I will give the *Soryu* what CAP we can as long as she is in range, but I am not losing four carriers to save another."

Kaku nodded, then exited the compartment. Yamaguchi turned to regard the Indian Ocean map on the starboard bulkhead.

Regardless of what happens the next few hours, we own Ceylon. If the Italians continue to move their fleet south into the Indian Ocean, the Americans will not be able to surprise us like this again.

Pacific Fleet Headquarters
2130 Local (0330 Eastern)
9 August (10 August)

"Bill, I got the message and came over as quickly as I could," Admiral Dunlap said as he walked into the Pacific Fleet's status room. "Now tell me what was so urgent you had some poor ensign drive from this building to my house at reckless speed."

Vice Admiral Halsey turned around from where he stood at the map. The look on the man's face made Dunlap's stomach drop. He kept his own face confident despite Halsey's funereal appearance.

Oh shit, Fletcher has gotten his ass kicked. But panic is contagious, and there will be none of that in this headquarters.

"Frank has gotten himself in a bit of a bind," Vice Admiral Halsey said, holding up a message flimsy. "It's roughly an hour old."

Admiral Dunlap took the message and read it quickly, then shook his head.

"I'd say it's a mixed bag," Dunlap said. He turned to the young officer Halsey had sent to fetch him.

"Ensign MacDonnell, I need you to go back to my quarters and collect Vice Admiral Wake-Walker," Dunlap said. "He may bring his aide or a flag captain, *but no one else*."

"Aye aye, sir," the ensign said, his blue eyes earnest. He hurried out of the headquarters, and Dunlap looked back at the message once more.

Mixed bag indeed, Dunlap thought as he finished rereading Vice Admiral Fletcher's report. Looking up, he regarded Halsey, then the other man standing with him. Like Halsey, Vice Admiral John Towers looked like he was about to attend a funeral.

"How did we get this status report?" Dunlap asked. "Please tell me Fletcher did not break radio silence to send something this long."

"Jack dragged the *Curtiss* out from Brisbane to operate with his tankers," Towers explained.

"The *Curtiss*?" Dunlap asked, confused for a moment. Halsey and Towers looked at one another.

"Gentlemen, pretend that I'm someone who just got dragged off the retired list and has yet to receive the full update from the staff," Dunlap stated with a smile. "Because you may recall, that is exactly who I am."

"Sorry sir," Vice Admiral Halsey said, his tone sincere. "When war began, I detached the *Curtiss* to the Asiatic Fleet once we were sure that the Japanese weren't coming back to Hawaii for an extended stay."

Which, to be fair, some would say we're still making a big assumption on. However, they hardly even nicked the Army's air forces back in March, so they'd have needed all those big carriers again.

Admiral Dunlap allowed himself a small prayer of thanksgiving that his predecessor had at least managed to bag one Japanese carrier and mauled another.

Even if it seems like the damaged vessel got back into action quicker than we expected, it sure has kept the Japanese from being overly aggressive in **this** *direction.*

"So Fletcher is using her as a relay station?" Dunlap asked. "How?"

"I assume some sort of flying relay, sir," Vice Admiral Towers answered. "Put a dispatch on a SBD, fly it back to the *Curtiss*, she transmits the message."

Dunlap considered the map of the Indian Ocean that was now stapled to a rolling blackboard and wheeled in front of the main Pacific map.

I am still at a loss on how half my fleet ended up in the Indian Ocean. Although I'm sure that's exactly what poor Husband is thinking right now as well. He's going to be super happy to find out he's fresh out of battleships.

Pushing thoughts of Admiral Kimmel's likely reaction from his mind, Admiral Dunlap turned to his own staff.

"So explain to me why you both look like your dogs died right after your wives filed for divorce," Dunlap said.

Once again, Halsey and Towers shared a look as if they were wondering about their new commander's mental facilities.

"Yes, it sounds like the *Massachusetts* is pretty hard hit and the *Indiana* is going to need some time in the repair yard," Dunlap continued. "Both of which triggers Fletcher's orders to disengage. But he thinks he's severely damaged or sunk three Japanese carriers, and last I checked he has all four of his left to pursue."

"Sir, that's part of the problem," Halsey said firmly. "Unless you release Fletcher from Admiral King's orders, he cannot catch the remaining Jap carriers."

Now we come to the meat of it. They want me to authorize Fletcher to disregard Admiral King's last directive.

"I am willing to admit my ignorance of carrier operations, gentlemen," Dunlap said. "That's why I have you both. If that map is correct, the Japanese are still well within range of Fletcher's forces."

Halsey and Towers looked at each other as Dunlap continued.

"Even if he is forced to start shepherding some cripples, it seems like he has more than enough firepower and time to finish the job," Dunlap stated. "Tell me what I'm not understanding before I agree to countermand a former superior."

Towers must be a helluva poker player. However, Vice Admiral Halsey I can read like a book.

"Sir, with all due respect, Admiral King is dead," Vice Admiral Halsey exploded, gesturing at the map. "We have a chance to *finish the Jap fleet off.*"

Halsey did not answer my question.

Dunlap briefly considered whether he wanted to push harder in the face of the man's near insubordinate response, but decided to take a different tack.

"I have a distinct advantage that neither of you gentlemen possess," Dunlap said. "Namely, I got to speak both with Secretary Knox and President Roosevelt before I got on a plane to fly out here."

Dunlap paused to make sure both men understood the implications of what he was saying. Seeing that both of them recognized that it was not only *King*'s orders that Fletcher had been given, Dunlap continued.

"So, yes, Admiral King, like Winston Churchill, belongs to the ages now," Dunlap stated. "The first did not want any British vessels taking part in what he considered to be a two party war between the United States and Japan."

Both Halsey and Towers' expressions indicated they could imagine one Admiral Ernest J. King's likely profane statements in favor of British exclusion. King's disgust with all things British had not exactly been a secret among the USN's senior officers.

I hope it's not true that he cursed at the Queen back when Secretary Knox and he went to collect that poor Cobb kid back in August. Still, I could easily believe it to be so.

"The second was quite willing to parlay some of the last heavy units the Royal Navy had left to support our Central Pacific advance if it meant we dispatched vessels to the Indian Ocean."

Dunlap turned and gestured out the window of the headquarters towards where the *Nelson* and *Rodney* had tied up along Battleship Row along with the *Maryland* earlier that evening.

"The British kept their end of the deal," Dunlap stated. "It was made clear to them that we were only upholding our end provided it did not result in the loss of the *Massachusetts* or *Indiana*."

Dunlap walked over towards the map, grabbing a long pointer from the bin where they were kept.

Time to educate both of them on how averse to risk I am. This will teach me not to have a staff meeting before I have a meet and greet with my subordinates.

"Yes, Admiral King belongs to the ages," Dunlap began, then pointed to the icons representing the Japanese force off of Ceylon. "However, these Japanese carriers don't, and despite my clear question neither one of you have explained to me why Fletcher can't attack the other flattops he's surprised from where he's at right now."

"He doesn't have enough fighters for both missions," Towers said, his tone defeated. Dunlap saw Halsey start to turn and look at Towers before the other vice admiral caught himself.

Ah, now I see. Guess ol' Bill thought that was something to keep from the boss. Best nip that in the bud.

"Now gentlemen, that sounds dangerously like you were wanting me to gamble with money that doesn't belong to me," Dunlap said, trying to keep his tone conversational after a long, pointed look at both his subordinates.

"Sir, those Japanese carriers up by Ceylon have their hands full with the invasion," Halsey spat in response to his rebuke. "We asked the G-2 and he's sure of it."

Dunlap considered the map, then pointed at the fleeing Japanese force.

"I bet you, unless he got killed by Fletcher's first strike, there's a Japanese admiral who regrets listening to whatever his G-2 told him several hours ago," Dunlap said. He then smacked the map where Vice Admiral Vian's force was.

"Yesterday, before he got himself killed, Vice Admiral Cunningham probably wished he'd ignored all the reports that those same Japanese carriers you guys want Fletcher to "bag" were up by Ceylon.."

With that last comment, Dunlap fixed Vice Admiral Halsey with a glare that could have welded a battleship's turret armor.

"At least my predecessor's intelligence officer had the courtesy to die from his mistake," Dunlap said. "Of course, he did get Admiral Greenman killed doing so. I *guess* distance will keep the same from happening to me, but that's going to be cold comfort if I *have no carriers left*."

Vice Admiral Halsey exhaled heavily, his jaw clenched.

I think I've made my point.

He turned back to the map to give Vice Admiral Halsey a chance to rein in his temper.

I need to get this man back to sea before it kills him or makes his relief necessary.

"Tell me more about this fighter problem," Dunlap continued, changing the subject. "I see the numbers on this report, but they don't tell me anything."

"It seems like Vice Admiral Fletcher lost quite a few fighters in his first strike and trying to defend the surface ships," Towers said. "It's likely they weren't all shot down and the numbers may change between today and tomorrow, but there are only so many planes to go around."

"Roughly twenty-five to thirty percent losses," Vice Admiral Halsey further explained. "Problem is, a large number of those are the new *Hellcat* and *Corsairs*, which are the only aircraft that can match up with that big Japanese fighter they showed up with back in March."

Speaking of intelligence failures.

Dunlap watched as Halsey reached into his pocket for a pack of cigarettes. Taking one out, the Vice Admiral offered the pack towards Dunlap.

"Sir?"

"No thank you," Dunlap said wistfully. "Decided to quit after the heart attack."

Halsey nodded sympathetically as he turned and offered the pack to Towers.

Well, guess that confirms they've asked around about me.

The heart attack that had contributed to his retirement wasn't common knowledge, even if the feud between Admiral King and he was.

Might have been a bit embarrassing to ol' Ernest's memory if the circumstances came to light. Most men don't nearly kill themselves chasing a superior officer out of their marital bed.

"So you're telling me even if Fletcher could strike, he would likely lose more of his fighters because they're inferior?" Dunlap asked, resuming the conversation.

"Between us and the British, I'm sure we've reduced the Japanese numbers," Halsey said after a pause. "Their other carrier fighter, the *Zero*, is only slightly superior to the *Wildcat*."

Slightly *superior isn't going to be a whole lot of comfort to young men expected to fight it.*

"So when will we have some of the new *Corsairs* and *Hellcats* for Fletcher's carriers?" Dunlap asked. "Since it appears the Atlantic Fleet's supply is going to need some replenishing before the *Bonhomme Richard* and *Independence* go back east."

"The first two replacement air groups are expected to arrive in the next week," Vice Admiral Towers said without missing a beat. "There will be another twenty each of *Corsairs* and *Hellcats* in reserve."

"But the carriers will have to come back to Pearl to get these aircraft, yes?" Dunlap asked.

"Yes, sir," Towers replied. "Unless we send them south on one of the escort carriers."

"Which would mean the battle line would have no air cover as opposed to very poor air cover, apparently," Dunlap noted. Towers stiffened slightly at that.

"Not your fault, Vice Admiral Towers," Dunlap said, then gestured towards the Royal Navy symbol near the Maldives. "But given our allies' reports, the *Enterprise* and *Yorktown* will be the only two serviceable modern carriers remaining in the Pacific when the *Bonhomme Richard* and *Independence* head home."

"Yes sir," Towers replied.

"Well, as Vice Admiral Halsey knows, I was already planning on bringing the *Enterprise* and *Yorktown* back to Pearl," Dunlap said. "This only reinforces that decision."

"Sir, is there a reason we're not asking the Combined Staff to allow those two carriers to remain out here?" Halsey asked.

"Yes," Dunlap snapped, then caught his temper. "Namely that I was told the answer would be 'absolutely not' and that asking would be frowned upon."

In an instant, Halsey's face went back to forlorn.

Wondered if you were going to remember the Atlantic Fleet's carrier problem.

Once more Dunlap looked at the map, watching Halsey angrily puff on his cigarette while clenching his left fist.

I see part of the reason I was sent out here was Vice Admiral Halsey would lose the entire fleet in a fortnight. Sure he'd take most of the Japanese fleet with him, but that still wouldn't help the Nervous Nellies back in Washington.

"There was a terrible rumor that you'd ordered torpedo tests to begin next week, Vice Admiral Halsey," Dunlap said after a moment.

"Yes sir, I did," Vice Admiral Halsey replied, stiffening.

"Yes, the head of BuOrd had apparently petitioned Admiral King to order you not to waste weapons," Dunlap stated, referring to the Bureau of Ordnance. "Given that the Atlantic Fleet has also reported torpedo problems at the Battle of Iceland, Admiral King had a very blunt response to that."

Dunlap looked back at the map, then shook the dispatch in his hand as he spoke.

"Would you say, Admiral Towers, that based on the losses to the torpedo squadrons that Vice Admiral Fletcher also sent most of them with the first strike?"

"Yes sir, I would," Towers replied.

"Does he have enough remaining to do a second strike?" Dunlap asked.

Towers looked at the notepad he had in his hand. Dunlap watched as the man's brow furrowed, much like a secondary student doing a difficult algebra problem. Halsey crushed out the cigarette in his hand and immediately lit another.

I think Halsey knows what this answer **should** *be and is not happy about it.*

"Raw numbers, yes," Towers said. "But I would need to know what the squadrons each had left."

"How much damage can the dive bombers do?" Dunlap asked.

"Quite a bit to carriers, sir," Towers replied. "Especially if they're caught while refueling and rearming."

"But it's typically not fatal without torpedo bomber help?"

"No, sir," Towers replied.

"To go back to my earlier question, Vice Admiral Halsey," Dunlap started, "I want you to start the tests *immediately*. I want you to figure out a way to put dummy warheads on the British torpedoes, and test them alongside ours."

Halsey looked at Dunlap in surprise.

"I want you to select the torpedoes at random, and I want you to test submarine, surface, and aerial torpedoes. At least *twenty* of each."

Both men looked at Dunlap in shock.

"Sir, that's going to make some people quite annoyed back in Washington," Halsey said quietly.

"Then those people can get on a plane and come out here," Dunlap snapped. "And I'll put their asses in the back of a damn *Avenger* or aboard a submarine going out on patrol as an observer."

"Sir, are you going to direct Admiral Hart to make the same tests?" Towers asked. "That might make him a little short on aircraft torpedoes if the *Bonhomme Richard* and *Independence* resupply in Sydney before going home."

It's probably about time I get ol' Thomas used to the fact he now works for me.

Technically Admiral Hart, as the commander of the Asiatic Fleet and a four star, had been senior to Halsey. Nominally to avoid overloading Hart during the defense of the Dutch East Indies, the Combined Chiefs of Staff had enacted a dividing line between the Southwest and Pacific spheres. In reality, it had been to keep Hart from meddling with the Pacific Fleet while he was senior. Dunlap's assumption of command orders explicitly directed that Hart was subordinate to him while still maintaining the Southwest Pacific Area's responsibility.

Glad they outlined the command relationship in the orders. Seniority gets kind of sticky when they've brought you out of retirement with a promotion to boot.

"Yes, direct Admiral Hart to carry out the same tests," Dunlap said. "I expect that he can have it completed within two weeks."

Vice Admiral Halsey scribbled down the note with a smile. Seeing Dunlap's curious expression, Towers spoke up.

"Rear Admiral Christie is not going to like your orders, sir," Towers explained. "He was the former head of torpedoes at Newport and has been loudly insisting that nothing is wrong from Brisbane."

"If he or anyone else down there wants to get a free reassignment to the Great Lakes, they can go ahead and raise a fuss," Dunlap replied sharply. "While BuPers is being their usual stupid selves about personnel rules, I've been told by Secretary Knox himself that anything I ask for, I'll get. I don't think the man who might be the root of our problems wants to test me."

There were several long moments of silence as Halsey continued scribbling.

I can only imagine how amused the Army is that their requests to put a four star down in Australia were denied by the President himself. Might have been a vastly different discussion if MacArthur had lived, but for now this will be a Navy show.

"Next order of business, since we're issuing directives: I want the staff to prepare an estimate for retaking Wake Island," Dunlap continued.

Halsey stopped writing and looked up.

"Bill, you'll be in charge of putting together the plan," Dunlap ordered. "You'll also likely be the person running the carriers."

"Sir, what about Vice Admiral Fletcher?" Towers asked, shocked.

"Vice Admiral Fletcher will be planning the subsequent operation," Dunlap stated.

There was the sound of running feet down the hallway. An out of breath commander dashed through the door, waving message.

"Sir, update from the *Curtiss*," the man panted, looking at Vice Admiral Halsey.

"Well, you may want to give it to your new fleet commander, Commander Curts," Halsey said genially. Curts turned, his face apologetic.

"Sorry sir, old habits die hard," Curts said, handing over the message.

"I understand we have you to thank for the ability to even communicate to the Indian Ocean," Dunlap said, taking the message.

"Sir, there are those who pass that scuttlebutt," Commander Curts replied, his tone humble. "I'd like to think I've had good subordinates and bosses who listened."

Dunlap nodded as he took the message. Reading the first two lines, he stopped and looked at Halsey and Towers.

"Well, seems like Vice Admiral Fletcher has made any thoughts on possibly intervening superfluous," he said, handing the message to Halsey. "Indeed, if he kept to this intended schedule, he's already launching as we speak."

9

DROWNING DRAGON

Even the bravest cannot fight beyond strength.

— **HOMER**

U.S.S. YORKTOWN
1315 LOCAL (0405 EASTERN)
10 AUGUST

"GATHER AROUND, gentlemen, it's time to find out how we're going to go make history!" Lieutenant Commander Brigante shouted over the din of *Yorktown*'s flight deck as he strode out of the carrier's island.

Eric turned away from where he'd been letting the breeze over the carrier's deck blow into his face. The air was strongly tinged with exhaust as *Yorktown* began launching her contribution to TF 24's Combat Air Patrol. The eight CAP *Wildcats* had been arranged in the front of the *Dauntlesses* spotted near the end of her deck, and Eric had been certain they'd have been the dive bombers' escort.

Guess the range was too far even with drop tanks. Hopefully by next battle we'll actually have **Hellcats** *too.*

"Looks like some *Kingfishers* off the *Baltimore* and *Tuscaloosa* found your former lady friend, Lieutenant Cobb," Brigante said as the group gathered around. "Either that, or someone else hit her sister and didn't make it back."

Eric felt a palpable sense of relief as the gathered group looked at Brigante.

Glad he's back on board. Otherwise I'd probably be the poor bastard expected to lead this strike.

Brigante had landed his damaged *Dauntless* aboard the *Enterprise*, his gunner dead with shell fragments through his neck and the aircraft a write off. VB-11's squadron commander had then bullied his way aboard an *Avenger* and flown back to *Yorktown*, arriving about 20 minutes before TF 25's cruiser scouts had made their report. This had made Brigante, as the senior ambulatory officer, de facto CAG-*Yorktown*.

Helluva way to get promoted.

"If the cruiser boys can be believed, she's bleeding oil like a gutshot deer," Brigante said, pointing at the map.

The cruiser pilots will have to carry their balls home in wheelbarrow after this.

Eric had glanced at the map twice, finding it hard to believe the initial reports when they came in. The Vought *Kingfisher*s off of the *Baltimore* and *Tuscaloosa* made his own *Dauntless* seem positively swift.

Sure you can spot a carrier from well outside of the range they can see you, but they had to fly through that front between both sides.

The line of thunderheads Brigante had sketched on the map caused him to shudder. Looking around, he could see his concern was shared.

"Of course, one of them got too close and got himself shot down, but another one's been ducking in and out of clouds updating her position every twenty minutes," Brigante said.

Or you fuck up and the CAP kills you.

The gathered group shared glances and murmured about the dead pilot's bad luck.

"Even if he's a bit off, that trail will lead right to her."

"What about the rest of the Jap carriers?" one of the gathered pilots asked.

"This bitch is just at two hundred miles," Brigante said. "The guy shadowing her wisely decided not to go looking for trouble given what happened to his buddy, but I'm guessing the other carriers are probably trying to rearm after punching the shit out of the surface ships."

Brigante looked at the gathered group.

"Good news is, another one of the other *Kingfishers* found a huge oil slick, a bunch of debris, and a couple dozen bodies near where we bombed the first group," Brigante said. "So pretty sure we got at least one more of those damn carriers this morning."

The lieutenant commander paused at that and looked up at Eric as if expecting him to confirm the statement. After an awkward pause, Brigante turned back to his map.

"The staff is certain the other Japanese carriers are coming down from Ceylon," Brigante continued. "So they're not going to launch everything just to finish this one off. That's why I selected you men rather than just launching one or the other *Dauntless* squadrons."

And there aren't enough torpedeckers left to really justify asking them to make another attack.

He'd pointedly not counted noses in the VT-11 ready room when he'd briefly ducked to look for Seward. However, in addition to confirming his ersatz roommate had not landed back aboard *Yorktown*, Eric had been given a stark reminder of just how deadly torpedo bombing was.

Lots of empty seats in that ready room. Way too many.

Brigante turned to make eye contact with every man as he made his next statement.

"All of you are experienced and have put a bomb into something this cruise," he declared. "If we're only going to launch fourteen *Dauntlesses*, I want to make sure that we get enough hits to put this damn carrier down."

Eric nodded as he continued looking at the line of thunderheads.

"What has got your attention, Lieutenant Cobb?" Brigante asked. "You've been looking at that map like you're trying to memorize every freckle on your girlfriend's chest."

"Those thunderstorms, sir," Eric said. "Gonna be fun flying back through them if we get damaged."

"The weather's not going to be that bad, Cobb!" Brigante chided teasingly. "You act like you've been shot down twice or something!"

Eric glared at his superior officer.

"I've also *hit* my target, sir," he shot back, leading to several jeers and laughs from the gathered pilots. Brigante took the comeback in stride, looking at a couple of the gathered group.

"Well since our good friends from VS-11 will be joining us rather than screwing up our dives," Brigante replied, causing the four men standing around Eric to shift. "I think this will go a lot better."

"You can go fuck yourself," Charles muttered from beside Eric, his voice raw but still just low enough for Eric to hear. Eric made sure he didn't glance over at his friend, suddenly glad the engine roar from the last *Wildcat* taking off made it difficult to hear. For a brief moment, the *Yorktown*'s flight deck was quiet.

"Well, let's get this show on the road, we're already late!" Brigante shouted, stepping away from his map. "Hurry up and get the position copied down, then man your planes."

The gathered pilots quickly complied, each pilot swiftly marking down the damaged carrier's position then turning towards their respective *Dauntless*. Eric grabbed Charles' arm as the younger officer angrily finished sketching the necessary bearing and heading. Moving away from where Brigante knelt, Eric waited until they were definitely out of earshot.

"He didn't mean anything by it, Charles," Eric said. He watched Charles' nostrils flare as the man turned and looked back at Brigante.

Man goes out there with a temper like that, he won't be coming back.. He suddenly felt a moment of terror.

"You lost your squadron leader," Eric spoke rapidly. "Lieutenant Commander Brigante has lost several good friends."

"And I fucking haven't, Eric?" Charles nearly shouted.

"Goddammit, push it out of your head," Eric replied, annoyed at how desperate he sounded. "I don't want to deal with Toots losing the man she loves."

Charles looked like he was going to snap something else, but stopped. Face still flush, he nodded stiffly.

"Judging from what she told me about you as kids, you'd probably just make her angrier," Charles said with a wry grin.

"Toots cleans when she's angry," Eric said. "I don't think Jo would appreciate the spotless house *that* much."

Charles extended his hand, and Eric took it.

"See you when we get back," he said.

"You better," Eric replied. "Someday I'm going to have kids, and it'd be nice if they had at least *one* sane uncle."

Charles shook his head.

"You sure it's too late to let your sister down easy?"

"Cobb! Read! Hurry up gentlemen!" Lieutenant Commander Brigante shouted.

With a final glance, Eric turned and continued back to Blue One. He briefly looked over to where the *last* Blue One had been pushed over the side, then once more shook himself out of reverie.

Going to walk into a damn propeller if this keeps up. This day was supposed to be over by now, and I'm starting to get loopy.

Eric was startled to see Brown sliding gingerly off his wing as he walked up to Blue One.

"Goddammit Brown," Eric muttered. "I thought they told you to stay in sick bay?"

Brown shrugged, then cursed in pain.

Yeah, maybe not shrug with a partially dislocated shoulder, hmm?

Brown had not realized he'd injured the joint at some point that morning until the adrenaline rush had worn off. From what Eric understood, two of the squadron's gunners had threatened to drag Brown to sick bay rather than let him fly again in such a state.

"I'll be all right, sir," Brown said, clearly angry that he was missing the attack. The scowl left his face as he gave one more glance towards the clearly petrified young man checking the *Dauntless*'s rear guns yet again. "I was just explaining to Radioman 3rd Class Constanza how he needs to subtract 1000 feet from the *actual* altitude if he actually wants to get back here alive today."

"You did *not* tell him that," Eric said, his drawl deepening. Brown nearly shrugged again but caught himself.

"Well, guess you'll find out when you get to that damn carrier, sir,"

Brown replied. "Sounds like it's the same one we hit earlier. This time, punch that bitch like you just caught her poking a hole in the rubber."

Eric's eyes widened as Brown walked past him towards the island.

Jesus, I hope that was the morphine talking.

He'd known Brown was a hard man, but that simple sentence told him more about his gunner than their many conversations while flying. Shaking his head, Eric quickly got in the dive bomber and went through his preflight ritual with the crew chief. Satisfied, he clicked the intercom.

"So Constanza, where you from?" Eric asked, fighting the urge to cough as he inhaled exhaust from the section of *Dauntlesses* in front of him.

"Minneapolis, sir," Constanza replied.

Kid sounds like he's twelve.

Fear and responsibility jumped on Eric's proverbial shoulders with hobnailed boots at that moment. Shrugging it off, he tried to keep the conversation light.

"Minneapolis?!" Eric asked. "How'd you find yourself out here in the middle of the Indian Ocean from Minneapolis?"

"It was volunteer for the Navy or get drafted for the Army," Constanza replied. "I wasn't expecting them to get me through training as quickly as they did though."

"Quickly?" Eric asked, watching as Brigante started down the flight deck.

"My high school graduated me early back in March on account of me being already 18," Constanza said. "So here I am."

Eighteen. He can't even vote and he's stuck here in the back of some plane hoping I don't get his ass shot off.

"Here's to hoping you can tell your grandchildren about the time you sailed with Fletcher," Eric said, watching as the last of the *ad hoc* Yellow Flight trundled down the *Yorktown*'s deck. Advancing forward slightly under direction of the plane director, Eric spared a quick glance up towards the island. He recognized Vice Admiral Fletcher and his staff all watching the takeoff but did not have time to study their faces before it was his turn to advance the throttle and roll down the *Yorktown*'s deck.

I'm really starting to wonder about my life choices, Eric thought as he left the teak deck behind him. Raising the gear and looking over the *Dauntless*, he listened closely to the engine and gently waggled the wings.

Well, looks like this lady is none the worst for wear having been suspended from the hangar roof, Eric assessed as he searched for the rest of the strike. Acquiring the circling *Dauntlesses*, he turned into the oval and waited for the rest of the scratch Blue Flight to join up. Blue Two was Lieutenant Lang, a tall, gangly man from VS-11 Eric had only seen a couple times in passing he'd joined the *Yorktown* in Sydney. Blue Three was Lieutenant Silverstein, also from VS-11.

I guess drawing heavily from the experienced pilots makes sense given how far of a strike this is, Eric mused as they climbed up to cruising altitude. Double-checking to make sure he had good oxygen flow, Eric glanced towards the sun.

At least there's plenty of daylight to get back in.

It took roughly twenty minutes for the *Yorktown*'s *Dauntlesses* to finish joining up, another five for them to tuck in under the eight *Hellcats* that were their escort.

Surprised Fletcher's staff is allowing any of the new fighters to come along. **Bonhomme Richard** *must have lowered some spares from the hangar ceiling.*

The combined force flew along a half hour before Constanza spoke from the rear cockpit.

"Sir, Radioman Brown said that he hoped my affairs were in order as trouble keeps finding you."

Not an unfair statement, Eric thought bitterly as his gunner continued.

"But that you, being an officer and all, could take down my last will and testament if I thought of anything on the way to the carrier if I just waited until we were in formation."

Brown you son of a bitch.

"Brown is an evil man who is just upset he didn't get to come shoot at more people," Eric muttered. Before he could say anything else, he saw a slight smudge of white smoke begin to drift back from Yellow Two's engine. The stream thickened quickly as the *Dauntless* broke formation and jettisoned its bomb as it turned back towards the *Yorktown*.

"Sir, does that happen all the time?" Constanza asked, his query slightly high-pitched.

"All the time, no," Eric replied. "But we also don't fight a carrier battle every day either. Don't worry, they'll be fine."

Mild white lie.

No one had broken radio silence to report the damaged *Dauntless*, not even the in distress crew. He hoped that the VS-11 bird made it back in one piece, but if it went down the two men aboard were screwed.

With the surface boys forty miles north and west of us, I'm not even sure their floatplanes are this far out.

He pulled out his plotting board and made a quick notation on the side, hoping that someone had paid better attention than him to navigation.

Get your damn head in the game, Eric! War means fighting, and fighting means dying. Stop thinking about Stratmore, Strange, and Van Horn or you'll be joining them.

Glancing back at Lieutenant Commander Brigante's aircraft, Eric saw the rear gunner fumbling with something in his lap. A moment later, the man fired one yellow flare then, a few moments later, a red one.

One small thing Hitchcock got right was establishing procedures for signaling without radio within the squadron. Sure I hope he's burning like a greasy newspaper in Hell, but he at least got that right.

"Constanza, get ready to write this down!" Eric barked. He heard a rustling in the back of the aircraft, followed by a surprised curse.

"Constanza? What the hell was that?" Eric asked, thinking he already knew. There was a long pause.

"Sir, I just lost my logbook," Constanza replied.

Goddammit, Brown with a bum shoulder might have been the better option.

Before Eric could say anything else, Red One's gunner began signaling.

STORM AHEAD. LINE ABREAST
FORMATION, RENDEZVOUS TWENTY
MILES ON THE FAR SIDE.

Eric waggled his wings, then advanced his throttle to lead his section to starboard of Red. Leaving enough room for Blue Two and Three to formate on either wingtip, Eric glanced across at Brigante. The squadron commander flashed him a thumbs up that Eric returned before looking back forward.

Okay, that storm looks like it's getting worse by the minute.

There were no less than four thunderheads in front of them. The clouds' upper structures were visibly continuing to billow upwards, an ominous sign for anyone getting ready to fly through them. Looking upwards, Eric saw the escorting *Hellcats* starting to climb and angle to the south.

Brigante should probably follow them. The *Hellcat* leader was attempting to lead his group between two of the towering cumulonimbus. As the sleek fighters accelerated away from the *Dauntlesses*, Eric had another terrifying realization.

If we don't link back up with them, we're going to be meat on the table for any Japanese fighters over that carrier.

"Sir, shouldn't we close our canopies?" Constanza asked. Jerking out of his focus on the F6Fs, Eric quickly looked around to see he was one of the few pilots who had not already closed things up in preparation for the storm.

"Good call, Constanza," he replied, reaching up and sliding the cockpit shut. The dark clouds in front of them continued to swell in the windscreen, and for a brief moment he was back aboard a different *Dauntless* entering a squall over another ocean. Shaking his head to force away the memory, Eric forced himself to relax.

Just a storm. You've flown through squalls before. It's just a another...

What happened when the *Dauntless* was still five miles away from entering the cloud swiftly disabused him of that notion. One moment he was in level flight. The next a giant's fist was shoving the dive bomber's nose down in a flat descent so sudden it made the entire airframe shudder and creak. The impact of his legs into his lap belt was so sharp and sudden he cried out involuntarily, even as his pilot instincts kicked in and he brought the nose up. It was only his conscious brain catching up that prevented him from advancing the throttle, as just as suddenly the *Dauntless* soared upwards from an updraft.

Then the world was a cacophony of darkness, lightning flashes, and rain lashing at the dive bomber. Through the noise of their ten minute transit in the heart of the storm, as his arms and legs grew sore fighting the dive bomber through updrafts, Eric could hear Constanza screaming in terror from the rear seat, then gradually descending into helpless sobbing as the *Dauntless* nearly flipped over a half dozen times. In each instance, he managed to fight the updraft or downdraft just long enough to avoid an inevitable death plunge. It was only on the final iteration, as the plane hovered vibrating on the edge of a stall, that he briefly considered jettisoning the 1,000-lb. bomb that made its handling so much more precarious.

I did not come this far to turn around and leave.

His resolve wavered as the dive bomber hung vibrating on the edge of a stall. Fighting his fear, his bladder screaming for relief, Eric fought the dive bomber back to level.

Don't know if I can do that...wait, we're coming out.

Eric looked over the rainbow hue briefly wreathing his propeller as sunlight caught on moisture. Beyond he could see the Indian Ocean's majesty, blue waters stretching off into the horizon. Pulse racing from adrenaline, any thoughts of fatigue gone, Eric felt a sense of awe even as Costanza continued to sob incoherently.

What a time to be alive.

"Constanza," Eric said, fighting the urge to yell at his gunner. He repeated the man's name more firmly as the teenager continued to panic in the rear cockpit.

Like calming a startled horse.

To Eric's relief, the sobbing gradually stopped.

"Yes sir," Constanza said, then yelped as the *Dauntless* bucked with turbulence again.

"I need you to help me find the rest of the squadron," Eric stated, once more trying to keep his voice from being too severe. "Get out your binoculars and scan from nine to four, I'll take from nine to three."

There was the sound of shuffling equipment in the rear cockpit, then a moment later Constanza attempting to shove his canopy forward. The gunner strained mightily in the *Dauntless*' rear cockpit, and Eric began to grow concerned until, with a large *snap!*, whatever was obstructing the canopy's passage gave and it slammed forward. Opening his own canopy, Eric was struck in the face by the warm moisture coming off of the *Dauntless*' nose and into the cockpit.

Like a dog shaking itself off from the pond. Maybe I should have taken Secretary Knox's offer and stayed back home. Probably be married with a kid on the way by now.

"Sir, I don't see anyone," Constanza said, his tone worried. "Are we the only ones left?"

Wouldn't be the first time a storm ate an entire squadron, would it?

Eric's stomach churned as he considered the possibilities.

Goddammit Charles, you better have gone back home if you're not coming out this side.

"We'll give it five minutes," Eric said, setting course towards where he believed the rally point might be. Five minutes later, just as he was getting ready to give up hope and set off towards the Japanese carrier by himself, Eric spotted several dots descending from the heavens above.

"Constanza!" he barked after several seconds of nothing from the rear cockpit.

"Yes sir?" Constanza asked nervously as Eric put the *Dauntless* into a gentle turn.

"Get your damn guns out!" Eric ordered. "Never, *ever* assume bogeys are friendly."

"What bo...*oh shit!*" Constanza said. Eric gritted his teeth as he heard the twin machine guns being taken out of their stowage and hurriedly prepared for combat. Already Eric could tell the eight shapes were not *Dauntless* from the speed of their closure. With great relief, he quickly recognized the *Hellcats*' outline. The two flights of fighters zoomed over his *Dauntless* while waggling their wings.

"Sir! I've got three...no five *Dauntlesses* astern!"

Eric turned and saw the aircraft behind him. As the small strike group joined up, he felt his spirits soar as he sighted Blue Two and Three. The pair of pilots were trailing Yellow section. As the group joined up with him, Eric realized he was the senior officer present and the clock was not on their side.

"Constanza, signal all aircraft we're going to go find that carrier and then go home," Eric said. He heard Constanza grabbing his signal lamp, followed by clicking back and forth between Constanza and Yellow One's tail gunner.

"Sir, Yellow One is ready to follow you," Constanza said as the *Hellcats* began flying a protective weave overhead. Eric brought his nose around to the southeast, hoping that he had guessed correctly which way the storm had blown them. Fifteen minutes later, he was not disappointed, as he could see the glittering hue of floating oil beneath them.

Like a gutshot deer indeed. Well, time to go put Bambi's Mom out of her misery.

"Sir, more *Dauntlesses!*" Constanza said, pointing off to their south.

Dear Lord, please let Lieutenant Commander Brigante be among them, Eric thought, looking at the three approaching planes.

Two minutes later, in a sure sign that maybe he should be on better terms with the chaplain, Eric watched as Red One swung around to take the formation lead. He also noted that only one of the other bombers was part of the original Red section.

Hoping the Japanese can't call up any more divine weather. Or maybe I just need to accept God's not playing favorites today.

I.J.N.S. Soryu
1415 Local (0605 Eastern)

"You there! Pilot! You need to put out that cigarette!"

Isoro took a deep drag of the cigarette in question before turning around to see who was shouting at him from halfway down the *Soryu*'s flight deck. Seeing a mere ensign striding towards him, he exhaled the smoke in his lungs like an angry dragon.

This carrier smells like someone set fire to a meat shop, she's so low in the water I feel like I nearly ditched rather than landed, and I'm sitting here twiddling my thumbs while they refuel my fighter.

Isoro took another defiant drag of the cigarette as he watched the man continuing to close.

*But yes, let's talk about how my **one cigarette on an open flight deck** may be the demise of us all.*

"Are you deaf, you idiot?" the ensign screamed, his face starting to color as he strode forward. Although Isoro was sure the man was probably only a couple of years younger than him, the junior officer's outraged demeanor and ill fitting helmet made the gap seem much larger.

I am about to cuff you like we are back on the school yard.

Isoro took yet another drag, then again exhaled upwards so the man would see it. The ensign, truly incensed, began moving even quicker.

"I will *kill* you..." the man shouted, starting to break into a sprint down the *Soryu*'s damaged deck. Isoro was aware of several men turning from the gun tubs at the spoken threat. He ignored them and continued to focus on the stouter, shorter man he was about to come to blows with. To his shock, the officer stopped, looking past him.

"Ensign Tokugawa, I think that striking a superior officer would not improve your day," a wholly unfamiliar voice said from behind Isoro. "Even if you win, Vice Admiral Yamaguchi would have you flogged for removing Lieutenant Honda's services during this battle."

Isoro turned around to see another pilot, likewise outfitted in his flight suit and helmet, standing looking at the scene with a bemused expression. Face expressionless, Isoro took another drag of the cigarette, then turned to look at the ensign.

"As for you, Lieutenant Honda, clearly you cannot smell the fuel fumes coming from below," the man observed, looking at the cigarette in Isoro's hands. "I know it's likely because of the charred flesh, but I assure you the fuel truck refueling our fighters has a very impressive leak."

Isoro considered the man speaking, then the cigarette in his hands. He stubbed the latter out on his life jacket, then placed the unsmoked half in his pocket. Ensign Tokugawa, satisfied that the problem was solved, pointedly looked at the man next to Isoro before bowing and turning back towards *Soryu*'s island.

"Forgive me, I do not recognize you..." Isoro said.

"Lieutenant Iyozoh Fujita," the man said, then added with a slight smile. "I am not surprised you do not know of me. The leader often does not see those who are giving chase."

Isoro found himself smiling as well.

"I believe Warrant Officer Nishizawa holds that distinction," Isoro replied. "Especially after this morning."

"Glad to see someone had a decent flight then," Fujita replied, his face clouding. "The new American fighters were a very unpleasant surprise."

"Yes, yes they were," Isoro replied. "I ended up taking a swim."

*I am just glad I did not face them in a **Zero***, he left in his thoughts.

"At least your carrier did not get hit," Fujita observed. "While I am glad that *Soryu* is still nominally functional, I can only hope those worsening storms between us and the Americans will keep them at bay."

"The torpedo pilots claim to have sunk a battleship and severely damaged the *Repulse*," Isoro replied. "Maybe that has given the Americans pause."

Fujita looked astern.

"We can only hope so," the other pilot replied. "I don't know how bad the casualties were aboard *Akagi*, but it appeared the *Kaga* air group got very shot up attacking the surface vessels before I returned here."

Isoro shrugged.

"I was busy getting into dry clothes," he said. "Then I was told I was to fly a *chutai* of *Shinden* over here. Last I saw the *Soryu*, I did not think she would be conducting flight operations anytime soon."

Fujita pursed his lips and was silent for several seconds. Isoro could see the man struggling to hold in his emotions.

"I am told the damage control measures were arduous and we were quite fortunate our executive officer hoarded wood for the flight deck," Fujita stated. "The fires were intense but we managed to get them out. It was the casualties that were problematic."

I'd imagine a hundred or so burn victims would indeed be a problem.

He glanced to the newly repaired portion of the flight deck. He was about to speak when the carrier's after elevator began cycling.

"We shall see which one of us gets to take off first," Fujita said with a smile.

"I would expect that the hangar crew would take care of their own first," Isoro replied. "Especially since they're more familiar with your *Zeroes*."

"Perhaps," Fujita said. "Unless their mothers taught them to take care of guests first and foremost."

Isoro laughed at that.

"That is a very fair observation," he replied, then grew pensive as he looked up at the sky. "I will be honest, I do miss the *Zero*'s range. We'll be back here almost twice as many times as you will."

"I am sure that you'll be sent back to the *Akagi* after this," Fujita said somberly. "Quite frankly, I am surprised that you were sent to reinforce us at all."

"Vice Admiral Yamaguchi is doing his utmost to save every carrier he can," Isoro said. "You are in far better shape than the *Shokaku*. She burned for hours and her flight deck is completely gone."

Fujita visibly shuddered at that report.

"The stench aboard her must be terrible," the pilot noted. "Any word on casualties?"

"I understand many of the air group's support personnel are dead," Isoro replied. "I overheard that as Rear Admiral Kaku was taking my report."

"Your report?" Fujita asked.

"I was asked about the new American fighters," Isoro replied with a shrug. Looking over as the elevator rose, he smiled. "It looks like your hangar crews have manners after all."

Fujita glanced over and smiled himself as the plane handlers shoved the third *Shiden* in Isoro's scratch *chutai* astern off the elevator.

"Well, you've hardly been down long enough for the engine to get cold, so looks like you'll be taking off shortly," Fujita stated, envy dripping off every word.

Isoro scoffed.

"The less the engines are run, the better," he said. "They can be very temperamental."

Fujita shook his head.

"But look at how fast you are and how well they accelerate," he said, gesturing as Isoro's fighter was brought up on the center elevator followed by the final member of his *chutai* being brought up astern. "Even with temperamental engines, it is a major improvement over the *Zero*."

"Be careful talking about your lover that way," Isoro said, looking around in mock horror. "She'll abandon you when you least expect it."

Fujita rolled his eyes.

"My lover has a salty face when the only thing she can do is outturn enemy fighters," Fujita stated, then nodded his head at the plane handler gesturing towards Isoro. "But it appears *your* lover's manservant wishes to get the door."

"May neither of us score anymore today," Isoro solemnly, looking up at the partially cloudy sky.

"Indeed," Fujita said. "Hopefully the cruiser plane those lucky bastards from *Hiryu* shot down will allow us to get away."

With that, the two men bowed to one another. Isoro saw his wingmen, Warrant Officer Okamoto and Petty Officer Takahashi already going through their pre-flight routine. Moving at a rapid walk that was just short of a run, Isoro clambered up into this own *Shiden*. He quickly ran through an abbreviated preflight, then looked down *Soryu*'s flight deck for the signal to launch. As the carrier's bow made the slight adjustment to port to come fully into the wind, Isoro considered the visibly patched portions of her deck.

They flew off what remained of the air group and several fighters have already landed and taken off today. Why am I sitting here nervous my fighter might fall through the planks?

Isoro glanced at the smoke plume wafting back from the carrier's bow to help the helm align fully into the wind. Seeing it align down the center of the deck, Isoro shook off his feeling of foreboding.

That's as good a wind as we're going to get.

The *Shiden* shook with the *Soryu*'s hull vibrations as the flattop increased her speed. Judging the wind over the flight deck to be sufficient, the carrier's air officer hoisted the white flag with a black ball. In a carefully choreographed dance, the flight crews removed the chock blocks beneath all three fighters. This was followed by the island hoisting a plain white flag that granted Isoro permission to launch.

At long last.

Isoro released his brakes and advanced his throttle to the limit.

*Thank goodness for that strong wind out of the east. Otherwise this might be a very difficult launch given **Soryu's** condition.*

Even with the wind, Isoro could tell the heavy *Shiden* was going to use all of the *Soryu*'s flight deck. It was when he was three quarters of the way there that he saw activity out of the corner of his eye in the gun galleries, with men pointing upwards and barrels starting to elevate. He glanced upwards and nearly peed himself at the glint of sunlight off cockpit glass.

What in the...helldivers!

Wisely Isoro did not panic, continuing his normal take off even as the carrier began to change her helm over. He swore that the *Shiden* didn't take off so much as *Soryu*'s deck heeled over just beneath his fighter. With Isoro out of the way, the guns all along the flight deck began opening up in a ripple of fire as *Soryu* began turning to port.

Where did they come from?

Isoro again glanced upwards. He immediately regretted *that* decision, as it seemed like a long snake of SBDs was falling from a sky just darkening with flak. Concentrating on operating his landing gear switches, Isoro briefly sensed a shadow passing across his rear view mirror as first one, then two waterspouts erupted just off the *Soryu*'s starboard side before a third bomb hit the carrier forward on her flight deck.

"*Chikusho!*" Isoro cursed as debris arced past this fighter. With his gear up and airspeed well above stalling, he slammed the *Shiden* into a turn. The maneuver saved his life as the fourth dive bomber turned and attempted to draw a bead on his *Shiden* as it pulled out of its dive.

Behind the SBD, the American's 1,000-lb. bomb obliterated Okamoto's fighter in a brilliant orange fireball.

You son of a whore!

Isoro felt the *Shiden*'s controls start to vibrate as he approached stall speed. The offending SBD, realizing that discretion was the better part of valor, turned away. Isoro leveled off as he headed south to clear the *Agano*'s anti-aircraft fire, making continued glances upwards to see if any more Americans were diving on the *Soryu*.

Where in the Hell did they come from?

A quick glance around revealed smoke trails across the sky at altitude and a final section of *Dauntlesses* pulling out of their attacks. Behind them, the *Soryu* convulsed from at least two more blasts.

She's done for.

Isoro's eyes burned with unshed tears of frustration, rage, and mourning. Gritting his teeth, he began a gentle turn around to the west.

Now to find that bastard who dared to attack a samurai.

ISORO'S ASSESSMENT WAS MORE OR LESS CORRECT. THE AMERICAN air strike, taking advantage of the scattered clouds over the *Soryu* and her escorts, had stalked to the carrier's north. Detaching from the dive bombers, the *Bonhomme Richard*'s fighters had bounced six of the *Zeroes* on CAP to clear a path for the *Yorktown*'s strike group. Due to those fighters notoriously finicky radios, the only warning the rest of the CAP had that Americans were about was the descending comets from the two dying *chutai*. Just like their American counterparts attempting to cover TF 25 earlier that day, the remaining three *Zeroes* and same number of *Shiden* were too busy fighting for their lives to either warn the surface vessels or interfere with the *Dauntlesses*.

The *Soryu*'s late turn saved her from being hit by Red One or Red Two. The next ten dive bombers scored a total of five hits on the already damaged vessel. Being in the midst of flight operations but with empty hangars, the carrier at least had the good fortune of not having ordnance strewn about her hangar decks to create secondary explosions. Indeed, despite the spectacular, fiery destruction imparted by the destruction of Isoro's wingmen and the three *Zero*es below deck, the possibility of salvage existed through four of the big half-ton bomb hits. It was the last bomb, fuzed for maximum penetration, that ended *Soryu*'s career. Detonating just above the carrier's fire main, the blast immediately dropped the pressure to the fire hoses and sprinklers. With blazes being fed by perforated avgas lines on the hangar deck, the carrier began the rapid process of transforming from man-of-war to crematorium.

There you are, Isoro thought angrily, sighting the *Dauntless* that had attempted to shoot him down. Noting several more of the American dive bombers making their exit, he made sure none were in range while accelerating ahead of his prey. Zooming upwards, Isoro killed his speed then dived to come around in a high beam run. The dive bomber's tail gunner swiveled his twin machine guns towards the attacking bomber, but his burst went wide even as the *Shiden*'s did not. Flame blossomed at the *Dauntless*'s port wing root as Isoro pulled up and over the descending dive bomber

He is finished.

Isoro glanced back to confirm its destruction...then immediately snap-rolled to starboard as an American fighter and his wingman tried to kill him.

Ah, new Grummans.

Both fighters rushed past Isoro as the *Shiden* arced away from them. Isoro traded some altitude for speed as he increased the separation. A saner man would have run, but Isoro felt nothing but rage towards the Americans at the moment. The Grummans, for their part, whipped around in a tight turn that bled off their airspeed as they reversed.

Today is a good day to die if it comes to that.

Isoro's face broke into a feral smile as he craned his neck to watch the two enemy fighters. As they finished their turn, Isoro went into a split-S to reverse his own direction, then chose an angle that would bring him into a head on run with the American leader from just above the same level. As the two fighters hurtled towards one another, Isoro saw the Grumman's nose start to come up.

Too late for you.

Isoro squeezed his trigger, the *Shiden* shuddering from his bust. The American responded just as Isoro's fire raked the Grumman's fuselage. There were several loud impacts on Isoro's wing as he passed both Americans, but a quick glance told Isoro the damage was minimal. Another glance behind him showed only one Grumman that was running away at full speed and a crash site.

Now where was I? Isoro thought, blood rushing in his ears as he did a quick scan upwards and around his fighter. A glance at his fuel gauge gave him pause, the needle pointing at 75 percent.

Those idiots didn't fully fuel my fighter!

Slamming his hand against his canopy rail in frustration, Isoro began cursing the men on the hangar deck...until he had a sobering realization.

If they had fueled me fully, I would have probably still been on deck when the dive bombers arrived. Like my men were.

He looked at the burning *Soryu*. The carrier was slowly drifting to a halt and obviously in distress. As Isoro watched, another eruption of flame burst from her amidships, splashing onto the destroyer attempting to come alongside.

"All fighters, all fighters, immediately return to the *Kido Butai* by order of Vice Admiral Yamaguchi," his radio crackled. "Fly bearing oh eight oh true to be met by a navigation craft."

Hope there aren't more Americans coming. Otherwise that order is condemning every individual aboard that cruiser and the two DDs to die.

He watched as the *Agano* cut a circle around the burning *Soryu*.

Once more looking around to make sure an American was not lurking to jump him, Isoro began heading out in the proscribed direction. As he began his journey, he looked back and saw a *Shiden* ditching next to the *Agano*.

Must have been low on fuel. He did his own quick calculations.

Half my fuel should get me to the task force with plenty of time to spare. I don't want to be here if there is another strike.

JAMES YOUNG

U.S.S. Houston
1515 Local (0705 Eastern)

Goddammit these stitches still hurt, Jacob thought, clenching and unclenching his bandaged left hand. *Houston*'s skipper caught himself once more attempting to shift his new steel pot off swollen knot on his head as the XO gave him an assessment of the *Houston*'s damage.

"Sir, if I'm totally honest, Lieutenant Commander Sheldon thinks he can give you eighteen knots easy, twenty in a pinch," Commander Sloan said, speaking of *Houston*'s engineering officer. The XO paused to wipe his face with a handkerchief.

"But if Vice Admiral Godfrey is wanting someone to go hunt that light cruiser and the two DDs that are standing by that burning carrier, we'd have trouble catching anything besides the flu right now," Sloan finished grimly.

Jacob pursed his lips, turning to look over at where the *Repulse* was also limping along behind the damaged *Massachusetts*. The signal from the British battlecruiser had led to a flurry of assessments among the task force. With both the *Massachusetts* and *Repulse* clearly worse for wear, Vice Admiral Godfrey was stuck on the horns of a dilemma.

Have to send a strong enough force to overwhelm that light cruiser, but not so strong to overly thin the escort if the Japanese come back.

Jacob tried to put himself in the Japanese cruiser captain's shoes.

*However, I don't care what the **Baltimore**'s pilot said, there's no way that cruiser is still going to be there in the over six hours it would take us to get there. Sucks for the men who are about to drown or be shark food, but have to save his own vessel.*

"Signal the *Repulse* that we can make only eighteen knots," Jacob ordered. "As much as I'd like to beat up on a couple of destroyers and a light cruiser, I'd also like to make some more repairs before that next round of storms catches up with us."

"Aye aye, sir," Commander Sloan said, also turning to look off the heavy cruiser's port side at the advancing weather. The swells the *Houston* was moving through were starting to cause the heavy cruiser to pitch and roll slightly as TF 25 continued southwards. Jacob strongly suspected that the storm was only going to make that worse.

Not quite looking like a gale, but certainly above a minor squall. Don't know how the fly boys are making it through that.

The storm's lightning was wreaking havoc with the task force's radars. The electronics had still worked well enough to track the USN's carrier strike both coming and going.

Glad the flyboys stayed well clear of this task force. Gunners are a bit on edge.

"Sir, the *Repulse* is replying," a lookout called out. Jacob turned to look at the battlecruiser as her blinker light sent a rapid message. As it reached its end, the *Houston*'s master exhaled heavily.

"Well that's sorted," Commander Farmer said sadly. "Thankfully it appears someone convinced Vice Admiral Godfrey it would be bad form to send a bunch of vessels on a sail to nothing."

Here I thought you'd be the most eager for revenge.

"I think that this battle is all over except for getting the cripples home," Jacob stated.

"Burying the dead, sir," Commander Farmer noted morosely. Jacob watched as the man closed his eyes for a moment, visibly upset. "We still have to bury the dead."

His service has been beaten bloody. At least one carrier gone from yesterday, another crippled. How much fleet do they have left?

"Speaking of, sir, Chaplain O'Malley has finished the list of the dead," Commander Sloan said somberly. "Are you still wanting to conduct services at 1600?"

Jacob looked over at the *Repulse*.

I don't think there's anything else the flag is going to ask of us. At least, I sincerely hope not.

"Yes," Jacob said, looking at the clock. "You have the Conn, XO."

TWENTY MINUTES LATER, JACOB GRADUALLY MADE HIS WAY AFT along the *Houston*'s port side. The damage control parties had managed to clear the main deck, but the smell of burnt materials and flesh wafted upwards from below decks.

We've been in a fight but we're far from out.

Jacob nodded at work parties moving debris to be tossed over the side as he passed aft. The *Houston*'s fires had gutted several storage compartments, and he tried not to think about the hundreds of dollars' worth of equipment the crew was committing to the Indian Ocean's depths. Part of the starboard catapult had already been cut away in order to facilitate damage control, an act Jacob would not have believed possible before it happened.

Even if we could have somehow salvaged some of the equipment, it's not feasible in the middle of combat. The only reason we're burying the dead now is the lack of anywhere to put forty-three bodies.

Jacob tried to keep his face impassive as he thought about the cruiser's dead. In a way the *Houston* had been lucky, as none of the torpedoes that had missed the *Massachusetts* had carried on to hit the heavy cruiser. Still, as Jacob considered the four neat rows of canvas arranged on the vessel's stern, a brief wave of melancholy caused him to pause and regain his composure.

They died under my watch. Even having done everything we could to train and prepare, there are still almost fifty telegrams that will be getting sent out sometime in the next thirty days.

"Make way!" someone shouted from a hatch behind Jacob. Jacob turned to see a Chaplain O'Malley holding one end of a stretcher bearing yet another casualty. The man's face was red, and Jacob could tell it wasn't only from the exertion of carrying yet another victim of the Japanese attack.

Forty-four confirmed dead, four missing. Sixty-two...no, sixty-one wounded, ten of those critically.

"Sir, we have one more coming from the wardroom behind us," Captain O'Malley stated after setting the stretcher down. "One of the new mess stewards."

Forty-five. For what? So some young woman can eventually get married and give birth to different children than the man who sitting on a throne in England?

"Thank you, chaplain," Jacob said, glancing over at *Repulse*.

"Poor bastards," O'Malley said, also looking over at the *Houston*'s companion.

Jacob looked to make sure none of the crew were in ear shot.

"I'm not feeling very sympathetic," he replied. "Indeed, I'm feeling a lot like a lieutenant who is now eating his food through a straw because his buddy got mouthy on shore leave."

O'Malley looked pensive for a moment.

"Well, sir, if you don't mind me saying so, that's a relatively asinine way of looking at it," O'Malley replied.

"Excuse me?" Jacob said, turning to glare at the chaplain. The priest did not flinch, meeting his captain's gaze with his own.

"You can lash me to that damn mast if you want to, sir," O'Malley said, gesturing forward. "Won't change my mind, and won't have me think any less of you if you can't tell the difference between the two sides in this little discussion our species is having."

Jacob was about to speak, but O'Malley clearly wasn't having any of it.

"I mean, those men over there?" the priest said, nodding angrily towards *Repulse*. "Their government is led by some right assholes, and I'm not saying that because their 'royal' forebears beat, starved, and generally acted like bastards towards mine."

O'Malley gestured towards the bodies on the deck, then stopped, clearly gathering himself.

"But the shits who did *this*?" O'Malley hissed. "They raped and murdered their way across most of China before the Russians beat their ass back in '41. My brother was a missionary in Nanking, and he can tell you stories that would make you puke."

The chaplain gestured vaguely to the northwest.

"Those other sons a bitches they work with? They gassed women and children in one of the world's finest cities. So, no, I'm under no illusions which side *I* want of fight with."

O'Malley fixed Jacob once more with an unrepentant, determined look.

"I don't think anyone who calls themselves a civilized man should have to think long and hard about it either, sir."

Jacob was surprised to find that he was not angry at O'Malley's near insubordination.

Sometimes a person can get lost in their dejection. Strange how chaplains always seem to know how to bring a person out of it.

"I think Senator Lindbergh would be quite surprised to find out you consider him uncivilized," Jacob replied drily.

"Senator Lindbergh is making me sympathetic towards the man who kidnapped his baby," O'Malley said, then covered his mouth. "Sorry sir."

"I don't think I'm the superior you need to apologize to for that one," Jacob said, slightly aghast. "But I'll chalk that up to the stress of today."

Before O'Malley could reply, there was a very loud round of thunder from the approaching storm.

That line is probably closer than I thought. Maybe thinking it's not going to be a gale was too optimistic.

Looking at the surrounding swells that were also starting to increase, Jacob pursed his lips.

"Well, I guess we had better hurry chaplain," Jacob said.

There were roughly twenty or so sailors milling about the canvas shrouds. Some were leaning down to say final goodbyes, tears running down their cheeks as they kneeled down next to what used to be their friends. Jacob watched as O'Malley gently, but firmly, got the gathered group together with a couple of chief petty officers' help.

"Friends, we are gathered here to say goodbye to our comrades and fellow sailors," O'Malley began. "Let us pray..."

As O'Malley recited the Lord's Prayer, Jacob considered the man's earlier words.

He is right. We are truly the side fighting against an evil ideology. Doesn't mean we're ideal.

Jacob considered the dead steward's canvas shroud as a corpsman finished sealing it.

Hell, that young man he just brought out here would have to get up and move to a different car if he was catching a train from Portsmouth to Charleston. But at least we wouldn't shoot him out of hand like the Germans would.

"Sir, would you like to say any words?" O'Malley asked. An almost immediate peal of thunder and freshening wind caused a few nervous titters among the group.

"I don't know whether to take that as a sign of endorsement or warning, chaplain," Jacob said. "But a few short words, yes."

As the gathered enlisted men looked at him, Jacob keenly felt the weight his position.

A prudent captain speaks seldom and chooses his words carefully, Jacob recalled a mentor advising him at the War College. *Like flooding, unwise speech will pass through a vessel with great speed and threaten her stability worse than any tempest.*

"Gentlemen, we say goodbye to our friends and comrades today secure in the knowledge that they have passed in achieving a great victory against the forces of tyranny," Jacob began, briefly glancing at O'Malley. "It is not my place to speak to you of our foes' depravity, for it is well documented. Nor will I attempt to assuage your grief, for that can only be done with the passing of time."

Jacob paused to meet every man's gaze.

"What I can tell you is that as long as I am privileged to be the captain of this fine vessel, I will do my utmost to make sure we employ her in defending liberty, righteousness, and all that is right with mankind against those who would drag us into barbarity," he finished. "Due to circumstances, we must commit our comrades to the depths this afternoon. May our actions always rise to the standards set by their sacrifice. Chaplain."

Looking at the gathered throng, Jacob was unsure if he'd reached the men. However, the increasing wind and first drops of rain told him that he certainly wouldn't be finding out that afternoon.

"May our comrades find repose with the sea in which they gave their lives so that others might live in freedom," O'Malley said solemnly. "Into thy hands, oh Lord, we commend the soul of thy servants departed, now called unto eternal rest, and we commit their bodies to the deep."

At the chaplain's gesture, a chief petty officer began to play taps from beside *Houston*'s aft turret. As they did so, the funeral detail set about their grim task. Jacob noted with satisfaction the efficiency with which each litter team solemnly placed a corpse on the litters, then under American

JAMES YOUNG

flags, secured the ensigns, then waited for the signal from the senior chief in charge of the ceremonies. Behind him, the *Houston*'s Marines fired three volleys, each timed with the deposit of bodies into the vessel's wake, then stood at attention as the final series of burials took place.

It's a small thing, but I'm glad someone properly weighted the bodies.

As a young ensign, he'd been part of a burial at sea where the canvas wrapped corpse had bopped for what seemed forever before finally sinking into the Atlantic. Although Jacob had not seen it, one of his fellow officers had sworn they'd sighted a dorsal fin during the proceedings the body had taken so long to sink.

It's not like the bastards will feel it, but I'd rather not get sharks used to the taste of human. Not even Japanese.

I.J.N.S. AKAGI
1715 LOCAL (0905 EASTERN)

THE DOOR TO VICE ADMIRAL YAMAGUCHI'S DAY CABIN OPENED.

I am sure that what I am about to hear is no good news. Then again, if it's word of an attack perhaps I may still perish in battle.

"Sir, the *Agano* reports that the *Soryu* has been scuttled," Rear Admiral Kaku said solemnly.

Yamaguchi continued to stare at the map in front of him, nodding once because he did not trust his voice.

My first flagship. Is this how it feels to hear that your childhood home has burned to the ground?

"Captain Takashige is among the dead," Kaku continued. "The fires trapped many of the command team on the *Soryu*'s island, and he elected to remain with the Emperor's portrait."

Yamaguchi took a deep breath, biting back the angry words that nearly spilled out. The pen in his hand began to bend ominously, and he set the writing implement down.

"How many of her crew did the *Agano* and the destroyers recover?" Yamaguchi asked once he had control.

"Five hundred, sir," Kaku replied.

Over half the crew dead.

Yamaguchi was suddenly glad he had not ate much that day.

"How many aviators?"

"Captain Takashige had ordered the transfer of all possible aircrew a half hour before the American dive bombers arrived," Kaku replied. "All told, roughly forty-five percent survived."

Yamaguchi did the math in his head and did not like the number. He looked up at Kaku.

"How long did the *Agano* stand by for survivors?" he asked. Kaku recoiled back from the look on his superior's face.

"The captain stood by for thirty minutes, sir," Kaku replied. "That was in accordance with the standing orders I had the staff broadcast to him."

Which was a prudent and sane decision. Light cruisers do not last well against either aircraft or surface ships.

"Have we recovered the last of the fighters?" Yamaguchi asked, leaning forward to rest his hands on the desk.

"Yes, sir," Kaku replied. "The new American fighters caught much of the *Soryu*'s CAP by surprise, and two *chutai* were in the midst of launching when the dive bombers struck."

Will the disasters never cease?

"How bad?"

"We recovered two *Shiden* and four *Zero*es," Kaku said. "Three more fighters ditched around the *Agano*, and one of the destroyers recovered another survivor. He is grievously wounded, however."

"How many Americans did they shoot down?"

"The *Agano* and destroyers claimed to have shot down eight dive bombers," Yamaguchi said. "The fighter pilots claimed another six with Warrant Officer Nishizawa allegedly shooting down four enemy fighters himself as well."

Yamaguchi saw a flicker of emotion cross Kaku's face.

"You seem skeptical, Kaku-san," Yamaguchi said.

"Sir, if we total all the claims put in today, we should be turning this force around as the Americans are out of planes," Kaku replied bitterly. "The *Agano*'s captain specifically mentioned Nishizawa, so I have reason to believe he saw or heard *something* that leads him to mention the man."

"But?" Yamaguchi pressed.

"I think, before we send our claims higher, we should be very judicious in our reports," Kaku continued. "I have walked down to the hangar decks and know how much our squadrons have suffered, but we also have been outmaneuvered by our enemies today."

Kaku looked up in shock as he realized what he had said out of fatigue.

"Sir, I am..."

"You are truthful," Yamaguchi cut the other man off. "I have been thoroughly outthought by both the British and Americans today."

"Sir, that is not fair," Kaku replied. "There is no way you could have expected *four* American carriers."

"Expect, no," Yamaguchi stated, his voice breaking. "But I should not have let my annoyance at the British to cause me to fixate on their forces when I knew at least *two* American carriers were still out there."

Yamaguchi gestured at the map.

"If not for the *Taiho*'s radar and bad American torpedoes, we would have lost this entire force today," he stated emphatically. "I fully expect Admiral Yamamoto to demand my resignation when this is finished."

Kaku drew himself up to attention, then bowed quickly at the waist.

"Then I, as your chief of staff, shall resign also," he replied stiffly. "You have led this force with aggression and honor, sir. It is your staff that has failed you."

For the first time that day, Yamaguchi felt a sense of pride push itself through the pall of anger, frustration, and sadness. Drawing himself up to attention, he returned Kaku's bow.

"Kaku-san, if Admiral Yamamoto retains me, you will always have a position as my chief of staff," Yamaguchi said.

"Then it is my fiercest hope that we will be able to apply the lessons the Americans taught us today," Kaku stated.

ROYAL HAWAIIAN HOTEL

0405 Local (1005 Eastern)
10 August

"Nicholas, you are going to give a woman a complex," Agnes said drowsily. Her lazy smile belied the admonishment as she shifted under the covers. "No one likes to be stared at first thing in the morning."

"I don't ever want to forget your face," Nick responded, reaching over to stroke Agnes' cheek. "I'm burning it into my memory."

Agnes' eyes shot open, and she grabbed his hand.

"You sound like a man who is thinking about it as if it will be the last thing he sees," she said quietly. It was hard to see her face in the room's darkness, but Nick could hear the sadness in her tone.

Whoops. I guess a problem with actually talking to someone every day for months is they figure some things out about you.

Realizing his error, he quickly scooted forward to embrace Agnes as she gave a strangled sob. After briefly struggling against him, she wrapped her arms around him tightly, burying her face in his chest. Nick held Agnes as she cried, shuddering in his arms. Gently, he stroked her hair as she wept for a good twenty minutes.

"I'm sorry, Nicholas," she said lowly into his chest. "I beg your forgiveness for bringing a ghost into our marital bed."

I'm pretty sure that's not a line most men hear on their wedding night.

Nick barely caught himself before he let out a chuckle at the gallows humor of it all.

"I'm pretty sure I'm the one who called him on the telephone," Nick replied sheepishly. "Told him to come over for breakfast, I'm sure the missus wouldn't mind."

Agnes gasped and leaned back up to look at him, her eyes wide.

"I think it is fortunate that we found each other, Nick," she observed archly. "Me a woman with a broken heart. You a man with an *incorrigible* wit."

Nick looked at her in mock surprise, his eyes having adjusted more fully to the darkness.

"You mean, you didn't think that someone who grew up the

smallest of four boys with two louts as brothers would be a smart aleck?"

Her eyes narrowed as he continued.

"Why, to think there's probably someone who is still convinced you're a spy over at fleet intelligence," Nick finished.

Agnes cocked an eyebrow at him.

Uh oh.

With a snort of derision, Agnes sat up and let her sheet fall from her body.

"Are you saying I'm not as fetching as Mata Hari, Nicholas?" Agnes asked haughtily, then broke into giggles.

"Why are you laughing?" Nick asked, feeling his cheeks warm.

"Because the look on your face was the epitome of confusion, desire, and stupefaction," Agnes answered. "You didn't know what the right answer wa–"

When in doubt, attack, Nicholas thought as he kissed his wife.

Two hours later, the firm knock on the hotel room door brought Nick and Agnes both of their slumber.

"Mr. and Mrs. Cobb?" a voice said from the other side of the door. "Our apologies, the phone system is down. This is your six o'clock wake up."

Whose bright idea was that?

He slid out from under Agnes as the mumbled something about a few more minutes.

"Thank you," he called out, listening as the man walked off. There were a few other individuals starting to move around in the hallway, including at least one still drunk sailor whose comrades were trying to shush him.

"It is probably fortunate we only have a couple of days off work," Agnes observed, her voice muffled by the pillow.

"I know," Nick said, moving gingerly himself. "I feel like I just had my first day of boxing all over again."

Nick just barely dodged the pillow hurled at his head, and immediately regretted it as his leg muscles tried to cramp. Agnes giggled at the expression on his face, then again at the wholly different expression it changed to when she stood up.

"Nicholas..." she chided him, her tone warning. "We must get presentable if we want to catch the shuttle to the Dole plantation. Please turn on the radio, I'm going to take a shower."

"We could both—"

"No, no we both cannot, Lieutenant Cobb," Agnes replied. "I am apparently a wanton hussy and you are an insatiable brute."

"Don't let anyone hear you say that at the office," Nick replied.

"If 'anyone' at the office heard me say that I'd be fired and you'd be brought up on charges," she replied. "As far as anyone at the office is concerned, we are like most married couples and never speak of such things with one another, much less do them."

There are days where it's obvious you're the only child of older parents. As opposed to the poor child who had the small former closet right next to your parents' bedroom.

"I am not sure I want to know what you are thinking about, but something I said clearly killed the mood," Agnes observed with a slight frown. "Did you suddenly have fear that this will change?"

"No, actually," Nick said, shaking his head. "I just remembered when I was three and asked my mother if we kids did something wrong?"

"Okay?" Agnes said, looking at him in obvious befuddlement.

"My mother used to say, when we were doing something bad, that she was 'going to go pray to Jesus for patience, because if she asked for strength someone was going to be the first man on the moon,'" Nick explained.

Agnes raised an eyebrow.

"Or, at least she did. Then that morning, three-year-old me asked my Dad if we kids had done something wrong the day before."

Agnes' confused look deepened.

"Dad asked me, 'Nick, why would you think you kids did something wrong?' 'Well, it's just I heard Mom talking to God a lot last night, Dad, so I figured she was asking for a lot of patience.'"

Agnes covered her mouth, eyes going wide as Nick continued.

"My father turned as red as a tomato, my mother dropped the dish she was washing, and my brothers all looked confused. That's when they all started asking questions, and it was the last time Mom mentioned God and patience in a sentence together."

Agnes' laugh started low, then rose to a huge guffaw as she sat down on the bed.

I love the way she looks when she laughs like this. Hell, I love everything about her.

"Anyway, once Dad got us all to calm down, he looked over at Mom with a small smile. 'Boys, I think your Mom just had a religious experience or four last night is all.'"

"Stop...stop...it's too late for me to get the marriage annulled," Agnes said, starting to hiccup.

"I've never seen a man take such a calm sip of orange juice while contemplating his imminent demise in my life," Nick continued deadpan. Agnes, realizing there was only one path to relief, came over to kiss him, pointedly swatting his hands away from her.

"I love you, Nicholas," she said. "I cannot wait to meet your parents."

With that, she grabbed one hand and put it on her abdomen for a moment.

"And to someday bear your children."

I...I don't know what to say back to that.

"Although I am glad twins are a maternal thing," Agnes said. "I do not know how your mother did it."

"Mom is just like Patricia..."

"I doubt that despite how often you and your brothers swear to it," Agnes interrupted with a smile. "Your sister is very...*unique*."

"Stubborn. Stubborn was the word I was going to say."

"In any case, I look forward to meeting her when this is all over," Agnes said.

Part of me wonders if it will ever be over.

Rather than saying anything this time when she read his expression, Agnes simply kissed him tenderly.

"I'll try to hurry," she said, then looked at the time. "Well, I guess you'll catch up on Gibson and the Octopus."

Nick laughed as he looked over at the radio. KGU, the Hawaii radio station, had begun to rebroadcast episodes of "Speed Gibson of the International Police" in the morning back in March. It was a radio serial that had begun shortly before Nick started the Naval Academy, and he'd never had a chance to listen to it all the way through. Much to Agnes' chagrin, Nick had just happened upon the broadcast when his previous boat, the *Nautilus*, had been in harbor.

"Anything that will keep me distracted from a beautiful woman in the shower," Nicholas said with a smile. He switched on the radio...and was immediately disappointed to hear a familiar male voice.

Why is Senator Lindbergh on the radio?

"...investigate this waste of federal dollars while our brave young men are fighting with outdated equipment to protect some teenager's colonies!"

The passage of wind coupled with the whir and click of cameras told him that Lindbergh was apparently standing outside in front of microphones.

Probably grandstanding at the Capitol Building.

Nick clenched his fists.

*Let's not forget that the reason we've got **obsolete** equipment is you cut President Roosevelt's request by 25 percent to stop his 'adventurism' back in January.*

"Senator Lindbergh, how did you find out about this 'Manhattan Project?'" a reporter shouted.

"Brave citizens concerned about this country's direction shared information with us," Senator Lindbergh replied. "That's all I will say about President Roosevelt's Folly until our committee calls its first witness on Thursday."

There were so many additional shouted questions that Nick had trouble making them out. An unidentified man whose voice Nick did not recognize called for the gathered reporters to ask their questions one at a time, and there was a moment of bedlam while the gathered throng figured out what they were going to ask.

There are days I wish D.C. was a lot closer to the action. Maybe goddamn German bombers overhead would stop some of this idiocy.

"Nicholas, what's wrong?" Agnes asked from the bathroom door. "You look like you want to kill someone."

Nicholas looked sheepishly down at his clenched fists.

"Politicians being idiots again," he said.

"This has you sitting there like you're expecting Tojo to walk through the door?" Agnes asked lightly, reaching up to dry her hair while looking straight at him.

She did that on purpose. I should be angrier that it worked.

Seeing her mission accomplished, Agnes grabbed a bathrobe, slipped it on, then sat down beside him. Nick started to reach for the radio, only to have Agnes put her hand on his.

"I want to listen," she said. Nick slipped his arm around her, and they listened while Senator Lindbergh continued to answer questions.

"Do you think it's true he's a German sympathizer?" Agnes asked after about a half dozen inquiries.

"No," Nick said without hesitation. "I think that he saw some things in Germany that he thought would be more efficient or should be enacted here, but Senator Lindbergh is an American patriot first."

Agnes nodded at Nick's words.

"Then why has he and his party been so resistant to President Roosevelt?"

"Because President Roosevelt did a lot of things without Congress' approval that set the table for where we're at now," Nick said sorrowfully. "I mean, if we're being honest, the man nearly got Eric killed because we interfered so strenuously in a war we were allegedly neutral in."

"But the Nazis are terrible people," Agnes noted.

"There are still rules," Nick replied. "When you start having a President giving nations arms and having our warships fire on German submarines, that sounds an awful lot like war."

"Didn't he say something about a garden hose and a neighbor's house?" Agnes asked with a smirk.

See, this is why people think you're a spy. You actually pay attention.

"Yes, well, he assumed the neighbor didn't have gasoline in the attic," Nick replied, then stopped. "Wait, how much did Senator Taft just say we've spent in Manhattan?"

MORTON RESIDENCE
0735 LOCAL (1335 EASTERN)
10 AUGUST

SAM JERKED AWAKE AS THE PILLOW HIT HIM IN THE FACE. His arm reflexively cocked back, ready to deliver a counter blow before Jo's startled yelp of surprise stopped him.

"What the hell Jo?" he asked, still trying to gain his bearings. Jo stood in front of the sofa bed, pillow clutched in both hands halfway between another swing and a potential block.

"You didn't wake up when I said your name five times, Sam," she snapped. "It was clear stronger measures were needed. Make yourself decent, we've got to talk."

Sam looked at Jo incredulously as she turned to go into the kitchen, setting the pillow on the chair in the corner.

What the hell has gotten into her? he wondered. Looking at the small table next to the sofa, he saw that Jo had left him a glass of water with a pair of pills.

Wrong twin you're leaving those for. Although thank goodness we got David back to the bachelor's officer quarters without running into Shore Patrol.

Surprisingly, David had gotten very, very hammered at Admiral Dunlap's party. Not without good reason—there'd been some English drinking game the Marines had been challenged to by the H.M.C.S. Norfolk's wardroom.

That's sure as hell not the '21' I was expecting.

Looking at the end table, Sam shrugged, then swigged down the glass of water.

Apparently Major Haynes has played before...and I suspect David was the sacrificial lamb in that particular gambit.

Grabbing his robe from the top of the sofa, Sam went to the bathroom first. It was only when he was washing his hands that Sam had a sudden start. Drying quickly, the eldest Cobb stepped back into the hallway and confirmed what his peripheral vision had told him.

"Jo!" he called, trying to keep his voice level. "Where's Toots?!"

"That's one of the things we need to talk about!" Jo called back.

Uh oh. I recognize that tone, and it's not a good one.

He walked into the kitchen right as Jo finished stirring a coffee mug to hand to him. Regarding her suspiciously, Sam took it.

"Sam, do you really think I'd poison you?" Jo asked, raising an eyebrow.

"I'm not sure of a lot of things right now," Sam replied evenly. Jo gave him a shocked expression.

This. This is why I'm still single.

"What is it with you Cobbs?" Jo asked archly. "Am I that much of a conundrum that *not a single one of you* can figure out how to talk to me? Or is it that neither Eric nor you give a fuck about my feelings?"

Oh shit. I've done touched off a powder magazine someone else has packed for me.

"Now Jo, that's not..."

"What, fair?" Jo snapped, slamming her coffee mug down on the counter. She stalked towards Sam, her fists clenched and face wild.

"You fucking asked me *in a letter* if I was a *prostitute*, Sam!" she said, her voice all the more intense from the effort of not trying to scream. "Somehow, I doubt that Patricia got the same letter."

Sam took a step backwards in reaction to Jo's fury.

Oh God, why did I think that was a good idea?

"What life lesson did *Nick* get that both *Eric* and *you* did not?" Jo asked. "Because seeing the way Agnes looked at him, I *know* last night was not the first time those two had sex, she's been engaged, and somehow he doesn't treat *her* like she's scratched and dented furniture."

"Now hold on a second," Sam said, setting his own coffee cup down with a *thunk*! "You don't get to lecture me about treating someone like damaged goods just because I asked if you needed help."

"Help?" Jo asked, cocking her head and widening her eyes. "Sam Cobb, my father has paid for rent on this house through the end of this year. There is enough money in a savings account that I *never* touch to pay for another two years."

Jo looked down for a second, her eyes briefly clouded.

"I've put your sister's half of the 'rent' in a separate account," she continued softly. "I figured if she had to go back to the States because they forced us all to evacuate, she'd have some start up money so there'd be options besides Alabama."

"What?!" Sam asked, incredulous. "But why wouldn't she want to go back to Alabama?"

"Gee, I don't know, the same reason she bolted out here?" Jo retorted, shaking her head. "Namely a mother that thinks she needs to be someone's prim and proper wife and a father who allows it?"

"Hey!" Sam said.

"Is for horses, Sam," Jo cut him off sadly. "Who was going to stop it, you? You're too busy whoring around with anything that will stand still."

I think that's a bit harsh.

Sam grit his teeth as Jo turned away from him to glance out the kitchen window.

Guess I'm just going to take this ass chewing and find someplace else to sleep.

"Okay, that wasn't fair," Jo said after a moment. Her back turned towards him, she took a deep breath. "That's...I think that's the anger of you thinking I'd disrespect my father that way plus having the audacity of double standards."

I think Eric is in there somewhere...wait, what?

"Double standards?"

"Yes, that's what us Yankees call it in when you think a man can just stick it in anything he wants but clearly a woman who has had... well, that's none of your business," Jo continued. "So let's just say, a woman who has not been *chaste* is the type to be giving three minute rub and tugs down in the red light district."

Sam looked at Jo aghast.

"I'm a librarian, Sam," Jo said, turning around to face him. He could see emotions flit across her face as she made a mental correction. "Or at least I *was*. Sailors really don't pay attention to who's around when they talk."

Which leads to the whole thing that got this mess started. That stupid note.

"If I'd known that your rent was taken care of, I wouldn't have asked if you needed me to send you money," Sam replied. "I mean, they told me about Patricia going to work at the docks, but they said you'd just basically vanished."

"Gee, and the first thing that crossed your mind was..."

She has a point, Sam realized, suddenly horrified.

"That wasn't the first thing that crossed my mind, Jo," Sam muttered defensively.

"But it was on the list," Jo pressed. "I mean, how did you know I hadn't gotten a job as a school teacher? Or a nurse's aide? Or just started drafting with your sister and not told anyone about it?"

Sam held up his hands plaintively.

"Okay, okay, that was stupid," Sam admitted. "I am sorry."

And not just because I haven't been read the riot act that effectively since I nearly pranged a bird during training.

Sam could see Jo searching his face to see if he was sincere. Apparently satisfied, she held up one finger.

"That's the first thing," Jo said, then added a second finger. "The next thing..."

"No, wait a minute," Sam interrupted sharply. He paused to take a calming breath. "How about we discuss just where in the hell my sister is right now?"

"Oh, you mean the woman who left me a lovely note calling me names that were not exactly pleasant? A message which informed me she had packed an overnight bag, and would see me at work tomorrow?" Jo asked. "All because her siblings and I conspired against her?"

Sam whistled like a descending bomb.

Vintage Toots. Got Mom's temper without Dad's long fuse. Didn't help that she had most of us wrapped around her finger.

"Yes, that sister," he replied sorrowfully.

"Well, given she told me to enjoy 'fornicating with whatever brother suited my fancy," Jo began evenly, "but would ask that I not break up the family's marriages...'"

Jo stopped to collect herself, lip trembling.

Oh my God!

Sam stepped forward to wrap Jo in his arms, shocked at Patricia's callousness. After a moment's resistance, she grabbed him back, burying her face in his chest as she sobbed. The smell of her hair shampoo and lotion wafted into his nostrils.

"I am going to have words with her," Sam snarled, feeling his own temper rising. "Dad only made me give her a switch once when we were kids, but maybe that needs to be revisited."

Jo pushed back and looked up at him, snorting in a completely unladylike manner. Sam started to smile until she began speaking.

"Gee Sam, I have *no idea* why I would set aside money for your sister to possibly start her own life somewhere," Jo said, incredulous. "I mean, you're talking about giving a *grown woman* a switching for what is a relatively reasonable response to what we did."

Sam looked at Jo in surprise.

Reasonable? I don't think that was very reasonable at all.

"She basically accused you of passing yourself around between us," Sam responded, his eyes wide. Jo just looked at him with a slight smile. After a moment, Sam started grinning in return.

"I guess that's rather hypocritical given...uh..."

Jo let him struggle for words for a few moments.

"Here, I'll say it for you: 'Given I, Sam Cobb, believed you were basically performing acts of sodomy on half the Pacific Fleet,'" Jo said.

Sam felt the heat rise in his cheeks even as his smile became a broader one.

Jesus Christ I missed how blunt she is. But I was mainly thinking about the fact that I enjoy you being in my arms.

"So, with that being said, I think we need to agree *maybe* you shouldn't be treating your sister like she's eight and giving you back talk," Jo chided. "It's not right to her as a woman, and I am fairly certain I can fight my own battles, thank you."

"I wasn't intending to fight your battles—" Sam began, only to have Jo interrupt him with a gentle finger to his lips.

"Whatever you want to call it, Sam," Jo said. "It's not okay. If I wanted to have some Sir Galahad sweep in and save the day, I'd be long married by now."

Jo stepped fully out of his embrace and backed up to the kitchen sink. Sam fought the urge to step forward and close the space again.

She's moving like some townswoman facing Frankenstein's monster.

"Which leads to the crux of this discussion," Jo said. "What are we?"

Wait, what?

Jo looked at him expectantly for five long seconds.

"The fact that you're not immediately answering *friends* is why I'm asking, Sam," Jo said. "I mean, I haven't seen you and Sadie much together, but somehow I doubt you just pat her leg and leave your arm there in mixed company."

Sam widened his eyes at that very thought, then realized what he'd done. Jo pressed her advantage with a slight smirk.

"Or hold her like she's a life preserver and you've been dog paddling in the Pacific for two hours when either of you are hardly dressed for being around the opposite sex. Tell me, Sam, would you have just held Sadie like that in the middle of her kitchen?"

I feel like that one time the Anders kid jumped me in 8th grade. No idea why he was mad at me or where he came from, it was just suddenly all fists and screaming.

"I'm sorry, I didn't think that would bother you," Sam said. Jo's bemused look told him that his response, while honest, was not the right one.

"See, that's the problem—it *didn't* bother me," Jo said. "Indeed, the only reason I moved your hand when it was on my knee is Agnes looked over at us with a faint approval."

Jo's smirk became a full smile.

"And the only reason I just stopped you from holding me is I think we were both starting to enjoy it a little too much."

"Oh," Sam said.

"Yeah, 'oh' indeed," Jo noted, then took a deep breath and turned around to grab her coffee. The delaying tactic was so obvious, Sam nearly commented, but stopped as Jo made a face after her first sip.

"Stone cold?" he asked with a smile. Jo gave him a frustrated look, then motioned as if she was going to throw the mug at him. Only as he flinched did he see the amusement in her expression.

"Look, we can't keep doing this," Jo said suddenly, shaking her head.

"I'll go get a room at the bachelor officer quarters tomorrow," Sam replied.

"Oh, okay, and then what's your excuse going to be for why you're not coming to dinner before you leave?" Jo asked. "Sorry Toots, Jo basically called me out for acting like we're a courting couple which made me feel all awkward. Off to harm's way!"

"Are you asking me if we're going steady?" Sam asked.

"No, I'm saying if you want to go steady, then I'm enough of a traditionalist *you* can ask *me*," Jo replied. "But, given Lord knows putting a Cobb man in a corner is a *bad* idea, you need to ask or stop making people wonder."

Sam started to speak, then stopped. It was his turn to reach for the coffee.

"Yep, stone cold," he said, putting it back after making a scrunched up face.

"If you have to stall, Sam, that's my poi–"

Oh God, I'm going to regret this.

Jo, seeing something in his face, had stopped mid-sentence. Sam took two big steps forward and wrapped Jo in his arms before he could reconsider. As she looked up in surprise, her mouth still open from being caught mid-sentence, Sam kissed her. After a moment's stiffness, Jo kissed him back, molding herself to him.

This is going to be messy.

He pushed his hand into the front of Jo's robe, surprised to find her naked breast. She whimpered as he cupped it, kissing him back even more fiercely.

So incredibly, inextricably messy.

"Sam..." Jo said breathlessly as his thumb found her nipple. He started to pull his hand back at her saying his name...until her own hand worked inside the flap of his pajama pants. He gasped as her cool fingers found him.

"Dammit...Sam...I just wanted...to..." Jo continued.

"Yea..." he started, this gasped as she made a frustrated sound and it his neck.

Samuel Cobb, what in the hell are you doing?

He lifted Jo on the counter, bringing his other and up afterwards once again to her chest. Then he had no more time for consideration, her hands firm but gentle on him.

"Are..." he gasped, then was silenced as she kissed him, one hand on the back of his head.

"Yes," she gasped. "Oh my God, stop talking and hurry up before someone comes home!"

Oh shit. His hand moved up the outside of her thigh, quickly grabbing her underwear. Jo pushed her legs together and pulled her right leg up. The underwear caught on the counter edge, trapping her foot.

"Goddammit," she muttered, then giggled when their hands collided reaching to help her foot through them. That task done, Jo quickly brought her leg back around to pull Sam towards her, kissing him urgently again. He nearly jumped as her hand gripped him firmly, then with a desire-filled mewl aligned him.

We are really doing this!

There was a brief moment where he considered stopping, then he was inside her. Jo made a strangled cry in his ear as he thrust forward, then bit down hard on his shoulder.

"I'm not...sure...we...should have done that," Sam panted a few moments later, voice trembling. He leaned back to look into Jo's eyes. In them he found the same sense of shock, surprise, and satisfaction that he felt as well.

Definitely shouldn't' have done that. But I'll be damned before I'll regret it.

Inhaling her lotion and perfume, Sam was almost intoxicated with lust. Without another thought, he tenderly kissed Jo. For a brief moment their tongues dueled. Then as if regaining her senses, Jo pushed him back.

"I have to go take another shower," Jo said quickly, casting a nervous glance over her shoulder at the empty walk. "You probably should too, but only after you open that window."

Sam was taken aback for a second as Jo bent down to collect her underwear.

"Uh..." he said, befuddled.

"Talk later, move now," Jo said, walking quickly towards the back of the house. "And wipe down the counter too."

With that, she was gone, leaving Sam feeling bewildered before he did as he was told. Jo's wisdom was apparent just as Sam finished mopping the floor.

"Some brother you are," David said from the front foyer, causing Sam to jump.

This is why I joined the Corps rather than lead a life of crime. He felt a rush of relief as David turned to put his uniform cap on the hat rack by the door.

"Major Haynes had you well in hand when I left," Sam replied.

David gave him a wry look.

"He said it was the least he could do after making me the 'weaving trailer' last night," the smaller Cobb replied.

"The what?" Sam asked, perplexed. David rolled his eyes.

"Apparently our friends in the RAF used to fly in three plane formations," David replied. "The Germans got really good at picking off the guy tasked to weave behind the other two to stop a bounce."

Sam looked at his brother aghast.

"That poor bastard," Sam said. "Anyway, I just got up."

"I could kinda tell from the robe and boxers," David said. "Mom would kill us both for how casual we've gotten around Toots and Jo."

Casual. That's a whole new slang for it.

"Speaking of which, did Toots and Jo ever make up?"

"No, we did not," Jo said airily, walking into the room with her hair up in a towel. Sam noted she was wearing a different dressing gown. "You want breakfast, David?"

Jesus, that woman could murder someone without giving it away. He was slightly horrified at Jo's cool demeanor, her quick thinking and, most terrifyingly, the mixture of pride and awe he had with both.

The smell of breakfast is going to cover up anything else.

"If it's not too much trouble, Jo," David answered. He turned to Sam.

"Anyway, Major Haynes gave the squadron liberty for an extra day," David said. "Apparently there's a front moving in sometime tomorrow, and he doesn't feel like trying to fly in bad weather."

"Yes, I don't think we suddenly forgot how to use instruments on the way over here," Sam noted.

"Sam Cobb, you spent all morning complaining about how long it takes me to get out of the shower, now here you are standing in *my* kitchen," Jo said, turning around from where she'd started some eggs. Sam looked at her to see her pantomiming a shooing motion.

Don't look suspicious, Sam repeated to himself, turning to head towards the back of the house. David shook his head, then looked as if he immediately regretted it.

"I'm going to lay down for a nap, if no one minds," David stated. "Where is Toots, anyway?"

"She didn't come home last night," Sam said. "I'll let Jo explain."

"No, you'll let Jo cook," Jo snapped, then gave Sam a smile to indicate the tone was totally for David's benefit.

I like that smile. I like that smile way too much.

For the second time, Jo shooed him away, brandishing the spatula. This time Sam obeyed her, heading for his own shower.

10

RESTITUTION AND REMNANTS

One more such victory and we will be undone

— **KING PYHRRUS OF EPIRUS**

Pacific Fleet Headquarters
1000 Local
10 August

"With God as my witness, I hope I don't look nearly as bad as I feel, Frederick," Admiral Dunlap said, squinting as he stood on the second floor balcony of the Pacific Fleet Headquarters building.

It has literally been decades since I've been this hung over, he thought. *I am never drinking with a man who has fundamentally lost his country ever again.* Vice Admiral Wake-Walker and he had retired to his office after the Royal Navy officer had received the final update on events in the Indian Ocean.

"Sir, to be fair, if you looked as bad as you felt, I would be calling for a corpsman," Commander Powers said, handing Admiral Dunlap a large mug of coffee. Dunlap nodded in appreciation, took his first healthy swig of coffee, and almost spat it out.

"Who made this?" Dunlap asked, looking in the pitch black cup he held.

"I did, sir," Powers replied, his face blank.

Clearly he's not going to dime out some poor mess steward. But this coffee could almost get up and walk across that yard to the road.

Dunlap took another swig as he met his aide's gaze.

"Well, you should really learn how to make better coffee, commander," the flag officer said. "It's not quite sentient like Frankenstein's monster, and I don't feel my heart about to explode out of my chest from the caffeine."

"Yet, sir," Powers replied. "You don't feel your heart about to explode out of your chest yet."

Dunlap smirked at Powers' comment.

"So do you have any actual reports for me, or are we going to continue having a discourse about cardiac arrest and Secretary Daniels' favorite drink?"

Powers smiled faintly, then stepped to close the door back into the building.

"Vice Admiral Fletcher has been disengaging all evening and into the night," Powers said. "His last update until morning, his time, is as follows..."

As he listened to the butcher's bill, Admiral Dunlap winced inwardly.

One hundred seventy-five aircraft shot down or written off. Severe damage to one battleship, a likely yard trip for the other, similar damage for three cruisers. That's not even counting what happened to the poor Royal Navy.

"Vice Admiral Fletcher, speaking frankly, believes he's out of commission for at least four months unless we have another air group on stand by."

Powers looked up and, seeing he had guessed right at Dunlap's forthcoming question, continued on.

"Vice Admirals Towers and Halsey state they could cobble together two carrier air groups out of what we have available here in Hawaii," Powers stated. "However, they believe a better use for the airpower here is to reinforce the garrisons at Espiritu Santu and Noumea."

"Why?" Dunlap asked, eyes narrowing.

"There are indications the Japanese may try to expand south from their current base at Rabaul," Powers replied. "Both the British and our own submarines have spotted a large amount of shipping in the area. With their carrier losses and ours, it's unlikely that anything would happen immediately, but it can't be ruled out."

What I would not give to be able to read their code like we almost could a couple years. Stupidest thing we ever did, letting the British know about that. Of course they'd have that information at Singapore when it switched hands after Kent.

"How many squadrons does he want to send south?" Dunlap asked. "As I assume we're going to have to put something aboard the *Yorktown* and *Enterprise*, especially now that the Royal Navy is out of the carrier business for awhile."

Powers looked down at his folder, then back up at Dunlap.

"Sir, Vice Admiral Halsey had a very profane directive in here that I was to let him talk to you about that," Powers replied.

I'm not going to put my aide in the middle of two admirals.

Dunlap looked down at motion out of the corner of his eye, then slapped the mosquito on his sleeve. Swiping the dead insect off his khakis, he gestured for Powers to continue.

"As Vice Admiral Halsey predicted, your directive to Rear Admiral Christie was not well received," Powers said. "Admiral Hart—"

Dunlap motioned for Powers to stop talking.

I see that ol' Thomas wants to do things the hard way.

After a few moments of thought and swigging coffee as he counted to ten, Dunlap set the mug down with a *thunk* so audible it caused an orderly to look up from the walkway below.

"Immediate message, Admiral Hart's eyes only," Dunlap stated so only Commander Powers could hear. "Rear Admiral Christie is to report to this headquarters as soon as possible, but no later than one week from receipt of this message."

Powers was writing furiously in the margins of the paper in front of him. He paused and did some mental calculations.

"Sir, that's not a lot of slack time," Powers observed. "He'll have to catch one of the Pan Am clippers, and the next one leaves in about four hours Australia time, doesn't it?"

Dunlap smiled.

There are many reasons you're my aide. One, your father was an impeccable comrade and the Navy lost a great man when he was lost at sea. But two, your slide rule brain means you immediately know just how thoroughly I'm fucking someone over at the same time I do.

"I think Rear Admiral Christie should have a chance to fix his fuck up personally," Dunlap said. "Or the bastard should be consigned to some distant backwater up in the Aleutians and get to freeze his ass off until this war is over. The choice will be mine, not Admiral Hart's."

I was probably a little heavy handed there.

He watched as Powers made additional notes.

"Mind the padding on that message, Frederick," Dunlap stated. "It's going to be insightful enough, I don't want some stupid phrasing causing Admiral Hart to misconstrue it as a deeper admonishment than intended."

Powers started to smile at that, but caught himself before losing his bearing.

"Yes sir," he replied.

Everyone jokes about that until it goes awry. Hart has a better temper than most, but best to get the staff in the habit of checking these things now.

"The *Intrepid* delivered two squadrons of the new *Helldivers* to Midway last night," Powers noted.

*Maybe we should have sent those birds south instead of **Wildcats** and **Dauntlesses**. I'll have to ask Halsey what intelligence told him that made him think the Japanese might come to Midway. Especially with what appears to be most of their fleet in the Indian Ocean.*

"Be a great time to try and retake Wake if we had the tankers for it," Dunlap noted bitterly. "Especially if Fletcher is correct in thinking he bagged three carriers."

Powers flipped back through the G-2's notes.

"Sir, the Japanese still have five large battleships that no one has accounted for," he noted.

"Make a note for me to take that up with the staff today," Dunlap stated, finishing the last of his coffee.

*I'm going to have to figure out if we'll need to send **Rodney** and **Nelson*** *south to replace the Commonwealth losses.* It's not a lot of fun trying to guess what your enemy is going to do when he apparently has a plan.

"Remind me again—when did Halsey tell me the floating dry docks will get to Sydney and Canberra?"

"The 14th, sir," Powers said.

At least that will ease some of the repair problems.

The two floating drydocks, ABSD-1 and ABSD-2, had both been completed months ahead of their planned schedule in late June. When their sections were joined in Sydney, they would theoretically allow for the repair of two more capital ships in Australia.

Still going to be a problem getting resources there, but that's another discussion for a different day. Armor steel doesn't grow on trees, unfortunately.

"Another item on the agenda will be whether Vice Admiral Towers or Vice Admiral Halsey assumes chief of staff duties full time," Dunlap said. This time Powers could not help himself as a short chortle escaped.

"Sorry sir," Powers said quickly, his face coloring slightly.

"I know, Vice Admiral Halsey would pace every day like a lion trapped inside a cage," Dunlap observed. "But I also know if I send him south, he's going to get up to mischief of some sort."

"Yes sir," Powers replied, his expression thoughtful.

"Sometimes you save your strongest horses for a journey's final leg," Dunlap stated. "We'll see what I can glean from Fletcher's final report on just how worn out he appears to be. I don't want him dropping dead in the traces, so to speak."

"Sir, permission to speak freely?" Powers asked.

If he's feeling the need to ask, it's probably going to be pretty harsh.

"Permission granted, Frederick," Dunlap said with a smile. "Just let me know if I need to grab this railing lest I pass out from shock."

Powers smirked but did not fully smile, something that further conveyed he thought what he was about to say was sensitive.

"Vice Admiral Fletcher has just spent the last couple of weeks rampaging across the Indian Ocean," Powers noted. "He's now sank four enemy carriers, counting those small British ones off of Africa, a whole bunch of smaller shipping, and is the only admiral we have who has faced the Japanese carriers twice."

Powers paused, making sure he had not overstepped his bounds by recounting what his superior probably knew. Dunlap waved him on.

"Sir, whether he thinks he's tired or sounds as such, he's gotta be worn out," Powers said. "In addition, if he dropped dead tomorrow, there's a lot of hard earned knowledge that would go with him."

"You don't think most of that work has been done by his staff?" Dunlap asked with a slight smile. "I mean, no one is indispensable, especially in our line of work."

"That may be true, sir, but I'm betting right now the Japanese admiral running from Vice Admiral Fletcher is probably one of the smartest people in *their* navy," Powers said.

Unfortunately, you're probably right, and I doubt Isoroku Yamamoto is going to can him. He had met his counterpart when the Japanese admiral had been at Harvard, then again when he'd been part of the embassy detail in Japan.

"I think Vice Admiral Yamaguchi's boss would beg to differ about the smartest man bit," Dunlap replied. "Indeed, given that Yamamoto's plan killed my predecessor, mauled this fleet, and bought him a great deal of time to do what he wanted, I'd say this Indian Ocean excursion hasn't been horrible."

Powers paused for a long second. Dunlap felt another mosquito on the nape of his neck and startled his aide by striking at it. Bringing his hand back, he confirmed that he'd indeed gotten the bloodsucker and wiped its remains on the balcony rail.

"Out with it, Frederick," Dunlap said finally. "You're more reluctant than a former nun on her wedding night."

"Sir!" Powers said, taken aback.

"I'll talk about my mother how I like," Dunlap said with a smile. "Clearly she got over it at least five times. Anyway, continue."

Powers looked completely discombobulated at Dunlap's tangent, but found his rhetorical footing again after a moment.

"In any case, Vice Admiral Fletcher learned some things from the last few months," Powers said. "I think we could all benefit from him returning here to Pearl."

"Put it on the agenda," Dunlap said. "Also make an appointment for me to meet with Towers and Halsey separately."

"Aye aye, sir," Powers said. "Speaking of appointments, General Short would like to have a word with you at your convenience."

Dunlap smiled.

"Well, I suppose I should eventually talk to the Army," Dunlap said. "I'd rather have dental work without sedatives, but we're allegedly all in this war together."

"Quite kind of you to extend that olive branch to a service that hasn't done a whole lot in this war yet, sir," Powers noted angrily.

"Now, now, Frederick, I'm pretty sure there are 10,000 soldiers who drowned and a captured Icelandic garrison that would disagree with you," Dunlap replied. "Plus that's just opening the door for the Army telling us to do our damn job so they can get around to doing theirs."

"I think getting around to doing theirs is why the Atlantic Fleet keeps pointedly asking when we're handing their carriers back," Powers noted. "Or why the pipeline for replacement air groups is only moving at a trickle for the Pacific."

"I think Senators Taft and Lindbergh's budget shenanigans back in January are the reason for that, actually," Dunlap stated. "Oh well, we'll get more ships and planes soon enough."

TRINCOMALEE
CEYLON
0705 LOCAL (2035 EASTERN)
12 AUGUST (11 AUGUST)

THE SILENCE IS UNNERVING, VICE ADMIRAL YAMAGUCHI THOUGHT as he stepped out of the *Akagi*'s *Tenzan*. The torpedo bomber had ferried him to a grass field just outside of the British port, departing from the *Akagi*'s flight deck a mere hour before. Other than the crackle of a couple of nearby raging fires and the distant ripple of small arms, the small runway could have easily passed as a graveyard for the amount of noise upon it. With a start, Yamaguchi realized what the fires were consuming and realized just how apt the comparison was.

Why are we burning the British dead?! The Army is truly a bunch of walking jackals.

With a start, Yamaguchi realized that the smell of burning flesh had become so familiar to him over the previous two days that it hardly registered.

*Visiting the **Shokaku** was completely a result of my desire to assess her seaworthiness, and had nothing to do with feeling like I needed to atone to the carrier's crew.* His staff had mightily protested the transfer between *Akagi* and the damaged carrier, but Yamaguchi had needed to see the vessel's damage for himself.

It will be at least six months, if not longer, before I see her again. At the rate this war is going, she may be the final fleet carrier we have remaining.

"Welcome to Ceylon, Vice Admiral Yamaguchi," a smiling Japanese officer stated as he walked up. Yamaguchi did not recognize the stocky man, but did note his lieutenant general rank. His peer's uniform also looked as if he'd been doing a lot more than just directing the assault on Ceylon from afar.

"Thank you," Yamaguchi said, bowing. The gesture was politely returned.

"I am Lieutenant General Akira Nara, and it is a pleasure to finally make your acquaintance."

I cannot tell if the man is being sarcastic or not. Of course, one never knows with any of the Army these days.

"Likewise, General Nara," Yamaguchi stated. "Your offensive in the Philippines was of great service to the Emperor. I am surprised, however, that you requested my presence here for the British surrender."

"*I* did not request it," Nara said. "Field Marshall Wavell did."

Yamaguchi raised an eyebrow at that.

"I've never met Field Marshall Wavell in my life," he stated. "Why would have request my presence at the surrender?"

"It would appear that the Edwardian general, Percival, spoke highly of the Navy's conduct during Singapore's turnover," Nara said.

His tone, so even for a voice that holds that much venom.

Yamaguchi stopped and looked at Nara, eyes narrowing.

"Has it occurred to you that one's enemy asking for a senior officer by name could be a ruse?" Yamaguchi asked.

"Are you frightened, Yamaguchi-san?" Nara asked sarcastically. "I mean, surely a great warrior such as yourself is not concerned with the possibility of death in the Emperor's service!"

Yamaguchi smiled.

"If I respected any of you Army jackals as men, I would challenge you to a duel right here," he replied. "But I do not strike animals, it is beneath me."

He saw that his words had struck home, Nara's face starting to darken as his hand unconsciously dropped to the sword at his side. Yamaguchi raised an eyebrow as he looked at the Army officer, seeing the veins starting to bulge at the side of the man's neck. The Army squad accompanying them stepped backwards from the two officers as if to give them room.

This is why our nation is in our current situation: Army hotheads who say stupid things, act even more foolishly, then just expect the Navy to accept their idiocy.

Nara gripped the sword tighter. Yamaguchi made no move for his own weapon.

The nation prospered when the Russians killed so many of you back in 1941.

"It is indeed fortunate for you that my desire to see our nation succeed in this war far outweighs my own sense of honor," Nara spat. "Perhaps you should be more grateful at the nice new harbor the Army will be providing for you shortly."

"That harbor may be the only thing that makes any of this worthwhile," Yamaguchi said. "Lead on."

Nara looked as if he wanted to argue, but the distant *crump!* of artillery appeared to have him think better of it. Turning on his heel, the Army officer strode off at a brisk walk. Yamaguchi followed, the squad of soldiers falling in behind him.

After about ten minutes, Yamaguchi followed Nara around a curving path into an open park. Two British soldiers stood behind a table, with one holding a Union Jack and the other a white bedsheet nailed to length of lumber. Both men looked angry, as if they were being forced to participate in an act of utter perversion.

I imagine large white flags aren't standard issue in any military.

Seated at the table were a pair of older British gentlemen, neither of whom he recognized. Squinting for a brief second, Yamaguchi deduced that the officer wearing Army versus RAF rank was likely Field Marshal Wavell. Both men stood as Nara and Yamaguchi approached.

"Vice Admiral Yamaguchi, I presume?" Field Marshal Wavell said evenly. Yamaguchi noted that the man did not extend his hand nor offer any other honors.

Even in this situation, when they are about to be defeated, the insulting behavior continues. Perhaps it is time to ensure all parties present have the proper mindset.

"I am Vice Admiral Yamaguchi," Tamon responded. "I assume you are here to discuss the terms of your surrender, should we offer any."

Wavell's expression faltered at that last comment. The RAF officer with him regarded the Army squad behind Yamaguchi and Nara wearily, while the two men holding flags glared with even more hatred.

"Yes, I am here to negotiate a cease fire within the parameters given to me by Her Majesty's government," Wavell replied. "I assumed by your acceptance of free passage for me and this party that you wished to negotiate."

"His Majesty's Imperial Navy are not barbarians," Yamaguchi stated. Yamaguchi had to fight not to smile as Nara stiffened beside him at the insult of not electing to use "forces" in lieu of his specific service. "As I am the senior commander in the area, I assure you that you will be returned safely to your lines regardless of this meeting's outcome."

Wavell nodded, and Yamaguchi could see that he acknowledged both the guarantee and the implicit threat of what continued resistance might bring.

"It would appear that your forces have managed to defeat the Far Eastern Fleet and currently control the seas around this island," Wavell said slowly, as if trying to talk while simultaneously remembering something he'd read. "As such, continued resistance will only serve to further increase our casualties while having no effect on the issue at hand."

My aviators must have done almost as much damage as they believed.

One of his continued issues of doubt had been pondering just how badly his fliers had actually damaged the Royal Navy's forces. But if Wavell was surrendering almost wholly due to the damage done, it was obvious the *Kido Butai* had administered a great shock.

"Would you really dishonor your nation by surrendering while you still have the means to resist?" Nara burst out, incredulous. Wavell turned and regarded the man coolly.

"I follow the orders of my rightful sovereign, sir," the British officer replied. "My Queen has directed that we are to limit casualties while simultaneously receiving guarantees that prisoners are well treated."

There's something he's not telling me.

"We cannot offer you a parole or any similar repatriations," Yamaguchi stated. "Indeed, at present we would likely have to place your men in temporary holding while we arranged shipping for you to be returned to more permanent camps in Siam or Burma."

Wavell's face showed a moment of hesitation and surprise as he looked at the RAF officer beside him.

"We were under the impression that the Usurper's government had arranged parole with the Emperor himself," Wavell stated. "At least, that is what was communicated to us..."

"That is what was stated to us by an emissary from *His* Majesty's Government," the RAF officer stated hurriedly. "That all of us would be repatriated by shipping arranged by King Edward's government pursuant to your handover of Ceylon to His Majesty's forces."

"What?!" Nara roared, standing up. Yamaguchi did not even bother looking at the man as he considered regarding Wavell.

"I do not know what has been negotiated between our governments," Yamaguchi stated simply. "What I do know is that the Imperial Japanese Navy currently controls the waters surrounding this island and the Army is in the process of wresting control of it from your forces."

Yamaguchi looked at Nara, his face impassive as he waited for the Army officer to sit back down. Face flush and hand gripping his sword, Nara returned to his chair.

While Nara having a stroke would be amusing, the likely outcome would be a bloodletting that is helpful to no one at the moment, Yamaguchi thought.

"Given those circumstances, what King Edward's government may or may not have negotiated is of little concern to myself or Lieutenant General Nara," Yamaguchi stated. "I can promise you that if you surrender, here and now, your men will not be mistreated. The Imperial Japanese Navy will personally guarantee their safety."

The rattle of Nara's sword vibrating against his chair was audible to all present.

"However, as you have noted, we have defeated all Allied forces in the area," Yamaguchi continued. "Every day you make us resist is another day that we will have to expend supplies and shipping for Lieutenant General Nara's forces. Eventually, those ships will dwindle as we conduct other operations."

Yamaguchi smiled, and hoped Wavell could tell there was no mirth in his expression.

"Which, of course, means when you do surrender there will be far less available shipping for prisoners' supplies or transport," Yamaguchi said. "Then, of course, we just may have to let the Army take certain expediencies in order to preserve our own soldiers' rations and those of the civilian populace."

"You bastard," Wavell said, starting to stand up. The IJA soldiers behind Nara and Yamaguchi starting to raise their rifles caused the man to think better of whatever he was planning.

"I realize it may be difficult for you to accept that Ceylon is, shall we say, under a different sun than the British Empire's," Yamaguchi stated. "But we did not suffer our own losses just to hand this island over to *anyone*, much less so your men could go be employed elsewhere."

"Even if that elsewhere is fighting against your Soviet enemies?" the RAF man snapped.

Yamaguchi raised an eyebrow.

Well that's a surprising twist.

Out of the corner of his eye, he saw Nara turning to face him. The Army officer's eyes were narrowed, as if he too realized there was something very amiss.

Seems like there is a bit of both alliances having countries with their own interests. Or, alternatively, what we've heard about the Germans tying grain shipments to British participation in war is true.

"I leave that for the diplomats to figure out, Field Marshal..?" Yamaguchi said, his voice rising to indicate he did not recognize the man.

"*Air* Marshal Boyd," the man spat. "*His* Majesty's government."

Ah yes, I forgot their Royal Air Force has their own flag rank. Very foolish of me.

Wavell looked at his companion with no small bit of annoyance.

"Dangerous decision to come to an island without notifying your erstwhile allies," Yamaguchi said. "Nevertheless, I am glad to meet the *emissary* in question."

"King Edward has been quite clear in his communications with your government as to expectations regarding this island," Boyd continued. "Your ambassador in London was rather reticent to commit to any course of action, so I was dispatched here on behalf of the rightful government."

Yamaguchi kept his face impassive even as he felt goosebumps raise along his arms.

How in the Hell did you get here?! I will have to speak to Ozawa-san regarding his patrols.

"So, as an allied officer now under my command, I will have to formally request that you leave these proceedings," Yamaguchi stated, then turned to Nara. "I assume you can provide Air Marshal Boyd with an escort back to your headquarters?"

Boyd looked positively apoplectic at Yamaguchi's statement.

"I am not under *your* command," the man sputtered, starting to color.

"Well, then the alternative is you are here as a spy, Air Marshal Boyd," Yamaguchi said. "Lieutenant General Nara, what is Imperial Army policy on spies?"

"We shoot them out of hand," Nara said eagerly. He turned and spoke in rapid fire Japanese to the men behind him. A lieutenant responded with an abrupt "Hai!" and began drawing the Nambu pistol at his waist. Yamaguchi noted the well-disciplined officer kept the weapon pointed down at the ground until he was standing beside Nara. The weapon's cocking was loud as he began to bring the pistol up to aim at the senior British officer.

"What?!" Boyd stated. "You cannot just shoot me! I am–"

Yamaguchi was proud of himself for not flinching, either at the shot or Boyd's scream as the pistol round struck him in the chest. Wavell sprang backwards, holding his hands up as the two officers behind him immediately began to reach for weapons that were no longer at their sides. The Japanese lieutenant, for his part, cursed and rapidly fired two more shots, the second ending Boyd's screaming as the British officer slumped forward.

"What are you doing?!" Wavell asked. "Are you *mad*?"

Yamaguchi looked at Nara. The Japanese Army officer was regarding him with a newfound respect.

"For too long, your nation and the United States has treated ours as if we were second class or somehow subservient to yours," Yamaguchi said. "Now one of your officers, nominally an ally, has deigned to arrive in *our* operational area and tried to tell us what *we* were going to do as if we are somehow servants."

Yamaguchi looked at Boyd's body. Flies were already starting to alight on the corpse. As Yamaguchi watched, the man's breeches began to darken as his bowels released.

I am half tempted to leave you there to rot, symbolic of your Empire and its ability to dictate terms to anyone.

"Now, unless you wish to be the second general officer who dies for either of the two monarchs you both served, I strongly suggest we conclude these proceedings," Yamaguchi said. "My patience wears thin. Let us begin with discussing the condition your men will leave the port facilities in."

U.S.S. YORKTOWN
SYDNEY HARBOR
1225 LOCAL (2225 EASTERN)
18 AUGUST (17 AUGUST)

"One thing about the Australians, they're always happy to see us," Charles shouted over the din of the ship's whistles and horns as the *Yorktown* entered the Sydney Harbor channel. The carrier's crew was manning the vessel's rails as she moved through the channel, with most of the available shoreline filled with joyful, waving Australians.

It makes me think of Pearl.

Eric felt a wave of homesickness wash over him.

"I'd be happy to see someone too if they were all that stood between me and annihilation," Lieutenant Commander Brigante observed. His arm in a sling, VB-11's face was also visibly pockmarked from the shards of glass that had been blasted backwards from his canopy taking a direct hit.

*Couple milliseconds sooner and that 25mm shell would have taken his head clean off. It's been a week since we put paid to that **Soryu**-class carrier and I can only just now look at his face without staring.*

Eric glanced to where the squadron's enlisted stood and looked at Constanza and the young man standing beside him with his head wrapped in gauze.

*Brigante is lucky he didn't lose **another** gunner. Would have had to become a fighter pilot because no one would fly with him at that point.*

"I can almost taste the beer," a pilot called out.

"And the perfume!" another responded, drawing whoops and whistles from his comrades.

"I think I want to go find someplace far away from the rest of these idiots," Charles murmured beside him. "I don't want to just drink my troubles away. Not enough beer in all of Australia for that."

Helluva battle.

Eric could only nod in assent as he once again thought about what they'd done over the last few days. The USN was referring to the engagement as the Battle of the Laccadive Sea, while the Royal Navy was referring to it as the Second Battle of the Maldives. Whatever it was called, Eric just knew many of the young men he'd left Hawaii with were either confirmed dead or 'missing' somewhere over the vast Indian Ocean.

"You know, Eric, you look like you're sorry we're still alive," Charles observed. Eric could see his former wingman was concerned, and he tried to force a smile that was nowhere near authentic.

"I just hope it was worth it," Eric rasped. "Might be having to box up way too much stuff this past week."

Lots of letter writing going to happen.

Sam and David had included a personal note with each set of property they'd boxed up. Eric had thought that was a particularly kind touch and made it a family tradition when boxing up dead men's effects. Charles had helped once he'd realize what Eric was doing.

Man is going to fit in real well with the family, Eric thought. *That is, whenever we get the Hell back to Pearl.*

"We creamed at least two of their carriers," Charles said. "Didn't lose any of ours."

Well, depends on your definition of 'ours.'

Eric looked across Sydney Harbor towards Cockatoo Island. The *Illustrious* was in place, having managed to limp into Sydney under her own power earlier that day. The *Ark Royal* was not so fortunate, and had been towed to the Maldives pending arrival of a Royal Navy or American repair vessel. Vice Admiral Fletcher, with Admiral Hart's vehement backing, had believed it highly unlikely the carrier would survive a journey from the Maldives to Australia while under tow.

The Commonwealth forces started with five carriers, if one counts **Unicorn**. *They ended the battle with one and a half. It's been awhile since I've read my Greek classics, but some guy named Pyrrhus comes to mind.*

"There goes the *Houston*," someone noted. Eric jerked his head around at that comment, almost breaking ranks to get a proper look at the heavy cruiser as she passed the *Yorktown* heading out of Sydney Harbor.

"Lucky bastards," Brigante stated.

"What?!" Eric asked, turning to look at his squadron commander, then back at the departing heavy cruiser.

"Not enough dock space here, even with the floating dry docks," Brigante replied. "They did a quick patch job on her, then got her out of the way so they could put the *Illustrious* in the dock."

As he watched the *Houston* pass by with her own crew lining the decks to cheer at the *Yorktown*, Eric had decidedly mixed feelings.

On one hand I avoid having an awkward conversation with some officer about how I think I love his daughter.

He shook his head at that thought.

Then again, who knows whether there's actually any conversation to have given the lack of letters.

"Cobb, you look like you're seeing a ghost," Brigante noted. "I mean, she's heading back to Pearl, not Tokyo."

"Without an escort, looks like," Charles noted grimly. He gave Eric a knowing look of concern.

"Yeah, not enough tin cans to go around if they actually have to try and tow that Brit carrier and some battleship back from the Maldives," Brigante said. "I hope that doesn't happen anytime soon."

"Even if it does, I don't think we have enough pilots to help," Eric said.

"I'm so glad of the times we live in," Brigante sighed.

"Could be worse," Charles said, drawing an incredulous look from Eric and Brigante before he elaborated. "We could be Russians."

Both men nodded sympathetically at that. The news reports from the Soviet Union weren't good.

No sympathy for most Reds after hearing the Duchess talk about what they did growing up.

"The Duchess" was one of his parents friends, a White Russian émigré who had married an American navy officer then settled in Alabama. She was a kind woman, and had nothing good to say about Lenin, Stalin, or just about any Communist.

I'm sure she's thinking the Germans are making lots of "good Communists" as she put it. Still, gassing is a horrible way to go, and somehow I doubt it only killed soldiers or commissars.

"I can't imagine someplace like St. Louis getting gassed," Charles remarked.

"Or New York," Brigante replied with a visible shudder.

*One of those is a lot more likely. Which is horrifying, especially since it's a long way home for the **Independence** and **Bonhomme Richard** now.*

There had been intelligence reports that the Usurper Forces had dispatched two battleships and a fleet carrier through the Suez Canal sometime in the last week. With the Japanese forces around Ceylon,

Admiral Hart had determined he didn't want to risk borrowed assets getting pinned near the Cape of Good Hope. So the Atlantic Fleet carriers and their undamaged escorts had not even disembarked their crews when they'd stopped in Sydney to reprovision en route to the Panama Canal.

Almost a month at sea after having already been at sea all the way from Norfolk to around Africa.

Eric looked at the departing *Houston* as he did the math in his head.

They're going to need one hell of a refit when they get back to the Atlantic. Almost makes more sense to just have them stop at Pearl if the Usurpers' heavy ships are in the Indian Ocean, but that's above my pay grade.

"Eric, I'm sure even if her dad gets back to Pearl before us she'll still love you," Charles teased.

"Who?" Brigante asked, clearly confused.

"Eric's dating the daughter of *Houston*'s captain," Charles replied, then realized what he'd said. Eric gave him a quick glare.

Didn't we agree not to share that little fact?

"That explains why you've been seeming a lot less happy than the rest of us about getting back to civilization," Brigante remarked with a knowing smile. The man looked like he was about to say something else until he realized the way both Eric and Charles were looking at him.

No, generally being involved in a kill or be killed business is why I've been pissed off. Missing the woman I...love is just icing on the cake.

"I'm sure there will be plenty of mail waiting for us when we get to Cockatoo Island," Charles said, his tone apologetic. Eric could see the man was genuinely remorseful for spilling the beans.

Gotta let it go.

Eric clapped his friend on the shoulder.

"But the real question is, will Patricia have sent us some of Mom's famous brownies after you asked?" Eric replied.

Pacific Fleet G-2 Building
1130 Local (1700 Eastern)
17 August

"You know, at some point we're going to have to have to at least talk about when you're moving your things out of my house," Jo said, her tone sounding like she was discussing the weather.

What the hell?!

Patricia snapped her head up from *Tarzan and the Forbidden City*.

"Excuse me?" Patricia asked, looking up to see it was only Jo and her in the lunch room.

"I did not stutter," Jo replied. "While I appreciate that your nominal presence allows your brothers to stay with me without running afoul of any blue laws, Sam and David have both stated that they're ready to get rooms in the BOQ. And you're moving out, I would like time to find a renter before next month."

Count to ten...must count to ten.

She took a deep breath, hating that her face was likely already revealing her temper rising.

"If this is your way of getting an apol..." she began.

"I don't give a flying fuck if you're sorry, Patricia," Jo snapped, then stopped. Patricia could see the other woman visibly reining in her temper.

So, even the imperturbable Josephine Morton has her breaking point, Patricia thought with some degree of satisfaction, then realized she should have kept a better poker face.

"Namely because I recognize that smug superiority when I see it," Jo bit out, causing Patricia's smugness to fall away. "Yes, congratulations! After a week of literally only saying five words to me before grabbing a bag and going back over to that nurse's apartment, you have finally established that you don't need ol' Jo anymore."

That's not what it is at all!

Patricia clenched her fists in frustration. Looking down at a sticky sensation on her hand, she belatedly realized she should have put her peanut butter and jelly sandwich down first.

"Goddammit Jo, is this *really* the time and place for us to have this conversation?" Patricia asked, disgusted. Looking around again, she shook her head angrily and started licking her fingers.

Undignified as hell, but it at least gets cleanup started and I don't interrupt the bigwig meeting going on outside.

She had no idea *why* Admiral Dunlap had made an impromptu visit to "the cave," but the man had shown up in a state of high dudgeon with Vice Admiral Halsey in tow.

Ever since that admiral up and had a plane crash last week, things have been insane around here. I almost asked Jo if she knew who Rear Admiral Christie was, but that would have involved actually giving her that apology. That she deserves.

Jo watched Patricia licking her hands with a raised eyebrow, then narrowed her gaze.

"Practicing for tonight?" the other woman asked archly. Patricia looked up at her, not understanding initially...then having a rush of cognition.

You bitch.

Her initial rush of anger turned to sadness, as she realized just how deeply Jo had to be hurt to hurl that insult.

"I think, with that comment, we are even," Patricia observed coolly, then paused. "No, actually, I *still* owe you an apology: I am sorry, Jo. I am sorry that I took out my frustration at my brothers on you."

Jo's mouth opened slightly before the other woman caught it.

At least you have the grace to not look completely dumbstruck.

"I realized that despite *knowing* Nick had gotten engaged, I never really processed it," Patricia said. "Nor did I treat Agnes appropriately for someone who was going to be my future sister-in-law."

Patricia could see Jo regarding her suspiciously.

I suppose I've played the 'oh everything is fine...let me bite your head off' trick one time too often.

Once more, she felt ashamed at her behavior.

"I know that might seem hard to believe," Patricia continued. "I can only hope that you'll accept my apology."

After a long pause, Patricia swallowed. Her eyes started to burn as she proceeded.

Goddammit. This is why the damn twins treat me like I'm twelve still.

"But if you want me to move out, Jenny can probably use a roommate," Patricia said. "I've been gone so much the last few days because I've been helping her roommate Rebekkah get ready for a wedding. Seems she is in the family way from a sailor off the *Salt Lake City*."

Jo winced.

"That's a fella who is going through a lot," Jo observed. "First he loses a bunch of his shipmates and all his stuff back in March, now he's about to be a father and a husband?"

"He was recently reassigned, disappeared for a few weeks, came back," Patricia said. "I think they celebrated his survival a little too enthusiastically."

Patricia saw a shadow cross over Jo's face for a brief second.

"You seem kind of judgmental there," Patricia said.

"Just never sure what it means when a woman gets herself pregnant," Jo replied. "There's ways to stop that."

Patricia raised an eyebrow, but decided to let that one drop.

"Anyway, I'm sure I can just move into Rebekkah's bedroom," Patricia finished. This time, the tears did come, and she grabbed at the napkin on the table to dab at her eyes...and just barely remembered the gooey remnants on her hand.

Jo covered her mouth to hide her laugh, then shook her head as she wiped at her own eyes.

"No one needs to leave," Jo said, quickly standing up to walk over to the break room's basin. She rummaged for a cloth, wet it, then brought it back for Patricia.

"Thank you," Patricia said, taking the cloth. After she wiped her hand, Jo reached out and took it in both of hers.

"I'm sorry too," Jo said. "I should have insisted they tell you, especially with me being the maid of honor."

Patricia saw her roommate swallow.

"It's all right," Patricia said, putting her hand on top of Jo's. She smiled. "I'm glad you got some experience in the job before Charles and I's wedding,"

Jo's eyes widened at that.

"He didn't formally ask, but there was at least a discussion about it before he left," Patricia said. "I just wish we'd get some damn letters from Eric and him. Or at least some confirmation that they're still alive."

As soon as she'd said the words, Patricia felt her lunch do a flip flop in her stomach.

Losing Eric is hard enough to think about. That I could conceivably have lost both Eric and Charles in the same day? It's terrifying.

With that thought, she put the peanut butter and jelly sandwich back in its tin. Jo glanced at the uneaten sandwich, then up at Patricia.

"It's terrible not knowing, isn't it?" Jo said quietly.

"Yes," Patricia replied. "The most terrifying feeling of all."

"I wish they hadn't made us leave while they had their pow wow," Jo said. "Kind of hard for us to maybe guess what some code might mean if we don't know what's going on."

"Probably thought our delicate sensibilities couldn't handled it," Patricia said, rolling her eyes.

"Yes, because us sitting in here thinking the worst is so much better," Jo said. "Eric, Charles, my dad…they could all be dead."

The door opened and Gunnery Sergeant Longstreet stepped inside. Nodding at the two women, he walked over to the coffee machine and started to make a pot.

"It was well past time for me, a lowly Gunny, to leave," Longstreet observed when he realized both women were staring at him. Pausing, he considered both Jo and Patricia.

"I'm sorry, I'm not interrupting something, am I?" he asked. "I assure you, with five sisters there's nothing you're going to say that will shock me, so please carry on."

Jo and Patricia looked at each other, then back at Longstreet, who was smiling at them.

"Yes, I am the mirror image of Miss Cobb," he continued. "Oldest child. Dad actually made me explain the birds and the bees to my three youngest sisters. Said I needed the practice if I was going to keep breaking young ladies' hearts."

Patricia looked at Longstreet in shock as Jo guffawed. Longstreet smiled at her knowingly.

"I imagine your father probably had the same problems I did with that speech. Except he didn't have his mother crossly correcting him from the next room. With anatomically correct phrases."

Longstreet stopped as there were rising voices from the next room.

Looking out the break room's small window, he nodded and walked over to both Patricia and Jo.

"By the way, I've seen the initial casualty reports," he said quietly. *Houston* is on her way back here by way of Samoa, and there were no Cobbs listed."

Patricia felt a momentary sense of relief that turned to dread. Longstreet looked at her quizzically.

I can't...I can't ask, Patricia thought.

"Read," Jo said. "Was there a Lieutenant Read?"

"Off the *Massachusetts*?" Longstreet asked, his face starting to grow horrified.

"No, he would have been off the *Yorktown*," Patricia said, her mouth feeling like it was full of ashes.

"No, there was a Lieutenant Read off of the *Massachusetts*," Longstreet replied. "Would have been from the Atlantic Fleet."

Patricia felt a sense of relief as Jo reached over and gripped her hand. Patricia squished her friend's hand back, then looked over when Jo jerked in surprise.

"You didn't get all the peanut butter," Jo observed with a relieved smile. She licked her hand, causing Patricia to start giggling. Longstreet looked at the two of them, but was stopped from asking any questions by Commander Tannehill poking his head in the door.

"Miss Cobb, Miss Morton, you are released for the day," Tannehill said. "Don't worry, you will get your full pay. Gunny Longstreet, let's take a walk."

Patricia turned to look at Jo for a moment, then started gathering her things as the two men left.

"What do you think is going on?" she asked.

"Who knows?" Jo replied. "I'm just glad that everyone is safe."

U.S.S. HOUSTON
300 MILES NORTH OF AMERICAN SAMOA
1655 LOCAL (2234 EASTERN)
29 AUGUST (29 AUGUST)

"GENERAL QUARTERS! GENERAL QUARTERS!" THE *HOUSTON*'S intercom crackled, causing Jacob to jerk upright at his desk. "All hands, man your battle stations! Direction of travel is forward to starboard, aft to port! Possible surface action!"

Surface action? Dammit XO, this is not the time to call a drill.

Looking down, he cursed, the smudge of ink marring an otherwise perfect line on the heavy cruiser's stationery.

Well, guess I'll be starting that letter to Mrs. Gooding again whenever I get back here. He grabbed his helmet and buckled it as he headed for the hatch leading out of his day cabin to the bridge.

"Report," he said resignedly before realizing Commander Sloan was standing behind the helmsman, not the Officer of the Deck.

That means it's not a drill.

Jacob felt a rush of adrenaline.

"Smoke, sir," Sloan said, pointing as Jacob grabbed his own binoculars from the captain's chair. "I left orders for the OOD to notify me before we bothered you, given what you were doing, but the lookouts also swear they saw an aircraft low on the horizon as well."

That's not good.

Jacob glanced at his watch, then studied the horizon.

No, that's *not good at all.*

It was far too late for any long range patrol aircraft from Samoa to be this far out given how close it was to sunset.

"Good call XO," Jacob said. "Did radar pick anything up?"

"No captain," Sloan said. "I've doubled the sky lookouts aft though."

"Best get back there to Battle Two to supervise them, I suppose," Jacob said with a grim nod.

*Not that if there's an enemy aircraft we're going to be able to do much. Given we had to leave all the new shells back in Sydney for ships not **allegedly** heading to safer waters.*

After her emergency repairs, the *Houston* had arrived in American Samoa a little under a week after departing Sydney. Jacob had personally delivered the sealed orders from Admiral Hart to Rear Admiral Giffen, American Samoa's current commander. After reading them, Rear Admiral Giffen had commandeered the *Houston* for an important mission: Figure out what happened to the U.S.S. *Trenton*.

"Sir, signal from the *Pillsbury*," the bridge talker said. "Do you see smoke bearing oh seven oh true?"

Jacob kicked himself mentally.

Have to remember I've got a second vessel with us.

"Respond in the affirmative, bring us around to course oh five oh true, then tell the *Pillsbury* to assume line ahead formation," Jacob ordered.

Not so sure sending an elderly destroyer and a damaged heavy cruiser out to find whatever ate a light cruiser whole is the best plan. Alas, that's why he's **Rear Admiral** *Giffen and I'm* **Captain** *Morton.*

The *Houston*'s propulsion plant had received some hasty repairs and her hull was patched. Still, the best the cruiser could do was twenty-two knots as opposed to her designed thirty-three.

"Sir, I must protest the safety of this transport," Commander Farmer observed drily as he stepped onto the bridge. "I was led to believe that this would be an uneventful transit to Hawaii, yet here we are going to action stations in the middle of the South Pacific."

Jacob favored Farmer with a smile. Initially, the powers that be had determined that the Commonwealth officer should be assigned ashore due to his brother's death. Jacob's action report to Admiral Hart had emphasized the utility of having a Commonwealth officer aboard and formally requested Farmer's retention.

Apparently I was persuasive. Or else he's now considered a deserter and might end up getting shot when we reach Pearl Harbor.

Jacob was glad to have the officer back aboard, even if the thick cast on the British officer's arm joined Jacob's stitches as reminders of their time in the Indian Ocean.

Plenty of time to heal on the way to Pearl. It's going to be a long haul, especially with this detour.

"It's not too late for you to be assigned as the Commonwealth liaison to American Samoa," Jacob replied. "We're getting close to where the *Pillsbury* has to turn around anyway."

Farmer drew back in mock horror.

"Is it an American Navy custom to throw an officer from the frying pan into the fire?" he asked. "I mean, yes she survived the unpleasantness in the Indies, but the *Pillsbury* is only a safe haven when compared to a rowboat."

Jacob raised an eyebrow.

"I'm pretty sure Lieutenant Commander Moran would have no mercy on you for that comment," Jacob replied. "Knew him when he was a plebe and I was a firstie. He boxed intramurals. Quite the wild man."

Farmer raised up his left arm.

"I've got a bloody club, Captain," he said, drawing a chuckle from the rest of the bridge crew.

"Sir, radar has two contacts, bearing oh two zero, range twenty-eight thousand yards," the bridge talker reported, then paused as the lookouts called out basically the same information.

Good to know sharp eyes beats the new fangled technology on a clear day still.

Jacob looked at the low cloud cover.

Well, mostly clear day.

"We're a little east of the usual shipping lanes, aren't we?" Commander Farmer asked after glancing at the map. "That is, unless it's a pair of merchants out of Chile bound for Sydney."

Something doesn't seem quite right about this.

"Come starboard thirty degrees," Jacob said, looking at the low sun. "Signal the *Pillsbury* to make sure she doesn't get more than ten thousand yards ahead of us."

Commander Farmer looked over at Jacob briefly, then quickly looked away.

"Yes, I am feeling slightly suspicious," Jacob said. The British officer cracked a small smile.

"Didn't want to sound any more paranoid than I already am, sir," Farmer replied.

The next ten minutes passed in tense silence as the *Houston* and *Pillsbury* continued to close with the two ships ahead. Bringing his binoculars up, Jacob once again studied the two vessels. Both had single stacks, the smoke pouring from them indicating both vessels were steaming near maximum power away from *Houston*.

"Signal both vessels to heave to," Jacob ordered, guessing the trailing vessel to be close enough to read *Houston*'s code. Jacob turned over to see Farmer staring intently at the two ships.

"Do you recognize their markings?" Jacob asked Farmer as his crew sprang to their work.

"No, sir, I do not," Farmer replied. Suddenly he jerked erect, as if he'd had an epiphany. After a moment, his shoulders slumped. "I don't expect your vessel has an Admiralty Book, do you?"

"A what?" Jacob asked.

"It's a handbook the Royal Navy provided to all of our cruisers at the start of the war," Farmer said, then corrected himself. "In '39, rather. Updated every year."

Jacob shook his head ruefully.

"I've heard that ONI was supposed to publish a merchantman recognition book sometime at the start of this year," Jacob said. "Intended to help our vessels know who had stayed and who had left in your fleet as well as what merchantmen."

Farmer's lips pursed.

"I'm guessing that never got done?" he stated.

"No, not likely," Jacob stated. "Or if it did, the books are a pile of ash someplace at Cavite or the East Indies."

Farmer was about to respond when both men spotted a flashing near the sternmost ship's superstructure. Bringing up his binoculars, Jacob first saw the vessel's black hull fill his field of view. A white band ran seemingly in an unbroken line around the ship, looking almost like a second waterline. The superstructure matched the band while the funnel matched the majority of the hull. Two light blue bands at the very top of the funnel completed the paint scheme.

Such a familiar coloring but I don't know why.

Then it struck him about the same time as he read the only part of the vessel's blinkering he could understand.

Those look like some of the Dutch vessels we saw in the Indies.

"*Abbekirk* is an odd name," Jacob said. "Can't understand a lick of the rest."

"Might be panic," Farmer said, relaxing somewhat. "I know I

wouldn't be expecting a heavy cruiser all the way out here, so they may think we're Japanese or Usurper."

I can't believe anyone would mistake us for a Japanese heavy cruiser. Then again, I haven't had my home country and colonies both conquered and become a vagabond.

"Tell that Dutchman to signal slower, and in *English*," Jacob stated. "Come starboard ten more degrees so she can get a better look at us. Then order the *Pillsbury* to get in closer. No one's going to mistake a four-stacker for enemy."

Farmer winced.

"You did give fifty of those destroyers to us back in '41," the man said. "But yes, bit far out for a *Town*-class destroyer, even if the Usurper still had forces in the Cook Islands."

The mention of the Cook Islands' former bases made Jacob consider his orders.

*Pondering whether we should break radio silence to Samoa. If there's something that sank the **Trenton** out here, these two merchants probably need an escort. They're fast vessels given how slowly we're catching them, which probably means a critical cargo.*

He glanced at the navigator's map hanging in the corner.

*Then again, if I make a transmission and there **is** a hostile force out here, that'd almost certainly bring them looking in this direction.*

"Signal the *Pillsbury* to close with all possible speed and make visual contact," Jacob said. "Bring us another ten degrees to starboard so they can get a good luck at our broadside. Not much that looks like a *Northampton*-class cruiser on the other side."

Once more, the *Houston*'s crew smoothly began to execute his orders. The *Pillsbury*'s stacks puffed additional smoke as the destroyer began to accelerate. Jacob noted the *Houston*'s turrets starting to swing to track the two vessels.

"Tell Guns to belay pointing the main battery at the two vessels," Jacob snapped. "They're jumpy enough as is."

"Aye aye, sir," the talker replied. There was a moment's pause.

"Commander Sloan asks if we should secure from General Quarters?" the talker asked. Jacob was about to speak in the affirmative, but something stopped him.

"Negative," he replied, dimly recalling an intelligence briefing from long ago. "Also, did that Dutchman ever send his signal again?"

Farmer looked over at Jacob.

"You still seem suspicious, Captain Morton?" he noted.

"Suspicious men live long, fruitful lives in war," Jacob replied. "Plus I remember reading somewhere that the Germans had a couple of 'Q-ships' or whatever that had the same punch as a light cruiser."

Farmer nodded.

"I believe they call them *Schiff*, sir," Farmer said. "Nasty little buggers. When the truce fell through, several of them were already at sea. Caused quite a bit of damage to the whaling fleet and some unescorted vessels."

Jacob pursed his lips.

"We'll stay at a bit of range," he said, turning back to the signaling rear vessel. Again the response was gibberish other than *Abbekirk* and, for the other vessel, *Antenor*. As he relayed the name to the talker, Jacob saw Farmer's brow knit.

"What's the matter, Commander Farmer?" he asked.

"That name is fam...*that's a bloody raider!*" Farmer shouted. "The *Antenor* struck a mine off of Espiritu Santo last month!"

Well shit.

"Signal the *Pillsbury*!" he barked. "Order her—"

Jacob did not get a chance to finish his sentence before both vessels ahead of them executed hard turns to port. Although at 10,000-yards the *Houston* was too distant for Jacob to make out details with the naked eye, he watched as both vessels sides flashed down their length. With that all too familiar sound of ripping canvas and steel on steel, the *Houston* shuddered and was surrounded by several water spouts.

"Damage report!" Jacob shouted, even as the main battery began to swing out. He saw black smoke already pouring from the *Pillsbury*'s amidships, the destroyer obviously struck by whatever guns had not fired on *Houston*.

Sailed us right into a damn trap.

"Sir! Guns reports they're flying the fucking Kraut flag!"

. . .

THE TWO "MERCHANTS" WERE INDEED FLYING THE GERMAN FLAG. The lead vessel, the *Kormoran*, had just entered the South Pacific in order to rendezvous with her sister, *Pinguin* prior to both heading for Japan. Both vessels were similarly armed with a half dozen 5.9-inch guns, giving them a total of eight to a broadside. Having had the *Pillsbury* wander well within maximum range, the *Pinguin*'s captain had taken the old four piper under fire with two of his guns and torpedoes while joining the *Kormoran* in firing half his broadside at *Houston*.

The *Pillsbury* had never been designed to take hits from her own battery, much less cruiser shells. At just under 6,000 yards, the first shell had exploded in her boiler room while the second had ruined her bridge. Even as the veteran crew was responding with a ragged salvo that splashed short, the *Pinguin*'s crew put another pair of shells into the battered *Pillsbury* that slowed the tin can's speed to a veritable crawl.

THE *HOUSTON*'S FIRING GONG SOUNDED JUST AS JACOB WAS TURNING to hear the talker's report. With a concussion that shattered the bridge windows and shook the cruiser, a full broadside flashed out towards the *Pinguin*. No sooner had that assault on the senses occurred then the air was buzzing with splinters and fragments from a *Kormoran* shell ricocheting off the front turret face.

Have to even the odds, Jacob thought, hearing the *Houston*'s secondaries belatedly entering the fray.

"Starboard twenty degrees, all ahead flank!" he shouted, the cruiser shuddering again as another *Pinguin* shell hit her. The helmsman spun the wheel...and there was no commensurate swinging of *Houston*'s bow.

"No response from–" the quartermaster started to say, just before a shell exploded just aft of the bridge. Whereas the ricochet had seemed like a minor passage of honey bees, this explosion was a swarm of hornets making its way through the bridge. Jacob felt at two sharp lances of pain across his chest and looked down to see his uniform slashed.

Is it too much to fucking ask for just one battle without getting hit?

The main battery roared again as he looked quickly around the bridge. One talker was a slumped ruin, his remains looking like what happened in a farm accident. The other was staring in shocked horror at his friend, mouth moving silently before he was struck from behind by a petty officer.

"You fucking idiot, tell Battle Two to take control before we're dead!" the chief shouted. Seeing the bridge was in hand, Jacob turned to see Farmer trying to stop blood spurting from a lookout's neck. Bringing his binoculars up, he focused on the almost drifting *Pillsbury*... then clenched his teeth in helpless fury. The destroyer's superstructure was a ruin and her forward guns were knocked askew in their mounts.

Goddammit Moran!

The *Pillsbury* suddenly leaped out of the water, the white spout tinged with a black just under the forward mount immediately telling Jacob the destroyer had been hit by a torpedo. There was no time to react before their companion's entire fore section exploded, her forward magazines touched off in an awful secondary explosion.

"Sir, steering restored!" the helmsman reported.

Houston's bow came to starboard, the movement sluggish but at least opening the range from the furthest German raider. The main battery thundered again, and Jacob realized he could see their intended target's superstructure in worse shape than *Pillsbury*'s had been. Two shells detonated low on the waterline amidships, followed by a tremendous cloud of steam from the vessel. Jacob was distracted again by two shells hitting the *Houston* forward, the blasts muffled. Looking, he saw the heavy cruiser's No. 1 turret lurch, then stay stuck in train even as the No. 2 turret began to swivel onto the forward merchant.

Willoughby must think we've damaged the first vessel enough. Or else he realizes that bitch will kill us if we keep letting her shoot freely.

WITHOUT THE BENEFIT OF THE *HOUSTON*'S DIRECTOR'S SIGHTS, Jacob had no idea how badly the *Pinguin* had been hurt. Willoughby was indeed switching targets after having turned his initial prey's superstructure into a chewed cauldron. Her captain dead, fires raging on the bridge, and power no longer to the mounts, the *Pinguin* began to coast to a stop. A final blow from the *Houston*'s secondary armament damaged the steering, and the big merchantman began an involuntary starboard turn that pointed her bows towards the distant American cruiser.

"Fire in the galley and crews quarters, sir," the talker reported. "We've been holed again in fire room number one, and–"

The main battery roared again, interrupting the talker just as the merchant's side flashed once more. The German fire arrived as a ragged volley, this time with a shell hitting the *Houston*'s stem. Jacob cursed as fragments and splinters from the deck cut down several of the men attempting to clear the obstruction in No. 1 turret's barbette. Turning to observe the fall of *Houston*'s shot, he was pleased to see two clear hits on the now burning enemy raider. For a brief instant he considered closing to finish the vessel off, then remembered what had killed the *Pillsbury*.

Have to keep the range open, plus he's shooting faster than we are.

As the German fired again, Jacob thought back to the War College. There had been vigorous debates between proponents of smaller, faster firing guns and those who believed in a weightier main battery. Jacob had been part of the latter group. Now, as his command was getting thoroughly riddled by faster gun crews, he could appreciate the former argument. Then the German salvo arrived, every one of the shells splashing short.

Opening the range is working!

Jacob saw *Houston*'s No. 2 turret correct slightly, then Willoughby's response roared back at the raider. Jacob mentally started counting down the time of flight...only to be utterly shocked as their target disintegrated in a ball of flame, smoke, and expanding debris in the twilight gloom.

"Holy shit! Holy fucking shit!" one of the lookouts screamed, his cries echoed by other cheers across the *Houston*'s crew.

Maybe the heavier broadside folks have a point after all.

Shaking himself out of his brief stupor from having likely watched a hundred lives snuffed out in an instant, Jacob turned to look towards the sole remaining German vessel. The raider was listing and smoking, but her fires seemed to be dying down.

"Port eighty degrees rudder," he ordered. "Tell guns to cease fire."

As he heard the order relayed, Jacob continued to study the area around the German raider. The crew was busy abandoning ship, and he could see them attempting to launch boats into the water.

"Sir, we should stop them from abandoning ship," Farmer said urgently.

"What?" Jacob asked, turning to look at the British officer in horror. "They're not *pirates*, Commander."

Farmer started to open his mouth, then stopped.

"Sir, you misunderstand me," he replied. "I am not saying we give no quarter. I am saying that if we board that vessel, we will likely find intelligence of great import. It will all be lost if we allow them to scuttle."

Ruthless man, but he's right.

"Order the XO to form a boarding party," Jacob ordered rapidly. "Tell guns to have the machine gun crews to stand by, bring us about and close with that vessel."

Two hours later, the *Houston* began to turn her bow back towards American Samoa as the *Pinguin* exploded three thousand yards behind her. The blast caused the raider's leaking bunkerage to ignite as well, creating a hellish pool of flame around the hull.

That would be her magazines. Farmer was right, keeping the Krauts from reboarding her was critical.

"Commander Sloan, you have the con," Jacob said, turning to his XO. "Set course for Samoa, wait an hour to send the report if I'm not back on the bridge."

"Aye aye, sir," Sloan replied, his jaw set.

"I don't think the captain's mast will take that long," Jacob said. "I might drag it out a bit so O'Rourke doesn't kill himself trying to be everywhere on damage control."

Sloan shook his head at that.

"Or alternatively, so you're stuck here rather than climbing all over the ship either."

"I may have learned that from my predecessor, sir," Sloan replied with a slight smirk.

"Yes, well, I have it on good authority that man is a heartless bastards," Jacob thought, glancing back towards the flaming oil.

I hate not staying longer to search the ocean near where that other Kraut bastard went down either. But we now have no escort, the ship is shot to shit, and I don't feel like finding out if there really is a third raider within seaplane range.

The mystery aircraft that his lookouts had sighted was allegedly a seaplane off the *Kormoran*. It had allegedly been sent north to try and rendezvous with another German supply vessel. At least, that was the scuttlebutt several *Trenton* survivors had immediately told him when they'd gotten hauled from the *Pinguin*'s boats.

Guess we solved that mystery of what happened to **Trenton**.

Jacob tried to cool his anger he headed across the *Houston*'s darkened bridge towards his day cabin. The smell of smoke, burnt debris, and blood once again permeated the *Houston*'s superstructure.

I'm never getting to Pearl Harbor. Couldn't make it if we wanted to right now, not with three hundred extra mouths to feed.

The *Pinguin*'s cruise had been lucrative according to the material Farmer and the *Houston*'s boarding party had recovered. The *Houston*'s shells had killed most of the senior officers, so there wasn't really anyone to ask for particulars. Jacob would leave it up to the interrogators in Samoa to figure out details. All he knew was that he had roughly one hundred and fifty Germans, over a hundred former merchant sailors and, last but not least, ten *Trenton* survivors aboard his vessel.

Terrible tragedy that the **Kormoran** *apparently took aboard a hundred or so other men off the* **Trenton**. *Add in the merchant sailors aboard* **her** *and we killed almost as many Allied sailors as German.*

Nausea at that realization rose and he had to swallow hard.

Nothing to be done for it. Even if I'll go to my grave thinking maybe I should have just spent a few more minutes looking.

It was grim consolation that *Catalina* flying boats would likely depart before dawn from Samoa after his report. Technically the waters were warm enough for anyone who had survived the blast to potentially live until the next day. Unfortunately, that very same warmth meant a plethora of predators and the specter of dehydration were almost equally likely to kill any survivors.

Lucky enough to survive getting sunk by a raider and a magazine explosion only to end up in a shark's belly. I'm sure someone would have words with ol' St. Pete when they got to the Pearly Gates. Do you go to Hell for telling an eternal gate guard to go fuck himself?

The two armed Marines outside his day cabin's hatch came to attention. Jacob nodded at both of them.

"Carry on, gentlemen," Jacob stated. Both Marines returned to parade rest as he opened the hatch.

"Carry on," Jacob repeated, waving the gathered officers back to their positions of parade rest. Two men stood in the center of the gathered group. One wore a set of ill-fitting USN khakis, clearly borrowed from someone aboard the *Houston*. The other was in manacles and wore a still wet *Kriegsmarine* uniform.

Plenty of witnesses here for what's about to be said.

He noted that at least two officers had notebooks and pens in hand. Moving behind his steel desk, Jacob took a seat, then gestured for everyone but the two men standing in the center of the room to do so. He noted that Captain Westerman, commander of the *Houston*'s Marine detachment, was under arms with a riot shotgun in his hands.

I really hope that he's got birdshot or something similar in that street sweeper. Also glad he had the common sense not to bring a rifle into a compartment this crowded.

Looking around the space, Jacob saw that two more of his officers were also armed, their .45 pistols secure in their holsters.

Commander Sloan is paranoid, but I'm also not interested in taking any chances with this lot.

"Sir, *Kapitänleutnant* Kruger asked to have a word with you as the senior survivor," Westerman stated. Jacob remained expressionless as he looked at he tall, muscular German in front of him.

"Do I need a translator?" Jacob asked.

"No, I speak English," Kruger spat.

Jacob continued to lock eyes with the man, the German's pure hatred and spite roiling off of him.

*Shame I couldn't have had him led down here by one of the stewards. I'm sure that would have **really** made him happy with all that stupid 'Master Race' talk.*

"You've got five minutes," Jacob said. "Speak your piece."

"I protest the treatment of my men and your refusal to allow us to return to our vessel in time of distress," *Kapitänleutnant* Kruger stated angrily, his accent growing slightly thicker with emotion.

"Your men ignored a clearly signaled order," Jacob replied.

"The law of the sea is clear," Kruger said rapidly.

"Yes, the same law that says, by virtue of you getting your flags up a split second before shooting at the *Pillsbury*, I cannot have you summarily hanged," Jacob stated.

"We conducted ourselves in accordance with the law of warfare," Kruger sneered. "It is not our fault that you fell for our ruse. Perhaps your destroyer captain should have paid more careful attention."

Jacob could have sworn the man standing beside Kruger was about to turn and throttle the German, long-term consequences be damned.

I'd better take control of this situation before Lieutenant Hoffner makes my life more complicated.

"And it's not my fault your scuttling charges didn't detonate," Jacob retorted. "Perhaps the responsible personnel forgot to check the fuses in their haste? Talk to them about why 'your' men are dead along with your XO."

Blood ran from Kruger's face, followed by what Jacob could swear was a brief moment of guilt.

"You have committed a war crime!" Kruger screamed. "You are—"

Jacob slammed his hand down on his desk as he sprang to his feet. The noise startled everyone in the room and stopped Kruger mid-rant.

*I will **not** be spoken to this way on **my** ship.*

Jacob let Kruger and the cabin's other occupants sit in silence for a couple of seconds while he considered his next words.

"You listen to me you little Nazi son-of-a-bitch," Jacob said slowly, his tone cold but level. "I will *not* be lectured on proper decorum or procedures on my vessel. If you *ever* speak to me in such a manner again, I will have you bound, gagged, and thrown into the brig. If you resist, I will have you shot."

Kruger's eyes widened at the clear threat as Jacob finished.

"*Do. You. Understand?*"

Kruger looked at him, defiance etched on his features. Jacob felt the vein on his temple starting to throb.

I just may offer up a three day liberty if you go into that brig with a few bumps and bruises.

Something about his face made the German officer reconsider his life choices.

"I understand, *Kapitan*," Kruger said, coming to a position of attention.

"Very well," Jacob continued. "Now, as to the matter of your treatment aboard this vessel—we will conduct a preliminary investigation and questioning of the merchantmen and sailors we took prisoner. If you or any of your men are accused of maltreatment, my officers will begin a charge sheet."

Kruger remained at attention, staring at the bulkhead behind Jacob.

"Understood, *Kapitan*," he said.

"If you attempt, in any way, to sabotage this vessel or harm a member of my crew, I will have the offender summarily hanged from the mainmast," Jacob continued. Kruger flinched slightly at that, then nodded.

"Understood, *Kapitan*."

"If any member of my crew mistreats you or your men, I am to be notified immediately," Jacob finished. "The offenders will be punished harshly, I assure you. Do you have any questions?"

Jacob saw a brief moment of skepticism cross Kruger's face before the German regained control of his emotions.

Again, if your executive officer had listened, he and everyone else in that boat would still be alive. Foster's pretty sure we have a fully functional codebook and current machine. I'd shoot my own mother for that.

Jacob had never worked in cryptography, but he had studied ciphers as a hobby in school. He was well aware of how important having a complete codebook was.

"Nein, *Kapitan*," Kruger replied after the short pause.

"You're dismissed," Jacob said with a gesture towards the cabin hatch. The German officer came to attention and rendered a salute, arm extended at an angle towards the bulkhead behind Jacob. As much as it pained him, Jacob returned the gesture with a hand salute. With as much bearing as a man in manacles could muster, Kruger turned and shuffled out of Jacob's cabin.

"Now, Lieutenant Clancy, your report," Jacob said after Kruger's guard had shut the hatch behind them. "No, first, someone give this man a damn chair, it's not a Captain's Mast."

There was a hurried shuffle as several of his officers started to give up their seats. He was not surprised that Ensign O'Rourke caught the proverbial short end of the stick as the junior man in the room. Even if, Willoughby aside, the young officer had done the most work in the last couple of hours of any of *Houston*'s wardroom.

We got shot to shit. Lucky we didn't end up crippled again.

Looking at Lieutenant Clancy, Jacob felt a wave of sadness and anger.

***Trenton** never had a chance.*

"Sir, I'm not sure where you want me to begin," Clancy stammered. Jacob could see an almost visible weight settling on the young officer's shoulders.

"I just need to get your impressions of what happened to your vessel," Jacob prodded gently. "I know Commander Sloan already asked you some questions and you were off watch when the shooting started. I guess we'll start there."

"Aye aye, sir," Clancy began. "As I told Commander Sloan, I was down in the wardroom when those bastards opened up..."

In Jacob's professional opinion, it took Clancy longer to describe the *Trenton*'s end than it had taken the light cruiser to die. The ensuing fifteen minutes was some of the most harrowing narrative Jacob had ever heard. As with *Houston*, the two German raiders had ran up the German navy ensign before opening fire. Their first salvo had been aimed at the *Trenton*'s superstructure. Jacob doubted the light cruiser's captain had lived past the fight's first sixty seconds. The cruiser had managed to get off maybe one salvo, then a pair of torpedoes had knocked out her power. Clancy had struggled his way to the deck just as *Trenton* was starting to capsize.

*The **Omaha**-class might need to function in pairs. That was not a battle, it was an organized murder.*

As soon has he had the thought, Jacob thought back to the Italian cruiser they'd jumped seemingly a lifetime ago.

Or maybe the real lesson from this is what I said to Farmer about paranoia and longevity being intertwined.

"Thank you Lieutenant Clancy," Jacob said. "Do you have anything else that you think might help a Board of Inquiry?"

"No, sir," Clancy replied.

"You're dismissed," Jacob said. The young officer stood up and saluted. Jacob returned the gesture, then waited for Clancy to be led out by O'Rourke. He looked at the gathered officers, many of their faces ashen.

"Gentlemen, let's get back to work," Jacob said simply. "It's going to be a long war."

RATMALANA AIRFIELD
0940 LOCAL (1640 EASTERN)
15 SEPTEMBER (14 SEPTEMBER)

"SIR, IS IT TRUE THAT THIS WAS ONE OF THE BRITISH SQUADRON'S ready rooms?"

Isoro turned from the window to look at the young petty officer who had asked the question. The man was languorously laying on a chaise lounge, munching on cookie he'd taken from a tin liberated upstairs. The small living area was filled with the sounds of Chopin, the short wave radio still tuned to whatever frequency the British Exile Government was using out of Sydney.

Isoro smiled at question. The petty officer looked concerned at the expression, unconsciously sitting up straight.

There is something wrong with our Navy that a non-commissioned officer thinks I'm going to beat him because I smiled. That or I'm no further from a breakdown than I was two weeks ago and it shows.

Commander Fuchida had drawn lots for which pilots would remain on Ceylon and which would accompany the *Kido Butai* back to Singapore then onwards to Japan. Isoro suspected some trickery, but he had been selected to lead the contingent of *Shiden* that were to remain until the Army showed up.

Ah, as if on cue, he thought, hearing the distant thrum of propellers. *Or at least, I **hope** that is the Army, and not the British, Germans, Americans, or all of the above.*

That Isoro worried about possible Nazi aircraft spoke to how crazy the war was getting. Although he was certain the rumor was wild, allegedly their erstwhile allies in Berlin had not taken kindly to Vice Admiral Yamaguchi's...*direct* methods of negotiating. Isoro wasn't sure of the details, he had just been advised not to assume any German aircraft sighted on patrol were friendly.

I hope we didn't pay so dearly for this island just to sell it dearly with our blood to some other colonizer.

Shaking his head, Isoro remembered he hadn't answered the question.

"One of their night fighter units, allegedly," he replied simply. "The Army never got this far south before the surrender, and the *Rikunsentai* just occupied the perimeter without checking the buildings."

The petty officer stopped, looking at the cookie in his hand. His companion laughed.

"Yes Heike, that means you could be eating a poisoned cookie as we speak," the thinner, taller noncom said.

*Murakami. Both of them off of **Taiho**. I hope they haven't used up their luck.*

There was a peal of thunder. Isoro glanced out the window into the gloom.

They'd better land fast or there's going to be an accident.

Monsoon season had officially begun a few short days before, and the rain gods had not disappointed. Isoro was pleasantly surprised that the bombers were all able to put down quickly, the complete squadron landing in a matter of minutes just as the rain began to cascade down in sheets.

"Sir, are we going out in this?" Heike asked as Isoro walked towards the door. The rain beating down on the roof was strangely relaxing, and he took a moment to just listen.

"No, I think our Army friends can come to us," Isoro said, opening the door. The dropping temperature made it feel as if a cool breeze was blowing into the humid building. As he watched men dash through the rain around the bombers, Isoro listened to the shortwave radio in the corner.

Those bomber pilots probably did not ever expect themselves to be sitting here, on Ceylon, as a hedge against treachery from a nation that no longer even had colonies before the Treaty of Kent. I can only hope that they enjoy their stay.

A formerly British lorry rolled down the runway towards the bombers. One man, clearly the squadron commander, waved wildly for it to come towards his aircraft. As the truck slowed, the squadron commander turned, saw Isoro, then gestured for one of his officers to head towards the opened door. Noting Isoro's naval uniform, the designated officer strode slowly and deliberately towards the squadron shack.

Ah yes, cannot have the Navy think that Army pilots are averse to a little rain.

A short, squat man, the young Army lieutenant's eyes narrowed as he regarded Isoro upon reaching the doorway. The officer then turned towards the two petty officers lounging on the couches and his face started to darken.

Why no, I am not wearing any of my insignia on my flight suit.

He gestured for the Army officer to step inside just the radio began to play Mozart.

Let's see how good you are at picking up on social clues, idiot.

"Are you the liaison officer who was supposed to be meeting us?" the lieutenant asked, his nostrils flaring as he removed his sodden helmet. "What are you doing in here?"

"What does it look like?" Isoro asked. "Not getting wet."

Locking eyes with Isoro and seeing no fear there, the Army officer gathered he was at least talking to a peer. The man began removing his gloves, wringing them out on the floor.

"I would think you'd be in a hurry to get back to your clean bunks and silverware," the Army man said disgustedly. "Heaven forbid the Navy have a little hardship."

"Both of these men are from a carrier that is on the bottom of the ocean," Isoro replied coolly. "I lost both my wingmen wresting this island from the British. What have you done in the last month?"

"Bombed Darwin," the Army pilot responded grimly, his demeanor relaxing somewhat. "Nice place to visit, if you don't mind *Spitfires*."

Isoro gave the man a nod of respect, and the Army officer returned it.

"I am to show you the ready room and the rather austere amenities," Isoro said. "Thankfully the British claimed to have thinned the snake population, so you don't have to worry as much about having a viper under your pillow."

The Army lieutenant looked at Isoro worriedly.

"Yes, that happened," Isoro said, shrugging. "Thankfully the pistol works on them."

The Army officer shuddered. Before he could respond, there was a fanfare from the radio in the corner. The man's eyes narrowed.

"That's the British Royal Family fanfare," he said, then looked back at Isoro with a raised eyebrow.

"We haven't changed the channel since we got here," Isoro said. "According to one of our prisoners, every pilot in this squadron died. Figured keeping the ghosts happy with their choice of music was a good plan."

The Army pilot laughed at that one.

"I understand mollifying ghosts," he replied grimly. "I am Lieutenant Hirohata, by the way."

"Lieutenant Isoro Honda," Isoro replied. The Army officer came to attention and saluted, which Isoro waved away.

"No, sir, please do me the honor," the man said, his eyes wide.

Oh shit, not this again.

Isoro returned the salute.

"The papers back home have talked a great deal about your exploits," Hirohata said. The man was clearly awestruck.

"I am sure they embellish some things," Isoro replied.

"Honorable sir, the Queen is apparently about to speak," one of the petty officers said.

Isoro and Hirohata turned to look at the radio, finally paying attention to what was being said.

"...Her Majesty's speech to both houses of the United States' Congress will begin at the top of the hour," the British radio announcer said. "Our Washington office has assured us that it is critical to the continued war effort in light of recent events. To our listeners around the Indian Ocean and in Australia, you may be hearing history."

"Maybe they are going to announce peace talks," Hirohata noted. "The Australians and Americans have been much less active attacking the East Indies since the operation here."

That's probably because someone believes we have the strength to attack Australia proper. Or they're just preparing to take this place back.

"We go now to our Washington Office and Mr. Denis Johnston, BBC."

There was a brief pause, the rain continuing to pour down on the roof as the four men looked at one another.

"Good evening from Washington, D.C.," Mr. Johnston's voice came over the radio. "Her Majesty has entered the American capitol building, where she is being escorted by Mr. Harry Hopkins and several armed agents of the FBI. We are told that these men are allowed here at the express permission of the Speaker of the House, Congressman Rayburn of Texas."

"Interesting that the Americans would need an armed guard for a foreign leader in their legislature," Isoro observed.

"Have you not heard what happened to the British Prime Minister?" Hirohata asked. Isoro shook his head.

"Americans shot him while trying to kill the Queen," Hirohata stated.

I missed so much here while we were on operations, Isoro said. Before he could speak, he could hear a gavel being banged on the radio and several shouts."

"As you can hear, ladies and gentlemen, there is a commotion from the Republican side of the Senate," Johnston said. Isoro noted the man seemed distressed and angry. Cursing his memory, he tried to recall how the American Congress was organized. His old school lessons were still evading capture when the Queen began speaking.

"Thank you, Speaker Rayburn, for inviting me to speak today."

She sounds so reserved and calm for someone who was just delivered a grave insult.

"Gentlemen, I pray you will forgive me for speaking plainly, as time is short. I come not to you today not, as some of your more intemperate members have recently called me, a beggar princess."

I recognize that tone. That is a woman who is deeply, irrevocably angry but is being polite. Several of those men have made an implacable enemy.

"As you can see I have not been, as Senator Taft stated yesterday in this very hall, rendered incapable of independent thought and movement due to Prime Minister Churchill's death. While Lord Churchill was my advisor, my tutor and, in his last act, my protector, I assure you that the woman who stands before you is a sovereign, not a 'puppet.'"

*Indeed, if I were **any** of the men who were so insolent, I'd hire a food taster immediately.*

He glanced over at Hirohata. The Army officer was pensive as the broadcast continued.

"Instead of a child's toy, let me introduce myself properly. I am Queen Elizabeth II, rightful ruler of the British Isles. A ruler who has now not only lost my father to fascism, but buried one of the greatest statesman my nation has ever known to radicals within in your own midst. Still, even to the last, Prime Minister Churchill considered the United States the key to the entire world's salvation."

There was a pause as someone shouted something indistinct. Whatever was yelled was immediately met with calls questioning the rude individual's courage and manners. The banging of Congressman Rayburn's gavel brought the bedlam under control, at which point Queen Elizabeth continued.

"As many of you, to include the gentlemen being escorted out, have taken every opportunity to remind me, my *right* to speak here was revoked by the events of 1776," the Queen stated.

She has become even calmer. Resolute to the level of being frightening.

"If it pleases you and allows you to consider my words, do not think then of me as a sovereign nor an empress. Indeed, as I informed President Roosevelt just over an hour ago, the Court of St. James has renounced any and all claims to overseas colonies."

*Wait, **what**?*

Isoro could hear that this statement had similarly shocked the Americans listening in the chamber. Giving them a moment to collect themselves, Queen Elizabeth continued.

"Instead, consider my statements those of a herald and beloved friend. If need be, think of me as someone who has suffered mightily at the hand of terrible people. A woman who is now beseeching you and your constituents to learn from the ruin that has befallen my own nation."

There was again murmuring, but the Queen's tone powered through the noise.

She has such power without seeming the least bit shrill.

"Before you today is a bill, brought by the President, seeking further loans to Great Britain so that we may continue this conflict. In opposition, many of your body have pointed out that the Atlantic and Pacific serve as natural depredations to the scourge of fascism. That despite your countrymen who have died and continue to perish alongside my own, the price is too great."

Yours are not the only people who are dying, Your Majesty.

For a brief moment his eyes burned, thinking about his dead wingmen.

"These naysayers sing to you soft songs of isolation, of an easier path than President Roosevelt has asked you to set yourselves upon. 'Let us build up our Navy and turn to our own affairs in this hemisphere,' Senator Lindbergh has stated, as if he himself has not flown from this land to Europe. 'We can reach accommodation with Himmler as we have with other nations in the past,' says Senator Taft, as if the path of appeasement has not been attempted before."

On the last, Queen Elizabeth's voice briefly faltered before she regained her strength.

"I more than anyone in this room understand the sweet succor that seems to be offered by these words. As we speak, Nazi forces have laid siege to Leningrad and begun reducing that city's defenses. The Red Army is in retreat on all fronts after the debacle in Poland and the eastern Soviet Union. Premier Stalin lies stricken by a stroke and their government appears in disarray. In the Indian Ocean, Japan has laid waste to the Royal Navy and forced Vice Admiral Fletcher to retreat to Australia."

"Hai!" Isoro shouted at the radio, the defiant call surprising even him.

"The situation is dire, the way ahead dark," Elizabeth intoned. "It would, given the circumstances, make perfect sense for your nation to deny my government additional resources and thus, by extension, seek a separate peace."

There was a long pause, enough for Isoro to wonder if the connection had failed.

"It would make perfect sense, that is, if *you were not dealing with monsters*. Monsters who have attempted to assassinate me, a young woman who is here as a guest, on your own soil. Men who have repeatedly brutalized unarmed women and children in every one of their conquests, then murdered prisoners with glee."

Isoro's stomach turned at those last words. Knowing it was his imagination, he still imagined everyone present was looking directly at him.

"Fascism is an ideology that will brook no remaining dissent, no further opposition, no possible threats until this entire globe is under their control," Elizabeth said. "As you look to your east and west to take comfort in the vast tracts of ocean that lay there, recall that the English Channel served as my realm's bulwark for almost nine centuries. Varied French kings, Napoleon Bonaparte, and the Kaiser were all stymied in their attempts to bring Great Britain to heel by *that* body of water. Ten miles of ocean backed first by wooden, then steel hulls of the finest navy in the world."

Unsurprisingly, that comment also brought some dissent, but Queen Elizabeth ignored it as she pressed her point.

"It was not only our fleet, of course. With our success in 1940, my nation grew complacent at the strength of our air force. Grudgingly, we made peace in the face of continued adversity once Herr Hitler had gone to his just reward. We had no idea of the depths of Himmler's depravity, nor of the devastation modern airpower has made possible."

Once more there was the long pause.

"I will leave you with the thought of how quickly doom befell my nation as you consider whether to remain our ally and supporter as we fight on," Queen Elizabeth stated. "For make no mistake, regardless of the vote here today, the Commonwealth will continue to fight against the darkest manifestations of our humanity, as *our* dead demand this of us."

Again, the strength of her words comes through even though she is thousands of miles away. This is a woman who will not rest until she is dead or she has regained her throne.

"Although your citizens of my generation will appreciate the peace, the Commonwealth will continue to fight bravely on. Our ships will gradually fall into disrepair. Aircraft will grow obsolete. Courageous men will die. Despite this, we will continue to do our duty with the hope that we so harm Fascism that it will come for you in decades, not years. For we know that trouble exists now, in *our* time, and wish that all our children will know peace in theirs. Thank you, and I bid you good evening"

Ironic she speaks of us as part of a group coming for others when **her** *'empire' has colonized so many.*

He saw the other men in the room similarly sneering at the sentiment as they stood on Queen Elizabeth's former property.

"Do you think they will vote to continue the war?" Hirohata asked, as applause from the American Congress spilled from the speaker.

Isoro looked at the radio, then at the Army pilot. With a start, he noticed that several more Army pilots had come into the room during the speech.

"It matters not whether they vote to help the British or decide to cower in their cities and farms," Isoro said. "I serve as the Emperor's blade. If they wish to send their pilots to challenge His Majesty's will, I shall continue to meet the challenge until I breathe no more."

As the Army pilots cheered his words, Isoro wished his heart believed the words as fervently as he'd spoken them.

AFTERWORD

It is said that every book is a labor. This one was certainly a trip through the salt mines and back. I thank you for joining me on this journey. It's always fun knowing that someone, somewhere, has had a chance to see the many ways World War II could have been different. Yes, I know that there's a lot of Europe alluded too but not quite dealt with. Don't worry, we'll be getting to that in another arc. Unfortunately there's no "Vinson Bill" that allows me to clone myself for a "two series author," but I think the "bread crumbs" are obvious enough you know the work's getting done.

As always, I'd like to thank Anita for her help with this. A lot of stuff went wrong during this past year, and I'm meaning beyond catching COVID-19. Throughout it all, Anita's supported this endeavor, even after having surgery (did I mention it's been a crazy year?) and wondering if I was ever going to finish it. Writing is hard, but having a helpmate makes it easier. Especially when she does the cover art and many of the book drawings while working on her own art projects.

Next, I'd like to thank my editors, Jennifer Frontera and Emily Swedlund. Both of them had to deal with Murphy not only screwing up my plans, but theirs as well. ("Gonna be late on that next chapter,

AFTERWORD

[insert Murphy].") Above all else, I told them both that this book was going to be 100,000 words, and let's just say it's a bit beyond that. Still, I hope you've found we made a very good book together.

Finally, contrary to previous plans, I'll not be alternating the Usurper's War with my Vergassy Universe sci-fi series. After writing *Aries Red Sky* and then starting this book, I've come to realize that just adds to the gestation time as I reacquaint myself with what I'd done a couple years or so before. So, after I knock out a short story to round out my upcoming alternate collection *Dispatches from Valhalla*, it'll be time to do the next novel in this series. If you're curious about it and also want to stay informed on my plans, you can sign up for my mailing list.

ABOUT JAMES YOUNG

Dr. James Young resides in the Midwest, sharing his home with fellow author and award winning artist Anita C. Young. *Against the Tide Imperial* is the third work in his *Usurper's War* series of alternate history. In addition to tilting World War II on its head, James has also co-edited the *Phases of Mars* series of alternate anthologies that consists of *Those In Peril* (naval warfare), *To Slip the Surly Bonds* (air), and *Trouble In the Wind* (ground). If you're a fan of military science fiction, there is also his *Vergassy Chronicles* series.

As a non-fiction author, he has won the United States Naval Institute's Cyberwarfare Essay Contest, placed in the James Adams Cold War Essay Contest (2nd and Honorable Mention), and been published in the *Journal of Military History* and *Proceedings*. When not working on the latest article, Dr. Young can be found hawking books and prints inspired by the series at various sci-fi and comic conventions. His blog is at vergassy.com, where you can also sign up for the Slinger of Tales newsletter.

Website: https://vergassy.com/
Newsletter: http://eepurl.com/b9r8Xn

facebook.com/ColfaxDen
twitter.com/youngblai
amazon.com/James-Young

ALSO BY JAMES YOUNG

USURPER'S WAR SERIES

Acts of War

Collisions of the Damned

Against the Tide Imperial

USURPER'S WAR COLLECTION

On Seas So Crimson

PHASES OF MARS ANTHOLOGY SERIES

(Editor and Contributor)

Those in Peril

To Slip the Surly Bonds

Trouble in the Wind

NOVELLAS

Pandora's Memories

A Midwinter's Ski

Ride of the Late Rain

VERGASSY UNIVERSE
An Unproven Concept

Aries' Red Sky

NONFICTION
Barren SEAD

Printed in Great Britain
by Amazon